Nina Milne has alwa[...] Boon—ever since she [...] stacks of Mills & Boo[...] to this dream Nina ac[...] her own, three gorgeous children and—somehow!—an accountancy qualification. She lives in Brighton and has filled her house with stacks of books—her very own *real* library.

Nina Crespo lives in Florida, where she indulges in her favorite passions—the beach, a good glass of wine, date night with her own real-life hero and dancing. Her lifelong addiction to romance began in her teens while on a "borrowing spree" in her older sister's bedroom, where she discovered her first romance novel. Let Nina's sensual contemporary stories feed your own addiction for love, romance and happily-ever-after. Visit her at ninacrespo.com

Also by Nina Milne

Marooned with the Millionaire
Conveniently Wed to the Prince
Hired Girlfriend, Pregnant Fiancée?
Whisked Away by Her Millionaire Boss
Their Christmas Royal Wedding
Baby on the Tycoon's Doorstep

Discover more at millsandboon.co.uk

ITALIAN ESCAPE WITH THE CEO

NINA MILNE

THE COWGIRL'S SURPRISE MATCH

NINA CRESPO

MILLS & BOON

All rights reserved including the right of reproduction in whole or in part in any form. This edition is published by arrangement with Harlequin Books S.A. This is a work of fiction. Names, characters, places and incidents are either the product of the author's imagination or are used fictitiously and any resemblance to actual persons, living or dead, business establishments, events or locales is entirely coincidental.

This book is sold subject to the condition that it shall not, by way of trade or otherwise, be lent, resold, hired out or otherwise circulated without the prior consent of the publisher in any form of binding or cover other than that in which it is published and without a similar condition including this condition being imposed on the subsequent purchaser.

® and TM are trademarks owned and used by the trademark owner and/or its licensee. Trademarks marked with ® are registered with the United Kingdom Patent Office and/or the Office for Harmonisation in the Internal Market and in other countries.

First Published in Great Britain 2021
by Mills & Boon, an imprint of HarperCollinsPublishers,
1 London Bridge Street, London, SE1 9GF

Italian Escape With The Ceo © 2021 Nina Milne
The Cowgirl's Surprise Match © 2021 Nina Crespo

ISBN: 978-0-263-29900-7

0121

MIX
Paper from
responsible sources
FSC® C007454

This book is produced from independently certified FSC™ paper to ensure responsible forest management.

For more information visit: www.harpercollins.co.uk/green

Printed and bound in Spain
by CPI, Barcelona

ITALIAN ESCAPE WITH THE CEO

NINA MILNE

To my family and friends
you are all very precious to me.

CHAPTER ONE

AVA CASSEVETI STUDIED her reflection in the mirror and tried out her trademark smile. *Fake it till you make it.* It was a mantra that had always served her well, had got her through an outwardly gilded life, and one that she now relied on to manage the trials and tribulations that had multiplied on a daily basis since her father's death.

Another look at herself and she reached out for her reddest lipstick, a fire-engine red, completely suited to the day ahead. With any luck people would be distracted from the tiredness in her eyes, the pallor of her skin that even her super-expensive, perfectly matched foundation couldn't completely conceal.

But she would keep it together, present the façade, convince the world that she was in control, a competent businesswoman able to hold the family company together.

Family. The word boomed around her head, clanged with irony as the complications of her family tree threatened to tangle her mind.

Why did you do it, Dad?

She closed her eyes, pictured her father, the bluff good looks, the boyish cheek he had maintained even into his sixties, the youthfulness that had survived his first heart attack four years before. His presence, his aura, her belief in him, all shattered when she'd learnt the contents of his will, her grief at losing the man she adored darkened by the confusion and hurt over his betrayal, wrapped in the legalese of his last will and testament.

Because instead of leaving Dolci, the dessert company he had founded, to Ava—the company she had put her heart and soul into for the past five years—he had left it to Ava *and* her two half-siblings, Luca and Jodi. Remembered shock, disbelief and the ice-cold stab of betrayal hit her again.

Luca and Jodi Petrovelli, children from his previous marriage, from his past, who had never been part of the Dolci venture. Children who hadn't even kept the Casseveti surname, instead had taken their mother's. Luca and Jodi, adults now, whom Ava had never even met. Though she had known of their existence, the shadowy threat of her childhood nightmares. Little surprise really—even now she could hear her mother's dire warnings.

'We have to be careful, Ava darling. Always. Those people would do anything to get Daddy back. And we won't let that happen, will we, sweetheart?'

Three-year-old Ava had shaken her head vigorously, her mouth dry with fear as she'd imagined Luca and Jodi kidnapping her father.

'So we'll be perfect, darling. A perfect family for Daddy. We have to be perfect.'

And Ava had watched Karen Casseveti reach for her make-up.

So that had become Ava's mission: achieve perfection to ensure a perfect family so the perfidious Petrovellis wouldn't take her father away. Her understanding was hazy but absolute as she grew into an implicit alliance with her mother—a joint determination that James Casseveti *would* stay with *this* family. Though there was always that doubt—after all, he had walked out on his previous wife and children, the precedent set. The doubts were worsened by the overheard conversations that permeated her consciousness as she grew older, the tears and recriminations from her mother.

'You never loved me. You still love her. Would you have married me if I didn't have money?'

Her father's muted, soothing answers that eventually culminated in exasperation and finally into goaded admission.

'I did love her and Luca—of course I did. They were my family. But now you've got me, we have a marriage, we have a daughter. Why can't that be enough? This is our life.'

And Ava had come to realise that her father had loved his first wife, but had left her regardless, had decided that wealth and connections trumped family. She'd wondered if he ever regretted it, wondered if she and Karen were second best, if the riches and success could compensate.

So she'd redoubled her efforts. Ava always looked perfect, acted perfectly, danced to the tune her mother played. In truth there was no need for complaint. Her life had been one of privilege and she knew how lucky she was.

Yet there had been times when the constraints had stifled her individuality, when she'd felt almost like a parody of her own creation—an impeccable mix of English aristocracy and Dolci heiress. She'd wanted a life where she could follow her own dreams, not those concocted for her, a life not governed by press and publicity and the need to be flawless.

Yet in the end, despite everything, Luca and Jodi had indeed been a threat to be feared; Ava had not been perfect enough and now her half-siblings once more threatened her peace. Two shadowy figures who refused to meet her, refused to communicate except through lawyers.

Ava pulled open a drawer on her dressing table, took out the letter she had read and reread so many times in the past months. The letter of explanation her father had left her.

Dear Ava

I know you must be hurt and angry, and I hope this letter will mitigate that in some way. Please believe that I love you. You have been the most precious thing in my life these past years. You showed me, proved to me, that I am capable of being a good father. You have done nothing wrong.

You did nothing wrong, Ava, but I did. I left behind another family, a wife I loved, a son I loved. Luca was five when I left and my wife Therese was pregnant with a daughter I have never met, Jodi.

However much I try to justify my decisions now, towards the end of my life, I know that they were wrong. I left my life with them to live a life of wealth and plenty, to achieve the success I craved. But Luca and Jodi are my family, my children, and as such they deserve a part in this family com-

pany. They should have been given that oppor-
tunity a long time ago.

I hope you can accept this and forgive me.

Ava placed the letter down and resisted the urge to rub her eyes, knew tears would simply necessitate a touch-up of the carefully applied eye shadow, the mascara that enhanced her already long eyelashes.

Her gaze flicked to her father's familiar scrawl and she sighed—talk of acceptance and forgiveness was all very well but that wasn't how real life was panning out. For a start Karen Casseveti had no intention of doing either. Her whole life was focused now on revenge for her husband's betrayal. All she wanted to do was overturn the will and oust the Petrovellis. Ava's refusal to do that had caused a rift between them. Karen could not comprehend her daughter's 'defiance'. Guilt touched Ava—she understood how her mother felt but knew that legally they didn't stand a chance. Knew that morally it wasn't the right thing to do. Yet she hated seeing her mother's bitterness and grief, even as she understood it. All through her marriage Karen had known that her husband still loved his first wife, but she'd concealed the knowledge, spun it into a sugar-coated illusion. In death James had torn that down, ripped away the gossamer strands to reveal the stark ugly truth.

As for Luca—who owned his own incredibly successful chocolate company—he seemed set on demonstrating just how little Dolci meant to him. He was refusing to engage, claimed that his sister was unsure of how to proceed and until she made up her mind, he would do nothing. In the meantime that left Dolci floundering in a mire of uncertainty, the Casseveti 'family' brand indelibly tainted, negative publicity and salacious gossip everywhere Ava looked, along with the damning verdict of the business world: that Ava Casseveti didn't have what it took. She was an ex-model, given a role in the company due to nepotism not ability. Otherwise why would her father have left the company to children he didn't even know?

Her perfectly manicured and painted nails curled into her palms as determination to prove everyone wrong clashed with the cascade of self-doubt. After all, it was a valid point—whatever he claimed in his letter her father wouldn't have left two thirds of Dolci to his other children if he truly believed in Ava.

But this morning wasn't about that.

Today was about the next part of her father's letter.

There is another wrong I did, Ava. One I haven't had the courage to rectify myself and so I ask you to do it for me.

Many years ago, when I was still with Therese, I had a friend and colleague named Terry Rourke, and it was he and I who came up with the idea of Dolci. It was a pipe dream, discussed over a pint of beer or a Sunday barbecue. I had no legal obligation to bring him in on it but I did have a moral one.

I believe Terry has passed away, but he leaves behind a son—please do something for him in my name.

Thank you, Ava. I ask you to show understanding to your siblings and support to your mother.
My love
Dad

Sometimes it felt to Ava as if she had never known her father, that her relationship with him had been an illusion, a con, a dream, and it was only in death that he was showing his true colours. Yet whatever his shortcomings she missed him with an ache of grief that seared and swelled inside her even six months after his death. A grief that made her determined to at least try to carry out his wishes. James Casseveti had wanted Luca and Jodi to be involved in Dolci—Ava had to give them that chance And now she would go and try to make amends for a wrong done before she was even born.

One last look at her reflection and Ava gave a satisfied nod. She was as ready as she would ever be—ready to face Liam Rourke, Terry Rourke's son. Another fun day in the life of Ava Casseveti.

In his sleekly furnished office, a careful mix of minimalist and comfort, designed to inspire client confidence, Liam Rourke read the email on his screen. Surprise and disappointment coalesced into a low but heartfelt curse—he'd lost the Daley contract. For an instant anger joined the mix but he resisted the urge to slam his fist onto his desk. He couldn't win them all, he knew that. But this one stung, because he'd lost it to a man he knew and despised.

Andrew Joseph Mason, known to his upper-class pals as AJ. AJ Mason, ex-army like Liam. Founder of a security company. Like Liam. And there the parallels ended. AJ Mason came from 'proper' gilded army stock. There had been a Mason in the British army since time immemorial. No doubt since the first battalion of cavemen faced each other. And no doubt even millennia before they had been officer material, clad in a more expensive brand of leopard skin.

Now here was AJ Mason muscling in on his turf and Liam knew exactly how he was doing it. AJ had influence, clout and connections. All of which were undeniably impressive, especially when put against Liam's, which were pretty much non-existent. Liam had no army officers in his family, didn't have that extended familial network. But that shouldn't matter—though it had to AJ.

For a moment, memories hit Liam, of officer training thirteen years before, and the hell AJ Mason and a couple of his thuggish friends had put him through. AJ had taken an instant dislike to Liam, an antipathy born of his belief that officers should come from an upper-class background. A dislike that had flourished because Liam had turned out to be *first-class* officer material, had excelled in the training and exercises, had showed AJ up again and again. So AJ had exacted revenge; he'd known Liam would never 'snitch', so he and his friends had caused him to be ostracised, forced him to endure humiliation time and again.

Well, he wouldn't take it again. He was no longer a vulnerable eighteen-year-old boy. He'd figured out a way to beat AJ then and he'd do the same now. Years ago he'd managed to persuade AJ to meet him in the boxing ring. Once there he'd won a hard-fought victory, one where he'd showed AJ up and beaten him fair and square, the land of each punch a relish and retaliation for the humiliations piled upon him. A relish he could still taste now.

But it was a defeat that had left AJ a laughing stock—worse, it had also come to the attention of senior army officers who had been less than happy with him despite his illustrious background and family. AJ had been livid at the time and it seemed that had festered over the years.

There was a knock on the door and Liam's PA pushed it open and entered.

'Hey, Rita.'

'Hey. I'm sorry about Daley.' The petite redhead shook her head. 'It sucks. I heard on the grapevine that AJ invited Old Man Daley over for dinner, brought out the family silver and had his wife name-drop like crazy. The tipping point was a promise to invite his daughter to the Henley regatta with a few minor royals in tow. Worse I heard AJ's going for the Beaumont contract too.'

Liam's jaw clenched. Beaumont Industries replaced their security providers every five years and had requested a tender from Rourke Securities. It would be the contract that took his business to the next level.

Rita hesitated. 'It gets worse.'

'Explain.'

'He's dropping insinuations as well as names over the port and cigars. About how tragic it was that you lost your wife. That the tragedy made you lose your edge and isn't it sad you can't bring yourself to even date anyone. Shows what a long way you are from recovery.'

The idea that AJ was using Jessica's death caused cold, hard anger to slide into his gut. Made worse as he realised the effectiveness of the tactic. Right or wrong, like it or not, clients wanted a man with edge to be in charge of their security contracts, not a man still swimming the depths of grief and guilt.

The ache of guilt, the sadness of what might have been, still pulsed inside him, part of the fabric of his being even though it was five years since Jess's death.

The knowledge that their marriage had been a disaster of his own making, that he had taken her love and given her nothing back, allowed her to waste her tragically short life on him.

The start of their relationship had been overshadowed by the illness and death of his father. Followed by their hasty marriage due to Jess's belief she was pregnant, though by that point Liam had already suspected their relationship was doomed. That in his grief he'd mistaken attraction and liking for love. That Jess's love for him had blinded him and made him believe he felt the same way. But Jess had been so happy, so grateful even, that she had touched his heart and so he'd squashed down the niggle of doubt, the growing realisation that he didn't love her. Besides, he would never abandon a child. And by the time they'd realised the pregnancy scare was a false one he'd known he couldn't reject her love, couldn't hurt her the way his mother had hurt his father.

A few years later Jess had fallen ill and her last words to him had been of love, an admonishment not to grieve for too long and not to feel guilt over their marriage. Perhaps her forgiveness should have absolved him but in some ways it simply weighted the load more. That final conversation had torn his heart, shredded his insides with sadness and frustration. He would have done anything to give Jess more time, a chance to follow her dreams instead of waiting for him to return her love.

But he wouldn't show anyone that pain and he knew damn well it hadn't caused him to lose his edge. 'Thanks for the info,' he said. 'I'll deal with it.'

'I know you will.' Rita glanced at her watch. 'Anyways, the other reason I came up here was to tell you that you have a visitor.'

'A potential client?'

'I assume so.' Rita frowned. 'She looks familiar but she's wearing sunglasses and a scarf. Didn't want to give me her full name either.' None of this was unusual—sometimes clients were loath to give their identity or be recognised. 'She just said her name is Ava.'

Ava. It took all of Liam's iron control not to react, even as he told himself he was being foolish. Ava wasn't that uncommon a name—yet to him it had huge significance. The name bandied about during his childhood: Ava Casseveti—daughter of the man who had betrayed his father, driven Terry Rourke to drink and bitterness.

Liam gave his head a small shake—there were plenty of Avas in the world. And why on earth would Ava Casseveti show her face here? Any Casseveti was definitively persona non grata in his world. 'Bring her in.'

Rita nodded and exited the room. Liam rose, paced, worked to clear his mind from thoughts of the past.

A minute later there was a brief knock, the door swung open and Rita showed a woman in. Designer sunglasses hid her eyes and a scarf covered her hair; her clothes were an explicit demonstration of her status. Clearly expensive, without being flamboyant, they combined power with chic. White blouse, long-sleeved and V-necked, tucked into a dark checked skirt that emphasised her slender waist and long legs. Cool, sleek, professional.

Liam rose and headed round the desk as Rita made a discreet exit. 'Liam Rourke,' he said.

Before he could hold out his hand the woman deftly removed her sunglasses, dropped them into her shoulder bag, then swiftly tugged off the scarf to reveal long glossy corn-blonde hair that fell in perfect waves to frame a heart-shaped face. But what arrested him most were her eyes. They were an extraordinary colour, a luminous amber flecked with copper. To his chagrin his jaw dropped of its own volition. There was no need for her to identify herself. This was definitely Ava Casseveti and she was stunning. Little wonder that a few years back she'd taken the modelling world by storm. He blinked and forced his brain cells to regroup.

'Ava Casseveti,' she said and held her hand out—long-fingered and elegant, silver rings on the first finger of her right hand and the middle of her left, perfect nails a pale brown. Liam shook her hand, registered the smooth silk of her skin and a sudden little zing shot through him at her touch. *Whoa.* His gaze met hers and for a fleeting second he saw a flicker of shock in the amber depths and he knew she'd felt it too.

Time to focus, however surreal this felt. But it was hard because in some strange way Ava had always been a part of his life, both a nemesis and a motivator. Hadn't he wanted to prove to his father, *to himself,* that he would succeed despite what James Casseveti had done? Driven to do better than James Casseveti's daughter.

All of which explained that jolt and presumably also explained why their hands were still intertwined. As if she too realised that fact she moved backwards and disengaged her clasp, inhaled deeply and met his gaze. 'Thank you for seeing me at such short notice. Before I explain why I am here, can I ask if your father ever mentioned my father?'

The words tumbled from generous lips outlined in the reddest of reds and the sheer irony of the question nearly startled a bitter laugh from him. Instead he merely inclined his head. 'Yes. He did.' On a daily basis. The story of James Casseveti's betrayal had been the equivalent of Liam's bedtime story, the tale of how

Terry Rourke's best friend had used *their* business idea to leapfrog to fame and fortune. And that act of treachery had destroyed his father's life, his marriage, his job…the success of Dolci had broken Terry Rourke. And broken his family with it.

Pulling himself to the present, he gestured to his desk. 'Why don't you sit down? Then you can tell me why you are here.'

CHAPTER TWO

AVA MOVED TOWARDS the chair Liam had indicated, tried to use the time to regroup, refocus, settle the thrum of her nerves. Wished she could figure out what the hell was going on. *Quit kidding yourself, Ava.* She knew exactly what was going on. For some inexplicable, unfair reason her hormones had decided to awaken from dormancy and fix their attention on Liam Rourke.

To be fair the man was gorgeous. Thick coppery brown hair, a face that held strength and determination in its clean planes and angles, firm lips and a body that combined lithe muscle, breadth and length and... And jeez what was she doing? An inventory? This was not what she was here for. She sank onto the state-of-the-art chair, prayed he hadn't noticed her practically measure him up with her eyes and pulled her thoughts together into the carefully rehearsed words.

'I want you to know that during his lifetime my father never mentioned your family to me. Not once. However he left me a letter to be opened after his death. In it he explained that he did your father a moral wrong. Apparently they discussed the idea for a company like Dolci together and therefore he felt it was morally incorrect of him to set up Dolci without any reference to your father.' She paused and continued, kept her voice even. 'I would like to stress that there is no legal obligation at play here. There was no partnership, no agreement and no legal need for my father to involve yours.'

'So why are you here?' A hard edge of anger lined his words and she couldn't blame him. 'Given legal obligations clearly trump moral responsibility.'

'I didn't say that. I'm here because my father did feel a moral responsibility, but I'd be a fool not to safeguard my company. I want to be clear I'd like to offer compensation without prejudice. I'd like to carry out my father's wish to make amends.'

'How noble of him.' Liam made no attempt to hide the sarcasm. 'Unfortunately he is too late. My father died ten years ago and the damage was done.'

'I'm sorry.' And she was, she had hoped against hope that Terry Rourke had been unaffected by her father's actions, but the anger, the bitter twist of Liam's lips belied that hope. Showed her the utter inadequacy of her words.

In an instant, though, his face donned a mask of cool neutrality. 'An apology won't help my dad now—you cannot compensate for what your father did.'

'There must be something.'

'Such as?' The question was cold and tinged with contempt.

Yet it was imperative she carried out her father's wishes; she knew she couldn't just slough this responsibility off. Knew she didn't want to. 'What about the rest of your family? Is there anything I can do for them?'

'No.' The syllable was instant and absolute and she saw a shadow cross his eyes 'My mother has remarried and she is happy—I will not let you charge in and dredge up old memories to make yourself feel better.'

'That is not why I am doing this.' Now anger surfaced and she glared at him, saw the clench of his jaw. 'I want to do something to atone for what my father did. That is what he wanted.'

'Then why didn't he do it?'

It was a good question and one she didn't want to answer. Truth be told her father had *always* been morally weak. He would have intended to make amends but he would have easily talked himself out of it, put it off, procrastinated. 'That is irrelevant now. He asked me to act for him and that's what I want to do.'

'You can't. Accept it. And accept that I don't want your bounty—because nothing can atone for that betrayal. His perfidy broke my father. He felt cheated and bitter, a bitterness that pervaded and corroded his life. He began to drink heavily, he lost his job, his marriage fell apart as he watched your father climb the scale of success and fame. I understand that he could have made different choices, but the choices he made were put into play by your father.'

Ava winced, felt her face scrunch, her body braced in an attempt to reject his words even as she recognised their truth and realised the impact this must have had on Liam. Then for a second she saw something flash across his face. A sudden shaft of sympathy that vanished before she could be sure it was there. 'I... I... I don't know what to say.'

'Then say nothing. This is not your fault—I understand that.' He rubbed his hand over the back of his neck and exhaled. 'But there is nothing you can do to "right the wrong". The man your father wronged is gone. This is too little too late. The best thing you can do now is leave.'

Ava nodded, realised that her very presence must

be dredging up memories for *him*. She rose and he followed suit, walked round the desk to usher her towards the door. Halfway there she stopped. 'Hang on.' Ava turned, reached into her bag and pulled out a card. 'Here. This…' The words dried up, and they both seemed to freeze. Her feet felt stuck as his sudden unexpected proximity assailed her. The scent of his aftershave with its woodsy overtone tantalised her, and for one moment her gaze snagged and held on his lips, the firm etched outline of them. What was she *doing*? Gritting her teeth, Ava tucked a determined tendril of hair behind her ear and then continued, annoyed that the slightest of wobbles tremored the words. 'This has my details on it. I know I can't make up for what my father did but if I can ever do you a favour, please get in touch.'

Not that that was likely to happen. 'I mean it.' She held the card out, saw his hesitation, wondered if he was as unsettled as she. Carefully he took the card, but despite his care his fingers brushed hers and there it was again, a frisson, and this time she was sure he felt it too, saw awareness jolt in the depths of his cobalt eyes.

'Sure,' he said, though she suspected he'd bin the card as soon as she left.

Without meeting his gaze she slipped on her sunglasses and headed for the door.

Two weeks later

Liam scrolled down his inbox, each email sending his anger up a notch.

Given the report in the financial press I have concerns…

As a result of the uncertainties facing your firm…

Hi, Liam. I just wanted to check in, mate. See if you're OK. I'm sorry to hear you haven't been well. Grief over the loss of a loved one is so hard and it's fine if you need some time off.

Anger slammed him. 'Uncertainties' and 'time off', his backside. Over the past two weeks AJ's smear campaign had escalated, cast a tightening net of doubt over Rourke Securities by targeting its CEO. He'd done all the sensible things so far, looked at the legal route, decided not to react as that might give credence to the rumours. But enough was enough.

He snagged his jacket from the back of his chair and left the office and an hour later he pushed through the glass revolving door that led to the plush lobby of AJ Security, headed towards the reception area and smiled his friendliest smile.

'Good afternoon. I was wondering if you could help me.' He pulled out his army credentials and flashed them at the receptionist. 'I'm a fellow officer of AJ's— we trained together at Sandhurst—could I run up and surprise him?'

The receptionist looked doubtful. 'I'm only a temp here. I'm not sure…'

Another smile. 'I promise he won't mind. But just in case I'll tell him you tried to stop me. Would that work?'

'Um…' Before the temp could say anything Liam headed purposefully for the lift, saw the temp press a button on the phone and start to talk. He hopped out at the first floor and glanced round the open-plan office, then strode purposefully through the line of desks until he spotted a door with AJ's name plate, guarded by a PA. The blond man rose to his feet. 'Excuse me, sir. I need you to stop right there.'

'Not happening.' Liam knew he needed to move fast. 'I just want a quick word with AJ.'

'I'm afraid that won't be possible.'

'We'll see.'

Before the man could do anything Liam vaulted over the desk and in seconds had the PA's hands behind his back. 'I'm sorry about this and I really don't want to hurt you. I'll be a few minutes, that's all.'

The man nodded and stood and watched as Liam released him and headed for the office door, pushed it open and entered. He turned and stood with his back against it, estimating he had a few minutes at best before security guards burst in.

'Hey, AJ.'

AJ's eyes were wide and satisfaction slid through Liam as he saw fear flash in their depths. 'What do you want, Rourke?'

'Call off your guards and I'll tell you. Or...' and now Liam stepped forward '...let's do this the old-fashioned way and see who wins. It didn't take me that long last time to kick your butt.' He eyed the other man with contempt. 'And you were in better shape then. So make your choice.'

AJ picked the phone up. 'It's all right, guys. I've got this.'

'Good choice. I'm here to say back off.'

'Back off what?' The upper-class drawl grated on his nerves but Liam kept a smile on his face.

'Back off my clients and my business.'

Now AJ spread his arms in a gesture of innocence. 'I'm not doing anything, Rourke. If I have a bit of chat with my potential clients about your very understandable grief over your wife's tragic death, that's my prerogative.'

'Leave my wife out of this.' Rage threatened and he tamped it down into a useable commodity. Took a step forward, fists clenched, saw panic cross AJ's face as he pushed his chair backwards.

'Sorry. Sorry.' Now he pressed a button under his desk. 'But the Beaumont contract will be mine. And there's nothing you can do to stop me.'

'Watch me, Andrew, just watch me. You're a coward who relies on Daddy's money and position. Always were, always will be. Much as I'd love to wipe that smirk off your face, I'm not going to. This time let's finish it in the business ring. The result will be the same.'

Liam turned and exited, walked back to the lift, descended and left through the revolving door. Adrenalin surged through his body and he unclenched his fists. There was no way he would let AJ Mason win this and take Rourke Securities down.

Whatever it took, Liam would win. As he climbed into his car his mind raced through options. Legal and IT routes were all very well but the most important part of his strategy was to show Ray Beaumont and everyone else out there that Liam Rourke was on the top of his game, in control and capable. He needed to combat, not only AJ's accusations, but also the force of his connections and lifestyle, which would impress and bedazzle Ray Beaumont and his wife.

He drummed his fingers on his steering wheel, and an idea niggled the corner of his brain, grew and expanded into a plan as he completed the drive back to Rourke HQ. A plan he recognised as a gamble that verged on the cusp of insane. But one thing he'd learnt in the army was that sometimes the risky way was the only way to go, however high the stakes.

Once in his office he lifted the keyboard on his desk

and pulled out Ava Casseveti's card. Studied it for a long moment. Daughter of aristocracy, ex-model, business-woman, celebrity... Beautiful, charming, intelligent, well connected... And she owed him. Could he ask a favour of an enemy? In these circumstances, yes, he could.

Decision made, he punched in her number.

One ring, two, and then the call was picked up. 'Hello.'

'Ava. It's Liam Rourke.'

A couple of beats of silence and then, 'Liam. Good to hear from you.' Her tone clearly belied the truth of the sentiment.

'You said to call if I thought of a favour you could do me. Well, I have.'

There was a silence, then, 'Go ahead.'

'I'd rather pitch this in person. How about dinner to-night? I can pick you up from work if you like?'

'Um...' Liam realised he was holding his breath, told himself if Ava refused then he'd come up with an alternative strategy. 'OK. But I'll meet you there. Just tell me the location.'

'I'll text details and how about we meet at eight?' He'd already picked the perfect place, the right back-drop to help explain his plan, a venue that also had the merit of getting him seen in the right circles.

'I'll be there.'

A few hours later Liam approached the restaurant, as a taxi pulled up to the kerb. He waited and watched as Ava alighted from the black cab. His breath hitched in his throat—she looked...stunning. Her blonde hair was up in an elegant sweep that highlighted her slanted cheekbones; she wore a simple fitted black dress made that little bit different by the subtle striped detail of the V neck.

She paid the driver and headed towards him, her poise still reminiscent of the catwalk, graceful and lithe. As she reached him he nodded. 'Thank you for coming.'

'No problem. I told you to call if you needed a favour.'

'Then let's go in and I'll explain.'

He stepped back to allow her to go first, forced his gaze away from the slender column of her neck, the tantalising sweep of bare skin, focused instead on the air above her head. That at least was safe. Once inside he signed them in, and led the way into the restaurant situated on the ground floor of the exclusive military club.

Ava glanced around the room, her amber eyes scanning the huge portraits of historic military figures on the walls, the plush leather theme of the room reminiscent of men's clubs from days gone by. 'The website said it's imposing and they were right. But it also feels as though it is a part of history.'

Liam nodded. 'The army, battles, war have been part of life for centuries. This gives people a place to be part of that community if they want to be.'

'Do you come here a lot, then?'

'No. I use it to meet clients sometimes. Particularly if they have an army background, or find this sort of thing impressive.'

'So why did you ask me here?'

'Well, partly because the food is incredible. And partly for a reason that will become clear later.' He wanted to be seen with Ava, wanted the news to trickle back to AJ and his clients.

'I did have a look at the menu online,' she said. 'For all the different restaurants. They all look great—I didn't think a military club would have a tea room. Though it looks amazing with the book-lined walls. The cream teas did look good too.'

'It sounds like you studied the website pretty thoroughly.'

'Absolutely. I like to be prepared.'

'Rather than surprised?'

'I'm not keen on surprises. Plus if I hadn't prepared how would I have known what to wear? Imagine if I hadn't checked and I'd turned up in a gold lamé cocktail dress.'

Startled, he glanced at her. 'You own a gold lamé cocktail dress?'

'That's for me to know.' Her smile was almost shy and he realised that somehow they had relaxed into easy conversation. The knowledge unsettled him—this was Ava Casseveti, daughter of his father's nemesis—it shouldn't be easy to talk to her.

He gestured to the menus. 'I guess we'd better choose our food. Then we can get down to business.'

She studied the menu, took her time and then gave a small decisive nod. 'I'll go for Chalk Stream trout and buttered kale and dauphinoise potatoes. What about you?'

'The oven-roasted duck with roast potatoes and broccoli. Would you like wine?'

'Yes, please. White for me. I'm happy for you to choose.'

A waiter glided up, so silent and discreet that as always Liam wondered how it was done, was tempted to ask to see the soles of the man's shoes, check if they were crepe. Indeed, discretion was the order of the day. The restaurant was busy but the tables were well placed and the music pitched so that it wasn't possible to hear more than a general hum of conversation.

Within minutes the waiter returned. Liam declined to go through the tasting rigmarole and the waiter poured the delicate golden wine into the crystal glasses before melting away once more.

They sipped the wine and both nodded approval at the same moment and then Ava placed her glass down. 'Tell me the favour.'

Liam took a deep breath. This was it. Time to put Campaign Insanity into play and let the chips fall where they would.

CHAPTER THREE

AVA TOOK A sip from her wine, savoured the floral overtone as it trickled down her throat. Studied Liam's expression and wondered what on earth he could be about to request. Premonition tickled the back of her neck—instinct warned that perhaps she should do a runner now. Yet she couldn't stop herself from lingering on the strength of his features, the line and shape of his lips.

He leant back slightly, his body relaxed though this was belied by a tension in his jaw and the guarded look in his eyes. 'As you know, I head up Rourke Securities.'

Ava nodded. Her research had shown her that his company was a massive success. Both admiration and envy tingled through her. This man had forged his own fortune—come up the hard way. Like Luca Petrovelli. And unlike Ava. Ava had been born into advantage and ready-made fame, her mother a Lady, a minor royal celebrity, her father founder and CEO of Dolci, rolling in success and riches. What would she have achieved in Liam's shoes or in Luca's? She pushed the thoughts away, focused instead on Liam. 'Go on.'

'In recent weeks I've hit a snag in the form of a competitor. Another ex-army captain, a peer of mine, has also set up a security company. A man with personal wealth, upper-class background, connections. Blah blah. That I can deal with.' Liam upturned his palms. 'I've got no issue with healthy competition but this guy plays dirty.

Now Liam's whole stance hardened, his jaw clenched and anger iced the cobalt of his eyes. But before he could speak the waiter returned and placed their dishes in front of them. Ava murmured thank you and waited for him to go before she looked expectantly at Liam.

'We are both in contention for a really important contract with Beaumont Industries and AJ Mason has orchestrated a smear campaign, designed to make me look vulnerable and weak.'

Ava stared at him and once again her hormones did a funny little flip. There wasn't even a hint of weakness or vulnerability in sight. The man was sheer power, from the craggy strength of his features to every sinew of his body. Compact lithe muscle, and now her eyes lingered on the breadth of his thigh, moved up to see the wall of his chest and the sculpted swell of his shoulders in the fine linen shirt. She blinked. *Get a grip.* What was wrong with her? Perhaps her starved hormones were so happy to have lighted on an attractive man they had decided to make hay whilst the sun shone. And who could blame them?

'The man sounds like a dirtbag. Surely you can get him for libel or slander or…something.'

'My problem is timing. My tender for the Beaumont contract needs to go in in a month. I don't have time to take AJ to court and, to be honest, even if I do it won't counter-punch the impact of all the online lies and the background venom. My reputation will be in shreds.'

'So where do I fit in?'

Liam looked down at his plate, pushed it away and topped up their glasses. 'I'm a widower.' His voice was flat, factual, and Ava kept her expression neutral, even as sympathy touched her. Liam could be little more than thirty; his wife must have been tragically young to die. There had been no mention of a wife on his company bio, no mention of a wife full stop in the Internet search she had conducted. 'My wife died five years ago. Since then I haven't had another relationship. AJ claims that I have never recovered from the tragedy and as time goes on it is affecting me more and more. So I need to *show* everyone that I am perfectly OK, on my game, my edge honed and nowhere near a nervous breakdown. I also need to counter his connections, his background and so on.'

'So what are you proposing? Exactly.' Ava remained still though every instinct told her not to wait for the answer but to push back her chair and run for it.

His gaze met hers full on; one deep breath and then he launched. 'I want you to pose as my girlfriend.'

It took all her social poise not to drop the sterling silver cutlery into her trout. Perhaps AJ Mason had a point. Perhaps Liam Rourke had lost the plot. But forget nervous breakdown—the man was bonkers. 'Excuse me?'

'I want you and I to fake a relationship.' The suggestion was uttered with a calm that quite simply did not gel with the sheer preposterousness of the idea. 'Unless of course you already have a partner? I did do some research of my own but I realise that may not have been sufficient.'

For a moment Ava considered simply making up a boyfriend, then dismissed the idea as craven. 'No. I am currently single.' Had been for the past four years. Since the Nick debacle, her one serious relationship.

Nick Abingworth had been a producer, met in the heady days of Ava's modelling career, and he was Hollywood handsome, charming and charismatic. Ava had fallen for the façade, believed it to front a good guy, a hero. Had harboured rose-tinted dreams of a happy ever after.

Had forgotten all the lessons learned from her parents' marriage. A marriage where Karen Casseveti's love for her husband had been an obsession. As for James, he'd loved Karen's wealth and connections, loved them so much he'd left his first family.

But Ava had forgotten all about the folly of one-sided love, disregarded the knowledge that love could be bought, faked with an eye to the main chance. Had believed she and Nick were different. Turned out she'd been wrong. When her dad had suffered his first heart attack and Ava had given up modelling to enter Dolci, had no longer been a celebrity party girl, Nick had shown his true colours and a swirl of dust as he'd legged it out of the door. Said he was sorry but she'd changed, was no longer the woman he'd fallen in love with. *Ciao.*

That had been that and, as far as Ava was concerned, that was how it would remain. 'Definitely single,' she added for emphasis. 'With no interest in a relationship. Of any type.'

'Think of it as a charade. A ruse to refute the idea that I haven't got over my wife.'

Have you? The question nearly fell from her lips and she bit it back. That was none of her business. Plus the man hadn't dated in five years—he didn't sound over it. But that was beside the point—the point was that this plan was granola nuts.

'It won't work. For a start, don't you think AJ will find the timing a wee bit suspect?'

'He might, but he can hardly suggest that I have persuaded or bribed Ava Casseveti to play along with a fake relationship. Why would you?'

'Well, there's an excellent question. Why would I?'

'Because you want to make amends for your father's actions. This is how you can do that. There's a certain poetic justice in the idea—a Casseveti *helping* a Rourke with a business plan.'

Touché. Ava closed her eyes as a swell of panic threatened. Every instinct told her this was not a good idea. Liam Rourke was too…much. Too good-looking, too attractive, and that was not what she needed right now. Her hormones were way too volatile around Liam. She could almost feel her carefully ordered world fraying at the edges. 'I see that, but this idea is… Well, it's pants. I mean, how would it even work?'

He shrugged. 'We fake a relationship, we go out for dinner, give some interviews, attend business functions together, get seen, generate some *positive* publicity for me. Right or wrong, people will be impressed by you, your position, your credentials.'

A stab of hurt pinged her ribs. Obviously all Liam Rourke wanted was the Ava Casseveti persona, the aristocrat, the celebrity model, the businesswoman. Not Ava herself. She gave her head a small shake at her own idiocy. Why would he want anything else? 'Actually, right now they may not be. The current public verdict on me is that I am a ditzy airhead who won't be able to keep her company from going under. A woman her own father didn't trust at the helm.' She met his gaze directly. 'So I may be a liability rather than an asset.'

For a moment he considered her words, his fingers

drumming on the snow-white linen of the tablecloth. 'Nope. I don't think so. You are still my best option. This may even help you.'

'How?'

'It will distract people from a consideration of your business problems.'

'Hah! They'll think I'm fiddling whilst my desserts flambé.'

This pulled a smile from him. 'Not necessarily. If we publicise our relationship properly we can orchestrate some interviews that will give you a real chance to put your case forward.'

'It's too high risk.' Ava contemplated him, realised that Liam Rourke represented danger, high risk, high octane. Everything Ava Casseveti didn't do. 'It wouldn't work. We are strangers. Worse than strangers.' Her gaze met his. 'There is too much history between us. We are natural enemies. We couldn't pull this off.'

His lips twisted. 'Sounds to me like an excuse. This is all about our history. You told me two weeks ago you wanted to make amends on your father's behalf. This is how you can do it. Your choice.'

What to do? What to do?

Liam's words came back to her.

'Nothing can atone for that betrayal. His perfidy broke my father. He felt cheated and bitter, a bitterness that pervaded and corroded his life.'

But it was more than that—it would have corroded Liam's as well.

Conflict warred within her—the desire to do what was 'right' versus the instinct for self-preservation. But this wasn't about self, wasn't about Ava. The crux of the matter was the wrong done by her father and his desire to try to make it right. If she walked away now she would fail, would let her father down. And herself. In reality there was no choice. 'Fine. I'll do it. I'm in.'

Even as the words fell from her disbelief caused her to clasp her hands together under the table, to resist the urge to pinch herself in the hope she'd wake up.

'Excellent.' His low voice held satisfaction and appreciation and a funny little thrill shot through her as he raised his glass; his cobalt-blue eyes held hers and the shiver of anticipation and panic intensified. 'To us,' he said, just as their waiter shimmied towards the table, dessert menu in hand.

Instantly she raised her own glass and smiled, her best 'Ava Casseveti thinks you're great' smile. 'To us,' she echoed. Once the waiter had cleared their table and glided out of earshot she nodded. 'I understand now why you picked here for dinner. You're hoping that word will get to AJ that you were here with me.'

'Not only AJ. People in general. Some of my clients are ex-military or have military connections. It will all help.'

Ava looked down at the glossy card as her brain grappled to come to terms with what she had agreed to. 'Right now what will help is a melt-in-the-middle chocolate pudding and an espresso.'

Liam smiled, the effect electric. Ava felt her pulse rate ratchet, as warmth flooded her body, and she reached for her water glass. 'You're right.'

Whilst that was gratifying she only seemed able to focus on his smile. Her gaze snagged on the firm contour of his lips. *Enough.* 'I know. There isn't much in life that chocolate pudding can't help.'

Once the dessert arrived Ava tasted it experimentally. 'This is good. Not as good as Dolci's, of course.'

His lips tightened imperceptibly and she wished the words back. Dolci was hardly the best topic to bring up. 'Sorry.'

He shook his head. 'Don't apologise. Obviously I can hardly expect you not to mention Dolci over the next three months.'

The chocolate melted to ash in her mouth and she dropped the spoon with a clank. 'Three months? Three weeks would be hard enough. Three months…is a quarter of a year.'

'We need the time or people will know it's fake.'

'But we can't sustain a lie of this magnitude for three months.'

'Surely it won't be so bad for you? You were a model. I assume you had to act, project, exaggerate feelings.'

'Yes. For *a photo shoot*, and I was projecting my love for perfume, or chocolate, not a real live person. For a very short space of time. For the benefit of the camera, not a live audience. *And* if I made a mistake I got another go.'

He raised a hand. 'I get it.'

'No. I really don't think you do. Besides, forget me.' After all, she'd spent her whole life playing the various personae of Ava Casseveti, perfect daughter, perfect girlfriend…celebrity…heiress, aristocrat. 'What about you? How are you going to pull it off?'

'That's my problem.'

'Nope. It is *our* problem. If we are exposed we will both look like idiots. Both be publicly humiliated. *We* have to make this look real.'

There was a silence and then he nodded. 'Fair point.' He picked up his coffee cup. 'How about we meet tomorrow for a brainstorming session? Give us both some time to think about a strategy to make this work. Per-

haps we could meet at Dolci headquarters? So I can get
accustomed to the idea I am dating a Casseveti.'

Ava felt a small tug of surprise. Liam had listened
to her, taken her comments on board. 'Works for me.
I'll see you there.'

CHAPTER FOUR

LIAM STOOD OUTSIDE the offices of Dolci's headquarters the following evening and looked up at the impressive glass-fronted façade. Memory rocked him. His father had brought him here once and for a few tension-filled moments twelve-year-old Liam had believed that Terry Rourke would storm inside and cause an affray. Remembered anxiety echoed a hollow ring in his gut.

Now, nineteen years later, Terry was dead and Liam stood here on the brink of a fake relationship with Ava Casseveti. About to gain entrance into the enemy's portals. Would his father approve of this? Of course he would—he would appreciate that a Casseveti had been forced into a contract with a Rourke. And his mother. How would she feel?

Liam had no idea. His relationship with his mother was too distant for him to hazard a guess. He loved his mum, of course he did, but that love was layered with strands of guilt and knowledge of how his selfish behaviour had impacted on her happiness.

As a child he'd hero-worshipped his father, blamed his mother for the breakdown of his parents' marriage, hadn't understood how hard it was for her to watch Terry Rourke slowly but surely give his life over to the bottle. Lose his job, his dignity, his body and soul vanishing into a maudlin, alcoholic haze. Liam hadn't got Bea's struggle to try and keep a roof over their heads and food on the table. All Liam had wanted was for his father to get better and his parents to be happy again.

Then, when Liam was twelve, Bea had met someone else, a plumber at the hospital where she'd worked as a nurse—John Malone—and they'd fallen in love. She'd been full of joy, had planned to leave her husband, had expected Liam to understand, to go with her.

Liam had been horrified at having his illusory bubble burst, had refused point-blank to leave his dad, and in the end Bea had stayed in the marriage. For Liam's sake.

Guilt at his actions tugged but before he could contemplate further Ava walked through the revolving glass door and headed towards him. And dammit again, she stopped him in his tracks, derailed his senses for a smidgeon of time, dressed today in elegant tailored grey trousers topped by a black top and cinched at the waist with a wide belt. 'Hi.'

'Hi,' he managed and for that fleeting instant they both simply stood and then she stepped back. 'Come on up.'

Through a marbled lobby, walls decorated with glittering photographs of Casseveti success. James shaking hands with a renowned global businessman, Ava in a photo shoot to promote Dolci products… Liam absorbed it all, ensured he kept his stance relaxed during the trip in a state-of-the-art elevator, a walk through a now empty open-plan work area, dotted with desks and equipment and then they entered a spacious meeting room. A large oval glass-topped table graced the centre, a tray with coffee, tea and biscuits had been set out, a whiteboard was ready at the front. The perfect setting for a business brainstorming session.

Liam placed his briefcase on the table. 'I think the best way is to sit down and swap some basic facts, the sort of information that it would be natural for us to have.'

Ava sat down and opened a leather-bound folder. 'Agreed. I've prepared a CV but with some extra personal information. Like how I like my tea.'

'I did a fact sheet. Though I have to admit I didn't include my tea preference. Good call.' That was the exact detail they would be expected to know. 'I take mine strong with just a hint of milk.' Ava already had a pen in hand and was jotting the information down, and for a moment he caught a glimpse of the column of her neck as she bent over the table.

For an overlong instant his gaze was caught and a pang shot through him, one he damped down immediately. 'Let's read each other's information and then try and learn it. We can test each other later.'

She nodded agreement and pushed her CV across the table. He noted that her nails were a different colour from the previous day and for a moment he wondered how hard it must be to coordinate her outfits so well. Wondered if attention to nails would feature on her fact list.

He watched her as she studied his piece of paper, the small fierce crease of concentration, the way she pressed her lips together. Dammit, now he'd snagged on those lips his gaze lingered for a moment and he quickly turned his attention to the paper on the table. Started to commit the facts to memory: her birthday, names of her schools, private education, top grades, various dance awards, excellent university, and then her two-year stint in the modelling world.

Then she'd quit modelling and gone into the family firm, where she'd held roles in different departments until her father's death six months ago. Never owned a pet, enjoyed dancing, fashion and shoes. As he came to the end of the sheet he looked back up at her and caught her studying him.

'Right,' she said. 'I think I'm getting the facts. I know your birthday, where you were born and a bit about your family. Your mum is called Bea, your step-dad is called John and his son is called Max and he is fourteen.' She stopped and he was aware he'd flinched as more memories cascaded in.

Two years after Bea decided to stay with her husband, John had married someone else, and Liam could still remember his mother's grief when she'd found out. He'd seen the anguish in her grey eyes, heard the sound of muted tears in the night, seen her feet drag and heard her voice snap. It had only been then that he'd begun to understand what his mother had sacrificed for him and he hadn't known how to handle that.

So he'd renewed his efforts to make his dad better, make him reform, make his parents be happy again. To no avail. So in the end at eighteen he'd done what he'd thought was right. He'd joined the army. He'd known that once he had a new 'home' and independence his mother would be able to leave. Finally accepted too that his father was not going to change.

Then Bea had reconnected with John, by then divorced and the father of a three-year-old son, Max. Bea and John got married and Liam was happy for them. But he knew that he had thwarted their chance of an earlier life together, a chance to have children of their own. And that created an awkwardness and a discomfort and so he stayed clear as much as he could, wanted to allow his mum a second chance to have a happy family life.

But he'd put none of the detail on his fact sheet. All Ava needed were facts, not the grim story that shadowed them. Facts were important.

'That's right.'

Ava nodded. 'I've been thinking about this. Are you going to tell your mum the truth about us?'

'No. The fewer people who know, the better. The best way to keep a secret is to make sure it is a secret.'

'I get that but she is hardly going to be happy that her son is dating a Casseveti. I'll need to meet her during this charade and that will be awkward, to say the least. So why put her through it? Surely you can trust her to keep the secret?'

'It's not just my mum. It's John and Max as well. It doesn't seem fair to ask her to keep it secret from them. And Max is only fourteen. It seems even more unfair to ask him to keep a secret like that or to lie for us. I won't ask her or her family to do that.' Wouldn't complicate her life or upset her family dynamic in any way.

'That is a fair point. But—'

'It does make it extra hard on you. I'm sorry. I'll shield you as best I can when we meet her. And we'll keep it brief.' That would hardly be a surprise to any of them. Liam kept his visits short and polite. 'And whilst my mum will have some negative feelings, she knows you aren't to blame for your father's actions.'

Ava hesitated and then shrugged. 'OK. This is your show. Could you arrange for us to meet them once we have figured out our act properly. Before we go public?'

'Sure. And what about your mum?'

'We will have to tell my mother the truth. She knows who you are and about my father's request.'

'Will she keep it secret?'

'Yes. My mum is the Queen of Spin. She will see that our relationship can be spun to Dolci's advantage. She won't mess with that.' Ava gave a decisive nod and glanced down at her printed agenda, then up at her computer screen, tucked a stray tendril of hair behind her ear. This must be exactly how she looked in a business meeting.

She looked up. 'Right, next on the agenda—we need to get our story straight. Get our facts lined up in a row.'

She rose to her feet and headed towards the whiteboard. 'I thought we could plot out a timeline, work out some plot points. Then I'll type it up.'

'Sure. Good plan.' And it was…yet something wasn't right with the current scenario. Sure, they now knew more about each other but…

Moving along a few seats, he watched the unconscious grace with which she moved. As she reached for the pen, again her nail colour caught his eye, the pale pink a perfect complement to the grey of her suit, the crisp businesslike white of her shirt. Her lips a perfect match. Liam frowned, tried to home in on what his instinct was trying to tell him.

Knew it was not that he had a nail fetish.

'Right,' Ava said. 'I've thought about this and it's really important we figure out when our "relationship"— she made quote marks in the air —started. The times have to add up and stand up to scrutiny. We can't say we were having a romantic dinner at The Ritz if that's the day they were closed for renovations.'

'Agreed.'

'Good. So…' She broke off. 'Are you listening?' she asked.

'Yes, I am, and you're right. All that is important but…' He hesitated. 'We're doing this all wrong.'

'I don't understand.'

He wasn't sure he did either, but he trusted his instincts and this was too important to ignore them. 'You are right to say that this will only work if we can pull it off, and to do that we need all these facts. But this isn't the way to collate them.'

'Why not?'

He started to pace. 'Because this is how we'd conduct a work meeting. And whilst this is a business arrangement, the fake relationship isn't a business one. If we spend hours in a boardroom we may come up with a good theoretical plan and a list of facts about each other but that won't help us be authentic. Because there's lots of information that we won't have included. For example, you didn't mention how much effort you put into your appearance. It must take time to change the colour of your nails on such a regular basis.'

Ava frowned. 'It didn't even occur to me to mention my nails.'

'Exactly. That's the sort of thing that takes time and being together for real.'

'But are my nails really that important?'

'I don't know. But I do know if you send an undercover agent in somewhere you send someone who knows the territory, understands the language and the community. I don't know about you but I haven't been in a relationship for a long time. It's unfamiliar terrain.' And one he'd completely destroyed in his marriage.

'So you think we need some hands-on practice rather

than studying the theory.' Her eyes widened and heat crept up her cheekbones. 'That came out all wrong. I didn't mean literal hands-on practice...' She raised her hands to touch her cheeks. 'Now I am making this worse.'

He couldn't help the smile that tugged his lips, even as desire sparked in his gut. 'I know what you meant. We can come up with the best story in the world, learn all these facts, but a play is only as good as the actors.'

'And we aren't actors.'

'Exactly, so we have to maximise our chances of managing to fake this. I think we need to get more... comfortable round each other, and that means spending time together outside a boardroom.'

'So what do you suggest?'

'Let's go on a date. Right now. A trip on the London Eye. We provided security at an event there recently and we were given a season pass for Rourke Securities employees. I'm pretty sure I can get us an upgrade. We can discuss a timeline, whilst looking out over London in a private pod.'

'Isn't it a bit risky? I don't think we are exactly ready to launch.'

'I get that.' Liam shrugged. 'But it's not as though we need to speak to anyone or give an interview. It will give us "relationship experience" and add evidence to our dating history.'

'Agreed.'

'Give me five minutes to make a couple of calls.'

Fifteen minutes later they were on their way, in the back of a chauffeur-driven car. Ava glanced sideways at him, ridiculously aware of his proximity. She'd watched him as he'd made this happen, the mix of crisp efficiency and charm that had secured them the private pod, and his sheer dynamism had sparked a frisson. Now her hormones were having difficulties mastering the concept of a fake date. But she had them on a tight leash, was sat squashed against the window, as far from him as it was possible to be. Hell, if anyone opened the door she'd tumble out. And Liam was no better. Yet the idea of moving across seemed way too fraught and relief swathed through her as the car glided to a stop.

They climbed out to walk the remainder of the way, the cool London evening breeze a welcome hit as they made their way towards the huge lit-up wheel. She tried to walk a little closer to him to get in character as their breath wisped white on the brisk February air.

Once there, a friendly member of staff approached and conferred with Liam, who then turned to Ava. 'Usually the pod comes with a host. Are you happy to sign a waiver to say you're OK without one?'

'Of course.' Minutes later they were standing in the pod, glass of champagne in hand.

'Are they really OK letting us on without a host?'

'Sure. I've said that we'll treat it as a test of their security and health and safety measures. Lots of people would rather not have a host so we're testing it for them. Last thing we need is to be observed close up.'

'Definitely not.' Ava looked out over the London night sky as the wheel began to move, so slowly it felt almost like magic, as if they were lifted by gossamer threads. 'It's beautiful by night. I came here in the day with a couple of colleagues once but this is completely different. All the landmarks look like a fairy tale.' Come to that, this all felt like a fairy tale. And it had nothing to do with the lights or the champagne and everything to do with Liam's presence. He was right. This was completely different from the boardroom, but she still wasn't at all sure it was in a good way. Or perhaps it was too good. Because here if she moved ever so slightly she'd be right next to him, would be able to feel the solid press of his muscular thigh against her leg, would be able to inhale the tang of expensive soap, study the way his hair curled over his ear and...

Time to talk, time to find poised, aristocratic, socially adept Ava, and she wrenched her gaze to the London landscape. 'It's amazing, really—I mean, who designed it? A glorified Ferris wheel that has become one of the main tourist attractions in London.'

'It was built by a husband and wife team. And it's about one hundred and thirty-five metres tall with a diameter of one hundred and twenty metres. The pods weigh ten tonnes and—' Five minutes later he broke off and ran a hand over the back of his neck. 'Jeez. Sorry. I didn't even know I *knew* all of that.'

'That's OK.' She was pretty sure Liam was as on edge as she was. 'You made all those facts interesting.' Seeing his eyebrows rise in clear disbelief, she smiled. 'Honestly. You did. You'd make a great tour guide.'

He gave a mock groan. 'And a terrible date.'

'Nope.' She shook her head. 'Actually...it's kind of sweet.'

'Sweet?' His tone mixed incredulity and distaste and she laughed.

'Yup. And it proves your point. Being here made those facts personal...and that is the best way to get to know each other. But it's also a bit...strange. Because it's a date that's not a date.'

'And we aren't natural around each other.' He took a deep breath. 'Yet.'

'Maybe it will just take time. A few more dates like this. Sitting in a car together...'

'And not squashing ourselves up against the doors,' he said and now they smiled at each other.

'Exactly. Maybe a week or so—we could walk round parks, hang out...get a bit more used to each other. I mean, we barely know each other, and our history makes it even more complicated. It's hard to base a relationship on—' She broke off as instinct prickled the back of her neck.

'What's wrong?'

'Nothing. Just keep talking. But I think we've been spotted.' Out of the corner of her peripheral vision, she saw someone point at their pod, camera in hand. 'We *have* been spotted.' Her mind went into overdrive; on automatic she appraised the scene. Champagne, private pod, the whole thing shrieked of date night. This was the perfect set-up for a launch of their relationship; discovered by accident, it would reek of authenticity.

Instinct took over and, leaning over, she kissed him. Her intent had been a simple, quick, featherlight brush of the lips but she hadn't bargained for her body's reaction. Or his. Because it wasn't enough—the sheer giddy sensation whirled her head. After a first startled second where he froze, he turned his body, raised his hands and cupped her face; the firm, cool grasp made her catch her breath.

Then he deepened the kiss, slowly, languorously, as if they had all the time in the world, and Ava forgot where she was, forgot everything except this heady moment in time where nothing mattered except the sweet sensations that glided through her whole body. Then all too soon it was over, the wheel literally stopped turning and Ava realised they were near the top.

As she pulled away she caught sight of his expression, knew it mirrored her own. Shell shock, surprise. *All wrong,* screamed the one bit of her brain that was still in gear. *Pull this together.* Seamlessly she pulled a smile to her lips and whispered, 'Don't look surprised.' Knew that a photo like that splashed on social media would give away too much.

To her relief Liam got it instantly, leant forward to hide his expression, looked as though he were whispering sweet nothings in her ear, and then he moved away to pick up the champagne bottle to top up their glasses, a smile of sorts on his lips.

Ava focused on breathing, sipped the champagne, wished it were the bubbles that were swirling her head rather than the aftermath of the kiss. 'Sorry. I reacted on instinct—I saw an opportunity to make this look real and I took it without thinking.'

'There's no need to apologise—you took me by surprise, that's all.' With an obvious effort he cleared his throat, brought his voice to a normal tone. 'What do you think will happen now?'

Ava shrugged. 'It's hard to know. It could be absolutely nothing, it could be the photo goes viral on social media. My feeling is it will land somewhere in between. There will be a buzz of interest because of who I am and it may or may not pick up.'

Liam rubbed the back of his neck, gave her a rueful smile. 'Sorry. You were right earlier. This was a bad idea. If interest is piqued we aren't ready yet.'

'No.' But it was impossible to feel irritation with a man who was willing to admit fault.

'Hmm…' She could almost see his brain go into overdrive. 'I've got an idea. Let's go back to my place—I need to make some calls.'

* * *

Forty-five minutes later the car came to a smooth stop and the driver opened the door. Ava smiled her thanks as she climbed out and looked around her at the large Edwardian London house.

She followed him through the front door and down a spacious hallway. "The lounge is through here. Drink?" he asked.

'A cup of tea would be perfect.'

'Coming up. Milk, one sugar, right?'

'Right.'

He left the room and she took the opportunity to look around. The room was functional and comfortable with clean lines and colours. Yet it could be a show room—there were no photographs or anything out of place or cluttered. Sitting down on a luxuriously comfortable arm chair she wondered where Liam was. Perhaps the kitchen was miles away or the kettle had broken or he'd run out of tea bags.

On that thought the door opened and he reappeared. 'Tea and biscuits.'

'Perfect.' He sat opposite her and she raised her eyebrows. 'You look pleased with yourself.'

'I am. I've figured out a solution to our need-to-get-to-know-each-other-fast problem.'

'Go ahead.' Ava eyed him and a sudden premonition tickled the back of her neck, told her that his next words were going to be humdingers.

'A mini break in Italy.'

'Mini break? Italy?' Parrot, anyone?

'Yes. Sometimes I have clients who need to meet away from the public eye. If two businesses are planning a merger and want to keep it under the radar they want privacy and security. I provide that—Rourke Security has a number of discreet, secure, safe locations. We can use one of those and spend the weekend there.'

'Um…'

'It's a little village in Puglia. It's beautiful and a tourist attraction so we can blend in as simple tourists. It's a low-key way to practise being a couple. I've got a flight sorted out for tomorrow evening and I've spoken to Elena, the housekeeper there. She'll have it all ready and—'

'Whoa.' Was he for real? 'Hang on a sec. You've done all that? I haven't even agreed—you haven't even asked my opinion.'

'That's what I'm doing now.'

'No. Actually it isn't. You've arranged everything. Sounds like it's a done deal.' It all felt like shades of her whole life, other people in control, deciding her actions and her future. Pleasing her father, her mother, Nick… Ever since she was a child she'd done what she was supposed to, done the right thing, worked so very hard to be the perfect daughter. She'd worn the clothes her mother bought her, taken dance exams, played the violin. To please her father she'd studied hard, made the right friends, walked the path her parents sent her down. Jumped when she was told to jump. Because she had always known she was the glue that bound the Casseveti family.

Now this man had done the same, made decisions for her and suddenly Ava was furious.

Liam sighed. 'There would be no point wasting time in a consultation if I couldn't deliver.'

'Well, how do you know *I* could deliver? You don't know me—I could be afraid of flying. I could be allergic to Italy. I may not want to spend the whole weekend with you in a strange place. Or anywhere, for that matter. *I* may have had some ideas.'

A pause and then Liam held up his hand. 'You're right. I sprang it on you as a fait accompli.' Now he shook his head. 'Discussion was never my strong point.' The words were muttered under his breath and she was sure she wasn't meant to hear them. 'I apologise.'

Ava blinked; she could practically feel the moral high ground drop from under her feet.

Then he smiled, a small quick smile, and she could feel her ire start to lose its heat. 'So let's start again,' he said. 'Are you scared of flying?'

Ava looked at him. 'No. I was speaking hypothetically.' Plus as a model she had done photo shoots all over the world—Liam had been well within his rights to assume air travel wasn't an issue.

His gaze met hers. 'Any allergies?'

Now Ava sighed and saw his lips quiver ever so slightly in clear amusement and her eyes narrowed.

'Perhaps an allergy to pizza. Pasta, spaghetti or lasagne.' He put on an Italian accent and now Ava couldn't help it—her own lips turned up in a reluctant grin.

'Ha ha! OK. You got me. No allergies.'

'Then on to your next point. Here you are completely correct—I should never have assumed you would feel safe coming to Italy to spend a weekend with a stranger. If it makes you feel better I have a housekeeper there who can stay in the house—Elena is a lovely woman.'

'Thank you. I appreciate all of that. But it wasn't my physical safety I was thinking about. It just feels a bit intense to spend a whole weekend together. A bit daunting.'

'Agreed,' he said.

The word gave her a sudden hard kick of reality. If

this was hard for her it would be doubly so for Liam. The last woman he would have gone on a mini break with was his wife. This whole charade must be incredibly hard for him on so many levels, which prompted the question: 'Are *you* sure you want to do this?'

'I'm sure. I won't let AJ Mason get away with this. He will not take my company and my reputation away from me. I won't let that happen. Or at least not without a fight.'

Ava had to respect that determination, had to concede as well that the idea had merits.

They would be tucked away out of the public eye and it would give them much-needed time to get comfortable around each other and practise their roles.

'Then, Italy, here we come.'

CHAPTER FIVE

THE FOLLOWING DAY as they approached the airfield Ava tried to quell the butterflies that flitted around her tummy in a maelstrom of panic. She sneaked a sideways glance at Liam. His gaze was focused on the road and there was no indication of any nerves in his demeanour. For a moment her gaze touched on the firm line of his jaw, the sweep of his nose and the surprising length of his dark eyelashes. For one stupid moment she wondered what it would be like if this were real, and a little shiver ran through her body.

All in all it was a relief to arrive at the airfield. 'So this is your plane?' she asked as they approached the craft.

'It belongs to Rourke Securities. A client has asked for an item to be delivered privately in Europe. My pilot will drop us off en route.'

Soon after, the plane started its ascent and Ava looked around the compact but comfortable area, complete with a small table and soft leather reclining chairs.

In the interest of showing that she was back in control of her nerves she put on her best social expression. 'So do you own a lot of planes?'

Liam shook his head. 'Just this one. Sometimes I have clients who want to broker a deal and they figure high up in the air is the best place to do it. Sometimes I have to move a team of people fast and safely and discreetly. Or move cargo. I do try to combine assignments where I can to limit the ecological impact. I need this plane to run my business but I minimise airmiles. If I can transport by land or even sea I do. And the company does support a number of environmental charities.'

Surprise touched her. 'I didn't have you down as someone who would care about the environment.'

'I think we all have to. Don't get me wrong, I'm not giving up air travel, but I figure every little counts.'

'I agree and I'd really like Dolci to do more. I'd like to use more local suppliers and really look at how much unnecessary plastic we use. Analyse how we can minimise impact to the environment.'

'Then do it.'

He made it all sound so simple, as if she could wave a magic wand. 'It's not that easy.'

'Why not?'

The slight quirk in his voice goaded her, as if she were all talk and no skirt. 'For a start I am not in sole charge. My half-siblings have equal shares.'

'According to press reports they aren't exactly showing up to work—maybe they wouldn't object? Have you asked them?'

Ava pressed her lips together—her 'family' problems weren't to be shared. 'No. They'd probably lawyer up.' Or simply stonewall her. At the moment Luca Petrovelli would only communicate through lawyers and his standard response was that he couldn't give an opinion until he came to an agreement with his sister. As for Jodi, she didn't respond at all, after her initial reply that simply said to refer to her brother. Frustration gnawed Ava's insides and tensed her muscles and she forced her body to relax. 'But I did ask my father and he was less than keen. He wanted to do the minimum needed to "look good", believed profit trumped ethics.' Even an appeal to his conscience hadn't worked. He'd listened to her ideas and then he'd vetoed them. Instead he had donated privately to an environmental charity.

'You don't still have to do as your father wanted. This is something you clearly feel passionate about. So own it. Make Dolci a forerunner on the environment.'

'It doesn't feel right. Dolci was built on the foundations of my dad's ethos, his drive, his ideas and beliefs. And they worked. I don't want to go against his wishes and I'd probably be a fool to do so.'

'But times change and people change. Your father had his vision, now it's time for yours.'

'Just like that?' Her whole life had been spent being the perfect daughter, following her parent's wishes, or at least ensuring they coincided with her own—she wasn't sure she knew how to stop. 'Dolci is his legacy. I can't trample over that. My vision may send Dolci down the pan. Then that would be my responsibility. My fault.' Because she wasn't good enough, wasn't perfect and would finally be exposed in all her lack of glory. The idea shivered panic-stricken fear through her and she clenched her nails into her palms. Sparked determination—Dolci would not go under, not on her watch. 'And that isn't going to happen.' She shook her head. 'Anyway, right now we need to be talking about our fake relationship and how to make it believable.' In truth she had no idea how this conversation had gone so off-piste.

Liam waited a heartbeat and for a second she thought he'd demur, pursue the topic of Dolci. Then, 'You're right. Where should we start?'

'It's all about the detail. The only way to spin a fabrication is to make sure it stands up to scrutiny.' A rule she'd learnt in the cradle or possibly even the womb. After all, Karen had spun the Casseveti story into a fairy tale and that had been no easy task. Somehow she'd managed to completely gloss over James leaving his first family and painted instead the magical romance of a lifetime between the Lady and the entrepreneur. Compared to that this should be a walk in the park. 'Let's start with our first meeting.'

'Three months ago you consulted me on a security issue. Maybe you were worried about industrial sabotage. That makes sense. After your father's death that would be a legitimate worry, a good time for someone to strike. Then let's say a few weeks later, when you were no longer my client, I asked you out.'

'I wouldn't even have considered dating that close to his death. I was too caught up in grief.' The soul-shaking realisation that her father was gone for ever combined with the ramifications of his will.

'It doesn't work like that. There is something about death that makes the living clutch at life, affirm it, want to live it.' The depth of his voice told her that he spoke from experience and yet she shook her head in refutation.

'I wouldn't have, couldn't have agreed to a date just a few months later.'

'I met Jess when my dad was dying—we got married a few weeks after his funeral.' Impossible to tell what emotions underpinned his factual tone, but his blue eyes shadowed and clouded, reminded her of how much he had lost.

'I can't imagine how difficult, how complicated that must have been for you both. But I am glad that you did have Jess, that you had support and love and comfort.'

'Yes.' The harshness of his voice shocked her and she saw the shadow cross his face and ravage it. 'My point is that it is possible to start a relationship even when you are grieving.'

'Accepted.' She gestured with her hand, then did a quick calculation. 'So our first date would have been about two months ago. Where did we go for dinner?'

'Does it matter? Any random restaurant.'

His voice held impatience, perhaps a leftover from the emotions this conversation must have awoken, but she knew she couldn't let that go. 'It does matter and that really wouldn't work. One of the stock questions we'll be asked is where was our first date? We'll look a bit idiotic if we say it was at a "random restaurant".'

'OK.' But she could tell he still thought she was over-reacting. 'Where did we go?'

Ava looked at him between narrowed eyelids. 'That's up to you. Where would you have taken me on a first date? If this were real. Really real.' In the silence that followed she sensed the atmosphere shift. Pictured the meeting in his office, the dawn of attraction, the moment he asked her. 'Would you have called me? Emailed me? Where would you have taken me?' This was becoming too real and she needed to move, to walk, to leave this illusion. 'I'll pop to the bathroom whilst you come up with an answer.'

Liam watched Ava walk away, knew he only had a few minutes to conjure up a scenario for a hypothetical first date. *Chill.* He was CEO of a multinational company. He'd been in the army for eight years. How hard could this be? All he had to do was pick a restaurant—an impressive restaurant, not a random one.

He'd narrowed it down to a shortlist by the time she

returned. He held out the phone. 'Take your pick. London's most exclusive restaurants.'

She glanced down and shook her head. 'It won't work. How come no one spotted us? Given someone spotted us on the London Eye. Plus would you really have taken me to a glitzy restaurant when I was grieving?'

Liam sighed. 'No. You're right.'

'It's all in the detail. That's what makes a story feel authentic. That's why you have to really think about it.'

Problem was he didn't want to think about it, didn't want to imagine what it would be like to take Ava on a real first date, a date where the attraction was allowed, in the open, a date where they could flirt and banter and encourage the spark of attraction to ignite into a flare. Because even now Liam could sense the bubbling undercurrent of awareness that seethed between them, urged and tempted, beckoned him to...to where? Nowhere he wanted to go. Liam pressed his lips together. This was a purely hypothetical situation, a business exercise, no different from a military campaign or a security detail for a client.

'If we couldn't go to a restaurant maybe I'd have cooked you a meal. With candles.' That flickered and glinted and highlighted the corn colour of her hair. The strum of music in the background, a chilled bottle of wine on the table. Fresh flowers as a centrepiece. Her hand brushing his as pulled out her chair. Discomfort edged his gut at the sheer realness of the image and it was an effort not to squirm on the aircraft seat. After all, the last woman he had cooked dinner for had been Jess and he'd never felt like this, however hard he'd tried, and he had tried. Had convinced himself that the love would grow, that he could make himself love her. But every 'romantic' dinner had been a construct, an attempt to make something out of nothing. And all the candles had illuminated were the awkwardness and falsity.

Pulling himself to the present, he looked at Ava. 'Would that work?'

'I'm not sure. It doesn't ring true. Would you really ask someone to your house on a first date?' She leaned forward, placed a hand on his arm. 'This is hard for you, isn't it?' Ava said gently. 'I'm sorry. If you haven't dated since Jess this must bring back memories.'

'I'm fine,' he said. 'Give me a minute.' This was important—this was the way to defeat AJ Mason, salvage his reputation and win the Beaumont contract. Liam forced his brain into gear. 'How does this sound? A moonlit picnic in Hyde Park. A thick tweed picnic blanket, a hamper from an exclusive emporium, chilled white wine in crystal flutes all under the stars. We sat and talked and looked at the stars and discussed constellations and...'

'It was magical,' she said softly.

And for a moment it was; he was there. Could see himself laying the blanket on the grass. Could see them eating, feeding each other bits of food, then lying back and gazing up at the stars, side by side, so close that a tendril of her corn-blonde hair tickled his cheek.

There was a silence and now their gazes meshed and, dammit, instead of the neutral air of the cabin he could feel the fresh evening breeze, smell the scent of evening flowers almost taste the food. 'Detail is important,' he said. Aware of the husk in his voice.

'Yes.'

Did we kiss? The words so nearly fell from his lips and he swallowed them down just as Ava gave a small shaky laugh.

'Actually detail is important and that scenario won't work. Because two months ago it would have been December.'

Liam groaned. 'Dammit. I thought I had it down perfectly.'

'You did.' Her voice was soft. 'But it's back to the drawing board.'

'Not for long.' To his own consternation he already had the exact answer, his mind inexplicably now fizzing with dating ideas. 'This is it.'

'Go ahead.' Her eyes were wide now, her lips slightly parted.

'I would take you in a horse-drawn carriage through the park. We'd have a cosy blanket and sit side by side. There would be mince pies and mulled wine and we'd hear the clip clop of the horses' hooves…'

'And the jingle of the sleigh bells and smell the tang of snow in the air and watch the winter scenery go by whilst we talked and…'

Did we kiss? Again he swallowed the words, saying instead, 'Does that work?'

'Yes.' Why did he have the feeling Ava had answered his unspoken question? *Enough. Stop.* Relief swept through him as the pilot's voice came over the Tannoy. 'We'll be landing in ten, Liam.'

Ava's head whirled as they disembarked from the plane and it had nothing to do with the dusky Italian breeze and everything to do with whatever the hell had just happened. For a moment she'd been sure he'd kiss her; hell, for a moment she'd wanted him to kiss her. Had been so caught up in the imaginary magical moment that a real spell had been cast.

The breeze was welcome, and with any luck it would

blow her mind back to order. Liam headed towards a car. 'Pierre is going to give us a lift. He is Elena the housekeeper's husband.'

The idea of a chaperone allowed her to gather a polite, friendly persona together for the ten-minute journey. As she chatted to the middle-aged flamboyant Frenchman the tension seeped from her shoulders.

'I miss my country,' the grizzled man said. 'But I know my Elena could not move from her home, her family, this beautiful place, and so I have adapted. That is the power of love.'

His declaration brought a smile to her face even as she marvelled at them. A sudden pang of envy touched her for what this man and his wife had. Even as she knew it wasn't for her. She did believe in the power of love and she'd seen how destructive that power could be. Seen her mother's love for her father send her to the verge of brittle breakdown. Karen Casseveti's whole life had been defined by her love to the exclusion of all else. Her fear of losing her husband had dictated her every move, even down to the decision to have a baby. And once she had Ava she had seen her as an asset in her quest. As Ava had grown up she had seen the fear in her mother's perfectly made-up eyes as her gaze tracked her husband across a room.

A justified fear because she had known how precarious her position was. Known that James had loved his first family and yet that love too had been destroyed, defeated by the power of ambition and the lure of wealth. James had needed Lady Karen Hales's money and connections to start Dolci and so he'd deserted his first wife and family.

So, yes, love was definitely a powerful force, but like any force it could cause pain.

The car glided to a stop and Ava blinked back to the present as she took in her surroundings. The white-washed stone-walled building took picturesque to new levels of meaning. Iron balconies fronted the first floor and pretty trees lined the pavement outside.

Inside the rustic wood-panelled front door an elegant grey-haired woman bustled towards them, a welcoming smile on her face. '*Buona sera*, Liam. It is good to see you again.'

Liam stooped to kiss the woman on both cheeks. 'You too, Elena. How are the children? How is the latest addition?' He turned to Ava. 'Elena welcomed her fourth grandchild into the world two months ago.'

Ava smiled and stepped forward. 'Congratulations. I'm Ava.'

'Welcome, Ava. And thank you. Arianna is gorgeous, my first granddaughter and she is beautiful. Now to business. I have prepared food, done the shopping and stocked the bar and freezer. The beds are made up. If there is anything you need, call me. Or Pierre.' She smiled at Ava. 'This is my number. Please feel free to contact me as well. I live nearby. I can come any time.'

'Thank you, Elena. I'll input that now.'

'Then I will leave you to it. Unless you wish for me to wait and serve the food.'

'No need.' Liam paused and looked across at Ava. 'Unless you would prefer it.'

For a craven moment she wanted to say yes, didn't want to be left alone with Liam in this cosy, intimate setting to share a meal, just the two of them. *Ridiculous.* This was a working dinner and she and Liam had a lot of ground to cover and the whole *point* was for them to get comfortable around each other. *Alone.*

'No, I'm good, and thank you, Elena. The food smells incredible.'

Now Elena beamed. 'Thank you. I have made *focaccia barese* and *orecchiette con cime di rapa*. And a salad to accompany it. The dessert is my speciality—I will let that be a surprise. I will bring fresh breakfast pastries and bread in the morning.'

With that Elena left and Ava forced a smile to her face. 'So,' she said brightly. 'If it's OK with you I'll freshen up and unpack and then we can reconvene our discussion.'

'Sounds good.' He pointed. 'The kitchen is through there. I'll meet you down here in half an hour.'

Thirty minutes of reprieve and she needed every single one.

CHAPTER SIX

LIAM GAVE THE pasta a quick stir and lifted the lid to check on the simmering pan that emitted a waft of herbs with a hint of garlic. Anticipation clashed again with guilt and he reminded himself again that this was not a date. It was a working dinner.

The kitchen door opened and he looked up and there it was again, that little kick to his gut when he saw Ava. She'd changed into black trousers and a tunic top, her hair now pulled up into a bun. A kind of smart-casual-cum-business look. Her face looked a little different and he frowned as he tried to pinpoint it—perhaps a different lipstick and something about her eyes. Maybe a touch more eye shadow.

In the same moment he realised he was staring he also clocked that so was she, that her amber eyes watched him with…appreciation.

'Do I pass muster?' she asked.

'Yes. Do I?' he countered.

'Yes. Sorry to stare. There is just something great about a man at the kitchen stove. I know it's considered normal nowadays but in my family it wasn't.'

'I'd love to say I cooked it but you know I didn't. There is a bottle of wine in the fridge if you'd like a glass.'

'Thank you. I would. But I'll set the table first.'

'Great. The cutlery is in that drawer.'

The drawer that was right next to him, in a kitchen space that could best be described as cosy. Now what? If he moved away too abruptly it would look awkward. If he stayed put things could get even more awkward. Jeez. He was behaving like an adolescent. The whole point of this was so that they could get more comfortable together. Yet he could feel his body tense, brace itself for impact as Ava came closer. He could smell the scent of soap, a hint of elusive light floral scent. And now she was closer still and his muscles ached with tension when he heard her sudden intake of breath and knew his proximity affected her. The reminder that this attraction was mutual ratcheted his pulse rate.

'I…um… I…' She stood stock-still and he could see her gaze flick over him. Her hand lifted as if she were going to place it on his chest and then she dropped it quickly, masked the movement into a reach across to the drawer. He tried to move away and inadvertently his hand brushed against hers, his fingers swept over her wrist and she made the smallest of noises.

She leapt away as he did and somehow stepped back straight into him, her back pressed against his chest and he instinctively wrapped his arm around her waist to steady her and himself. And for one glorious second she pressed against him and all he wanted was to hold her and nuzzle kisses on the tantalising allure of her neck, to bury his face in the glossy, silken strands of her hair.

The instant vanished. He released her immediately and she sprang forward. 'Sorry,' they both said, their voices vying for supremacy.

Ava busied herself at the drawer, snatched up what looked like a random selection of cutlery and moved at pace towards the table, her back to him, whilst he dished up the food.

Eventually she cleared her throat and turned to face him, and for a moment there was silence as their gazes locked. 'So,' he managed. 'Do you cook?' It was the best he could do.

'Yes.' The assertion was over-emphatic, as if it characterised her relief that he'd initiated conversation. 'My mum insisted on me doing extensive cordon bleu courses. She believed a woman should be able to cook for her man.'

'You don't sound as if you agreed with her.'

'I didn't have a problem with learning a necessary skill—I just didn't understand why my dad never had to cook just because he didn't want to, but I had to learn how to make a soufflé when I didn't like it. To be fair I suppose Mum did a lot of the cooking as well.'

'I always imagined your family as having an array of staff, a butler and a cook and—' He broke off, knew the words were a mistake even as he said them.

'Did you imagine my family a lot?' Her voice held no judgement or censure yet the question irked him.

'Yes. I did. It was hard not to. In my father's mind your life of huge privilege should have been ours and he tended to dwell on it. His imagination fed by the numerous articles depicting the glittering life and times of the Cassevetis. It felt as if your success had a direct inverse correlation to my family's decline.' He knew his tone was bitter but right now he didn't care. 'Whilst you were learning how to bake a soufflé I was learning how to make nutritious meals on a shoestring. Meals that my dad would eat to soak up the booze. If I didn't cook he wouldn't eat.' *Whoa. Let's not turn this into a pity party.* And yet...it rankled. The realisation that whilst Karen Casseveti was cooking for her man his mum was working more and more extra shifts to try to pay the bills.

'I'm sorry.' Ava's voice was small but clear. There was compassion in her amber eyes and he didn't want that. It was too close to pity and his dad would have hated that from a Casseveti.

'There is no need for you to be sorry. You didn't do anything.'

Ava hesitated, ate a mouthful of the pasta and then looked at him. 'No, I didn't. But my father did. His actions were the catalyst that drove your father to alcohol.'

Innate honesty compelled Liam to point out, 'No one forced the whisky bottle to my dad's lips.' He did know that, would never understand why that was the choice his father had made. Had vowed it would never be his—he would always stand and fight. In Terry Rourke's place he would have taken the fight to the Cassevetis, proved himself to be the better man. 'That was his choice.'

'A choice that impacted on you and your mum.'

There was that compassion again and he wanted none of it. Neither would he brook any criticism of his father however implicit. Liam had loved his dad and known, for all his faults, Terry had loved him too. 'Yes, it did, but looking after my dad helped me too. Kept me off the streets. I got a Saturday job so I could get him vitamins.' All in his quest to try to get his dad better, back to normal, so that his parents could reunite, so that his father would become the man he had once been. 'The shop owner was in the army reserves and that got me interested in the army. You don't need to be sorry for me.'

'I'm not. But I am sorry for my father's actions. More to the point, so was he.'

'Perhaps.'

'What do you mean "perhaps"?' Now anger sharpened her tone. 'He asked me to come and make amends. He regretted his actions.'

'But not enough to apologise in person, to contact my dad or to meet me face to face. Or pick up the phone himself. Over all the years.' His anger matched hers now. Say what she would, James Casseveti had been a coward and a cheat.

'My father found it hard to face his past. I think he tried to block it out. Seeing you would have evoked memories he didn't want to think about.' Now her voice was sad. 'So he decided to make amends for his wrongs after he was gone—that way he wouldn't have to face the consequences himself.' Liam saw the confusion, the resignation that shadowed her face and he realised that now it was Ava who had to do just that. Ava who was left at the helm of Dolci, undermined by her father's shock decision to leave two thirds of her legacy to his first two children. Children who the press alleged he had deserted in their childhood. Ava who was faking a relationship. Anger with James combined with a sharp and unexpected desire to offer comfort.

What the heck? This was a Casseveti.

Ava pushed her empty plate to one side, leant forward, reached a hand out and then pulled it back. 'I know my dad was far from perfect and I know he did wrong. But he was my dad and I loved him.'

Hell. Those were words that could have fallen from his own lips.

'But I do believe he felt genuine regret. I wish...'

'That you could ask him. Talk to him.' He could see the grief in her eyes, recognised the shell-shock look of the finality of loss, the creeping realisation that the person was gone. The meaning of for ever took on new dimensions. And suddenly his anger disappeared. Ava had lost her father. However flawed he had been Ava had loved him. Just as Liam had loved his own dad. James Casseveti had done wrong but Ava hadn't and it was time to lay the past to rest. In order to make this work, but also because that was the right thing to do.

'Yes.' For a second her voice registered surprise and then understanding dawned in her amber eyes. 'You understand because you've been through it. Does it get easier? All I want is to somehow bring him back and ask him what I should do. Why he did some of the things he did.'

'I used to go Dad's grave. I'd sit there and ask him questions, try to imagine the answers. It gave me a level of peace. Still does sometimes.' Surprise touched him that he was sharing this, but how could he ignore a grief he recognised all too well? 'Although he's gone he is still part of you. For better or worse he helped shape your life. Nothing can change that or erase the good memories. As for the grief, it doesn't go but it compacts, becomes a small part of you that you carry, a mark of respect and love for the person who is gone.' He rubbed the back of his neck to mitigate the prickle of embarrassment. 'That's my two pennyworth.'

'It's worth a lot more than that.' He looked across and saw that tears glistened in her beautiful amber eyes. 'That has helped more than you can know. It's been hard—I don't have any siblings, or at least not any who will share this grief. My mother is devastated so it feels wrong to burden her. So thank you—it means a lot to talk to someone who gets it.' Now she did reach out to cover his hand with hers. 'Especially when I know your feelings about my dad.'

'That doesn't matter. My dad wasn't perfect either—he made some pretty bad choices in his life, but that doesn't alter his love for me or mine for him or how much I grieved for him. You loved your dad and he loved you—your grief is real and valid.' He took a deep breath. 'And whilst I do have issues with his choices, I do know they aren't your fault. From now on I'll act like that. Let's try and put the past behind us.'

'I'd like that.' A smile illuminated her face, though sadness still flecked her eyes. 'I really would.' Simultaneously they both seemed to realise that her hand still covered his and for a moment all he wanted was to increase that contact, to move round the table and hold her.

The desire caused a warning bell to klaxon in his brain. *Bad idea.* The knowledge hit him like an iced bucket of water on the head. Ava was grieving, was as vulnerable as he had been in the aftermath of his father's death. That meant her perspective would be skewed just as his had been. In his case he had ended up believing himself in love, had ended up in a marriage that had been a mistake. Guilt touched him. Maybe he should never have asked Ava to be part of this charade, perhaps in itself that had been taking advantage. But it was too late to change that now. All he could do was ensure he acted honourably and with sensitivity. That meant keeping their latent attraction in check and that in turn meant keeping their physical contact to a minimum. It would be all too easy for a hug to morph into something more. This he knew.

But perhaps he could try to make the sadness recede from her eyes—there could be no harm in that. 'Dessert?' he suggested. 'And then I suggest we should test each other on our fact cards.'

'Sure.'

'But let's make it a little more fun than a straight-forward test.'

Now curiosity surfaced and sparked her eyes. 'How?'

'I'll get the dessert and I'll tell you.'

Ava watched as Liam stacked the plates in the dish-washer, her body and mind in turmoil. Emotions swirled, grief and a warmth at having had that grief understood—a sense of a connection that somehow prompted her body to hum anew at the memory of earlier. Of being pressed back against him, his arm around her waist Just those few seconds seemed to have branded her in some way. And now…now she needed to get a grip, had to be careful.

They had agreed to put the past behind them but it still existed. Plus Liam was a widower—a man who hadn't dated since his wife died. And Ava wasn't on the market for a relationship with anyone. Yet when he returned bearing a dessert that looked utterly delicious she knew the adjective 'yum' was directed at him by her unruly hormones.

And somehow her gaze landed on a curl of his cop-per hair, shower damp on the nape of his neck, and it mesmerised her. She snatched her glance away only to land on the tantalising bare V of his neckline.

'It's one of Elena's specialities—' He broke off as he looked at her, must have read something in her gaze, or perhaps she was drooling or sending out some sort of smoke signal from her ears. But as he paused their gazes locked and she saw desire in the depths of his cobalt eyes.

Say something. Break the spell. 'Um…you look

amazing…' *Oh, for Pete's sake.* 'Not you. *It* looks amazing. The dessert, I mean.'

'So I don't look amazing?' Amusement laced his deep voice and she glared at him.

'I… I don't know.' Ava closed her eyes and wondered where twenty-seven years of poise had vanished to. Seemingly cancelled out by one curl of hair, some understanding, a sculpted face and an even more sculpted body and… There she went again.

'Sorry,' she said. 'I am a dessert sort of girl and this clearly fuddled my brain. It looks amazing. What is it?'

'*Barchiglia.* It's a chocolate and almond tart with a pear and sort of almond meringue filling.'

'That sounds to die for.'

'It is. That's why I thought we could use the dessert as a bit of an incentive.'

'How?'

'We cut it up into small pieces and every time we get a question right we get a piece. If we don't get it right we forfeit to the other person. And you really don't want to forfeit any of this.'

'Bring it on.' She watched as he cut the cake, appreciated the deft, confident movements, but even more she appreciated what he was doing—knew he was trying to distract her from her grief.

'OK. You ask first,' he said.

'What's my favourite colour?'

'Amber.'

'Correct.' He picked up a small piece and popped it into his mouth, and she smiled as he made an exaggerated *mmm* sound.

'My go. Where did I live as a child?'

'Surrey.'

'Also correct.' He pushed the plate towards her and

she picked up a square of the confection. Nibbled it and closed her eyes. 'That is absolutely divine.' She took another small bite, savoured the taste of the almonds mixed with the tarter tang of the pears. Opened her eyes to find his eyes centred on her lips and she felt heat touch her face. Ate the last bit and returned to the questioning.

As the hour went on and the *barchiglia* reduced in size it became a challenge, both of them trying to find harder, more difficult questions until finally there was just one square left.

'All to play for,' he said.

'And it's my question.' She leant back in the chair, her eyes narrowed as she thought of a question that might flummox him. 'Name three products that I modelled.'

Liam paused, thought for a moment. 'Sahara clothes, Madeline cosmetics and…you were also the cover girl for lingerie, but the name of the company escapes me. Something to do with Temptation, I believe.' His voice was deep and husky as he said the word and she found herself leaning forward.

'It was called Allure.' And she couldn't help it, she said the word with a deliberate emphasis, and now the atmosphere seemed to cloud and haze with the simmering fog of tension. The urge to reach out, to touch, was almost too much. Almost.

He pushed his chair back, the scrape of wood against the marble dispelling the mist of desire. 'We need to talk about this.'

'About what?' The question was disingenuous but she needed to be sure she hadn't misinterpreted the signals.

'This chemistry. This attraction.' Against her will

the words sent a small thrill of satisfaction through her. The idea that this desire was mutual, that he felt the same pull, the same yearning strummed a triumphant chord through her whole body. 'Because if we don't figure out how to deal with it, ironically it will undo our whole act.'

'You're right. So we need to work out a way to feel comfortable with the attraction. Accept it and control it. Switch it on and off for the camera.'

'How?'

Ava inhaled a deep breath. 'First we need to get used to being in the same space. Let's give it a try.' His expression was so ludicrous she almost sighed, until she glimpsed her own reflection and saw the proverbial rabbit-in-the-headlights glint in her own eyes. 'We look terrified and that is *not* a good look for the camera. So let's start small. We need to smile.'

'Like this?' His lips turned up, the line forced and rigid but at least pointed in the right direction.

'That's not a bad start, but it looks a little forced and your eyes are still...' *shadowed, hard* '...not relaxed.'

'OK. Show me how it's done.'

'Easy. What sort of smile do you want? Girl next door, sultry, loving, flirty?'

'You pick.'

Ava closed her eyes for an instant and then smiled, a smile that she knew held a hint of fun, a touch of flirt and a dollop of come hither. 'So that's flirty. This is girl next door.' She widened her eyes and her smile, conjured up the idea of fresh-faced and wholesome. 'It's all about showing teeth without being toothy.'

'That's incredible.'

'I figured it out from a young age. I started family photo shoots when I was a toddler. I worked out the quickest way to get them done was to achieve whatever look the photographer and my mother wanted.'

And then she'd worked out the power of smiles— they could be used to impress people, to make people believe she was happy, to make other people feel good. A smile was a perfect disguise. She had learnt to keep her thoughts private and her smile on display. Hidden her hurt that she knew her mother's love was not really for her, for Ava. Her mother had loved her as long as she played her part. Her father would only love her as long as she was perfect. And so she'd smiled until her cheeks had ached and she'd looked perfect.

'But how does anyone know when it's genuine? How do *you* know?'

The question took her aback and as she considered her answer a level of discomfort tinged with uncertainty touched her. When was it genuine? Her smile, her façade so much part of her daily life she didn't even think about it. 'Because I mean it.' The answer was lame and she could see he was about to question it. 'But that's not the point. It's your smile we need to focus on. Try again.'

This time the attempt was woeful and she raised her eyebrows. 'Is that really the best you can do?'

'Right now, yes. Perhaps you could pass on some helpful tips.'

'Think of something happy.'

Liam looked up at the ceiling and then a smile did tip his lips, but it was not a smile that implied relaxation or joy. There was a grimness to it, an edge that held more than a hint of danger. A smile that sent a shiver down her spine.

'What are you thinking of? I mean, that's better but

not exactly what I was after. That's more the smile of a man who has won a fight.'

Two raised eyebrows and a nod. 'Ten out of ten. I was picturing AJ's face when I win the Beaumont contract.'

'OK. But now try for a different sort of happy. Maybe think of a more relaxing activity than a fight. Such as…' Oh, hell, the only image that entered her head right now was definitely not appropriate. 'Um…think of chocolate.'

'Chocolate?' The word was flat.

'Yup. Doesn't chocolate make you happy?'

'Not really. I mean, I like the occasional chocolate orange, but I wouldn't say that would make me smile.'

'OK. What do you do to relax?'

'The gym. Or I may work out in the ring, or do some sort of obstacle marathon.' He sighed. 'I'm guessing that's not what you're after.'

'No. I was thinking more about bubble baths or watching a film on a rainy day or lying on a beach.' Now she sighed. 'Let me guess. You're more a shower sort of person.'

'Afraid so. I don't think I've had a bubble bath since I was a kid.'

'Then we'll have to try another method. There was a time on a shoot when I couldn't get the smile right. It was one of my last assignments.' Her dad had just got out of hospital after his first heart attack, her world had been turned upside down and she'd been angry, sad and scared. 'There was a coach who helped me.' She gestured. 'Stand up and smile.'

He did as she asked and she stood and moved closer to him, told herself this was necessary. Any minute now she was sure her brain would find the off switch and in the meantime she'd focus on keeping her breathing even.

'Hold still. It's all about your mouth and facial muscles and knowing which ones to relax. You're too tense. Try to relax.' Telling herself this was purely professional, utterly clinical, she reached up and touched his jaw. 'Clench and relax your jaw a couple of times.' The feel of bristle under her fingertips, the sheer strength and determination of him made her clasp her lip between her teeth. No way would she actually moan.

She dropped her hands to his shoulders, both left and right. 'Drop your shoulders.' Now their bodies were scant inches apart and she tried to breathe normally. Knew this was playing with fire.

She could hear how breathless her voice was and when she met his gaze she saw a spark ignite there, his cobalt eyes darkened and she knew he was as affected as her.

'Anything else?' he asked, his voice more croak than depth.

'You need to engage the muscles round your eyes. Try crinkling them slightly.'

'Ava.' The smile, real or fake, had dropped and there was a seriousness to his expression that made her breath catch. Her brain ordered her to move backward but somewhere down the line the command got confused and instead she stepped forward.

'Another tip is to massage your forehead and cheeks and...' She was now so close she could smell the bergamot of his soap, could see the slightest dent in the sweep of his nose, the hint of a seldom seen dimple, and her voice ran dry, shuddered to a stop as she took the final step forward.

Then she wasn't sure who kissed who, but his lips

were on hers and it felt as if her body were melting, fusing with his as she pressed against him, wrapped her arms around his neck as he deepened the kiss. It was as though she'd been waiting for this ever since that first kiss, the feeling of rightness inexplicable.

Her senses competed and then soared into sensory overload, the experience blew her mind, as she tasted the hint of wine, of chocolate, of almond, felt her tummy clench in the need for more. More of this exquisite, gorgeous torture. Torture because she could hear the voice of common sense clamouring, knew that the need for more was doomed to failure, knew that what she had to do now was pull away.

As she suited action to word they stood, her breath coming in ragged gasps, and she could see the rise and fall of his powerful chest as they stared at each other and Ava knew no amount of poise could rescue her now. Mortification suddenly roiled through her. That had been a disaster, a complete loss of the composure she was famed for. Hadn't she been the one to advocate acceptance and control? But perhaps, just perhaps, she could rescue the situation, use every iota of her acting skills. Somehow she forced herself to raise her head and meet his gaze.

'Sorry about that.' She searched her bank of smiles and came up with rueful, embarrassed, but hopefully with at least a semblance of sophisticate. 'That is obviously not the "look" we are going for. Bit too full on. I was hoping we could practise the sort of kiss that looks good for the cameras. I didn't expect us to get so…carried away. It's a while since I've been in a relationship so it was obviously some sort of strange reaction to that.'

There was a moment's silence and she thought he'd challenge her assertion, force an admission that she'd kissed him because she couldn't help herself. Then, perhaps realising there would be nothing to gain, he nodded and his body relaxed. 'Well, it certainly brought a smile to my face.'

Recognising his attempt to relax the atmosphere, she smiled, this one of relief. 'On that note, I think we should call it a day now and regroup in the morning.'

'Agreed. I'll see you then.' Hard to say who ran for the door faster.

CHAPTER SEVEN

LIAM OPENED HIS eyes and as always went from sleep to awake in an instant, his brain scanned the surroundings for danger and landmarks—a trait honed in his army days, part training and part defence against AJ and his bully-boy cronies.

Today though a different type of danger pervaded the air, in the shape of a beautiful woman who had aroused a storm of passion in him. Perhaps Ava had it right—the kiss had been a simple scientific release of pent-up need; neither of them had kissed anyone else for a long time. Perhaps if he kept telling himself that he'd believe it.

A quick shower and he headed to the kitchen, where breakfast was laid out and the scent of coffee permeated the air. Ava turned and smiled. 'Elena left us all this. It looks amazing.' She waved him to a seat. 'Sit. I'll bring the coffee over. I thought you could tell me a bit more about Rourke Securities over breakfast.'

'Sure. What do you want to know?'

'How did you start?'

'After I left the army…' he'd crawled into an abyss of self-pity, grief and self-recrimination, had finally pulled himself out '… I set myself up as a one-man security band.' Lured by danger, fuelled by adrenalin, he'd accepted assignments where death had been a constant risk, the only way he could feel alive. Until injury had halted him in his tracks and his old army commander had made him rethink his path. 'It grew from there. I built a team of operatives and it spiralled. I branched out into non-military contracts. I bought a fleet of vans and started a transportation sideline that grew and grew. Then I started offering security for events and so it went on. And here I am.'

'Starting your own business, making it yours…that must be…fulfilling.' She sounded wistful. 'That feeling of achievement, of building something on your own.'

'Sounds like that is what you would like to do.'

Her look was slightly defiant. 'I've thought about it. I mean, I know how lucky I am—but sometimes it does feel like I've been handed everything on a silver platter. I wonder if I could have achieved success on my own.'

Liam considered. 'I'm not sure it matters. There are different parameters of success. You could take Dolci on to bigger and better things, make a success of it your way, with or without the Petrovellis. You could count your modelling career as a runaway success—that was down to you.'

'Not really. That is down to genetic luck and, let's face it, my connections probably helped me.'

'You are who you are and life deals you the cards it deals you—all you can do is play the best hand you can. Is heading up Dolci what you want to do?'

'Yes.'

'Then do it to the best of your ability. If you had started Dolci, what would you do with it?'

'I'd like to grow the company differently, sell more organic, fair trade produce. Be way more ethical. I'd also like to set up some small high-street shops that sell our products. Maybe even launch out from desserts to a few good quality ready dinners for families and people who live on their own.' She grinned. 'Kind of like Elena's food, but in bulk. I know it will lose some of its authenticity if it's mass produced but I'd do everything I could to keep it as "real" as possible.'

The ideas poured out of her, the spark in her eyes, the way she moved her hands to emphasise a point exuded a vibe or energy, piqued his admiration and interest.

'Then that's what you should aim for. Look into those ideas.'

'Maybe.' But the enthusiasm had gone and now she rose to her feet. 'Anyway, enough of that—it's more information than you need and definitely more than I meant to say. You should have stopped me.'

'I didn't want to stop you. I enjoyed listening. You are full of ideas—good ideas.'

'Thank you.' But he could see she hadn't taken the words on board, wondered why someone like Ava Casseveti found it so hard to believe in herself. 'So what's the plan for the day?'

'My idea for the day was to go into town. Practise being seen and spending time together so it starts to look natural.'

'Then give me ten minutes to get ready and let's go.'

CHAPTER EIGHT

AVA CHECKED HER reflection in the pretty full-length mirror in her bedroom and gave a satisfied nod. The white dress with the poppy-red pattern was perfect: swirly, flirty, fun and it made her look good without being overtly revealing or too noticeable. Topping it with a fleece-lined denim jacket for warmth, she would blend into the tourist crowd. She tugged her trademark blonde hair into a ponytail. One last swipe of lip gloss, a press of her lips, and she exited the room and headed downstairs. Twenty minutes later they were on the cobbled streets of the town and Ava gasped as she took in the architecture of the buildings.

'I had read about the *trulli* but the pictures don't do them justice.' She halted to appreciate the sheer unique quality of the small stone whitewashed buildings topped with conical roofs. 'They are straight out of a fairy tale.'

'Maybe they are—they were built centuries ago, just in this part of the world as far as I know. Some people believe they were built in order to avoid tax.'

Ava turned to him in question. 'I assumed they were houses or storage units.'

'The story goes that the King charged the local lord a dwelling tax. So they figured out a way of building dwellings that could be dismantled whenever the tax inspector paid a visit and put back up when he left.'

'Ingenious.' She gazed at the cluster of buildings. 'I can't believe they are still standing.'

'Yup. It does show that, for all the gains we have made with technology, there are still plenty of structural wonders that come from our history. And these definitely count.'

'Do people still live in them?'

'In some of them, but they are mostly used for commercial purposes—shops, restaurants or holiday lets.'

'Could we go to the shops? I'd like to pick up some gifts before we meet your family tomorrow.' The idea rippled nerves through her and she reminded herself that it was essential to do a 'meet the family' with Bea before their relationship became properly public.

As they made their way along the sun-drenched streets she sensed his glance and turned to look at him. He nodded towards a couple walking ahead of them, arms draped around each other's waists. 'In case we are spotted, and also as a kind of practice, do you think we should...hold hands?'

Ava bit her lip. 'Yes. You're right. We should.'

'Yet you didn't suggest it. And you're the detail guy.' His cobalt gaze held a perception that was becoming all too familiar. 'So I'm guessing the idea doesn't appeal, which is fine by me.'

Ava hauled in breath. 'No. You're right. It's a good idea. It shows affection and proves we are close. I'm just a bit funny about it. I remember being asked to hold hands for a modelling shoot—the idea was to show a married couple's intimacy and it made me realise there *is* something really intimate about it.' It had also made her question her own capacity to be intimate. Because after that shoot she had realised that she and Nick never held hands. Because it hadn't ever felt natural. 'I guess there's also a bit of worry. I mean, what if your hand is sweaty, or uncomfortable to hold or...?' She held her hand out and surveyed it. 'And now I've managed to make something insignificant into something huge.'

'Nope. I think you're right.' He frowned and she sensed a sudden pain in his voice, wondered if he was remembering walking hand in hand with Jess. 'Holding hands is intimate. It links you, creates a connection, an implication of a bond, a desire to be close. It's also a way of communicating—you can squeeze someone's hand to show support or commiseration or in warning. So yes, it is a big thing and maybe that's why some people don't feel comfortable with it. If we were really a couple I guess we'd both have taken a while before we felt ready to hold hands.'

'But we have now supposedly been together for three months and it would be a bit strange if we didn't hold hands.' Yet she'd been with Nick for eighteen months and hadn't held hands even once. 'So we're going to have to do it.'

'Maybe, but not now.' Liam indicated ahead of them. 'This shop looks like what you're looking for.'

It did indeed. The whitewashed *trullo* was bedecked with vivid hand-painted signs and wooden shelves stacked with intriguing pottery that tempted the eye. They entered the shop and Ava gave a small cry of delight. The shop was filled with local items, textiles of every hue, ceramics painted with vivid imagery, miniature *trulli* completed in exquisite detail, alongside black and white photographs of the village in times gone by. 'It's like a treasure trove.'

The proprietor stepped forward. 'Many of the items have been made by local artisans. The linens have been hand-woven and there are also some beautiful examples of filet lace.'

'They are all beautiful.' She turned to Liam. 'Let's start with your mum.'

'Um…' He glanced round, a slightly helpless look on his face. 'We don't usually do holiday gifts.'

'Yes, well. This is different. You're bringing a girlfriend home. And not any old girlfriend. A Casseveti. Your mum will hardly be thrilled to see me—the least we can do is take her and the rest of the family gifts.' She picked up a jug, beautifully hand crafted with a picture of a rooster and a flower on the side.

'Maybe not that. The symbols represent fertility.'

Ava placed it down hurriedly. 'OK. But there is plenty to choose from. What did you get her for Christmas?'

'Mum sorts out the gifts for me—she tells me what everyone would like and I give her the money.' He shifted from foot to foot. 'That way everyone gets what they want. Seems easier.'

'OK. But you must have some idea. What does she like? What makes her smile? What's her favourite colour? Does she have any hobbies? Does she like clothes?' Ava walked over to a selection of beautiful patterned scarves. 'Perhaps a scarf?'

Now finally she saw Liam engage as he studied the scarves. 'She is very elegant,' he said finally. 'She always made a point of looking good. She'd go out and scour the charity shops and find amazing things. She even taught herself how to make her own clothes.'

He tugged his phone out of his pocket and Ava looked at the photograph. Liam's mum was pretty, her copper hair faded with age, but her grey eyes were still bright. Her smile was slightly wary, but there was a serenity about her that Ava liked. She studied her clothes. Elegant grey skirt with a white blouse. Nice and simple, but livened up by a bright red cardigan.

'I think she'd definitely like a scarf or some jewellery. You pick.'

Liam studied the items on display, picked a couple of scarves up and held them to the light, chose a dark red patterned one. 'I think she'd like this.'

'Perfect. Now for my mum.' Ava sighed. 'I wish I could get her a magic wand that would make her feel better. Less miserable.' Less vindictive, less angry… Perhaps she could cast a spell that would somehow make her mother forgive Ava for refusing to try to overturn the will.

Liam pointed at a display of crystals. 'Maybe a crystal—some people believe that crystals have healing properties or can help in times of grief.'

'Do you believe that?' The man really was a whole heap of surprises.

'I don't know. I do think that it is possible.'

'I think that's a brilliant gift.' Ava looked at the crystals and then back at him. 'I don't think Mum is a believer but I think I'll get one anyway. Maybe they work even without belief.' She tried to keep sadness from her voice, knew she'd failed when he looked more closely at her.

'I assume she has taken it hard. Every article I ever read showed how close your parents were.'

'Yes.' No way would she expose the illusion her mum had so painstakingly set up, tell Liam that her father had still loved his first wife, just not enough to stay with her. Had loved Karen's money and connections more, but hadn't loved Karen herself. Sometimes Ava wondered if it had been worth it—he had sacrificed love to live a life cushioned by money, but also trapped by it. The fate of Dolci caught up in his marriage, in the Casseveti brand. And so he'd been a prisoner of his own ambitions. Had he ever just wanted to break free, abandon his second family and return to his first?

'I'll get Mum this as well.' She picked up a simple terracotta jug. 'I think we should get something for your stepdad and brother as well.'

'I really wouldn't have a clue what to get John or Max. I never lived with them and there is no blood tie so we aren't close.' There was an emptiness to his tone, a careful flatness, and his eyes held trouble in their depths.

'I know you didn't choose their gifts but you must have watched them open them.' His expression was one of reluctance and a sudden suspicion touched her. 'I mean, you did spend Christmas there, didn't you?'

'I popped in a few days after.' He rubbed the back of his neck. 'I was away over Christmas.'

'Where did you go?'

'Business trip.'

'On Christmas Day?'

'Yes. I was in a five-star hotel in India and that was fine.' His stance suggested the subject was closed. 'But looking back, I do remember that Max thanked me for my gift. I got him a pair of Rollerblades. He is roller skating mad. He plays roller hockey and does speed skating. Works as a skate guard at a local rink.'

Ava pointed at a small table with trays of beaded bracelets. 'Look. They look cool and I bet he could wear that to rollerblade.'

They walked over to them and she watched as Liam

went through the merchandise, a small frown of concentration on his face. 'I'm pretty sure the Rollerblades were this colour, so this should work.'

'What about John?'

'I'll buy him some Italian beer or some interesting food ingredients. He does a lot of their cooking.'

'Good idea.' It occurred to Ava that in actual fact Liam knew more about John and Max than he cared to admit, or perhaps even realised. She waited whilst Liam paid for his purchase.

'Where would you like to go now?' he asked.

'I thought we should get some photos of us. We can post them on social media as evidence of our relationship. I think that's the best way to let people know—a kind of subtle approach, rather than an official announcement.'

'Makes sense.'

'Where would be a good place for some photos? I was thinking somewhere romantic.' A flush heated her cheekbones. 'Just for the detail.'

'How about a beach setting? There is a beach not too far from here though I've never been. It's a nature preserve, so it's fairly secluded.'

'Sounds perfect.'

'I'll call Pierre to drop us off.'

CHAPTER NINE

AN HOUR LATER they stood and stared at the expanse of beach. White sand stretched before them, sloping to the near transparent turquoise of the sea, dappled and flecked by droplets of the February sunlight.

'This is absolutely beautiful,' Ava breathed.

'Yes.' But Liam realised he wasn't looking at the view. Instead his gaze had settled on Ava and something tugged inside him. *She* looked beautiful, her blonde hair ruffled by the breeze, her wide amber eyes entranced by the scenery. *Get a grip. Think of some facts.* 'It's a protected area so there are no beach bars or any developments allowed.'

'It's an ideal setting for some photos. I am going to do a collage and then post them up with a suitably cheesy message. Let's start simple, pose sitting on those rocks over there.'

They made their way across the sand and the feel of it crunching between his toes, the fresh sea breeze, all instilled a sense of calm. Dispelled the thoughts of his mum and John and Max, the reminder of Christmases spent away to allow them the space to have a proper family Christmas. Unlike those they'd endured when Liam was a child, marred by the alcoholic rants of his father. The most memorable the time Terry Rourke had flung the turkey at the wall. They reached the rocks and she sat down and inhaled a deep breath. 'How about we sit quite close, look at each other and make funny faces?'

'Funny faces.' Despite his best effort Liam could feel his face pull itself into a scowl, the thought of looking like an idiot not one he relished.

'Yes. You know. Kind of playful and like we're having fun.'

'No. I don't know. I've never taken a selfie and I haven't pulled a funny face since I was a kid.'

Ava stared at him. 'Never taken a selfie. Ever?'

'Nope. I run a security firm—social media isn't my thing. I'm more of a low-profile kind of guy.'

'It's not just about social media—I take loads of selfies with friends because it's nice to have quickly accessible memories. Look. I'll show you the sort of thing I mean.' She rose lithely to her feet and he caught his breath. She stood straight and slender, the dress she wore floated in the breeze in a swirl of colour, one hand caught her hair back to keep it from her eyes and in that second he got what she meant. Wanted a picture to capture this memory.

Desire tugged at his gut, but it was more than a physical need. Her smile, the teasing glint in her eyes combined, made him want to catch her in his arms, twirl her round, see laughter illuminate her face. *No point.* Once the charade was over he and Ava would go their separate ways and he would gain nothing from staring at a picture that simply marked an illusion. This wasn't real. Yet for one poignant instant he wanted it to be. The very idea caused a trickle of panic, urged him to flee, to distance himself from temptation.

Focus. Liam Rourke didn't flee, he fought, and

he would do that now. Would remain calm and still, wouldn't let Ava so much as suspect the sheer stupidity of his emotions. Yet he couldn't keep his brows from lowering into a frown at his own idiocy. How could he even contemplate a relationship with Ava? A vulnerable woman caught up in grief and complexity. The last thing she needed was man who had no idea how to navigate the shoals of a relationship. Come to that it was the last thing he needed. His relationship with Jess had been a mistake from start to finish. His mistakes had compounded, one after another and ended in tragedy. Never again would he take that risk.

'Here we go.' Ava tilted her phone and he pulled himself to the present. 'These are the sort of selfies I take—because they're fun.' She scrolled down and he saw images of Ava with a pretty dark-haired woman. They were both beaming at the camera and the other woman was making a gesture over Ava's head. In another they were posing, dressed in pyjamas, a big bowl of popcorn next to them.

'That's Emily,' she explained. 'She's my best mate. This is the sort of thing I'm looking for—a fun photo. So you need to stop channelling your grumpy-old-man mindset and give this a try.'

'Grumpy old man?' Belatedly aware that his face was now set in a scowl, though not for the reasons Ava believed, Liam tried to change his expression to relaxed.

'Yes,' Ava said firmly. 'Though actually perhaps that is an insult to grumpy old men. Come on, Liam. Selfies are part of our world and it's time we got some evidence that you know how to have fun.'

'I do know how to have fun.' Was that a hint of gritted teeth he could hear in his voice?

'Prove it.' The challenge in her voice was unmistake-able. 'When was the last time you had fun? And work-related events don't count.'

Dammit. Liam racked his brains, and didn't like the answer that kept coming up no matter how much he ransacked his memory banks. Last time he could re-member having fun was with Ava, laughing, talking and then, of course, those two kisses. But before that… He was coming up blank. 'This is a daft conversation.'

'In other words you can't come up with anything. Can you?'

'I am having a temporary memory blank.' For Pete's sake—his brain didn't even seem capable of making up anything fun.

Ava glanced sideways at him; a mischievous smile played on her lips. 'Then let's start now. I'll race you to the waves. Last one there pays a forfeit.'

Before he could even factor in the challenge she was off and running and he wasted further seconds caught flat-footed watching her as she sprinted forward, hair streaming behind her.

Quickly he started after, marvelled at her speed on the sand that seemed to slow him down, and Ava got to the cerulean sea with a couple of seconds to spare, turned to watch him, laughter in her eyes and on her lips as he reached her. 'I win,' she crowed and he gave a sudden laugh.

'So what's my forfeit?'

For an instant her gaze snagged on his lips and he knew what she wanted to suggest, could see it in her eyes, in the unintended provocative tilt of her body to-wards him, the instinctive step forward and then she shook her head, a small decisive admonition to herself.

'A funny face. You need to pull a funny face.'

That made him pause as he thought about it. 'What sort of funny face?'

'Any sort. Like this.' She stuck out her tongue and put her hands to the side of her face and wiggled her fingers.

'Fine.' Feeling like a complete idiot, he copied her actions, was rewarded by her spontaneous peal of laughter. He stepped forward into the water, felt the cold swish of the waves as they covered his toes. Without thinking he held out his hand and she took it, and together they stepped forward until the water reached their knees.

He turned to her, looked down at their clasped hands and their previous conversation unrolled before him. Following his gaze, she too stared down and for a moment it all felt too intimate, too close, and then before it could morph into awkwardness Ava smiled.

'It's OK. Let's not overthink it. Let's use this as the perfect photo opportunity.' Gently she dropped his hand and moved closer to him. 'You need to put your arm round my waist.' But now all he could think about was her closeness, how right it felt, and the panic resurged; his brain felt fuzzed by the conflict of emotion inside him. A desire to hold her close, a yearning to kiss her buffeted the knowledge that this was all wrong. A mirage.

Carefully, gingerly, he did as she said; his heart hammered his ribcage, and nerves and anticipation tightened a band across his chest as her arm slipped round his waist. His pulse pounded as her corn-blonde hair tickled his nose and a series of images flashed through his brain. All of Ava, in the shop, laughing as she raced over the sand, her expression when they'd kissed, her response, the sensations. Everything fused into an intensity of reactions and as she looked up at him, he smiled, just as the camera clicked.

He didn't want to move, wanted to gaze on her up-turned face, lean down and taste those lips, lips that enticed and tempted. The instant froze in time; it seemed to stretch and pull to urge him to act. He blinked, tried to break the spell and now she dropped her arm from his waist. Stepped back slightly shakily and shook her head so her hair hid her expression. Turned slightly away to study the photograph.

'Look. It's pretty good.'

Ava was right. It was good; any observer would see what they were supposed to see. A relaxed couple smiling each other. A qualm struck Liam—his smile was genuine, whilst Ava's had obviously been her model's pose, an illusory rictus. The knowledge felt stupidly bleak and he forced a lightness to his voice.

'Not bad. I've got the hang of this. Maybe I should sign up with an agency.'

'They'd snap you up,' she agreed, matching his tone, though her expression was still partly obscured. 'A few more and I think we're good to go.'

'Excellent. I'm not sure about you but I am hungry. There's an amazing pasta place in town if you fancy it?'

'Sounds good.'

And so a few photos later Pierre picked them up and took them back to the town and Liam led the way to small, discreet restaurant. 'You get great food in the more touristy places but, according to Elena, this is the best place to eat in all the town.'

'It smells incredible,' Ava said as they followed a waiter to a small table in the window. She looked around, took in the simple rustic interior, the wooden tabled topped with jugs filled with sheaves of wheat.

'The pasta is all handmade in our kitchens,' the young man explained as he handed them menus. 'From Cappelli wheat, which is both delicious and healthy. It used to be known as "meat for the poor".' Another smile and, 'I'll be back in a few minutes for your orders.'

'Thank you.' Ava studied the menu and frowned. 'I may as well just close my eyes and jab. They all sound incredible.' Quickly she suited action to word. 'I'm going to have the *laganari alla Martinese*. Dry-cured ham, dates, local cheese and exotic-sounding mushrooms.' She glanced at him, saw that his gaze held both amusement and warmth and for some reason she felt colour rise to her cheeks. 'What about you?'

'Why don't you choose for me? You could use the same method.'

She looked at him suspiciously. 'Why?'

Now he smiled and the heat deepened. 'Honestly? I want to watch you do it again. You had a really serious frown and you look like you probably did when you were a child opening her Christmas presents.' He gestured to the menu. 'And it seems as good a way as any to choose.'

She shook her head. 'Then you do it. And I get to watch you.'

He raised his eyebrows in an exaggerated movement and she replayed the words. 'OK. That sounds a little weird, but go ahead.'

His broad shoulders lifted in a shrug and then he closed his eyes and for that instant Ava took the opportunity to study his features. The strength and determination of his jaw and the thickness of his dark eyelashes. His finger hovered and then descended and he opened his eyes. '*Sagna al baccala.* Salt cod and pine nuts and broad beans. I like it.' Now suspicion tinged his tone. 'You didn't take a photo for your collage, did you?'

'No, but I should have.'

'I'm not doing it again,' he said firmly. 'You have enough photos.' Once the waiter took their orders he looked at her. 'What exactly will you do with them?'

'We need to talk about that,' she said, and for a moment she felt a sudden pang of regret. Instead she wanted to discuss the menu, the weather, what books she liked, films, music. *Like a date? A real date?* Was that what she wanted? A small swirl of confusion spiralled in her—the very fact she had to ask the question generated further panic. She had to get a grip. This was fake and she had to remember that. The very last thing she wanted was a relationship with a man who was still in love with his dead wife. All that could lead to was misery. Her own mother had fallen for a man in love with his first wife and had spent her whole life striving to keep him, lived in fear of losing him. But with Liam Ava would already have lost.

'Go ahead,' he said and she pulled herself to the present.

'Well, once we do the "meet the family" tomorrow I'll start posting the photos on social media.' She hesitated. 'I'm not quite sure what may happen next but I think you need to be prepared.'

'Prepared for what?'

'There may be quite a bit of publicity. I've been in the press recently and in the past.'

'Exactly. That's kind of the point.'

'Yes.'

Liam looked at her. 'What am I missing?'

'It's not a lot of fun. I've spent most of my life in the public eye and it's…intrusive.'

'OK. Define intrusive.'

Ava hesitated. 'Let's say we get asked to do an interview for a glossy magazine. They will ask questions.'

'Sure. Like our first date and where we met, et cetera, et cetera.'

'Yes. But they won't stop there. They will also ask about our past and that will include past relationships.'

'Oh.' Liam exhaled a sigh. 'Of course it will. I should have realised that.'

Ava could see his discomfort at the very idea and she didn't blame him. In the past days he had barely mentioned his wife at all and she sensed for Liam his marriage was intensely personal.

She sat back as the waiter approached and served their pasta dishes, smiled her thanks and waited until he was out of earshot.

'It's not just the questions—there will also be interest. People taking pictures, people talking about us, and it won't always be positive commentary. When you're part of a couple people seem to think they have the right to comment on your private life, assess your every move.'

'You're speaking from personal experience.' Liam frowned. 'Your last relationship was pretty high profile, wasn't it?'

'Yes.' Ava took another forkful of her pasta, focused for a moment on the sheer pleasure experienced by her taste buds in the hope it could counter the bitter taste generated by thoughts of her last relationship. Another mouthful and she sighed. 'On that note I suppose we should share some information about our past relationships. A real couple would have done that by now.'

He nodded, his face unreadable apart from a grim twist of his lips.

'I know it will be very hard for you to discuss Jess, and I'm truly sorry. Please know I am not trying to pry.'

Another nod. 'I get that.'

'I may as well go first.' She sensed from his silence that he needed time to gather his thoughts. 'How much do you know? It was a fairly well publicised romance.'

'If I remember right he was a producer or something to do with acting.'

'Yes. His name was, well, still is, Nick Abingworth and he was every girl's dream. Handsome, charming... he had the ability to make you believe you were the world to him. He was an on-the-up producer—he'd done a very successful series and was about to film the next season. Just beginning to get some recognition. I was the perfect girlfriend for him.' Her gaze met his and now she allowed her lips to turn up in a cynical smile. 'For all the same reasons I am the perfect one for you. I was famous, I raised his profile, I had the connections he wanted, and I came from money.' The reminder of exactly why they were sitting there was a welcome one. 'He was trying to get a new project off the ground so I did my best to help him—I partied, I introduced him to people, I was photographed with him, and I did everything I could to promote him.'

'It sounds like you did a lot for him. What did he do for you?'

A small frown creased her brow. 'It doesn't work like that. I loved him, I wanted to make him happy, wanted us to work out, so I did my best to make that happen, be who he wanted me to be.'

His flinch was unmistakeable, as if her words had caused him physical pain, and then he shifted, reached for his fork, and she wondered if she'd imagined it. Then he said, his voice tight, 'But surely you should just have been yourself.'

'That was me being myself.'

'But did you enjoy the parties, promoting Nick?'

'I… I didn't really think about that. It was the right thing to do so I did it. I mean, I like the occasional party but I'm more a "curl up in front of a film with a big bowl of popcorn" kind of girl really.' Not that she and Nick had ever done that. Somehow Ava had convinced herself that all the socialising, all the networking had only been temporary, that once Nick had achieved his goal they would settle into a 'normal' life, maybe even get married, have kids. Because she'd believed he loved her.

'What happened?'

'We broke up. I asked my father to invest in Nick's project and he refused. Said he didn't think it was viable.' Ava had been stunned and then furious. Especially when James Casseveti had explained his other reasons.

'I'm sorry, Ava, but I don't believe the project is viable. I also don't believe in Nick. I think he is using you.'

Her father's face had been unusually grim.

'I won't let that happen. You deserve real love, a man who loves you—not your money, or your public persona, or your connections.'

It was in that moment that Ava had known with certainty that her father had married her mother for all those reasons, a confirmation of a suspicion she'd harboured and resisted all her life, and anger had heated her veins.

'Just because that's what you did it doesn't mean Nick is the same. It doesn't.'

She'd waited, hoped her dad would deny the accusation, would agree with her, but he hadn't.

'I'm sorry, Ava. I hope I'm wrong, but I won't back Nick's project.'

'Nick was devastated so I backed it myself.'

Used up a vast amount of her savings, gave him a lump sum and loaned him the rest. Told herself that there was a difference between buying love and trusting love. Told herself that Nick's easy acceptance of the money was all right, that she didn't want gratitude because, as he pointed out, he was giving her an opportunity to invest. Told herself that she was imagining a change in their relationship, a withdrawal from Nick.

'Then Dad had his heart attack. I gave up modelling to enter Dolci. Life changed and Nick couldn't handle it. Couldn't cope with my "emotional neediness" so he left.'

The flush of remembered humiliation touched her anew and she pulled herself back to the present, saw the understanding in his eyes as he watched her. Nick had only been interested in what Ava Casseveti could get him and she'd been taken for a fool. That wouldn't happen again.

'I'm sorry,' he said. 'But he sounds like a scumbag. You're better off without him.'

'Yes, I know.' But it hadn't felt like that at the time. Yet, 'But compared to what happened to you a break-up is nothing. My situation was sad, yours is tragic.' Without thinking, she reached out and placed her hand over his. 'I'm sorry to ask, but do you think you could tell me a little bit about your marriage? I know it must be painful but it will look odd if I don't know anything.'

There was a silence as he took the last sip of his sparkling water and then he nodded, as the sun vanished behind a cloud and a small shiver touched her. 'I get that. But how about we move on from here first? There's a bar a few streets away with a heated rooftop terrace—we can watch the sunset.'

The words held a sense of poignancy and she nodded.

CHAPTER TEN

As THEY WALKED across the now dusky streets Liam appreciated Ava's silence, appreciated too her closeness as they made their way through the residential area, along pavements decked with potted plants and shrubs. The idea of discussing Jess was both unwelcome and strange, because for years he hadn't spoken about her to anyone, his ill-fated marriage and its attendant grief and regrets for his own consideration only.

Now that had to change—Ava needed some information—the key would be to try and keep it factual. They entered the small *trullo* that housed another souvenir shop and followed the signs to the back where a makeshift bar was in place.

'What would you like?' he asked.

'A glass of white wine, please.'

He ordered the same for himself and then gestured for Ava to climb the narrow spiral staircase before him. Once on the rooftop he watched Ava as she took in the setting, knew he had brought her here because she'd love it, that speaking of her relationship must have been painful. Anger swiped him at the thought of the man who had used her, used her money and position under the guise of love, left her when she would have needed him most. Even as guilt jibed, pointed out that he too was using her, even if he was at least being honest about it.

'This is stunning.'

The terrace was decorated with twinkling fairy lights that illuminated the early evening dusk. Potted evergreens and trellises arched and they could see the rooftops of the *trulli* spread below them. They were the only customers as they sat down at the small wooden table near the comforting warmth of an outdoor heater to counter the February chill.

For a moment they sat in contemplation of the view, sipped their wine and somehow Liam found a certain peace and tranquillity. 'OK,' he said finally. 'Let's talk. Maybe if I just tell you the facts.'

'Whatever works best.'

Liam stared out over the panorama. 'I met Jess when I was twenty-one. I'd been in the army for three years. My dad fell ill and I got leave to come and look after him.' He could still remember his shock when he had seen how much his dad had suddenly deteriorated. 'The alcohol abuse had caught up with him. The last weeks were pretty bad. His brain cells were fried, his memory was shot. He got so confused, was living in a myriad of memories. My mum wanted to help, but by then she'd been gone a few years, had already remarried. And my dad refused to even let her cross the threshold. So it was down to me. That's when I met Jess. Or, rather, reconnected with her. We'd gone to the same school. I bumped into her at the doctor's, we got talking and one thing led to another. Turned out her granddad had been an alcoholic so she understood what my dad was going through.'

'And what you were going through.' Ava's voice was quiet but full of understanding.

'Yes.' And he'd mistaken that connection for a deeper one. He'd been lonely and sad and confused and Jess had been like a lifeline. But even then he'd never thought about marriage—hadn't really thought at all. He'd just been happy to have someone there.

'You fell in love.'

'Yes.' What else could he say? For a time he'd believed it to be true. A mistake that he would carry with him all his life. But as he looked at Ava's beautiful face, illuminated by the last rays of the setting sun, just for one insane moment he wondered if he would ever utter words of love again. Shook his head. Surely this story of his past should cement the knowledge that he would never be so foolish again. Couldn't, wouldn't take that risk. 'We had a very quiet wedding because it was so close to the funeral and then Jess came and lived with me nearer my barracks.' And Liam had determined to stand by his vows, to do as he had expected his mother to do. 'Jess fell ill whilst I was on a campaign abroad. I came back as soon as I could but there wasn't much time left.'

For a moment he was back there in the hospital, with the distinctive smell of disinfectant, the beep of monitors echoing in his ears. Jess, gaunt and pale, her blue eyes so large in the pinch of her face. Her smile so sweet.

'I'm glad you're here.'

'Of course I'm here, Jess.'

She'd tried to rise and he'd carefully moved her, propped her up against the pillows.

'There are some things I want to say, before...before it's too late.'

'Anything.'

'I just want to say I'm sorry. When we met I rushed you into everything. I took advantage of you.'

He'd smiled through his tears. *'And I enjoyed every minute.'*

Her hand, so skeletally thin, had squeezed his.

'But that wasn't enough. You were grieving and confused, but I was so happy that you wanted to marry me, happy to be wanted, that I decided that didn't matter. That we could make it work, that you would grow to love me, because I'd be the perfect wife. I shouldn't have done that. I'm sorry.'

'I'm the one who is sorry. All these years I haven't been there for you and...'

'It's OK, Liam. I love you. I've always loved you and you have been an honourable man—you stuck by me and that has honestly meant the world to me. So please, Liam, don't beat yourself up—you did good.'

She'd dropped back on the pillow, her face lined with weariness.

'I'm glad I said all that. Thank you for coming back.'

The conversation was one he would never share with anyone. Instead he simply said, 'I was with her at the end and I am glad of that.'

'I'm glad of that for both of you,' Ava said, her voice gentle. 'And I'm sorry, Liam, sorry her life was taken so soon and the whole life you could have had together is gone.' She looked away from him, at the sky touched by the orange rays of the setting sun. 'Would you like another drink?'

'Thank you.'

'I'll be back in a minute.'

As Ava walked down the winding stairs past the vintage sewing machines sadness touched her, for Jess's life snuffed out so tragically early, but also for Liam. The haunted look in his eyes as he'd spoken of his marriage and his wife's death had been all too apparent, and underlined the fact that Liam had not got over Jess and most likely never would. The knowledge added an extra layer to her sadness, made her wish she could help him, made her wish…wish what?

That he weren't a man weighed with grief, that somehow this were a real date, an attraction that could be pursued in the hope of the possibility of a future. That way lay madness. Ava would not even set a toe on that path of delusion, take a single step on the way to one-sided love ever again. That would be nothing short of utter foolishness. She might as well put a target on her heart saying: *Break me now.*

So from now on she had to focus on the fact that this was fake, that the attraction between them couldn't be acted upon or built upon or go anywhere. Full stop. So she would go back upstairs and concentrate on making this the best fake relationship she could, paying her father's debt to the best of her ability.

With a smile of thanks to the bartender she headed back to the terrace, handed Liam his glass and sat back opposite him.

'Thank you.' He smiled at her. 'For this and for being such a good listener.'

'No problem. As I said, I am truly sorry you had to talk about it and I'm sorry that there will be intrusive questions from the press.'

'It's their job, I guess. Any ideas what they may come up with?'

Ava sipped her wine, ran through the possible scenarios in her mind. 'I suppose one question may be, "What was it about Ava that made you re-enter the re-

lationship arena after the tragic death of your wife?"'
She gazed at the darkening sky now only tinged with
the very last of the sun's rays. 'Obviously that will be
somewhat awkward and I'll do my best to turn the conversation.'

'How?'

Ava thought for a moment. 'I'll say something like,
"Hey, guys, much as I would love to hear my virtues
extolled, Jess's death was tragic and I'd much prefer to
take the opportunity to highlight what readers can do
to help with research for the terrible disease that took
her."'

Liam stared at her in evident admiration. 'That's a
brilliant answer.'

'Thank you very much. It comes from practice. I've
been in the public eye for as long as I can remember.'

'Did you enjoy it?'

'I got used to it, because it's all I've ever known.
And hopefully it will come in handy now. I will do my
very best to deflect questions about Jess where I can.'

'I appreciate that.'

Ava sipped her wine, glanced at Liam and without
her even meaning them to the words spilled from her
lips. 'Do you think you ever will have a relationship? A
real one, I mean?' Once said, the words seemed to hover
in the air and she shook her head. 'Sorry. I shouldn't
have asked that.'

'It's OK. It's a fair question in the situation and easy
enough to answer. No. I won't. I've built my life on my
own and I like it that way. I don't want to rock the boat
with a relationship.'

How could she blame him? 'I totally get that.' The
fervency in her voice was too much and Liam raised
his eyebrows.

'So you're not looking for a relationship either?'

'Nope. For now I've given up dating completely. Like you, I am genuinely happy on my own. Why would I want to complicate that with a relationship?'

'Because you want the traditional happy ever after, kids, family life?'

All the things he must have once been looking forward to and had had taken from him.

'I don't know,' she said honestly. 'I do want that but only with the right person and I don't know how to figure out who that is.' She'd got it wrong once and she'd seen the unhappiness that could be generated by a bad marriage. 'Getting it wrong is not a risk I want to take.'

'But how will you ever work out who Mr Right is if you don't give anyone a chance?'

'That is an excellent question and yet another thing I haven't figured out.'

'Perhaps someone will sweep you off your feet.'

'Nope. No way. That sort of thing sounds all very well, but what if you get carried away by the moment and then you discover it's a mistake? When it's too late to get out.'

His expression changed and as he reached out for his glass his usually deft movement was a jerk that tipped his glass. Recovering, he caught it, lifted it and sipped. 'I think you need to take your time. Really get to know someone before you make a long-term commitment. But to do that you do have to go on that first date.'

'It feels too scary. Plus it doesn't work like that. However sensible you think you are you can get carried away—attraction, love…they can skew common sense, kid you into making stupid decisions.' As she had with Nick. 'I'd want to walk away the minute I felt my heart start beating a bit faster, the minute it felt even the tiniest bit out of my control.' She shrugged. 'It's easier to stay single.'

'Agreed. Though there are some drawbacks, unless you plan on a lifetime of celibacy.'

'That is a drawback.' The words seemed to whir across the table and take on a life of their own. Their gazes met and locked and her throat tightened. 'I assume you have no wish to join a monastery.'

'No.' He hesitated and then shrugged. 'The only solution I've come up with is an occasional one-night stand. One night means there is definitively nothing more than a brief physical connection.'

Ava looked at him. 'And that's enough?'

There was a silence and then he nodded. 'Yes,' he said finally as he drank the last of his wine. 'That is better than the risks involved in a relationship.' He shook his head, gave a sudden smile as if to lighten the mood. 'Listen to us. We are hardly advocates of true love. Yet we're about to try and sell the concept to the world. Or at least some of it.'

'It does sound a bit mad. But I just want to say. I… think we have a much better chance of pulling this off now. Italy was a good idea. It's given us a chance to get to know each other.' Which was a good thing, right? So why did it suddenly feel like a bad one?

She glanced at her watch. 'I guess we'd better get going. I need to pack and prepare. It's going to be a long day tomorrow.'

CHAPTER ELEVEN

THE FOLLOWING DAY, once again aboard the private plane, Liam surveyed Ava. As always she looked perfect, the outfit smart casual, dark blue jeans, tucked-in collared shirt topped by a pretty grey jumper with a floral edging, perfect for a meet the parent for the first time scenario. Her nails were a discreet neutral colour; her hair, freshly washed, cascaded in blonde waves past her shoulders and wafted an evocative floral scent across the table. Light make-up showed that she'd made an effort but without being over the top.

She frowned. 'Do I look OK? Should I have gone for something more businesslike?'

'You look fine. It's perfect for the occasion.'

'That's what I thought.'

He could see her nervousness though, the slight pallor of her skin and the amber flecks of wariness in her eyes. 'It'll be OK.' What else could he say?

'I hope so. I just know that this is going to be awkward.'

He hesitated, knew he was putting Ava in an unconscionable position. A few days ago it hadn't bothered him. Now scant hours away from bringing the two women together he felt...bad.

'You told me a bit about your mum. What about John and Max? What are they like?'

Edginess shifted inside him. 'Max likes rollerblading, he goes to school. He is a typical teenage boy, I guess. John works hard, he's quiet… I don't really know him that well. I was twenty when they got married. I…' The wedding was etched on his soul. When he'd seen the way John and Bea looked at each other, the love and joy in their eyes, their stance, their everything, seen Max wrap his arms round Bea's waist in a hug, Liam had realised with an intense visceral knowledge exactly what he'd cost his mother. That was when he'd vowed to stay clear, keep his distance, make up for what he had done. 'We're not really that close.' He tried for a smile, wanted to take the worry from Ava's eyes, rebury his own memories. 'It'll be OK. We go in, chat, leave. Look at it this way—if we can convince them, it will all be a breeze from there.'

'It feels like a pretty big if.'

'Hey, what's the worst that can happen?'

'I've considered that. How about this? Your mum sees through us in less than a minute… Your mum hates me because of my dad. Either way she throws me out.'

'Nah. Won't happen. My worst-case scenario is we succumb to the stress of it all and run around my mum's lounge clucking like chickens saying, "It's all a lie".'

The absurdity of the image caused her to give an involuntary chuckle. 'Speak for yourself. I guarantee I won't do that.'

A few hours later they pulled up outside a small well-maintained terraced house on the outskirts of London. Ava took in the bright red door, the clean paint on the walls, the small front garden replete with carefully tended flowers and shrubs. The elegant slatted blinds in the windows. 'It's lovely,' Ava said, though a part of her had expected Liam's mum to live in a larger house, had thought Liam would have given her a mansion.

As if reading her thoughts, Liam shrugged. 'It is. Though I did offer to buy Mum something bigger but she and John refused. Prefer to make their own way.' Impossible to be sure but she thought there was a hint of hurt in his tone.

Before she could reply he knocked on the door and sudden trepidation touched her. As if he sensed it, Liam took her hand in his just as the door swung open. A woman who was clearly Liam's mum stood at the door, a smile on her face. Her eyes went directly to Liam, rested on him for a poignant moment and Ava could see the love. Yet there was also a wariness, one that directly matched Liam's.

Liam moved forward, but she sensed an awkwardness in the jut of shoulder; for once his movement seemed stilted as he hugged the older woman.

'Mum, this is Ava. Ava, this is my mum.'

'Pleased to meet you.'

'And you.' Ava knew she had to avert the sense of discomfort in the air and it seemed clear that Bea felt the same way. The older woman smiled. 'John and Max are getting things ready in the kitchen. I thought maybe we should have a word in private first.'

Bea led them into the lounge, a tastefully decorated, comfortably cluttered room. She turned to Ava, her grey eyes clear and direct. 'Max knows nothing about what happened between your father and Liam's dad and I'd like to keep it that way.'

'I completely understand and I won't say anything about that,' Ava said, appreciating the directness of

Bea's words. 'But I would like to tell you that my father did regret his actions. I realise that is not particularly helpful but he was sorry. And I am too.'

'Thank you. It was a long time ago now and, whilst I won't pretend to any positive feeling towards your father, I know his actions are not your fault. I will do my best not to make this awkward.'

'Thank you.'

She broke off as the door swung open to admit a youth and a tall man with grizzled hair and a serious face, though Ava noted his eyes held both warmth and humour. Both held trays containing tea and coffee pots as well as plates of cakes and biscuits.

'Ava, this is Max and John They have been baking up a storm today—sadly I am banned from the kitchen due to my non-existent baking skills. Which Liam will also attest to.'

Liam simply smiled, a small tight smile. 'I am sure these will be delicious.' But the words walked on stilts and Ava flashed a quick glance at him, instinctively stepped a little closer to him. Irrationally wanted him to know that, whilst she definitely liked Bea, she was on his side. Though why there should be a side to pick, she wasn't quite sure.

Accepting a cake from Max, she smiled at him, saw he had inherited his dad's serious face. 'They are utterly delicious,' she said. 'Chocolate orange?'

Max nodded. 'Yes, and Dad made shortbread.'

'You are men of many talents.' She smiled at John. 'Liam did mention you love cooking and I understand Max, you rollerblade as well.'

The dark-haired boy nodded. 'I speed skate and I play roller hockey.'

Bea gave a small shudder. 'It's a pretty violent game.

But Max is brilliant at it. He's trying out for the county team next week.' Her pride shone through and Ava could sense how close she and her stepson were, wondered whether Liam minded on some level. Impossible to tell from his expression, which was one of courteous interest.

Max turned to Liam and she could see the curiosity in his eyes. 'Um… We had a careers fair at school the other day. The army were there. It looked really cool. I… I told them about you.' Another quick look. 'They were talking about the army reserves. I wondered if you joined them. Mum said to ask you.'

Liam glanced quickly at his mum and then back to Max, and again Ava sensed an undercurrent of unease, suspected Liam wasn't quite sure what to say, what his mum wanted him to say. And her heart twisted inside her in empathy—she knew he wanted to do what was best. Knew too that Bea simply wanted him to tell the truth, otherwise she wouldn't have told Max to ask him. But perhaps what seemed obvious to her wasn't obvious to Liam.

Without thought she intervened. 'Liam told me he joined up because his boss at his Saturday job was in the reserves. That it was a great thing for him.'

Another glance at his mum and then Liam nodded. 'It gave me structure and I loved the physical side of it. I guess a gym would do the same thing but I liked the outdoors element. I made some good friends too—people I'm still in touch with today.'

'Maybe I'll give it a go. I'll mention you when I enrol.'

It became clear to Ava that Bea and John and Max were a happy relaxed family unit, the banter and the chat easy, and Ava found herself laughing at some of the dry anecdotes John told about work and some of the plumbing disasters he encountered. Yet throughout Ava was, oh, so aware of Liam next to her, felt the palpable tension in his body, saw how little he participated. His laughter was a little forced, a beat behind everyone else.

And it tugged her heartstrings because this showed a vulnerable side to him and she wasn't sure what had caused that. Realising the topic had shifted once more, Ava quickly refocused.

'I've got to do some work experience as part of my course,' Max said. 'I wish I could roller skate for that. But I can't.'

'You could come to work with me.' Both John and Bea spoke at the same time and Max made a face.

'I really appreciate that but going to work with you or Dad isn't the same as…' He trailed off but Ava saw the quick glance that he cast at Liam.

So did Bea. Swiftly she leaned forward and Ava sensed it was to protect Max from potential rejection. 'We were wondering if you'd like to stay for dinner?'

'Another time,' Liam said. 'I've got plans for dinner tonight.'

For a moment a look of hurt flashed across Bea's face As if he too saw it, he said hurriedly, 'But definitely another time.'

'Definitely,' Ava added. 'And it's been so lovely to meet you. I truly appreciate how welcoming you've been.'

Final goodbyes said, she followed Liam back to the car, climbed in and buckled up. 'We could have stayed for dinner if you wanted. I like them.'

'Yes. I could tell.'

Ava frowned, saw the closed expression on his face,

sensed a taut undercurrent of emotion, saw the way his hands gripped the steering wheel.

'What's wrong?'

'Nothing.' He turned the key in the ignition and put the car into gear, each movement contained and yet she sensed that he wanted to crash and grind through the gears and accelerate away. Liam shook his head. 'There is just no point in them getting to know you too well— we're going to split up in a few months.'

For some inexplicable reason the words made her stomach dip, presumably at the idea of the media coverage of their split, the knowledge that they would have to manage it to minimise suspicion or negativity. 'Yes, but—'

'There aren't any buts. It's better to quit whilst we're ahead. We convinced them we're legit. Mission accomplished.'

For a moment Ava was tempted to let it go—then she looked at him again, saw the shadow in his eyes and knew she couldn't do that. Perhaps it wasn't her business but she'd liked Bea. And John and Max. And it seemed all wrong that Liam didn't feel close to them. Didn't spend Christmas with them.

'Could we stop somewhere before you drop me back home? Maybe go for a walk?'

The glance he gave her held a wealth of suspicion and for a moment she wondered if he would refuse, simply press his foot on the accelerator, turn the music on loud and complete their journey. 'We need to discuss our plan for the next few days.'

'Sure. There's a large National Trust park nearby. We can head there.'

Twenty minutes later Liam surveyed Ava as they walked along a pretty tree-lined path; evergreens dense and green edged a garden that still bloomed with co-lour despite the winter month. She'd pulled on a navy-blue duffel coat and her cheeks were tinged pink from the breeze.

She glanced sideways at him and he recognised this as an unconscious indicator of a preliminary skirmish. 'The planning that must go into these gardens so they look beautiful all year boggles the mind.' Her tone was innocent.

'Yes,' Liam agreed. Where was she going with this?

'Do you garden at all?'

'Nope.'

'I think your mum and John do, though. I spotted their back garden and it's full of flowers and pots.'

'Yes.' He'd wondered if Ava had really brought him here to plan the next few days or to discuss their visit and now it seemed he'd been right to suspect the latter. 'But we aren't here to talk about gardening,' he said firmly. 'We need to think about our next steps.'

'Yes.' Now her chin jutted out determinedly. 'Which includes talking about family.'

'No need. We met my mum and her family and that box is ticked.'

'No, it isn't. What are you going to do if your mum follows up and asks us round for dinner?'

Liam sighed. 'Put her off? We can always be busy and I don't think she will ask again.'

'But that will hurt their feelings.'

'Perhaps. But that's better than her getting close to you and then we spilt up.'

Contrition touched her amber eyes and she reached out, placed a hand on his arm. 'I am *so* sorry. Your mum must have been devastated when Jess died—of course, you are trying to protect her.'

Liam blinked, saw the compassion etched on her face and knew he couldn't let her believe that.

'No. It's not that. Truly. Of course my mum was upset when Jess died. But they weren't close.' Jess had always said Bea made her nervous and in truth Liam had wondered if Bea had known, had seen that their marriage wasn't all it should be. After all, she had watched her own marriage disintegrate, perhaps she could see the signs. The idea had made him uncomfortable, had reinforced his decision to let Bea get on with her new life, protected from his problems. And Jess had seemed happy with that, happy for it to be 'just the two of them'.

'Then what is going on?'

'What do you mean?' He kept his voice even. 'Nothing is going on.' He tried to inject finality into his tone, but Ava shook her head.

'Yes, there is. Otherwise why were you so tense earlier?'

'I wasn't. Apart from being a bit nervous—this is the first time we've "appeared" in public as a couple.'

'I'm not buying that. You have nerves of steel.' She raised her hands up. 'If you want to tell me to mind my own business do, but don't lie to me.'

The words caused him to pause, swallow the words of denial that sprang to his lips. Dammit. He was lying. Irritation sparked inside him—this was exactly why he eschewed relationships. They became messy and complicated and he didn't know the correct responses. But lying didn't feel right and neither did the unvarnished truth. 'Fine. I wasn't nervous. We're just not close.'

'Why not?' The words impacted the air, directed by a force he didn't fully understand. 'I don't get it. Before I met them I thought maybe they weren't very nice but they are nice. All of them.'

'I know they are.'

'Then what's not to be close to?' Her face was serious, a wistful look in her amber eyes. 'You're lucky. Your mum, John, Max. They are lovely, decent human beings. I don't understand why you don't embrace the chance to be part of it. To ask Max to come and do work experience with you. Go have a beer with John. A cocktail with your mum. Celebrate Christmas with them all.' He heard frustration, almost anger in the vibrancy of her voice and he stopped in his tracks.

Ava stopped too, turned to him and he studied her face. 'Why does this matter so much to you?'

Now those amber eyes blazed at him. 'Because I'm angry that you're being so stupid. That you're wasting a chance to have a family. When I would do anything to have that opportunity. All my life I wanted siblings, real siblings, not a shadowy, furtive half-family I wasn't allowed to meet. I wanted a mum who I could be close to, laugh with, shop with, confide in. What I do have now are two half-siblings who won't even speak to me. And a mum who is furious with me. And you have this lovely family you are refusing to be part of.'

Understanding hit him; he heard the pain that underlaid her words, could see it in the way she turned away from him, tried to hide her expression. 'I'm sorry.' The words were wholly inadequate and they both knew it. 'I didn't realise.' Had always assumed the Cassevetis were a close, happy family.

'There is no reason why you should.'

'Do you want to talk about it?'

'It doesn't work like that. You don't get to hold back and not talk about your family stuff, whilst I discuss mine.'

'That's not how I meant it.' God. He really did suck

at this. 'I just thought talking about it may help.' He stared at her as the penny dropped. Presumably that was exactly how Ava felt too. She wanted to help him. The idea was startling in its novelty. And suddenly he did get it, knew that he wanted Ava to understand that he wasn't blithely refusing something she wanted so much. 'Shall we sit down and I'll try and explain?'

Ava shook her head. 'Hell. Now I feel like I've forced you into this.'

'You haven't. Truly.' She sat down next to him. 'You're right. My mum, John, Max…they are all lovely people and they are a happy family, a happy family unit. They don't need me to be part of it.'

'It's not about need. You could choose to be part of that happy family unit. You would be welcomed in.'

'It isn't that clear-cut. There's history.' He wanted Ava to know that she wasn't alone, that the past had thrown its shadow over his family as well. 'You know that my parents' marriage disintegrated.'

Ava nodded.

'Well, at the time I didn't know or fully understand what was going on, didn't realise how cruel a thing alcohol abuse is, how it changes a person. All I saw as a child was my mum trying to get my dad to stop drinking—she wanted him to "be a man", pull himself out of the pit of self-pity he was wallowing in. The problem was, the less sympathetic she was, the more he tried to convince her the blame was all your father's and the more bitter he got. And as Dolci really took off it got worse and worse. My mum kept telling him to let it go and he just couldn't.'

Ava's amber eyes focused on his face and he sensed how intensely she was listening to him. 'And the more you must have felt in the middle.'

'I wasn't as fair as that. I landed on my dad's side.'

'Because that way you didn't have to give up believing in him,' she said softly. And with such understanding he knew she truly empathised. Knew how hard she had worked at believing in her dad.

'Yes, but that meant I blamed my mother for not being supportive enough, not being loving or understanding enough.' He shook his head. 'What I couldn't see was everything she was doing. All the extra shifts, all the worries about not being able to pay the bills, and all the while having to deal with the demands of living with an alcoholic. But she always got on with it. There was food on the table, and she still made me do my homework. But my dad, he let me do whatever I wanted.'

'You were a child—a child doesn't understand the responsibilities of bills to pay or adult emotions. You just wanted everything to be OK, for your parents to be happy again.'

The sympathy in her eyes shivered discomfort down him. Little did Ava know how instrumental he'd been in his mother's unhappiness. He rubbed the back of his neck, knew he needed, wanted to tell her. 'Perhaps. But it didn't work out like that. Instead my mum met John when I was twelve. They fell in love.' Ava's eyes didn't move from his face, her whole being focused on him. 'She wanted to take me and leave Dad.'

'What happened?'

'Dad went nuts, and I took his side. I told her I wouldn't go, that I'd run away, quit school, that my dad would die without her and it would be her fault. I said so many things and in the end she stayed. For me.' His voice was bleak.

'You were a child. You loved your dad. What you

did wasn't wrong. If your mother chose to stay with your dad that was her choice to make. It was not your responsibility.'

'I was still the reason she stayed. The reason she and John lost years of happiness and my mum gained years of misery. John met someone else, got married, had Max and Mum was devastated. It didn't work out because he'd never got over Mum. He and his wife got divorced and he got custody of Max.'

'But obviously they did reconnect.'

'Yes. When I joined the army Mum did finally leave Dad. A couple of years later she and John started talking again and very soon after that they got married.'

'That's a good thing.'

'Yes. It is. It's a wonderful thing and I am truly happy for them.'

Now her gaze held an awareness, an understanding that he didn't want. 'And you don't want to spoil it?'

'Yes… No. I don't want to intrude on it.'

'You wouldn't be. They like you. Your mum loves you. I could see all that.'

'In one visit?' He made no effort to hide his scepticism.

'Yes. I know what it feels like to have siblings who aren't accessible. Max looks up to you. I bet he'd love to have a hands-on older brother like you. You heard him when he was talking about the army. And joining the reserves. You're his stepbrother. Do something about it. Stop being scared. I know I'm right. They wouldn't feel you were intruding, they'd welcome you in. It's your family unit.'

For a moment her words slipped past all the barricades and guards, probed into a place he had blocked off long ago. He wondered what it would be like to be part of it, to fit in. Emotions dipped and waved. Envy? Sadness? Regret? Who knew? All he did know was that he didn't want to feel any of those emotions. Couldn't take the risk. Ava was right—he was scared. It was too easy to get it wrong. What if he encouraged Max to join the army and, God forbid, something happened to him? What if he somehow offended John and his mum had to take sides? Too many worst-case scenarios and he knew the best way forward was to make sure none of them were possible.

'Thank you for the advice, and I mean that. But I'm not a family kind of guy and I know they are happy, I know my mum is happy and that's what's most important to me. I'm not going to mess with the status quo. Because it's a good one.' He took a deep breath. 'But that doesn't mean you should do the same.'

'What do you mean?'

'Luca and Jodi—maybe you should try a different approach. Why don't you contact them direct rather than go through lawyers? Pick up the phone, leave messages, use social media. Talk to them.'

He wondered if his words even registered. Her head was shaking a denial before he'd even finished. 'I can't do that. The lawyers would have my guts for garters and my mum—I couldn't do that to her. She is already furious with me because I haven't tried to get the will overturned. She wants them out of our lives. I won't add to her sense of betrayal by doing something that would be a complete *et tu, Brute?* moment.' She rose to her feet, gave him a smile. 'Truly, it's better left.'

He knew the smile to be fake and the words to be wrong but what could he say? After all, wasn't her argument the exact one he'd advocated himself? *It's better left.* Conversations like this one tilted his ordered world, ones that reminded him exactly why relationships were a bad idea.

'Come on. I'll get you home.'

'Thank you. I'll post some photos on social media tonight. And I think from now on we need to be seen out and about a lot more. Dinners, parties, social events. I'll get it all set up.'

The business-like tone was exactly what he needed to hear.

CHAPTER TWELVE

LIAM OPENED HIS eyes the following morning, aware that he'd slept badly, but unsure why. In theory it should have been nice to have his own space, to know he could return to his regular routine for a few hours. There was an element of that, but he was also aware of a sense that something was missing over his solitary bowl of cereal. Or someone.

Ridiculous.

Yet that afternoon when his phone buzzed and Ava's name flashed on the screen he felt a sense of anticipation as he snatched it up.

'Hey.'

'Hey. My mum called. She'd like to meet you.'

'Any particular reason?'

'I'm not sure.' Her voice was guarded. 'But it's probably better to go and see—we don't want any surprises. I thought we could go on to dinner after. I've booked us a table at Muscat—it's showy but not too showy. We've had a lot of hits on my social media post and there is a definite level of interest.'

'Brilliant.'

'So how about I pick you up at four?'

'Sounds good.' Liam disconnected, aware of a sense of bitter curiosity about the woman he was soon to meet. Karen Casseveti, formerly Lady Karen Hales. The woman who had taken James Casseveti from his first family and thrown her wealth and position behind him, enabled him to set up Dolci, start the Casseveti fairy tale that had picked up pace in direct proportion to the Rourke family decline.

Liam tamped the feelings down. It was the past, over and done with, and he'd decided to put it aside. Yet by the time he climbed into the passenger seat of Ava's car he was aware of an edginess.

One matched by Ava. As ever she looked incredible, her blonde hair styled in a chic knot on the top of her head, the long-sleeved grey floral dress elegant with a hint of pizzazz. Yet he could see the slight strain in the set of her lips and the tension in her shoulders, though her smile was as flawless as ever as she greeted him.

'All set?' she asked.

'Yes. I'm a little curious and a little wary but I'm good.' He glanced at her. 'You OK?'

'Of course.'

He raised his eyebrows and she gave a small rueful nod of acknowledgment. 'OK. I'm a little wary too. I told you that my mum and I aren't seeing eye to eye at the moment and I'm not really sure how she is going to be.'

Half an hour later they pulled up outside a huge Surrey mansion. The gates opened with majestic splendour and Ava drove her small white electric car onto the expansive gravelled drive.

'It's a family house. My mother inherited it,' Ava explained. 'After Dad died Mum moved here. It's usually looked after by a housekeeper who's been with her since Mum was a child.'

The door was pulled open by a stately looking

woman, dressed in severe black, her grey hair pulled back in a bun. She bestowed a tight smile on Ava and graced Liam with a small nod.

'Hello, Ellie.' Ava's smile was wide, but he was sure it was strained. 'How are you?'

'I'm fine, thank you.' Ellie's smile was cold. 'But it's not me you should be worried about. It's your mother.' She pulled the door wider. 'Follow me.'

Once along a spacious corridor, with panelled walls and antique furniture, they entered a vast drawing room that imposed its plush richness. Velvet ruled and there was an indescribable air of wealth and heritage in the Georgian-style furniture and the heavy gold brocade curtains.

'Ava.' A woman stepped forward, a woman who shared Ava's blonde hair, though her colour was discreetly and elegantly aided and cut in a sleek bob. Her make-up was perfect, her figure svelte and stylish, though Liam could see the ravages of grief in the dark circles that couldn't be completely concealed. 'And you must be Liam.' The smile was a blend of welcome and appraisal with a hint of condescension, the blue eyes hooded as she rested her gaze on him.

'Mrs Casseveti. It's a pleasure to meet you.'

'Please, call me Karen. Then sit down and we can discuss the best way forward. Ava told me how you are hoping to use your fake relationship to help save your company and help spin Ava some positive publicity too. I'd like to help.'

'That's great, Mum,' Ava said.

'Yes. And in return perhaps you will feel more inclined to get rid of the usurpers.' The venom in the last word made him flinch.

'We've been through this.' Ava's voice was firm, but

he saw her nails clench into her palms, knew how hard this was for her. 'For a start, the will would be very difficult to overturn and would wipe us out in legal bills.'

'I have said I'll foot the cost.'

'Second, this is what Dad wanted. Luca and Jodi are his children.'

'Luca and Jodi Petrovelli are nothing. They didn't even keep your father's name. They do not deserve to even step into Dolci headquarters.'

'Perhaps. But they have the right to do so. I think we should make the best of it.'

'How can you be so disloyal? Your father made a mistake and I will not let the Petrovellis get their grubby hands on James's company.' Karen turned to Liam. 'You are an excellent businessman—you've come from nowhere and achieved a lot. I assume you must have a ruthless streak, a business sense. Show Ava the best way forward. The right way.'

Liam read the signs all too well; the same look had dulled his father's eyes with obsession. Quickly he stepped closer to Ava, hoped his body warmth could somehow shield her. 'I will support any decision Ava makes.'

Karen exhaled a long sigh; her eyes glittered with ice. 'Ava, show some family loyalty and together we will take that woman's children down.'

'I won't do that, Mum. I won't overturn Dad's wishes. Please, let's work together to try and make the best of this, do what is best for Dolci.'

Karen shook her head, emitted a sigh that gusted disappointment and anger.

But Ava persevered. 'Dolci is in trouble, will stay in trouble until we can get certainty and public confidence. Getting mired in a lengthy legal wrangle won't help.'

The words fell into Karen Casseveti's chasm of resentment. 'Just leave. Come back when you are ready to fix the mess you made. If you had been a better daughter, then your father would not have done this.'

Liam's heart ached for her as he saw the pain in Ava's eyes, the quickly concealed flinch.

'Perhaps that is true,' she said quietly. 'But at least I was given a chance to try to be a good daughter. They weren't given a chance to be anything, not even a peripheral part of his life.' She moved forward, approached her mother. 'I know how betrayed you feel, but this was Dad's fault, not Luca's or Jodi's.'

For a moment Liam wondered if Ava had got through but Karen shook her head. 'I cannot believe you would take their side over me. Please leave now.'

Ava hesitated and then nodded. 'I'll call you later.'

She headed towards the door and Liam followed, knew there was nothing he could say that would turn Karen. He had spent years trying to mitigate Terry Rourke's bitterness to no avail, sensed that Karen's hostility ran equally deep. But at least Terry Rourke hadn't blamed his son, hadn't directed his anger against Liam.

Sensing Ava didn't want to talk, he remained silent as she started the car and began the journey back to London, broke silence only when they were on the outskirts, had stopped to recharge Ava's electric VW. 'Are you sure you still want to go out for dinner?' He knew how much Karen Casseveti's words must have hurt Ava, but saw her expression close down into neutrality, knew she wouldn't talk about it.

'I'm sure. If we don't turn up that's the exact wrong message to send out. It won't help you. Or me.'

After that she adroitly changed the subject, manufactured small talk for the remainder of their journey, until they pulled up in the vicinity of the exclusive restaurant.

Ava focused on the click of her heels on the pavement, the cold February air that permeated the wool of her navy-blue button-down coat. Tried to push down and freeze the negativity and doubts swirled up by her mother. Allowed herself an awareness of Liam's strength and warmth, knew she needed to channel that to play the role of adoring and adored girlfriend, to cast the spell of an illusory love for the public eye to behold.

Because she was going to make this charade work, at least achieve something to help her embattled company. And so she entered the glitz and glamour of the star-studded restaurant with confidence in her walk and in her smile. Chose her food with care—there was no way Ava Casseveti would be snapped with spinach in her teeth, or a food stain on her dress.

When the drinks arrived she raised her sparkling water, aware that many of their fellow diners were watching. 'Cheers,' she said.

'Cheers,' he answered. 'Thank you for seeing this through.'

'No problem. My mother thought this charade a good idea and she knows what she is talking about. So this dinner is important.'

'Just because she knows about spin doesn't mean she knows everything. When someone is obsessed by bitterness their perspective is skewed. Looking back now, I know my father's was. I think your mother's is too. She didn't mean what she said about it being your fault. About you being a better daughter.'

The echo of her mother's words stung. 'Unfortunately the only person who would know that is my dad so I'll never know for sure. But as you said you're dealt the cards you're dealt in life.'

'Yes. Now it's up to you how to play the hand. Seems to me you've got a tricky one. Maybe I can help. Maybe talking about it will help.'

'I don't want to talk about my mother.'

'I meant help with Dolci. In my ruthless business-man role.'

'You want to help me rescue Dolci?'

'Yes. You don't deserve to be in this position. I wouldn't have lifted a finger for your dad but I'd like to help you.'

'I appreciate that.' And she did. 'But there is nothing you can do. I am caught between a rock and a hard place. My mother wants me to overturn the will, work to oust Luca and Jodi. Luca and Jodi are refusing to engage so I don't even know what they want. My dad seemed to think we would all miraculously become a happy family.'

'What about what you want?'

Ava paused, fork halfway to her mouth. 'Me? I'd like… I'd like us all to sit down and talk. But I'd also like world peace—neither is very likely.'

That pulled a smile from him. 'I admit it's hard to see your mother shaking hands with the usurpers. Right now. So maybe that needs to be your long-term goal. You need to think about what you *can* control now. Focus on a short-term goal, an obstacle you can overcome.'

Ava sat for a moment, tasted the succulent flavour of the perfectly cooked lamb and thought about his words. 'I'd like to show the world that I am capable, or at least more capable than they think I am. That my ideas could work.'

'Then pick an idea and do it. Your way.'

Easy to say—she wasn't sure she knew what 'her' way was. 'That's what you would do, but that's because you know what you're doing.'

Liam paused. 'No, I don't. Not always. I don't want to ruin my image but I certainly made my share of mistakes.'

'You did?'

'Yes. There was the time I nearly landed us with a lawsuit when I let myself get distracted and riled during a security assignment. The police tried to arrest me whilst someone tried to attack the guy I was meant to be protecting.'

'What happened?'

'I knocked the police officer out so I could protect the client. It eventually worked out but it nearly didn't. And another person may have handled it differently, figured out a less violent way. But sometimes you have to do it your way, take a stand, act on your own instincts, take a risk.'

'Maybe I am too risk averse. All I see is the worst-case scenario.'

Liam shook his head. 'I don't think it's that.'

'Then what do you think it is?'

He hesitated and she gestured. 'It's fine. Hit me with it.' She genuinely wanted his opinion, wondered how it had come to matter to her so much in such a short space of time.

'Right. I think you're too worried about everyone else. You want to please your father and your mother and the press and your staff and you've lost sight of you. That's what I told you from the start. Make the company yours. Show everyone you can do this—if implementing a new green policy is problematic, do something smaller first. But do something.'

Ava swirled her water thoughtfully, pushed her plate away, her mind racing. 'OK. So I need to do something to win their respect. I know what would help—I just have no idea how to do it.'

'Tell me.'

'My dad was about to close a deal with Leonardo Brunetti—he owns a chain of upmarket Italian emporium-type supermarkets. Since my father's death he's been prevaricating and now he's on the verge of pulling out. He's citing the uncertainty of Dolci's future and my inexperience. I can't help feeling that if Luca approached him he'd be fine.'

Liam could hear the bitterness in her voice. 'Because he's a man.'

'Yes, partly, but mostly because Luca has set up his own company, made a success off his own bat.'

'Then how about approaching Luca? You could go to see Leonardo Brunetti together, pitch for the deal.'

'No.' Ava needed to prove to everyone, including Luca, that she could do this herself. 'I need something different. I've done everything I can think of to win Leonardo Brunetti over. Short of giving him the damn products. I have written reports, costed spreadsheets, put together a presentation on why Dolci products are great. But I can't be my father and I can't pretend that Dolci isn't having leadership issues.'

'No, but you can be yourself. Stop apologising for your past and your father. You are a successful woman in your own right.'

'It doesn't feel like that.'

'Then fake it. Like you fake your smile.'

Ava stared at him—why on earth hadn't she thought of that herself? 'You're a genius. Fake it till you make it,' she said. 'I'm good at that.'

There was a heartbeat of silence as the words lingered in the air and the atmosphere changed. Liam leaned forward, raised an eyebrow. 'Really?' he said, his word a long drawl, a teasing glint in his cobalt eyes. 'Interesting.'

Heat crept over her face. 'I wasn't talking about… that.'

'Talking about what?' He maintained a tone of mock innocence but couldn't hold back a grin.

'I wasn't talking about sex,' she muttered. 'I meant that it's like modelling—sometimes you have to act, fake a smile and you keep doing it until it looks real and…then sometimes you find yourself genuinely…'

'Making it?' he offered helpfully.

'Yes.' Against her will she did smile. 'I need to stop digging this hole until it's so deep there's no way I'm getting out of it.'

'It's fine. I'll help you out. Any time.' He wriggled his eyebrows and she chuckled, then he joined in and it was as though they couldn't stop, the laughter an incredible and welcome release from all the pent-up tension and emotion.

'I needed that,' Ava said eventually.

'So did I.'

'Thank you for listening. It's really helped. I feel like I can think more clearly. And you're right. I need to jump off the treadmill because it isn't working. It's as though I'm running as hard as I can to maintain a status quo that can no longer exist.' So she needed a new Ava Casseveti—a new persona. Needed to do something different, eye-catching… 'I've got it!'

'Tell me.'

There it was again, the deep voice, the genuine interest that seemed to caress her skin.

'A fundraiser. A glamorous, glitzy fundraiser. I'll call in some markers in the showbiz world. I'll ask the Brunettis, I'll ask the staff, I'll use my aristocratic connections. Raise shedloads of money for charity. If Dolci goes under at least I'll have done something good that I believe in.'

'That's a brilliant idea.'

'You really think so?'

'Really.'

'So how about we do it together? It would give us something to focus on. We could promote it together, organise it together as a "couple".' And with any luck they could somehow transform all the sexual tension into an energy to create an amazing event. 'You can ask your clients and Ray Beaumont.'

He smiled. 'It's a great idea. Let's do it. First things first. What shall we fundraise for? What is a cause that means a lot to you?'

'I want to raise money for disaster victims and raise awareness about climate change. Given how many natural disasters there have been recently, fires, tornadoes and the devastation caused, I'd like to help.'

'Agreed.'

Sudden excitement fizzed in her, not only for the project, but because Liam hadn't dismissed her idea. Instead he'd encouraged it and she couldn't help but beam at him. And as she did her gaze took him in: the swell of muscle in his upper arm, the sheer masculine beauty of his strong, capable hands, the… Stop!

From now on it needed to be venues, ticket prices, food and canapés all the way. However hard that was going to be.

CHAPTER THIRTEEN

A week later

LIAM DISCONNECTED FROM the call and found himself whistling. This was all coming together. His relationship with Ava had definitely garnered a positive response from clients. He hadn't been so crass as to highlight it to anyone, but there had certainly been sufficient press interest and, of course, the invitations to the fundraiser clinched it.

Rita popped her head round the door. 'You sound happy.'

'I am. That was Ray Beaumont on the phone, accepting the invite. That has to be a good sign that we are back on a level playing field.'

'That is excellent.' Rita glanced at him. 'Is that the only reason you're happy?'

'Of course.'

Rita raised her eyebrow. 'Don't let Ava hear you say that. I saw the photos of both of you at Lady Mannering's ball yesterday. Mixing with aristocracy and celebrities—you both looked very happy. I'm glad for you, Liam.'

'Yes.' Rita's words took the whistle from his lips, a reminder that all of this was a campaign. A successful one but one that presented an illusion to the world. The smiles for the camera, practised and fake. At the end of each evening he dropped Ava home, made plans for the next day and discussed the fundraiser before heading home. 'Thank you,' he added.

'I came to tell you that Ava called whilst you were on the phone. She is on her way over.'

Liam frowned. They had no plans for today, which could mean a glitch.

Five minutes later Rita ushered Ava in and, with a small finger-wave, departed.

'Is everything OK?'

'Yes and no.' Ava looked perturbed and more than a touch annoyed. 'Emily called me.' Ava's best friend. 'Apparently a reporter called her, one of the more scurrilous ones, asking questions, about our "authenticity".'

'Meaning?'

'She's noticed that we don't seem to stay over at each other's houses.' Ava grimaced. 'I'm sorry, Liam. That is a huge detail and I overlooked it.'

'That's OK.' In truth he knew why she had, why they both had. Neither of them wanted to risk the intimacy of a 'sleepover'. 'So did I. The important thing now is damage limitation.'

'Yup. I thought maybe I could stay over at your house at the weekend? My flat only has one bedroom so... You'd need to sleep on the sofa.'

'That's fine. But to make a bit more of a splash, shall we go away for a night? Then return to my place? You look like you could do with a break.' She looked tired, he noticed with a flash of guilt. The effort of maintaining this charade was perhaps taking its toll. She didn't even like parties, was doing this for him. As she had for Nick. He pushed the guilt down. This was a finite time plan.

'I'm fine. Really.'

But the words didn't ring true and he frowned. 'I'm not buying it. I'll arrange it. Surprise you. I'll pick you up after work tonight. Think how good it will look on social media. And it will hopefully stop this reporter before she gets too close.' He frowned. 'I'm willing to bet that AJ set her on the scent.'

'Then we'd better head her off at the pass. The night away and staying over are great up to a point, but we need something more...girl next door.' Now she glanced at him. 'We could—' She broke off, a troubled look in her amber eyes.

'Could what?'

She shook her head. 'It occurred to me that we should do some more family things and then I thought I bet Max would love it if we went skating where he works as a volunteer skate guard. But I don't want to use Max and I don't want to raise his hopes that this would be the start of something. If we do it we need to keep it very casual and you should only do it if you are truly willing to engage with him.'

Liam looked at her and for the first time he wondered if Ava could be right. Was it possible that Max wanted a better relationship, any sort of relationship with Liam? The thought was scary but also...tempting? He forced himself to think—the one thing he wouldn't do was risk anyone being hurt, wouldn't raise expectations he couldn't fulfil.

'Let's see if we can think of anything else. You're right. It doesn't feel right to use Max.'

Ava thought for a moment. 'How about I organise something? Your mum says she watches that dance programme on TV. Do you think she'd like to meet one of the contestants? Anna Lise is a mate of mine from my modelling days.'

'She'd love that.'

'I'll sort it out. I'll take your mum out for a drink with Anna Lise.' She looked him straight in the eye. 'That way you don't have to be involved at all. If that's what you prefer.'

He could see challenge and sadness in her eyes, a sadness that reflected his own, that came straight from the part of him that wanted to be in a family unit, to be part of his mum's life, and for a moment he was tempted to go skating, to go for a drink, to…get involved.

Then common sense reasserted itself. Too risky. Involvement was complicated, painful, scary. It would invoke responsibility.

'That's what I prefer.'

The sadness intensified in her eyes and she nodded. 'OK. I'll speak to Anna Lise and your mum.'

'And I'll sort out a weekend getaway.'

Once Ava had gone, Liam sat at his desk, stared at the doorway for a while as guilt niggled him again. There had been shadows in her eyes and he had the feeling he'd put them there. Dammit! The least he could do was find the perfect getaway, give Ava a chance to recharge and maybe bring a genuine smile to her face.

By Friday evening Liam was confident he'd achieved his aim, sure that he'd found the perfect place to chase away the shadows from Ava's eyes. He looked sideways at Ava, pleased to see that she was fast asleep, had been since they started the journey.

He pulled to a stop and anticipation buzzed inside him as she stirred. For a moment sleep-clouded eyes dreamily stared at him and he saw something there, an elusive happiness that warmed something in him. The idea that someone could look at him like that triggered a strange sense of lightness.

Then Ava blinked and the look was gone, so ephemeral that he might well have imagined it. Knew he should hope he had.

'Here we are.'

As she took in the scene her amber eyes lit up and a sudden shaft of happiness touched him. 'It's like a tree house,' she said as she gazed at the wooden structure on stilts, whose roof peaked and nestled in the boughs of the trees.

'A tree house with five-star luxury guaranteed. Let's go check it out.' His lips were upturned in a grin that he suspected held a hint of goofiness and he didn't care. Just once he would give in to this unfamiliar sense of exhilaration, the precarious lightness of being.

He opened her car door and they headed to the stairs that led to the edifice, climbed the planks to the wooden door. Once inside they both paused on the threshold and gazed at the airy, sumptuous interior.

'I love it.' Ava gestured towards the spiral staircase that twisted up from the centre of the room, then at the iron wood-burning stove, replete with logs. She walked over to the window and glanced out at the view. 'It's beautiful. Sprawling fields, and a farm.'

Over to one side a simple Shaker-style kitchenette boasted a state-of-the-art oven and gleaming wooden worktops overhung with copper pans suspended on hooks. A separate section had been designated the dining area, complete with an oak dining table and matching chairs, whilst the other side of the spacious floor was the lounge with a soft, squishy sofa and a large television.

Another door led to a small second bedroom with twin beds. 'I'll have this one,' Ava said firmly.

'Let's look upstairs.' They climbed up the spiral stairs complete with pretty wrought-iron balustrade and into the master bedroom. 'Wow.' This room was magical; it would feel like sleeping nestled in the tree-tops. Triangular skylights showcased the clear late afternoon skies touched with the setting sun. And the enormous bed filled nearly all available space.

In tacit consent they both beat a hasty retreat back down the stairs into the lounge.

'Why don't I get the stove going?' Liam suggested.

'Good plan. I'll just pop to the bathroom and then I'll check the supplies.'

As the logs caught flame and the flicker of firelight danced across the sheepskin rug Ava returned with a platter. 'There are cold meats and English cheese and freshly baked bread and organic salad. All from the farm. Does that sound OK? We could have an indoor picnic.'

'Perfect.'

Once settled on the sumptuous sheepskin rug, she glanced at him. 'Thanks for finding this. It's perfect.'

'For social media posts?'

'Yes, but that's not what I meant. It's exactly what I would have picked myself. When you talked about making a splash I thought you might choose some-where more…public. Where we'd be seen, or snapped, or something.'

Liam shook his head. 'You've done enough of that. This is more about saying thank you. I know it must be a strain maintaining this charade.'

Now the sweetness of her smile trickled warmth over his chest. 'It's not the charade. Truly. And remember, this is benefiting me as well. At work everyone is really getting behind the fundraiser.'

'Then what is the matter? If it's not the charade?'

'It doesn't matter.'

'Yes. It does. Tell me.'

She hesitated, bought time by cutting a wedge of the tart farmhouse cheddar. 'I'm being silly. It's the same old story but this has made me feel...sad.' She tugged her phone out of her jeans pocket. 'I emailed Luca and Jodi about the fundraiser and today I finally got a reply. Here you go.'

She scrolled down and handed him the phone.

Dear Ms Casseveti

Mr Petrovelli has asked me to inform you of the following:

He is more than happy to endorse and support the fundraiser—please feel free to organise as you wish.

Unfortunately neither he nor Ms Petrovelli will be able to attend.

Liam handed the phone back as Ava sighed. 'It's so cold and formal. I mean, who would think we are related? I get that after what happened we aren't a family, but surely he could answer me himself. It just makes me feel sad.'

He got that. Yet... 'Of course it does, but I do wonder what's going on. Luca is a businessman, a successful one at that—his attitude to Dolci doesn't make sense.'

'Clearly his feelings about what my father did outweigh business sense. This is personal.'

Liam shook his head. 'If Luca was truly vindictive

he would have refused to endorse anything. It's formal, yes, but it's not nasty. It could be there is something else at play here that we don't know about.'

'Do you really think so?'

'I think it's possible.'

Ava scooped a spoon of chutney and added it to her plate. 'That hadn't occurred to me, but actually you have a point. It is all rather odd.' Now she smiled and he felt a small sense of satisfaction as she relaxed slightly. 'Thank you for your sense of perspective—I seem to have mislaid mine somewhere.'

As she finished speaking her phone rang and she glanced at the screen. 'Sorry, I'll have to take it. It's my lawyer.'

'Go ahead.'

'Vince. Hi.' He watched as her face creased into a frown of perplexity, then he rose to go and open some wine, returned with two glasses. 'She wants to do what? Can she do that?' She listened some more and then, 'Thank you for letting me know.'

She dropped the phone on the floor and shook her head. He could see a gamut of emotions chase across her face. Disbelief, anger and a weariness that made his heart ache.

'What's happened?'

'It turns out that Mum has decided to try and overturn the will herself—she wants to oust us all and try and get control of Dolci for herself.'

'Do you want to go and see her? Now? Talk to her?'

Ava shook her head and he could see tears glistening in her eyes. 'There's no point. There's nothing I can do to stop this and I'm not even sure I want to any more. Perhaps I should just hand her my share and leave them all to it.' She placed one hand on her tummy and quickly dashed her other hand against her eyes. 'I am not going to cry.'

For a moment panic threatened to engulf him as his comfort zone was cut from beneath his feet to leave him over an abyss. He didn't know how to deal with situations like this—never had, never would. But then, from somewhere, instinct came to his rescue with the inherent visceral knowledge that he had to do something to ease her pain.

Rising, he moved over, dropped down next to her. 'It's OK to cry. Come here.' It was so natural to pull her into his arms, breathe in the scent of her shampoo and offer what comfort and understanding he could. He heard the small hiccough and then the tears did come, gentle at first and then a torrent. He rubbed her back, made soothing sounds, held her close until finally she pulled away, swiped at her eyes.

'I'm sorry.' She opened her bag and pulled out a packet of tissues, blew her nose. 'I can only imagine what I look like. I doubt even my waterproof mascara can hold up to that.'

'You look beautiful.' The words were out before he could stop them and she shook her head.

'I look a blotchy, splotchy mess. But I do feel better. Even though I still have no idea what to do about it.'

'Maybe talk to your mum, tell her that this will be worse for Dolci. I very much doubt she stands a chance legally, but it could take years for it to go through the courts.'

'It won't make a difference. As you said—she is obsessed. She was obsessed when Dad was alive and she is still obsessed now.' Ava's voice was weary. 'All her life she's been terrified Dad would leave her. Leave us. Go back to his first wife, his first family. All her life she strove to be the perfect wife, to hold and bind him to her.' She shook her head, sipped her wine as she stared into the distance.

'And all your life you tried to be the perfect daughter.'

'Yes. We were an alliance, I guess. I can remember Mum telling me how dangerous Luca and Jodi were. I used to picture them lurking round every corner. I worried they'd kidnap my dad. Then I started to worry that I wouldn't be enough to keep him.'

Liam tried to imagine the burden of anxiety, could almost picture a wide-eyed child Ava, small hands clenched into determined fists, as so many things became clear to him. Her perfect smile, the way Ava always looked flawless, knew how to act whatever part was required of her, the way she still wanted to try and please everyone. The immense pressure she put on herself to do what was right. 'That should never have felt like your responsibility.'

'No.' She looked at him. 'But life doesn't always work like that, does it? It should never have felt your responsibility to try to get your father back on track. Your mother's happiness was never your weight to bear.'

'That's different. My mother had a chance of happiness that she gave up because of my actions and my existence.'

Ava shook her head. 'No, your parents' marriage and how it worked out was not down to you. They chose to have a child and actually it's OK for a parent to put their child first, to be responsible for their happiness. Your mum did the right thing and I am sure it is a decision she would make again.'

'Whereas your mum didn't put your happiness first.' The idea and its ramifications, the possibility that his mum had done what any mother would do, edged into his consciousness, only to be rebutted as he focused on Ava.

Ava shook her head. 'Nothing is as clear-cut as that. My father was her everything, and she believed I should feel the same way, that my happiness was also bound to him. She only had a child because she thought it would ensure my dad stayed.'

Liam shifted closer to her and draped his arm over her shoulders, as if he could belatedly shield her from the machinations of her parents. He loathed the idea that Ava had been a pawn in some obsessive game even as he struggled to understand it. 'But I thought your parents' marriage was a fairy tale.'

Ava shook his head. 'I told you my mother was the Queen of Spin. I believe the real story is he left his first family because my mother had the wealth and connections that would enable him to start Dolci.'

'He could have got a bank loan.'

'He took the easy option. I think my mother dazzled him. She told me it was love at first sight, that once she saw him she had to have him. And after that she had to keep him.'

As if he were some sort of prize specimen. 'Do you think he loved her?'

'I don't know.' Ava lifted her slim shoulders. 'Define love. Perhaps he thought the pay-off was worth it—he gained celebrity, wealth, his business, a beautiful wife who worshipped the ground he walked on. But he lived in a gilded cage with a replacement family. And I don't think we truly lived up to the original, however much he tried to convince himself we did.'

His heart tore as he listened to her, imagined how it

must have felt to always feel second best to one parent and a tool to the other. 'But he did love you.'

'Yes, he did. I helped him atone for his past.'

'Ava, I'm sorry. All of that is too much for one person to carry.' Only she had carried it and carried it without complaint. More than that, she hadn't let it blight her life.

'No. I don't want your pity.' She shifted to face him and the flicker of the firelight dappled her blonde hair, illuminated the classic beauty of her face, emphasised its strength and character. 'I've had a good life. I've never wanted for any material thing and my father did love me. We had good times together. Good family times. And my parents were happy in their own way. Their life was hardly full of hardship. I have friends, a job I love, if I could only figure out how to do it.'

'I'm not pitying you.' He needed her to believe that, understood exactly what she meant. 'I am full of admiration for you and the way you have dealt with everything life has thrown at you. Not just dealt with it—you've thrived.'

Now their gazes locked and he couldn't help it, she was so close, so beautiful, he leant forward and lightly brushed his lips against hers and an intensity of sweetness flooded him, as if he were afloat in sensory joy. He deepened the kiss, and her arms looped round his neck, her body pressed against his, and now the background faded and there was nothing except Ava. But this time he knew a kiss couldn't be enough, for either of them, could feel her need, her yearning, match his. He craved the taste of her skin, to touch, caress and revel in her body. To glide his hand over the satin sheen of her bare skin.

Her hand slid under the soft cotton of his shirt and

he heard his own groan as she placed it over the beat of his heart.

'Ava.' Her name was a whisper, a question, and she pulled away slightly.

Placed a finger against his lips. 'Shh. I want this, Liam. To lose myself in this, forget the world and reality and just feel.'

Now a muffled alarm rang in his head, trying to tell him, warn him, and he didn't want to listen, dammit. This was right, beautiful, wonderful… 'I want you,' she said.

'And I want you.'

'Then what are we waiting for?' Her voice was breathless, caught on a half-laugh, half-gasp of desire.

Then he remembered that he hadn't prepared for this moment, hadn't intended it.

As if she read his mind she pressed close to him. 'Don't worry. Five-star service includes a discreet stash of condoms. I happened to find them earlier when I went to the loo.'

Relief swathed him. 'Then what *are* we waiting for?' Rising, he tugged her up with him and they climbed the spiral stairs, entered the magical, beautiful bedroom and he tumbled her back onto the bed, under the canopy of the stars.

CHAPTER FOURTEEN

THE NEXT MORNING Ava opened her eyes, saw the twist
and tumble of the sheet, felt colour heat her cheeks as
she saw her clothes strewn haphazardly on the floor.
Closed her eyes for a moment and allowed herself to
savour the memories of the previous hours: the heat,
the passion, the laughter and the joy as their bodies intertwined, discovered each other. Explored, touched,
gave and received such intense pleasure.

But where was Liam? And, more to the point, what
now?

For a second Ava was tempted to lie back and hide
under the duvet, but before she could do anything Liam
popped his head round the door.

'Morning, sleepy head. I've got breakfast on the go.
A full English awaits, all local produce, all fresh and
all delicious.'

'I'll be right down. Give me ten minutes.'

Ten minutes to figure this out. Lord knew she didn't,
couldn't, regret the night just gone, but she also knew
it shouldn't have happened. Her mind whirred, told her
that it was impossible to analyse this situation until she
could gauge what Liam thought.

She had no idea how he felt—all she knew was his
preference for one-night stands and no emotional in-

volvement. Was that what last night had been? For Liam that was all it could be—the only way he could reconcile it with his feelings for Jess. Jess—would he be thinking of her now? Had he been thinking of her last night? No, she wouldn't believe that—couldn't believe it.

Shoving aside the whisper of doubt, she swung her legs out of bed, her mind analysing what to wear, how to project the right persona—cool, casual, the sort of modern mature woman who could separate sex from emotion. She settled for jeans and a long cream knitted jumper. Kept her hair loose and her make-up minimal.

As she entered the kitchen he smiled, but his cobalt eyes held caution even though his tone was light. 'Perfect timing.'

'It looks delicious. Thank you.' Yet right now the idea of food made her tummy ache and loop as she watched Liam. She could almost see the barricade he had put up. Gone was the man who had taken her to such heights mere hours ago, the man who had held her with such tenderness and stoked her to such passion. For a moment Ava wondered if the whole night had been a series of fevered dreams. 'We need to talk.'

'Yes.' Wariness played over his face, but it was more than that—she could see regret, apprehension, and that made hurt twist inside her.

'Last night was…wonderful and I don't regret it one bit.' His shoulders relaxed slightly and the worry made a small retreat in his cobalt eyes and gave her the impetus to continue. 'And I hope you don't either.'

His gaze met hers. 'I don't regret it.'

But she could see shadows in his eyes, and she wondered what he was thinking. Of Jess? Did this feel like a betrayal of his wife? 'I'm not sure that's true,' she said, careful to keep her voice gentle. 'I know you prefer one-night stands with women you don't know.'

Three strides and he had moved round the breakfast bar, was standing in front of her. 'Look at me.' Oh, so gently he raised a hand and placed a finger under her chin, tipping it up so she met his gaze. 'I swear last night was magical. I don't even know how to put it into words…and I don't regret it. But it wasn't planned or intended and I'm worried I took advantage of you. You were upset and you are still grieving and…'

Ava saw the sincerity in his eyes, and a thrill shot through her that Liam too had found the night magical. 'You didn't take advantage of me at all. I wanted last night.'

'I sense a but…'

He was right. Because whilst she did believe Liam's concern that he had taken advantage of her was legitimate, she could still see that he was haunted. 'But I know you must be feeling something about Jess.'

His flinch was almost imperceptible though his gaze stayed locked on hers. 'This isn't about Jess, this is about you.'

Leave it at that, Ava. But she couldn't. 'It's also about you and what you feel. Do you feel guilty?'

There was a fraction of a heartbeat before he answered and before he could Ava raised a hand. 'I'm sorry. I shouldn't have asked that.' Wished, oh, so much that she hadn't, but it was too late to swallow the question. 'Of course you feel guilt. You loved her. So a magical night with someone else must feel like a betrayal.' That knowledge hurt—too reminiscent of a lifelong awareness that, by being with his second family, her father was betraying his first family. But that wasn't Liam's fault. 'I'm sorry.'

'Ava.' His voice was hoarse. 'I—'

'It's OK. Last night took us both by surprise. We'll put it behind us and—'

He shook his head. 'Stop. I need to tell you something. I can't let you believe this any more.'

'I don't understand.'

He rubbed a hand over his face, inhaled deeply. 'My marriage wasn't the idyll you believe it to be.' Ava saw his pain, but she also sensed he didn't want comfort or interruption. He simply needed to get the words out. 'I met Jess when I was young and grieving. She was there and I mistook liking and need for love. When she thought she was pregnant I married her, even though I knew by then I didn't love her. It turned out she wasn't pregnant but by then the knot was tied. I'd made my vows and I wanted to stand by them.'

As his mother had done.

'I believed that I could make myself love her, force the emotion into being. Believed her love would somehow force me to do the right thing and love her back. It didn't work like that. The worst of it was that Jess still loved me and I was too much of a coward to admit I didn't. So I let her waste her life on me.'

'No!' The denial pulled from her as her heart turned at his words. At the pressure he'd piled onto himself, born of his own hopes and wishes that his parents would be happy together, would make their marriage work. Born of his belief that a person should never renege on a promise. After all, his father had been betrayed by a man who had done just that. So his word was his bond. Liam would have been incapable of breaking his marriage vows and as long as Jess had wanted to stay he would always have done his best. 'You did what you thought was right. You didn't want to hurt Jess.'

'But if I had, if I had been more honest, then perhaps she would have found real happiness.'

'It doesn't work like that. You can't second-guess something you can't change. Jess may have been miserable without you and…' she kept her voice gentle '… Jess had choices too. She chose to stay in your marriage as well. Neither of you could have known of the tragedy in store.'

'But she is the one who paid the biggest price.'

'Yes. But that is no fault of yours.' But she knew to Liam it felt as if it was, knew that he blamed himself for the failure of his marriage, the might-have-beens and what-ifs. She moved closer to him. 'All the worst-case scenarios. You don't really know them. If you'd left Jess she may have ended up more unhappy, if your mother had left your father she and John may not have worked out. It all may have been worse.'

'You're right. But it all may have been better. I'll never know. Because I can't change the past. But I can at least control my present and my future.'

And that was why he'd never risk a relationship or love again. Even as she understood that, the knowledge sent a sudden stab of bleakness through her, one she refused to give in to. Especially when she could see the demons that rode his shoulder, saw the haunted depths of his cobalt eyes.

'You're right. The past can't be changed and we don't know the repercussions if we could. We can imagine all the what ifs but we can't truly know. But we can make choices in the here and now.' And she moved closer to him, looped her arms around his waist, stretched up on tiptoe and brushed her lips against his. 'I think we should choose to enjoy our magic for a few weeks, forget the past and focus on the present.'

For a moment his body remained taut with a hard edge of tension and then slowly she felt him relax, the soft expel of breath, the release of tightness as he gathered her close.

'Are you sure it's what you want?'

'I'm sure.' And she was, knew that, whatever happened next, this was the right decision, the start of a heady few weeks that she would always remember. 'So how about we postpone breakfast and head back to bed?' And with a provocative look she sashayed to the door in her best model walk, stood in the doorway and in one fluid move unzipped her dress and let it pool to the ground, stepped over the material and continued to walk. She heard his sharp intake of breath, shivered in anticipation as she sensed his presence mere centimetres behind her, felt the brand of his hand on the small of her back as they walked towards the stairs.

A week later—the night of the fundraiser

Ava checked her to-do list yet again, told her twitching nerves that she had everything under control. She looked round the plush hotel room, tried to ground herself, smiled as Liam emerged from the shower.

'Need some distraction?'

'You'll do nicely.' It still seemed surreal to Ava that for now she had unlimited, unfettered access to Liam's sheer gorgeousness. That she had an intimate knowledge of the swell of every muscle, the sweep of his spine, the crook of his arm where she fell asleep each night.

His gaze devoured her with equal interest. 'Shame you're already in the dress,' he said.

For a moment she contemplated shimmying straight

out of it but a glance at the clock told her that was not a good idea. She needed to look poised, perfect, every hair in place, make-up pristine... 'Later, I promise I won't be.'

'I'll hold you to that.' The deep rumble of his voice sent a shiver down her spine and she marvelled at her body's response to him. 'You look stunning and I promise you've got this. It will be the event of the year. You've done a superb job.'

'We've done a superb job.'

'Nope. Own this. It's yours. You've brought flair and style and passion to it. The vegan canapés, the way you haven't used plastics, the fact sheets and talking points dotted around the function room—it all shows you believe in the cause you are raising money for.'

Ava smiled at him, touched by the sincerity in his voice. 'Thank you.'

'They'll enjoy the champagne, the food, the music and the company and having their awareness raised in a subtle manner that encourages them to part with their money at the auction.' He moved away and dropped the towel, pulled on boxers and a pair of tuxedo pants and for a moment she simply stared, caught anew by his unselfconscious nakedness. This could never get old.

Literally, she reminded herself. Because in a few weeks they would part ways, the fun would be over. In which case it made sense to make the most of it now, because discovering her body's capacity for Liam was a learning curve and she was enjoying every inch of the climb. He adjusted his cufflinks and a sudden pang hit her. It was so...intimate, so domestic despite the glamour, and it made her heart do a funny little hop, skip and a jump.

Whoa. Just sex and fun, remember?

And now she needed to focus on the evening ahead. 'Speaking of the auction.'

She sensed the hesitation in Liam's voice. 'Yes?'

'There's a last-minute addition to the donations. From Luca.'

'Luca?'

'I contacted him to ask. I didn't tell you because I didn't want to get your hopes up. Especially when I didn't hear back. But then earlier today an item arrived. A painting by an Italian artist. And an email message.'

He picked up his phone and showed her.

Dear Liam
I have dispatched a donation for the auction. I wish you and Ava luck in raising money for this excellent cause.
Best wishes
Luca Petrovelli

Ava stared at it for a long moment and the smallest tendril of hope unfurled. It wasn't gushing, it was bland, but it wasn't unfriendly and it wasn't vindictive. Happiness brought an extra spring to her step as she moved towards Liam and wrapped her arms around him.

'Thank you, Liam. That was good of you.' Kind. Thoughtful. Caring. Stop…leave it there. Stepping back, she turned to the mirror, warned herself to rein in emotion. One last glance at her reflection, a small adjustment to the folds of the dress, one final swipe of lipstick. 'Ready to go.'

'Ready to go.' He smiled at her and took her hand in his. 'So we meet and greet each guest at the door, then we mingle, then we eat, then we auction.'

'That's the plan.'

'Then we thank everyone, say goodbye and come

up here, where there will be champagne on ice waiting for us.'

A bubble of anticipation brought a smile to her face and she squeezed his hand as they left the room and headed downstairs to greet their guests. Ava cast a last glance of approval at the ballroom of the plush London hotel. Eco-friendly rose petals sprinkled the tables, the chairs were bedecked with bows and silver streamers looped and swirled from the ornate vaulted ceilings. Waiting staff were poised to circulate with glasses of champagne and soft drinks and plates of canapés.

'Here we go,' Liam murmured, and they stepped forward to greet their first guests. Twenty minutes later a compact grey-haired man barrelled in, a man with an aura of power. He had a woman on his arm, a woman who had decided to go grey naturally and was comfortable with her decision. As well she might be, Ava thought. Because she was beautiful, with classic features that endured with age.

'Hello, Ray. I'm so glad you could make it.' Liam turned to Ava. 'Ava, this is Ray Beaumont.'

Ray Beaumont. The man who led Beaumont Industries, the man whose business Liam wanted to win. The contract he was in danger of losing to AJ Mason.

The man held his hand out. 'Liam. Ava. Thanks for the invite. This is my wife of thirty years, Sophia.'

The woman gave a soft laugh. 'Honestly, Ray, you sound like you've been counting.'

'I have, my love. And every year I feel more thankful.'

There was obvious affection in the banter and Ava instantly suppressed a pang of what she really hoped wasn't envy. Reminded herself that this was a moment in their married life that might not even be real. Perhaps they stayed together because a divorce would be too expensive.

Reminding herself of her role, she smiled but judged it best not to overdo it. Ray Beaumont was a shrewd businessman. His small grey eyes looked twinkly enough but she sensed the assessment and matched it with a friendly but non-gushy smile of her own.

Once the couple had walked off she murmured to Liam, 'Do you want to go speak with him?'

'Nope. This is about fundraising for a good cause and allowing our guests to network, not about trying to secure a contract. In truth, when I think about the victims we are raising money for my business concerns seem petty.'

The words hit home as she acknowledged the simple truth of them and knowing that made the arrival of Leonardo Brunetti easy to deal with. Because this event wasn't about business—it was about fundraising. That was all that mattered here. There would be time enough for deals in the future. And so she greeted Leonardo and his wife the same way she had greeted everyone else and soon after that she and Liam joined the swirling throng of people.

Ava talked, smiled, chatted, mingled and all the while she was aware of Liam's presence, the calm way he dealt with any problems, the quiet behind-the-scenes preparations for the auction. All done without drama or fuss.

They had agreed to auction off the items together, taking it in turns, and Ava stepped up to the podium first, faltered as she suddenly spotted her mother at a table, realised Karen Casseveti must have slipped in late. Liam followed her gaze and stepped closer to her. 'Don't let her spook you. This is your show. Not hers.'

Liam was right. It was time to show her mum that Ava too could put on a show, organise an event for a good cause other than the Casseveti brand. If her mother did decide to bring down the edifice then this would be Ava's grand finale.

She brought the gavel down.

'Guests. Liam and I would like to thank you for attending and soon we hope to be thanking you for digging deep and paying for these amazing items so generously donated to raise money for what I hope you agree is a worthy cause. I'm up first and I'll be auctioning off a dress donated by my good friend and fellow model Anna Lise. Next up will be the camera used to photograph Hollywood icons donated by my wonderful friend and a fashion photographer herself, Emily Khatri. Unfortunately Emily can't be here tonight but she says, "Bid high!"'

The bidding began with lots of good-natured banter and generosity and by the end of it Ava's face wanted to crack from smiling so much, especially when she spotted Leonardo Brunetti win Luca's donation—and a bit of her wondered if her brother had picked something that he knew Leonardo would like.

When the final bid was made guests began to circulate again and the band struck up. On automatic Ava looked round for Liam, wanted to share her happiness, maybe have a glass of champagne and toast their success. Her eyes scanned the room and then she froze as she saw Karen Casseveti heading straight for Liam. For a mad moment she wanted to throw herself between them. Forced herself to turn away to talk to a guest. It was perfectly natural for them to speak with each other.

CHAPTER FIFTEEN

LIAM GLANCED AROUND the crowded room and a deep satisfaction rolled over him—the event was an undeniable hit and they'd raised a hefty sum for their cause. And he had stood by his decision not to discuss business with Ray Beaumont or any other of his clients. All he'd learnt about the charity had given him undoubted perspective. Honesty compelled him to admit that he still wanted to win the Beaumont contract, still wanted to mash AJ into the dirt, but if he failed he'd handle defeat a little better than he would have before.

'You look thoughtful.'

He turned as Karen Casseveti approached. Today she looked amazing, all ravages of grief hidden, though her dress was a deep sombre black that conveyed a sense of mourning combined with style.

'What a success. You must be proud of yourself.'

'I am. Though most of the credit goes to Ava—your daughter is an exceptional fund raiser.'

'Yes.' Karen's smile held a touch of resignation. 'She had a good teacher. Me. But that isn't what I would like to discuss with you.'

Caution warned him to tread with care. 'Go ahead.'

'I want to propose an alliance between us. I want your help. I want Ava to have what she deserves and that is Dolci. The company is her birthright and she should be the one at the helm. Not the Petrovellis.'

'That isn't what James believed. Or what Ava wants.'

'Tcha. James was a fool when it came to sentiment. I am not and I won't stand by and see Dolci destroyed and my daughter cheated. I want that will overturned. Even if I have to do it myself, then give Ava her rightful birthright.'

'I understand how you feel but it is not up to me. Or you.'

'But you could persuade Ava to see my point of view. My daughter loves you—you could influence her, guide her to do the right thing. It would benefit you both.'

Liam forced his expression to remain neutral even as panic blazed along his synapses and his brain scrambled. 'I think you're forgetting the truth about Ava and me.' He kept his voice low and the words as open to interpretation as possible.

'I am forgetting nothing. I know how this started but, whilst I may not be the world's best mother, I know my daughter. More than that, I recognise love. Ava loves you for real. I can see it in how she looks at you, the way her eyes follow you across the room.'

Liam stared at her, unable to say a word, his entire body frozen as he struggled to command logic to come to his aid. Ava did not love him. She was faking it. *Fake it till you make it.* Oh, God, was that what they had done.

They? Did he love Ava? The thought was too huge to compute. He couldn't have let that happen. Would never again subject himself or another to the vagaries, the complexities, the misery that love engendered. If he had been fool enough to let love slide, glissade under his skin, he had to get rid of it now. Before it took hold.

He saw Karen look at him and a small smile played across her lips. 'Why is this so bad? You and Ava make a great couple. You could do great things together. Like James and I did. You could end up on the board of Dolci—that would have made your father happy, wouldn't it? Your children could end up at the helm. As it should be.'

Liam wanted to shout, wanted to make the words cease. 'I wouldn't use Ava to win Dolci. I built up Rourke Securities on my own and my father would be proud of that.'

'But you are using Ava now. To win a contract.'

Oh, God. She was right. He'd used Ava, manipulated her need to make amends for her father's actions. Had forced her into faking a persona to the world. Just as she'd done all her life. For years she'd played the part of Ava Casseveti, perfect daughter, and now he'd made her play the role of perfect girlfriend, instead of allowing her to be herself. Worse, he'd done it whilst she was grieving and at her most vulnerable.

He pulled himself together. No matter what, he wouldn't be the reason this fundraiser failed, nor would it be because of him that the charade was exposed. He would not bring humiliation onto Ava. 'Mrs Casseveti, I think you have simply underestimated your daughter's acting abilities. In any case, I have no intention of influencing Ava, even if I could. I trust her to make the right decisions for Dolci. Perhaps you should consider supporting Ava and working with her. I know how important you are to her. Maybe it's time for a fresh start?'

Karen Casseveti shook her head. 'It's too late for that. The Petrovellis won't just disappear.'

'No. They won't. But you don't have to remain enemies—maybe you can all have a fresh start. The past can't be changed but you have a choice in the here and now.' Those had been Ava's words and they held good. 'Think about it,' he added.

The older woman said nothing, then unexpectedly she smiled. 'Perhaps I will.'

Liam nodded and with that he turned to find Ava. As he made his way across the room, with a smile and a word for the guests, he told himself Karen had got it wrong. Ava did not love him and he did not love Ava. As he reached her he saw the shade of worry in her amber eyes but before either of them could say anything Leonardo Brunetti approached them. 'I wanted to congratulate you, congratulate you both. This was an excellent event. Did you organise it yourselves?'

'Yes, we did.'

'Can I ask why you did it?'

'I wanted to do something good, Signor Brunetti. As you know, Dolci is in a complicated place and I wanted to achieve something positive. Something that has nothing to do with shares or profit and loss. Something that shows what I want Dolci to become. An ethical, good company. I believe in our products and I'll never skimp on quality but I must make sure we are doing our best for the climate, for future generations. I want to use potato-starch plastic instead of what we use. If we export to Europe—' and now she smiled at him, with a hint of mischief '—then I plan to do it in as environmentally friendly a way as possible. Perhaps start a manufacturing plant in Europe once we have enough interest, though I would also work on keeping our product exclusive. There's a lot to think about.'

'Indeed there is. But it sounds as if you have many ideas. Once I was like that. Now my wife tells me I am too hidebound. She has read all the documents here, she listened to your speech and she says I should stop being so set in my ways, should move with the times. You have done a good job, Ava. Accept an old man's congratulations.'

'Thank you.'

'Now we will take our leave. I will be in touch. And thank your brother for his donation—this is my favourite painter.' An old-fashioned bow and Leonardo Brunetti turned and made his way back to his wife.

After that there was little chance for conversation until all the guests had departed. The whole time Liam ensured he stayed in role, kept the smile on his lips, but for the first time in a long time he knew the smile to be fake. The practised smile that Ava had taught him how to achieve. Then finally the last lingering guest had departed, the final preparations for pick-up of the auction items had been squared away. For a mad second Liam wanted to chase after them, tell them to stay longer, wanted to put off the moment he and Ava would be alone.

The knowledge streaked sadness through him as he remembered how easy, how comfortable, how happy they'd been earlier. The intimacy, the banter, the talk, the anticipation of the night to come. All torn away by Karen Casseveti's words. Words that might hold no truth—yet he couldn't shake the sense of doom, the belief that the worst-case scenario was about to blow up in his face.

'Shall we go up?' Ava came and stood by his side. 'I think we deserve a glass of bubbly to celebrate.' Her tone was bright, strove for their earlier ease, but he could see the strain in her smile.

'Absolutely. This was an incredible success. You should be proud.' He paused. 'And whilst I know this wasn't the purpose, I believe that Leonardo Brunetti will sign on the dotted line.'

'What about Ray Beaumont?'

'I think he will give me a fair shot now and that's all I could ask for.'

Somehow each and every word felt like a prelude to goodbye, to the end he knew had to come.

As they'd talked they'd made their way up the grand staircase with its plush carpet and oak bannisters. He pushed the door open and allowed Ava to enter, careful—oh, so careful—not to touch her even by mistake. Saw the question, the insinuation of doubt and hurt in her eyes as she turned to him. Once inside their room he looked round, wondered that it looked exactly as they'd left it and yet everything seemed different.

Ava stopped, put a hand out to stop him as he headed for the champagne.

'Wait. Tell me what's wrong. What did Mum say?'

Now was the moment. He'd tell her, she'd scoff and they could…could what? Keep going with the charade that was no longer a charade? That was no longer a possibility—that he knew. Because even if Karen wasn't right the danger was too great. How had he been so blind? Had he really believed they could live together, sleep together, wake up together and it mean nothing?

Yes. He had. Because he was a fool, a man who did not understand how emotions worked. That was how he'd ended up in a marriage he'd had no idea how to navigate.

But this time he knew what to do, knew he had to tear all the fledgling, confusing emotions out before they took root and constricted and suffocated Ava. This time he would do the right thing. Wouldn't let the fallacy of love in. He'd mistaken other emotions for love—

he wouldn't let Ava do the same and neither would he. Love was not in this.

'Liam.' Now she stood right in front of him, though he noted she was careful not to touch him, and once again he marvelled how soon their closeness, their ease and comfort together, had vanished. Perhaps he should take hope from that, that all these unwanted emotions would fade away with equal bleak rapidity. 'What did my mum say?'

'She wanted me to persuade you to overthrow the will.'

'What did you say?'

'I refused.'

Ava frowned. 'But what made her think you'd do it?'

'She thinks you love me, thinks I should use that love to further my ambition. That we could be happy together.'

Ava's eyes opened wide in shock and she stepped backwards and for a timeless instant silence reigned.

Ava's brain froze, became a dark cavernous void where any form of thought was impossible. She knew she needed to act, to refute the absurdity of his words, but somehow she couldn't figure out how. The right phrases simply wouldn't formulate on her tongue. Because her mother was right. Deep in her bones, in her soul, she could see the truth. She loved him.

For one tiny moment she considered telling him, allowed her imagination to picture it. For a moment rose-coloured spectacles came into play. He'd declare undying love, go down on one knee, roses and violins would feature...

Then she saw his face and the pink-tinged illusion dispersed to ash-coloured shadows. His expression was full of a concern that couldn't disguise the underlying mask of panic-stricken horror. That would be his worst nightmare: another woman in love with him who he didn't love back. This time a woman he didn't want to love back—at least Jess had had a fighting chance. But Liam would never love Ava, would never let himself take that risk, and so she would end up like her mother.

That would not happen. Ava would not walk the path her mother had chosen, where love became obsession and need, where you sacrificed pride and allowed love to warp into a twisted parody. So now she needed to pull out every single acting skill, every modelling trick she had ever learnt or used, and she would play her part down to the last detail. Would not let Liam know of her love.

Her incredulous laugh was pitched to perfection. 'Well, that poleaxed me. Love? That is ridiculous. Mum is clearly desperate for a new alliance. So she is seeing what she wants to see.' Liam's blue eyes studied her expression, scoured her face and Ava forced herself to remain loose limbed, to keep any hint of her true feelings from show. Shut down the writhe of panic and self-recrimination and pain that twisted inside her. And smiled her very best 'faking it' smile. After all, people believed what they wanted to believe and the smile had never let her down yet. 'I'm sorry it put you in an awkward position.'

'Don't worry about it. I'm glad it was a false alarm.'

'Of course it was. Our relationship is a charade. True, the parameters changed along the way, but love was never on the table.'

'No, it wasn't.' His voice was heavy and she hoped, how she hoped, he was buying her act.

'But now the dreaded L word has reared its head I

think we'll both feel more comfortable if we wind the charade down.' There was no way she'd be able to be with him now, no way she could hold him, kiss him, fall asleep in his arms. Not now when she knew the dreadful truth.

'Agreed.' He nodded and she wondered what he was thinking, wanted him to say something, do something, tell her how he felt. But his expression was locked down and she forced herself not to ask. Knew she couldn't maintain this role much longer. She rose to her feet. 'Do you mind if we sort out technical details of how to deal with the press and roll out our break-up tomorrow? I think we need to phase out over the next few weeks, which means we will still have to see each other a bit. But perhaps we can plan some business trips, which will make it easier.'

'That sounds sensible. I'll sleep on the sofa and we'll regroup tomorrow.'

Ava nodded, knew that regrouping would not be possible for a very long time. But eventually her stupid foolish love would die. And until it did she'd pretend it had never existed—she could do that. Most supreme of ironies. She'd fake it till she made it. She was Ava Casseveti, after all.

CHAPTER SIXTEEN

LIAM PUT THE phone down, looked round his gleaming office and waited for the expected exultation to kick in. He'd won the Beaumont contract. Mission accomplished.

But the news felt...flat. Of course he was pleased—knew on a professional, practical level that his company was safe, was on its way up, and that did give him a deep sense of satisfaction. But the sense of victory he would have felt just weeks before was lacking. Now all he wanted was...to call Ava, to share the news. But he wouldn't because there would be no point.

Ava would say all the right things but... It wouldn't be real. He started to pace the office, in the hope that the monotonous strides would dull the ache of missing Ava. Because even though in the past two weeks they had seen each other, the meetings had been a true charade, a mockery of their previous closeness and camaraderie.

In truth it hadn't even felt like Ava—oh, the beautiful, perfectly dressed, perfectly poised woman had looked like Ava, sounded like Ava, but she had not been his Ava. His pace increased. Ava was not his, had never been his, could never be his.

He should be glad that she didn't love him, glad that

she had been spared that hurt. Glad that she was able to continue to play her part now that the 'fun' was over. Yet perversely he wasn't… Because there was nothing to be glad about. A part of him wanted to go and find her, tell her he loved her. But how could he take that risk? He who knew his inability to navigate relationships. He couldn't figure out how to be part of a family in any sense. Not as a son, a stepbrother, a husband.

Yet now he recalled Ava's words.

'Do something about it. Stop being scared. I know I'm right. They wouldn't feel you were intruding, they'd welcome you in. It's your family unit.'

What if she were right? Before he could change his mind he picked up the phone.

'Mum?'

'Hello, Liam.'

'I was wondering if Max is there.'

'Max?' His mum sounded understandably confused.

'Yes. I wondered if he wanted to go skating.'

'I… I'm sure he'd love to. I'm about to drop him off to the rink anyway—it's one of his volunteer nights. Why don't you meet him there?'

'Great. I'll bring him back and maybe could we talk?'

'Of course.' A pause and, 'Are you OK?'

'Yes. I think so.'

Half an hour later Liam arrived at the roller-skating rink, aware of nerves and a sense of the surreal, aware that this 'everyday' activity felt like a step into the unknown.

'Liam. Hey.'

Max walked towards him, a shy smile on his face, and he realised that, despite his casual bearing, his stepbrother had been waiting for him.

'Hey. Hope this is OK.'

'Sure. It's cool. Mum says you'd like a skating lesson.'

'If that's OK with you?'

'Let's get you sorted with some skates and we can get started.' Max gave a sudden grin. 'I teach a group of four-year-olds some days… I'll give you the grown-up version.'

Liam pulled the skates on, watched as Max followed suit, saw how confident the teenager was. 'Right. Don't try to do too much too soon. To start with, balance against the wall and move how you can. Next you need to let go and waddle like a penguin.'

'Hey, what happened to the grown-up version?'

'I meant waddle like an adult penguin,' Max said, deadpan, and Liam gave a snort of laughter.

'Like this?'

'Perfect.'

'OK. Whilst I practise my waddle, why don't you show me how it's really done?'

'Sure.' And then he was off, and Liam's jaw dropped as he watched Max weave in and out of the throng of customers in an incredible display of speed and agility before zooming back.

'That was incredible.' Liam shook his head. 'I know there's no way I'll ever be able to do that, but if you could coach me so I can at least do a circuit that would be great.' He glanced around. 'I know you're working too.'

He watched, saw how professional Max and the other skate guards were, watched the speed skating and realised Max had a real talent. And throughout Max came and offered encouragement and help until, 'I've got it,' Liam crowed.

'You have. You've clicked. Now it's all about practice and I'm pretty sure you'll get up to a good speed in no time.'

Liam held out a hand. 'Thanks, Max. You've been great. I appreciate it.'

By the end of the evening Liam had a happy sense of achievement, felt a connection to Max that he genuinely hoped to build on.

'Did you have fun?' Bea asked as they arrived back.

'It was cool,' Max said as he headed upstairs.

'Definitely cool,' Liam agreed.

'You said you wanted to talk,' Bea said. 'John's still at work.'

'That's fine. I… I just wanted some advice, I guess.' The idea was strange.

'About Ava?'

'Yes. How did you know?'

'I saw Ava a couple of days ago.'

'For drinks with Anna Lise. How was it?'

'It was fun. It was lovely of Ava to organise it. But Ava and I stayed and had a last drink and I got the feeling something isn't quite right between you. She said you're thinking of having a break.'

'Yes.' That was the story they'd agreed on, a kind of phased break-up. Pain jabbed at him and he tried to remind himself that you couldn't break up something that had never existed in the first place. 'But I don't want a break.'

'Then tell her.'

'It's not that easy.'

'Why not?'

'I'm scared.' The admission was terrifying in itself. 'I've always messed up relationships. I don't know how to do it.'

'So you're just going to give up? Throw away a chance for true happiness?'

'Like you did for me?'

'I am happy, Liam.'

'You are now. But you weren't—you spent years trapped in an unhappy marriage. Wasted years. Because of me.' Just like Jess had wasted her precious years. With him.

'No.' Pain touched Bea's eyes. 'That is not how it was, Liam. I stayed because I wanted to, because it was the right thing to do. For you and for me. Terry was your dad. He loved you. In the end I couldn't take you away from him. That was my choice and I've never regretted it. I loved you. I still love you. You were my priority and I do not regret that choice. If what happened then, between your dad and me, between you and me, is affecting your decisions now, then please don't let it. I know your marriage to Jess was both complex and tragic. But don't let that stop you now. Don't let what happened in the past take away from you and Ava.'

'There is no me and Ava. There can't be. I can't take the risk I'll mess it up again. It's not fair to her.'

'It doesn't work like that. Don't you think Ava deserves to make that choice for herself? Make her own risk assessment? Don't take that away from her.'

After all, wasn't that what he'd done to Jess? Not told the truth. Not given her a choice. Made assumptions.

'Think about it,' she said. 'Please.'

'I will.' Without hesitation he rose, could almost see the air clear between them as he moved over to her and hugged her. 'And thank you.'

Ava looked round, wondered if she'd lost her mind, imagined the wrath of her mother, the wrath of her lawyers if they knew her current whereabouts. She slouched down, pulled the brim of the designer sunhat a little further down and cast a furtive glance at the Italian offices, the headquarters of Luca Petrovelli's business.

Diligent research had uncovered an interview where he'd said he sometimes liked to eat his lunch in a nearby park—so here she was staking out the premises for the second day in a row. It at least gave her something to focus on apart from Liam, provided a small distraction from the pain that weighted her cracked heart.

She looked at the revolving door one more time and blinked in disbelief. There was Luca—in truth, she'd not really anticipated success. So now what?

Better to trail him to the park or he might simply turn and retreat back into his fortress or, worse, call security on her. Trying not to look furtive, she followed her half-brother until he seated himself on a bench. Her insides clenched with trepidation and swiftly she headed towards him and sat down. Cast a sideways glance at him. Dark hair presumably inherited from his mother. Grey eyes, ditto. But his nose was their dad's, and his lips, and she could see something of herself in him, something elusive that she couldn't quite place. Something that made them kin.

Now she was staring and Luca turned.

'Luca?' Ava heard the smallness of her voice.

'If you are a reporter I have noth—' He broke off as grey eyes met amber. He paled under the olive skin, and she felt the shock of recognition. 'Ava?'

'Yes.'

For a full minute they just sat and looked at each other, the birds in the background, the noise of the breeze rustling the trees. Ava locked the moment away—no matter what happened next, she'd done this,

looked for Luca and found him, and now she needed
to say what she had come to say. 'I'm sorry to surprise
you like this but it seemed important we talk, in private, face to face.'

'But not here. We could be spotted. Come. We'll find
a café, somewhere busy and anonymous.'

Once in a bustling café redolent with the smell of
pastries and hot chocolate and percolating coffee, he
turned to her.

'What would you like?'

'Black coffee and an almond croissant.'

His smile was tight. 'Jodi's favourite.' The words
jolted her, the idea that she shared something with a
sister she'd never met.

Once back at the table he sat down and stared at her,
his face unsmiling, his eyes hard. 'So why are you here?'

'Because the whole talking through lawyers isn't
working. Because I need to know what you want to do
about Dolci. Because I wanted to see you. Meet you,
even if it's only once.'

His gaze didn't waver. 'Do your lawyers know you're
here?'

'No. No one knows I'm here.' And only one man
wouldn't condemn her for it. For an instant she wished
Liam were here, waiting at the hotel. Someone to have
her back. But that wasn't to be. Couldn't be. 'Truly. I
just want to know what you and Jodi want.'

A shadow crossed his face and then he leant back.
'How about you tell me what you want?'

'I'd like to figure out a way for us all to work together. As a family. You, me and Jodi. I know there
will be tensions and difficulties. And obstacles. But we
could find a way to overcome them.'

'That won't be so easy.'

'I know. My mother—she will oppose this and I don't know how your mother will react. I don't know the answers. But I would like to try and figure them out with you and Jodi.'

Now Luca sighed. 'OK. I believe you. Though my own lawyers will have a hissy fit. But there is another problem. One you don't know about.'

Liam stood at the arrivals gate, his eyes scanning the travellers as they came through, some weary, some with smiles as they looked for their loved ones. His whole body was wired as if he'd drunk a bath full of caffeine; anticipation and terror tingled through him at the thought of seeing Ava. Then there she was, blonde hair pulled back in a ponytail, dressed in a cable-knit sweater, jeans and boots, tugging a suitcase behind her.

He knew that her nails were probably accessorised to her luggage and the idea tugged at something deep inside him. His heart cartwheeled at the sheer joy of seeing her even as nerves nearly caused him to remain out of her line of vison, flat-footed and petrified.

Swiftly he strode forward, stepped into her path. 'Ava.'

Her eyes widened and for a second there was his Ava. Her eyes held a fleeting happiness—joy, even— and then the emotion muted, vanished and he wondered if he had simply seen what he wanted with all his heart to see. 'Liam. What are you doing here?'

'I came to pick you up. I wanted to see you.' He'd vowed to tell the truth, not play with words or act a part, yet he didn't want to spook her, wanted to do this right. But the words of love wanted to escape right here and now and he swallowed them down. Better to stick to plan, maintain hope for longer. 'If you're not exhausted

I thought we could talk. Off script. If you are tired I'll drop you off home.'

'I'm not exhausted or even tired. I'd like to talk.' That sideways glance, her amber eyes flecked with curiosity.

'Good. Let's go somewhere more private.'

'Sure.' They walked to the car in silence, Liam simply happy to be with her, to have her close in this moment when he could still hope.

'Where are we going?'

'It's a surprise.'

Now a small smile tipped her lips and then vanished, replaced by a frown. 'Have I forgotten something? Is this part of our break-up plan?'

God, he hoped not. Nerves tautened inside him. *Jeez. Show some backbone, Rourke.* Worst-case scenario, he'd get hung out to dry, be humiliated. But he'd have been honest. He'd be able to look back without regret. There would be no what ifs to haunt either of them. 'We're here.' It didn't answer her question but it'd do.

Nerves crackled through him as he pulled to the kerb outside the London park. He climbed out and saw Rita and her boyfriend parked close behind him. The petite redhead waved, jumped out of her car, opened her boot and he walked over to heft the hamper out. He'd wanted the food to be chilled and the wine to be cold.

'Here you go. I'll drive the car back to the garage.' Rita caught the keys he tossed to her and turned to Ava. 'He chose it all himself. I'm just the delivery girl.' She stepped closer to him. 'Good luck, Big Guy.'

He'd take any luck going, though somehow the jangle of his nerves had calmed now his plan was under way, now he was committed to his course of action. Ava followed him through the park until they reached the place he'd chosen. He pulled open the basket, took out the portable heater and the thick tweed blanket, spread it on the ground. The late afternoon sunshine still touched the ground and air with a touch of early spring warmth but he knew soon enough the late March evening would turn colder.

Ava watched and he saw realisation dawn in her eyes. 'It's our first date,' she said. 'The one we couldn't have.'

'Because it wouldn't have been the right time of year,' he said. 'I am hoping that now is. The right time for a real first date. Not part of a charade or a pretence. Or an imaginary projection. Real. With a real blanket and a real hamper.' He gestured towards the wicker basket. 'I have chilled white wine. I have crystal flutes.'

'And soon there will be stars in the sky and we can sit and talk and…'

'Discuss the constellations.'

'And it will be magical.'

'Yes. Because I think we're good at magic. I want a chance for us to do this properly, to win your love the right way. If that's what you want.' *Stop talking, Rourke.* 'If it isn't, then that's OK too. I'll get it. Please don't go along with this because you don't want to hurt me.' He knew the damage that could be done that way.

'Love?' Her voice held surprise, shock, but also perhaps an undertone of hope.

'I love you, Ava.' He tried for a smile. 'I know it's a bit forward on a first date and I am not expecting you to reciprocate.'

She stepped forward, put her hand on his arm, her face, oh, so serious. 'I won't lie to you, Liam. Not now. Not ever. So I swear to you that what I am about to say is the truth. The whole truth and nothing but the truth. I love you too.'

For a moment he stared at her, unable to believe the

words, but then he took in her expression, the love in her eyes, the happiness that illuminated her smile, a smile that he knew was real. And a sense of joyous disbelief dawned inside him, pulled an incredulous chuckle. 'You love me?'

'Yes.'

'So you love me and I love you?'

'Yes.' Now her smile widened. 'This is the best first date ever.' She sank down onto the blanket and he followed suit, busied himself with switching the heater on, and then she snuggled next to him. Moved away, studied his expression. 'You are sure, aren't you?'

'Yes, I am. One hundred per cent and then some. This is real, Ava. And, hell, it frightened me. That's why I fought it for so long. Because I was so scared I couldn't handle it. Just like I couldn't handle my parents' relationship, just like I messed up my marriage. I thought the safest path was one I walked alone.'

'So you couldn't hurt anyone else.' Her voice was gentle now, so full of warmth and understanding. 'What changed your mind?'

'You. You've changed me, Ava, made me see things I couldn't before. I did make mistakes, but I don't have to bear all the responsibility. I have accepted that other people make choices too. My mum made her own decisions, so did Jess. She was part of our marriage too and she made mistakes as well.'

Ava shifted even closer to him, laid her head against his shoulder, and the tickle of her corn-blonde hair, her closeness, filled him with joy. 'You showed me that I don't need to cut myself off from everyone. You were right about my mum, about John and Max. They are my family. I've spent a lot of time with them in the past days. Max took me skating.'

'Really?' Now she laughed, the sound melodious and light in the evening air.

'Yup. Apparently I'm a natural. For someone of my advanced years. Something else I wouldn't have discovered if it weren't for you.'

Ava grinned at him. 'Well, you've done wonders for me too. Guess what happened on my business trip.'

'Tell me.'

'Well, I went to Italy to see Leonardo Brunetti and we signed the deal.'

'Ava, that is fantastic!'

'It gets better.' Her eyes sparked with happiness, her expressive face catching the light of the setting sun. 'I also saw Luca.'

He took her hands in his, held tight, knew how much courage that must have taken. 'You are incredible. How was it?'

'Amazing. Surreal. I can't believe I finally met him and there was an instant definite connection. And you were right. The reason he hasn't been in contact properly isn't because he hates me or that he is vindictive. It's because he really doesn't know what Jodi wants. He doesn't even know where she is.'

'She's missing?'

'No. She just won't tell Luca where she is. After Dad died Jodi took off to go travelling. Luca said she was having a great time and then suddenly she changed. Contact lessened and now she's asked him to leave her alone, promised that she is OK and she doesn't want him to pull his "big brother shit". He is really worried. It sounds like they are really close. But he won't make any decisions on Dolci without her.'

'That makes sense and I hope Jodi is OK. And I am so glad you have begun to sort things out with Luca.'

'Me too. We decided that for now I'll keep running the company but I'll keep him in the loop. We'll talk, conference call and he will have some input. Once Jodi is back in the picture properly we'll go from there. I even spoke to Mum, told her what I'd done. She wasn't happy but I did tell her that no matter what happens I will always be there for her. That I want her to be part of my life. But I realise that she will have to make that choice. And she didn't shoot me down in flames and she's agreed to hold fire on trying to overturn the will herself So I hope that we'll work it out. I know it will take time but I have hope.'

'I am so pleased for you.' And he was, knew how much this meant to her.

'But it's thanks to you I did it. You've shown me how to be me, to stop playing a part, to stop trying to please everyone else without taking my own views into account. You've shown me my opinion does count. You listened to me, encouraged and supported my ideas. That's one of the reasons I fell in love with you.'

He grinned at her. 'What were the others?'

'You make me laugh, you're loyal and caring and honourable and with you I can be myself.'

'Always.' He cupped her cheek. 'Because I love you for you. I love the way you smile, the way you care about everyone, the way you deal with difficult situations. I love that you have fun, take selfies. I love you, Ava. I want to wake up with you beside me every day. I want to be at your side for the ups and the downs. I want to have children with you, to grow old with you.'

'That's what I want too. You've shown me that love can be a good thing, a beautiful thing. That it isn't all about need or obsession. It's about a partnership, about reciprocity, about being there for each other. It's not a power struggle, it's about two people who want to be together, who work through their problems together. Because I know that's what we'll do.' Her gaze encompassed him with love and he felt an awe and wonder. 'For ever.'

'For ever.'

Then he kissed her, a kiss that sealed their love, marked the beginning of for ever. A kiss that filled him with pure happiness that this woman loved him. And so they spent their first date, began their for ever, lying under the stars and planning their future.

* * * * *

THE COWGIRL'S
SURPRISE MATCH

NINA CRESPO

Chapter One

Zurie Tillbridge opened the digital planner on her phone knowing exactly what to expect—"busy" written in bold letters across every day of the week.

As she scrolled through the tasks necessary to keep Tillbridge Horse Stable and Guesthouse at its best, her heartbeat consumed her chest and a small wave of burning unease churned the coffee she'd drunk earlier that morning in her stomach. The slightly off feeling had plagued her for over a week. She never got sick, not even with the common cold. What was going on?

Unbuttoning the navy blazer of her business suit, she sank into the beige chair and smoothed back a strand of her long black hair from her overly warm brown cheek. As the welcome cool air in her physician's private office seeped through her white blouse, she closed her eyes a moment, shutting out the slightly cluttered wood desk in front of her and the abstract paintings with splashes of orange hanging on the cream walls.

The side door opened, and Dr. Lily Westin walked in. Crisp and serene in a white lab coat, the midthirties brunette with a rosy complexion exuded energy.

Zurie waited until she sat down behind the desk. "So what's the verdict?"

"You'll live. I won't have your lab results for a couple of days, but my guess is your problems are stress and plain old exhaustion." Lily's green eyes held traces of humor and the candor of a friend. "What you need is a Mr. Tall, Hot and Irresistible in your life keeping you distracted so you'll stay where you belong right now—in bed, catching up on sleep."

A breath whooshed out of Zurie. *Whew!* She was just tired. But Lily's suggestion was hilarious. Even if she had time to lie around and do nothing, which she didn't, where would she find Mr. Tall, Hot and Irresistible in Bolan?

The image of a certain dark-haired guy flashed in her mind.

No way. Not him.

A laugh fueled another wave of relief as Zurie picked up her black designer tote from the chair beside her and put it on her lap. "That's an interesting diagnosis. Since Mr. Tall, Hot and Irresistible isn't available, are you giving me a B vitamin shot or a magic pill instead?"

"A shot or a magic pill won't do it. You need a break from Tillbridge."

"I have a stable and guesthouse to run."

"And you have capable people who can do more so you can do less."

"I can't." Zurie dropped her phone in her bag. "Especially now that there's a movie being filmed on the property."

Over the past few months, the filming of the sci-fi Western *Shadow Valley* had increased exposure and revenue for the stable, but it had also demanded more of everyone's time.

Lily leveled her gaze on Zurie. "Your body is trying to tell you something, and you need to start listening."

"Okay. I'll work on getting more sleep."

"What happens if Tillbridge loses you?"

Zurie's phone chimed in with a call, but the concern on Lily's face stopped her from answering it. "That would never happen."

"It could if you don't start taking better care of yourself." Lily got up and sat in the chair beside Zurie. "You're not eating properly. Your blood pressure is higher than it should be, and you're probably working on an ulcer. If you don't make some changes, there's a possibility the next time we have this conversation, you'll be in a hospital bed. You're only thirty-seven. You're too young to fall apart like this. Slow down before it's too late."

The voice mail alert pinged on Zurie's phone as Lily's words resonated. "You mean don't be like my dad."

Before her father, Mathew, had passed away, everyone had urged him to slow down, but he'd pointed to his full desk as the reason he couldn't.

Natural causes had been the official ruling. Some believed that as a widower, he'd worked himself into an early grave trying to hide from the pain of losing his childhood sweetheart, but still...

The image of her father burdened by stress wove through the tapestry of Zurie's memories like a too-bright thread, standing out. "If I had insisted he take time off, if I had begged, he might be alive today."

Lily lightly squeezing her arm alerted Zurie that she'd spoken aloud what she believed in her heart. "I know losing your father was a tough blow, but you can't blame yourself. No one knows what could have changed the past. I think the bigger question is, if your father were here right now, what would he tell you to do?"

Chapter Two

Zurie sat in the large brown leather chair that had once belonged to her father.

Sun from the window behind her glared off the financial spreadsheet displayed on the wide-screen computer on her desk. A few files and papers sat in the in-box on the left far corner of the desk while the out-box on the opposite side was full.

Not letting work pile up. Leaving nothing undone. That was her life as the co-owner of the stable. But today, for the first time in a long while, one uncertainty remained. The answer to the question Lily had asked her earlier that morning.

"What would he tell you to do?"

He'd tell her that Tillbridge had to come first. But if she didn't slow down and take a break as Lily suggested, she could end up letting down everyone who counted on her.

A knock at the door pulled Zurie from her thoughts. The meeting. She'd lost track of time. "Come in."

Her cousin Tristan, the stable manager and also a co-owner of Tillbridge, entered the office carrying his phone and a notepad. With his close-cut black hair and the strong angles of his brown face, he reminded her of their twin fathers, Mathew and Jacob.

From the faint smudges of dust on his standard work attire—black work boots, jeans and short-sleeved navy pullover—he'd come straight from the stable or one of the pastures.

He tipped his head toward the round meeting table on the other side of the room. "You ready?"

"Yes." Zurie took her padfolio from the left-hand drawer and grabbed her phone from the desk.

As she joined Tristan, she deciphered his slightly puzzled expression. She was usually already at the table, counting down the minutes to their 10:00 a.m. Wednesday meeting while squeezing in emails, calling her remote assistant, Kayla, and planning for the next meeting afterward.

Another knock sounded at the door and her sister, Rina, breezed in. "Good morning."

She laid her phone and keys on the table. Just like

Tristan, she had on jeans, plus she wore a lemon-yellow T-shirt with the white coffee cup logo and name of the café she owned, Brewed Haven. A matching headband held back her long braids, but the sunny color wasn't as eye-catching as the light of happiness in her brown eyes and the natural glow in her cheeks.

As Rina sat down, Tristan chuckled.

"What?" Rina shrugged at him. "Why are you looking at me? I'm not late."

"No reason. How long is he in town?"

She gave him a surprised look. "A couple of weeks. How did you know Scott was here? He flew in late last night."

Tristan winked at her. "Lucky guess."

Rina laughed. "How's Chloe?"

A huge smile took over his face. "She's great."

Feeling like the odd person out, Zurie opened her padfolio and powered up her computer tablet. A few months ago, when she'd made the last-minute deal with the movie production company to film *Shadow Valley* at Tillbridge, she'd never envisioned Tristan and Rina finding their significant others because of it.

Tristan had fallen for Chloe Daniels, one of the lead actors in the film, while Rina had gone head over heels for Scott Halsey, a stuntman who'd been a part of the crew until a knee injury had caused him to bow out.

Things were progressing in Tristan's and Rina's relationships. Soon they could both face a difficult choice—building their lives in California with the people they'd fallen in love with or staying at Tillbridge.

Images from her past she'd closed away about her own choices tried to get out. Zurie slammed the door shut. Tillbridge was more than enough to fill her life.

It was time to kick off the meeting. "Let's get started."

Zurie shared the information she'd received at the last chamber of commerce meeting in Bolan. An increase in tourism was anticipated later that year in the fall and winter months. Unfortunately, around the same time, major construction was planned on the primary road leading to Tillbridge, making the pothole-infested back road the main detour.

The route shift would surely deter the locals from visiting Pasture Lane Restaurant or holding events at the stable. Not to mention the bad impression it would make on the tourists. Luckily, at the mayor's weekly business mixer, she'd had a side conversation with him about it, and the mayor had promised to see if he could use his influence to change the order of construction to the back road being repaired first.

Tristan followed with an update on the stable and pasture management. The movie production was running behind. To accommodate the needs of the extended filming schedule, taking on new boarding and horse riding lesson clients was being delayed for at least four more weeks.

Rina took notes on her phone. Although she didn't participate in the day-to-day running of the stable, she was an equal third partner and still had a voice in the running of Tillbridge. "Are potential clients willing to wait that long or are we going to lose their business?"

"Most of them are willing to wait." Tristan sat back in the chair. "But no doubt we'll lose some of them."

"What if we offered an incentive?" Rina asked.

As Zurie worked through the financials of an incentive program in her mind, she couldn't stop a hand twitch. She missed her coffee. The caffeine jolt would have given her an energy boost and false comfort that she had the stamina to deal with the adjustments the film production was causing. But she had to lay off caffeine for a few weeks—doctor's orders.

As Rina and Tristan discussed possible incentives, Zurie remained in listening mode.

This time last year, their meetings had resembled a civil exchange between strangers instead of family. Actually, she'd been the stranger. Rina and Tristan had always gotten along. Lies and so many misunderstandings had nearly destroyed her relationship with them.

A few years ago, she'd believed Tristan had abandoned Tillbridge to pursue his bull-riding career, but then she'd learned about the sacrifices he'd made for their family. And with Rina—she'd failed to notice that her little sister didn't need her to resolve her problems anymore.

Memories of the illuminating and humbling conversations Zurie had had with Tristan and Rina over the past few months caused an internal wince. She'd been wrong about both of them, but it had been so easy to critique their actions and try to fix everything on her own.

As the oldest by five years over Tristan and almost ten years older than Rina, she'd often slipped into a parent-like role, especially when they were growing up. While her parents and her uncle, Jacob, who was Tristan's father, had handled business at Tillbridge, it had been her responsibility to get Tristan and Rina up and ready for school in the mornings and pack their lunches. At night, she'd helped them with their homework, and on weekends, when she wasn't practicing for the next barrel-racing competition or competing in one, she'd supervised them as they'd completed the small tasks they'd been assigned at the stable.

Sure, Tristan and Rina were adults now, but she still had the instinct to look out for them. Asking for more of their assistance at the stable so she could focus on improving her health felt…wrong. Tristan and Rina had experienced rough patches in their lives in the past, and now they were both so happy.

How could she do as Lily recommended without getting in the way of that and causing them to worry about her?

"I think those three incentives will work," Tristan said.

"I agree," Rina added. "What do you think, Zurie?"

Shoot! I missed everything they said. "I feel the same. As long as we keep an eye on expenses and continue to deliver top-notch customer service, we should be fine." Zurie closed her padfolio. "Unless there's anything else, I think we're d—"

A knock sounded at the door.

"Right on time." Tristan stood. "I asked someone to join us." He opened the door.

Chloe walked in, her dark curly hair bouncing near her shoulders. A similar glow to the one Rina had earlier lit up Chloe's pretty light brown face. Smiling next to Tristan in a fitted white T-shirt, skinny jeans, and high-heeled beige sandals, they were the perfect match as a couple.

He wrapped an arm around Chloe. "We have something important to tell you."

"Really?" Rina practically happy danced in her seat. "What?"

"We're engaged!" Tristan and Chloe said it at the same time as Chloe showed the sparkling diamond on her left hand.

Rina sprang from her seat. "Congratulations!"

She enveloped both of them in a hug, then turned to Chloe. "Girl, let me see that ring."

Zurie stood but hesitated in joining them, not quite sure where to interject herself into the moment.

Tristan's gaze met hers, and the happiness in his eyes was an irresistible invitation.

"Congratulations." Smiling, Zurie hugged Chloe first, then embraced Tristan. "So when's the big day?"

As Tristan said the date, he glanced to Chloe, confirming agreement, and she nodded.

"But that's just a little over six weeks from now," Rina said. "That's not a lot of time to plan a wedding."

"It is for a quick ceremony at the courthouse or in Vegas," Chloe responded. "When I'm done with studio work in California on *Shadow Valley*, I'm headed to Canada for my next production. Trying to juggle everything in our lives and plan a wedding is too much. And we don't want to wait."

"We don't need a big wedding." Love and pride shone in Tristan's face as he stared at Chloe. "She's agreed to become my wife. Nothing can top that." He briefly kissed her on the lips.

"But a wedding here would be so beautiful." Rina looked from Tristan to Chloe. "We can easily plan something small and intimate."

"We could." Chloe nodded. "But with the tabloids spreading false stories about me and the lead actor in the film being in a relationship, and paying for pictures and any scrap of news from the set, if we start planning a wedding, our personal life could be spun into some sort of crazy, jealous love triangle. We don't want that. We're even keeping our engagement a secret."

As Rina glanced down at Chloe's left hand, a glum expression took over her face. "So you won't get a chance to share the good news or show off that beautiful ring?"

"No." Chloe's gaze drifted to the platinum band with a marquis-cut diamond. "I'll have to keep this in my jewelry bag until we seal the deal at the courthouse or the twenty-four-hour chapel."

Chloe smiled, but Zurie caught the brief flash of sadness in her eyes. And the look of resignation in Tristan's.

He might not realize it now, but someday he would miss not seeing Chloe walk down the aisle. And they both might regret not sharing their vows with their family and close friends in attendance. But Tristan would take his disappointment to the grave to protect Chloe.

Before she could second-guess herself, Zurie let the words spill out. "It won't become a media circus if I'm making the plans instead of you."

Varying levels of doubt crossed Tristan's, Chloe's and Rina's faces.

"It's a lot of work…"

"We couldn't ask you to do that…"

"No. You're already doing too much…"

But the answer to Lily's question showed clearly in Zurie's mind. Her father would want her to make sure Tristan and Chloe had their big day. "Team Tillbridge."

The rallying cry her and Rina's father had used to motivate the family to get things done caught Tristan's and Rina's attention. The doubt in their faces melted slowly into smiles.

"Okay." Tristan nodded. "If you think we can team it out, I'm game."

Rina nudged his arm. "Of course we can."

Confused, Chloe looked at the three of them as if they'd suddenly started speaking a foreign language. "Team Tillbridge? Team it out? I don't understand."

Zurie reached out and squeezed Chloe's hand. "It means family takes care of family."

Chapter Three

In one efficient maneuver, Zurie parallel parked her gray Mercedes between two cars on Main Street. At seven forty-five on a Monday morning, the shops and residents in downtown Bolan were just starting to wake up. And she was beginning her first official day as Tristan and Chloe's wedding planner.

Five days ago, after she'd offered to handle the details of the ceremony and reception at Tillbridge, Tristan had insisted he take on more of her work as a trade. And then Rina had chimed in recommending Zurie take time off to work on the wedding and hand all her duties over to Tristan.

The remembered moment made Zurie smile. She

managed a horse stable and a guesthouse on a daily basis. How hard could one small wedding be? But seeing an opportunity to follow Lily's advice, she'd jumped on Rina's suggestion and feigned reluctance over taking time off. Then she'd bartered with them over how long she'd be out of the office. Otherwise they would have been suspicious. She hadn't missed a day of work in years. In the end, they'd settled on her taking three weeks off.

And they'd also decided to keep the engagement and the wedding a secret from mostly everyone until it happened. Tristan's birthday was a couple of weeks after the weekend he and Chloe wanted to get married. They could use that as an excuse to pretend that Zurie was helping Chloe plan an early "surprise" party for Tristan, since Chloe was leaving soon after filming of the movie ended.

Philippa Gayle, the guesthouse manager and executive chef of Pasture Lane Restaurant at Tillbridge, had been let in on the hush-hush ceremony. She'd agreed to cater the food for the reception and would handle most of the preparation herself.

Today's meeting at Rina's apartment above the café would start the ball rolling on ideas for the wedding cake Rina was going to make, as well as other ideas for the ceremony they would discuss later with Tristan and Chloe.

Zurie grabbed her black-and-blue animal-print bag from the passenger seat and got out. As she slipped the strap of the bag on her shoulder, she rounded the car and stepped onto the sidewalk. She joined the handful of dog walkers and joggers who were out for exercise and the employees heading to the shops linked together in strip-mall fashion that weren't open yet.

Sun glistened off water cascading down the stone fountain in the square located in the center of town. She would have cut through the space to reach the other side of the street, but workers mowed the grass around the benches and clipped pink and white flowering bushes lining the path.

A middle-aged jogger went around her without breaking his stride.

Maybe she should put running back onto her new healthy agenda. Years ago, she used to run three to five miles every other day. It would fit right in with not skipping meals, getting more sleep and enjoying time riding her horse, Lacy Belle. She'd even started meditating over the weekend…or at least she'd tried. Who knew breathing could be so darn challenging? She did it all the time.

Lily had suggested she try a variety of things to better her health, including a hobby. She'd never really had one of those. School, barrel racing and helping out where her parents needed her hadn't left time for much else. By the time she'd reached her mid-twenties, her focus had been finishing her master's degree in business and spending time with her father learning how to run Tillbridge.

Before she'd turned thirty, she'd been on a steep learning curve trying to catch up on all the things he hadn't gotten a chance to teach her. Trying to fit anything or anyone outside the stable into that equation had been impossible.

As Zurie walked past the ice cream shop near the left corner, the new manager, a dark-haired woman, gave her a quick smile before rushing into the establishment. The place had been sold, briefly closed for a few weeks and then reopened.

What was her name? She hadn't formally met the new manager yet. Tristan would probably be introduced to her at the mayor's business breakfast mixer at city hall that morning. She could find out the details about the manager and status of the ice cream shop from him. Wait. Tristan had said he couldn't make it this week. If she kept the wedding planning meeting to forty-five minutes, she could attend in his place.

A large pebble crunching underneath the sole of her low-heeled sandal drew Zurie's gaze downward. No, she couldn't go. Her jeans and short-sleeved peach-colored blouse were too casual for a professional gathering.

Fear of missing out started creeping in. She shoved it away. Aside from the wedding, her focus for the next few weeks was letting go of stress and taking in joy with every breath, like the beginner's meditation audio she'd listened to that morning had instructed.

She drew in a deep inhale, rich with the scent of freshly cut grass…and coffee.

Longing rose as she recalled the early-morning ritual of grinding her favorite blend of Colombian beans. Making the coffee in a French press and, when it was ready, pouring the steamy goodness into her A Yawn Is a Silent Scream For Coffee mug.

Disappointment pushed out an exhale. Drinking herbal tea, coffee's unfortunate step cousin twice removed, wasn't cutting it. She needed her caffeine fix. But she had to stick with the program. Her stomach was feeling better since she made the switch. Maybe the faint nagging headache she'd been experiencing lately, along with feeling jittery, would go away, too.

After waiting for cars to pass, she strode across the street toward Brewed Haven. Unlike the other businesses on the street, the two-story light-colored brick structure on the corner with large storefront windows on the first floor stood on its own.

A steady stream of customers entered and exited from the café with bags undoubtedly containing delicious pastries and cups filled with freshly brewed nirvana.

Thinking Zurie was headed inside, a friendly woman held the door open for her.

Suddenly, it was as if her feet had minds of their own and Zurie was propelled inside.

One small iced coffee wouldn't hurt. The one with extra whipped cream, chocolate sauce, caramel and a little sugar and sea salt sprinkled on top.

She slipped into the line leading up to the curved station.

Three baristas prepared coffees and grabbed desserts and pastries from the glass case underneath the counter.

When she placed her order, just saying the words *iced caramel mocha* gave her a caffeine-like buzz. Minutes later, the most beautiful creation ever to fill a clear plastic cup was in her possession.

Napkins. She'd better grab some. The cup was a little sticky. Weaving through the crowd, she made her way to the condiment station and snagged a few from the dispenser.

Taming the bag hanging from her shoulder with one hand while holding the iced coffee and napkins in the other, Zurie turned.

And smacked into a human wall.

Like a slow-motion scene in an action film, the clear domed top covering her cup of coveted mocha goodness came off, and iced coffee splashed up on a wide chest covered by a khaki-green athletic shirt.

Dang it. She hadn't even gotten a taste of her drink. Was it weird that she felt like crying about it?

She tipped back her head and looked up into the

naturally tanned face of Deputy Sheriff Mace Calderone. As she stared into his whiskey-colored eyes, Lily's cure flirted in her thoughts.

Tall...

"Excuse me." An attractive brunette squeezed by them to get to the napkins. She paused briefly and gave Mace a wide smile.

He smiled and nodded politely at the woman as he moved out of her way. "Good morning."

The woman looked at the wet spot on his shirt, then glanced at Zurie with an "ooh, girl, you didn't" smirk on her face.

Zurie stepped to the side with him, feeling like she wanted to disappear. But she needed to get over it and apologize for dumping coffee on him.

She set the half-empty plastic cup on the condiment station, dropped the soggy napkins in the trash and snatched dry ones from the dispenser. "I'm so sorry." She dabbed the wet spot on his shirt. "I can't believe I was so clumsy."

Mace took hold of her hand and the damp napkin. "It was an accident."

As the warmth of his fingers seeped into hers, Zurie's heart rate kicked up. But then she started free-falling into his gaze. Something that calmed and excited her all at once almost tempted her into leaning into him. "But I've ruined your shirt."

"I can wash it. I'm just glad it wasn't hot coffee."

His mouth curved upward into a wider smile that was even more intoxicating than his eyes.

Tall, hot... And her mind didn't need to go there. This was Mace—Tristan's good friend, whom she used to tutor when he was in high school.

She pulled her hand from his and stepped back. Droplets of coffee had landed on the front of his loose black athletic shorts and running shoes. She'd really made a mess of his clothes. "Now you're going to have to take everything off."

Mace's brows shot up. "Excuse me?"

"I meant, you'll have take off your clothes at home when you're alone...without me...because that's what you'll have to do to...you know...clean them."

What in the world had she just said, and did it sound as outrageous to him as it had to her?

His amused, puzzled expression answered the question.

"I need to go. Rina's waiting for me." Zurie headed for the exit.

Mace stood in line at Brewed Haven, ignoring the curious glances at his shirt, but the scents of coffee, chocolate and caramel wafting from him were harder to overlook.

The replay of Zurie bumping into him ran through his mind. *Well, damn.* That hadn't gone as expected. He'd just wanted to say hello to her. Actually, he'd wanted to confirm it was really Zurie. Seeing her away from Tillbridge and wearing casual clothes was unusual. She should wear jeans more often.

"Hi, Mace. The usual?"

He shifted his thoughts from how good Zurie had looked and focused on the upbeat twentysomething brunette behind the counter. "Please. Thanks, Darby. And can you give me one of whatever Zurie Tillbridge ordered?"

Fifteen minutes later he picked up his small coffee and Zurie's iced caramel mocha. After securing Zurie's coffee drink in a cardboard carrier, he left Brewed Haven.

As Mace stood at the curb of the sidewalk waiting for traffic to pass, he took a long sip from his cup. The small boost of caffeine would get him through his workout but not prevent him from getting sleep later on.

He'd planned on going to the gym near the sheriff's department after leaving work that morning, but a little over an hour ago, after his shift ended, Tristan had texted him, asking that he stop by Rina's place. After he met with her, he'd run a quick five miles in town, then drive home to get some sleep. But first he needed a clean shirt. Luckily, he had an extra one in his gym bag in his truck. Considering how the one he had on looked, Rina probably wouldn't mind him changing in her bathroom. And since Zurie had mentioned she was going to see Rina, hopefully he'd catch her there so he could give her the drink.

As he crossed the street, condensation glistened on the side of the plastic cup of iced coffee. With the swirls of whipped cream and stripes of caramel and chocolate packed under the domed lid, the drink could have passed for dessert. He'd never have guessed Zurie was a sugar fiend. Not that he spent that much time around her. But it hadn't always been that way.

Fifteen years ago, he'd been a starting sophomore quarterback more interested in chasing girls than passing his classes. When he'd started struggling in statistics, his attorney father had hired Zurie, who was a math whiz and in college, and issued an ultimatum—work with her as his tutor twice a week and get all his grades up or quit football.

At first, showing up at the Tillbridges' house to see Zurie instead of just hanging out with his friend Tristan had been embarrassing. But soon he'd looked forward to seeing her. She'd been easy to talk to, and she'd been patient with him and taught him how to study more efficiently. He'd finished that semester with a solid A average in every class. After she'd stopped tutoring him, they still had a good rapport. A little over twelve years ago, when he'd enlisted in the Marine Corps right after graduation, she'd been one of the last people to hug him goodbye before he'd left town.

Memories continue to roll in as Mace reached his red crew-cab truck and took his black gym bag from the back seat. Four years ago, when he'd returned to Bolan instead of staying in Nevada, where his family had relocated, he'd noticed a change in her. She'd lost the happy gleam from her deep coppery-brown eyes and didn't smile as readily anymore. The loss of her parents and Tristan's father, Jacob, along with the responsibilities of Tillbridge, had taken a toll on her. When he'd first gotten to town, he'd let her know that he was there if she needed anything, but she'd dismissed him.

He'd gotten the feeling she was seeing him as the teen he'd been instead of the man he'd become. That had disappointed him, but he'd accepted her decision. Since then, her interactions with him had been cordial but brief.

Hell, what she'd just said to him in the café was the first spontaneous sociable conversation they'd had in years. And it might not happen again, considering just how fast Zurie had rushed out of Brewed Haven.

Chapter Four

Upstairs in Rina's apartment, Zurie sat on the cream-colored couch, the only furniture in Rina's living room along with a wooden coffee table.

The sun shining through large tinted windows on the side wall gleamed on the clear packing tape strapped over the top and sides of stacked moving boxes.

Rina had purchased an older home just outside town about a month ago that needed some TLC. Now that the contractors were done, she was finally making the big move.

"It's mimosa time," Rina sang out as she walked through the archway on Zurie's left from the kitchen, carrying two tall glasses filled with the orange juice cocktail. "They're not as fancy as iced caramel mochas, but they're just as refreshing. It sucks that you spilled your drink on the way up here. Are you sure you don't want me to call downstairs and have Darby bring up another one?"

"No. This is good." Zurie accepted a glass from Rina.

The way her morning was going, a breakfast cocktail might help. They were meeting about Tristan and Chloe's wedding, so champagne was appropriate, and Rina's breakfast cocktails were legendary.

Bottoms up. Zurie took a long sip, and disappointment assaulted her taste buds. No alcohol? Rina never skipped putting alcohol in her cocktails, unless… Zurie took a good look at Rina. She hadn't gained weight, but she did have that glow about her. Maybe it wasn't just caused by Rina being in love.

Rina paused in taking a sip from her glass. "Something wrong with your drink?"

"No. It's good. But is there a reason you didn't put champagne in it?"

Rina followed Zurie's gaze to her flat tummy, and her mouth dropped open. "You think I'm pregnant? The only reason I used spritzer is because I took the champagne to the house. But a baby?" She laughed and shook her head. "Scott and I aren't there yet. We do want kids if we ever get married, but not right away."

An image came to Zurie's mind of Rina in the future, baking cookies with her young children and wiping the crumbs from their happy faces as they munched on the finished product. When the time came, Rina would be such a good mom. It felt like yesterday when Rina was a child and she was looking after her. But time moved on, and change came with it.

Pushing back nostalgia, Zurie took her phone from her purse sitting on the coffee table next to Rina's laptop. "I spent the weekend jotting down some notes about the ceremony and the reception."

Rina stalled her with a raised hand. "Hold that thought." She grabbed her laptop. "Tristan and Chloe want to FaceTime with us."

"I thought we weren't talking to them about the wedding until the end of the week?"

"We still are, but—"

The doorbell rang.

"I'll get it." Zurie set her phone and mimosa on the coffee table and stood. Hopefully, Tristan and Chloe weren't trying to micromanage the wedding. Yes, it was their ceremony and reception, but getting things done would become a lot harder if they were constantly checking in about the plans.

She opened the door.

"Hi." A small smile tipped up Mace's mouth. "I thought you might want this."

He held out a beverage carrier.

A frosty duplicate of the caramel mocha she'd spilled on him, her accomplice in crime that she'd abandoned downstairs, gleamed accusingly at Zurie in the sunlight. "You really shouldn't have."

Rina walked up beside her. "Hi, Mace. You made it. And you brought coffee."

His smile widened as he looked to Rina. "Now I feel bad. I should have brought you something, too. This is Zurie's."

Rina's gaze leveled on his stained shirt. "Oh, I see." She smiled at Zurie with a knowing look then turned back to Mace. "That's okay. Thanks for coming by on such short notice."

"Not a problem." Mace stepped forward.

Seconds passed before Zurie registered he wasn't just dropping off her iced coffee but coming inside. Like an awkward dance, he tried to come in then hesitated until she moved out of his way. She took the beverage carrier from him.

He walked inside and exchanged a quick peck on the cheek with Rina. "Do I have time to change before we talk?"

"Go ahead." Rina shut the front door and pointed down the entryway hall. "Bathroom's all yours."

"Thanks."

Once Mace was inside the bathroom, Zurie faced the humorous speculation in Rina's expression head-on. "Yes, that's my caramel mocha on his shirt. It was

an accident. The end." She went through the archway
on the left into the white marble–countered kitchen.

Rina followed. "It's kind of funny. You spilling
coffee on Mace, and him bringing you another one.
It reminds me of the day Scott ran into me." A sappy,
distant expression came over Rina's face. "I was so
mad at him for smashing my blueberry pies, but I
forgave him, and look where we are now."

Exasperation fueled Zurie's eye roll. "I can't take
it."

"Can't take what?"

Love. Tristan walked around with a perpetual
grin, and Rina wasn't any better. Not everything
was about love oozing happy vibes all over the place.
Some things really were just a clumsy, unfortunate
accident.

Zurie took the drink from the holder and stuck the
cup in the refrigerator. "It's not the same as what happened with you and Scott. Spilling coffee on Mace
was embarrassing. And to make it worse, I told him
he should take his clothes off. What I really meant to
say is that I'd gotten coffee on his shorts, too, and he
was going to have to wash them along with his shirt."

"You told him that?" Rina laughed, but empathy shone in her eyes as she propped a hip against
the counter. "I'm sure he didn't take it seriously, especially since you're not one of the women around
town drooling over him. Last week, when he was at
the café, from the looks a few of the women were

giving him, they really were imagining him without his clothes. But last I heard, the owner of the doggy day spa snapped him up. Wait…no. They might have broken up. Darby saw him having dinner with the new personal trainer at the fitness center. But that was weeks ago, too. I wonder who he's dating now?"

"You're right. I'm sure what I said didn't faze him." Zurie waved her hand over the top of the automatic trash can and dropped the cardboard carrier inside it. And she wasn't fazed by Mace. So what if he fit the description of Lily's prescription? That didn't mean that Mace was the cure, ridiculous as it was.

Rina gave her a contemplative look. "Mace may not be your type, but there's a cameraman working on the movie set who's single. Scott knows him well."

"I'm not interested in dating anyone. Period. Why is Mace here?" Zurie lowered her voice. "Does he know about the wedding?"

Rina offered up a shrug as they walked from the kitchen through the archway leading to the living room. "I'm not sure what he knows. When you got up to answer the door, I got a text from Tristan about Mace stopping by and that we had to bump the call fifteen minutes."

Zurie settled near the end of the couch and picked up her mimosa.

Rina sat closer to the opposite end and picked up hers.

A short time later, Mace joined them. As he

dropped his bag on the floor near the wall, Zurie forced herself not to stare, but it was hard not to appreciate how the white T-shirt he'd changed into molded to his pecs or how his shorts showed off his muscular legs.

Rina held up her half-empty glass. "We're having virgin mimosas. Would you like one?"

"No, thanks, I'll pass." He bent down and adjusted the laces on one of his light gray tennis shoes. "You're all packed up."

"I wish." Rina quietly chuckled. "I still have to sort through stuff in the bedrooms."

"Are you planning to rent this place out?" he asked.

"Not as an apartment. I'm converting the living room into an extension of the kitchen and putting in commercial appliances. Once the café starts taking online orders, we'll need the extra ovens and equipment to keep up. And this—" Rina swept her hand in a gesture encompassing the room "—will become a small conference space that I'll rent out for events."

Mace nodded. "I can definitely see it."

Zurie sipped her drink. She could, too, but what about the cost? Six years ago, she'd been totally against Rina buying and sinking money into remodeling the freestanding older building that housed the café and apartment versus renting one of the newer storefronts. Like she'd predicted, the upkeep of the place was more expensive.

Hadn't there just been an issue with the upstairs plumbing? Upgrading the pipes for the commercial kitchen was going to be a huge expenditure. Sure, Rina would have more income from the online business, but that could take a while to really kick off. And what about Rina's personal reserves? Surely she'd taken a hit to her savings with the renovation of the house. Had Rina thought it all through? Concern made Zurie fidget in her seat. Maybe she should talk to Rina about it?

No. She shouldn't. Not acknowledging Rina's success as a businesswoman in her own right had been one of the things that almost ruined their relationship.

Rina checked the time on her phone. "Tristan should be calling soon." She scooted over to the end of the couch and patted the middle cushion between her and Zurie. "Move over, Zurie, so Mace can sit down and see the screen."

Zurie hesitated. It did make sense for her to shift to the middle of the couch instead of Mace crawling over her. She scooted toward Zurie.

Mace sat down. A good twelve inches separated them, but his body heat reached across the space. "Tristan didn't tell me why I needed to be here. Does it have something to do with the engagement or the stable?"

Zurie looked to Rina in silent communication. He

knew about the engagement. Should they tell him about the private ceremony?

From the look on Rina's face as she answered him, she understood Zurie's unspoken question, too. "Not sure."

As if on cue, Rina's phone and her laptop rang on the coffee table at the same time. Rina answered from her laptop.

Tristan's and Chloe's faces appeared on screen. He was in the driver's seat, and she was in the front passenger seat of a car. "Hey," Tristan and Chloe said in unison as Chloe gave a wave.

"Mace." Tristan gave a bro nod. "Thanks for taking the time for this. I really appreciate it."

"You said it was important." Mace moved closer to the middle of the couch. His arm grazed Zurie's, and tingles expanded across her skin.

He peered down at the screen. "Where are you two headed?"

"Nowhere." Chloe laughed. "We're sitting in the car because it's the only place where we can talk about the secret wedding ceremony."

Mace reared back a little. "Secret wedding ceremony? Since when?"

Tristan chuckled. "Since Zurie talked us into it. She's our wedding planner."

"She is?" Mace looked to Zurie.

Growing overly warm under his gaze, Zurie grabbed her phone from the coffee table and focused on opening her notes app. "You should prob-ably bring Mace up to speed."

Tristan's expression sobered a little. "We're hav-ing a small private ceremony at Tillbridge in five weeks, but we're keeping the details a secret from the general public. If anyone asks what Zurie's up to, she's helping Chloe plan an early surprise party for my birthday. A party for me shouldn't be a big deal to anyone selling news to the tabloids, but once things start happening the day of the ceremony, and people figure out what's going on, word will spread. We need a security plan to screen out unwanted visi-tors. Chloe and I were hoping you could help us out."

Security plan. Zurie added it to her notes. She hadn't thought of that, and it hadn't been on the wed-ding planning checklists she'd looked at online. But this wasn't the usual wedding.

"Consider it done." Mace looked to Zurie. "We should get together soon to work through some de-tails. Do you have time tomorrow night?"

"Well..." Out of habit, Zurie pulled up her sched-ule on her phone. Seeing blank spaces on her cal-endar hijacked air in her chest. No. It was supposed to be that way. Kayla had remotely cleared all her Tillbridge meetings and tasks and handed them off to Tristan. She definitely had time. "Yes. I'm free."

In her suite at the guesthouse at Tillbridge, Zurie sat on her new blue yoga mat in the living room, legs crossed, feet not quite tucked into lotus position, but close enough for her to practice the new breathing exercise she'd stumbled upon online while looking up wedding planning checklists. The one from the beginner's meditation video she'd found on YouTube wasn't cutting it. This one was the heavy-duty upgrade she needed to take her mind off work…and Mace.

They were having an early dinner at his place at four thirty that afternoon. It made sense for them to meet there instead of a public place to discuss the wedding, but…

Stop thinking about Mace. You're meditating, remember?

Zurie recalled the instructions from the article. She hadn't read through every paragraph, just the important parts.

Back straight. Hands resting lightly on the thighs. Third eye open. *Third eye. That was one of the chakras. What was it about?* Maybe she should stop and look it up. *No, you shouldn't. Just breathe! Long exhale for three seconds… Inhale for five…hold for…*

A light tingling started in her nose, and she sneezed.

Dust…

Wiping down the furniture, vacuuming and doing some general cleaning would help fill the time until she went to Mace's house for dinner. Would his personal trainer friend be there? Of course she wouldn't.

The wedding was a secret. It would just be her and Mace. Alone.

Stop! You're losing focus again. Come on, Zurie, you can do this. Clear. Your. Mind.

Zurie wiggled into a more comfortable position.

If only Lily hadn't mentioned a hot guy that day in her office, having dinner with Mace wouldn't be a big deal. She had to stop thinking of him that way... but when did Mace turn into Mr. Tall, Hot and Irresistible, anyway?

Her thoughts went back to yesterday morning at the café when she'd bumped into him. Instead of being upset, he'd smiled and held her hand...kind of. He'd just stopped her from trying to do the impossible—clean iced coffee from his shirt. Still, for a brief moment, she'd felt comforted and attracted to him. And that's why her mind had gone rogue and she'd told him, in public, to take off his clothes. What had she been thinking?

Ha! You know exactly what you were thinking about. Ugh! This is impossible. Zurie stretched her legs out and flopped back on the mat. She couldn't keep her thoughts off him for fifteen whole minutes. And he wasn't even in the room. How was she supposed to make it through dinner at his place?

Chapter Five

Mace checked the whole chicken roasting in the oven then stirred the pot of *arroz con gandules* on the stove. Bay leaves, oregano, *sofrito* and other fragrant seasonings wafted from the rice and pigeon peas.

Home.

That's what he thought of whenever he made this dish. It was one of the ultimate comfort foods that brought up memories of sitting around the dinner table with his older brother, Efraín, their younger sister, Andrea, and their parents.

No matter how busy his father had been working as an attorney in Bolan or the number of cases his mother had on her desk as a school social worker, making time for dinner as a family most days of the week had been a priority.

He hadn't fully understood family meals as a teen, but once he'd moved away from home and joined the military, and experienced scarfing down MREs during training and deployments and eating in crowded chow halls, he'd come to appreciate the significance of those intimate moments during his childhood. There was something special about sharing a meal with the people you loved.

A text buzzed on his phone on the beige counter. As he glanced at the screen, he smiled. Even miles away, it was as if his mom had a sixth sense about when family was on his mind.

As he set down the spoon and picked up his phone, pictures buzzed in of his mom, dad and his mom's older brother, Dariel, standing outside the house where his uncle lived in Bayamón, Puerto Rico.

Past hurricanes had impacted the power grid system in the city. His parents were helping Dariel with the installation of solar panels on the roof of the pale green house that he'd painstakingly rebuilt with their help after Hurricane Maria had devastated the island. Once they left his uncle, they planned to visit other family members in the area over the next month. Then they were headed to Florida to see Andrea and her husband and their newest grandchild.

A flurry of texts and emojis went back and forth between his mom, Andrea and Efraín, who were also part of the group text. Mace joined in, asking questions about how the install was progressing. His mom texted back that things were going well.

The doorbell rang.

She's early. But then, he wouldn't expect anything less from Zurie.

After sending a quick text promising to catch up with everyone later, he set down his phone and went to answer the door.

He opened it and the greeting on his lips died out, leaving him speechless.

An inner radiance brought out even more of the beauty in Zurie's face, and her white sundress with splashes of sunflowers highlighted her tantalizing curves and silky-smooth-looking skin.

Maybe he should have made more of an effort and put on something other than a black T-shirt and jeans.

Holding a square pastry box in her hand, Zurie gave him a polite smile, then her gaze shifted to her brown sandals while tucking her matching clutch tighter under her arm.

Remembering his manners, he opened the door wider and stepped out of the way. "Come in."

"Thank you." Zurie walked inside, and the tantalizing scents of lavender and vanilla trailed after her.

He shut the door.

"I forgot to ask if I should bring something, so I

took a chance and brought these." She held the box out to him. "Nothing fancy, just cookies."

"The cookies from Brewed Haven are great."

"Oh no, they're from Pasture Lane. I didn't think about bringing dessert until it was almost time for me to leave, so I just ran to the kitchen and Philippa packed these for me. But you're right. The cookies at Brewed Haven are special." A look of doubt crossed her face, as if debating if she should give the box to him.

He slipped it from her hand. "Philippa's cookies are just as good. Thank you."

"Don't let Rina here you say that, and please don't tell her that I brought them to you."

The genuine look of discomfort on her face surprised him. Did she really think he would tell someone? He gave her a reassuring smile. "It's our secret. But make sure to leave room for dessert after dinner. I'm not eating these cookies all by myself." He gestured to the living room. "Take a seat and relax. Can I bring you something to drink? I've got flavored sparkling water, soda, wine, beer."

"Wine sounds good."

"White or red?"

"Red, please." She set her purse down on the wood coffee table in front of the dove-gray couch. "Can I help with anything?"

He had dinner under control, but from the way she lifted and dropped her hands, she needed something to do with them. Mace pointed toward the kitchen. "Sure, follow me."

As they walked inside, Zurie sniffed the air. "It smells amazing in here. What are we having?"

He set the cookies on the counter. "Oh, nothing fancy." Mirroring what Zurie had said to him a few minutes ago earned him a small smile from her. "Roast chicken, *arroz con gandules* and salad."

"*Arroz con gandules.* I like that dish."

"When's the last time you had it?"

"In Florida, a couple of months ago. I was filling in as a visiting professor at a college near Tampa. A friend that lives down there took me to dinner at a Latin restaurant."

"How was it?"

"Good."

Mace took a bagged mixed green salad kit from the fridge. "The chicken will be done in about fifteen minutes. All that's left is making this and setting the table."

"I can handle making the salad."

"That's perfect."

Zurie washed her hands in the sink.

Her methodical movements had a graceful quality that kept him glancing over at her as he slipped a bottle of merlot from the small silver rack on the counter. She was so deliberate he could practically hear her counting off the right length of handwashing time in her head.

Thorough. He could respect that.

As he popped the cork on the wine, she picked up the bag of mixed salad greens he'd left next to a bowl and wooden salad paddles on the counter. "It says prewashed, but I'll give them a quick rinse, just in case."

"Let me get you a colander." Mace found what she needed in a lower cabinet and went back to the wine. He poured her a glass, then filled another wineglass with sparkling water.

He handed her the wine. "I'd join you, but I'm working tonight. "*Salud.*" He lifted his glass in a toast to their health.

She clinked her wineglass to his and took a small sip. "Mmm. This is good."

"It's from a vineyard outside town."

"The one near Tristan's house?"

"No. This one's farther out. If you haven't already, you might want to take a look at their wine selection for the reception. I have their brochure somewhere around here. I can find it for you, if you're interested."

"Thanks." Zurie rinsed the salad in the sink. "Using wine from a local vineyard would be a nice touch. Details. I'm learning that's what planning a wedding is all about."

Her jumping in to plan the wedding? That's the last thing he'd ever imagined happening. As far as he knew, Zurie hadn't missed a day working at Tillbridge in years. Not even when she'd sprained her ankle a while back. Tristan had been so frustrated with her because she wouldn't even let him help when her crutches got stuck in the mud near the stable.

Prickles dancing on the back of his neck, a sensation that he got when something wasn't quite right, started up. Curiosity almost prompted him to ask her lots of *why* questions.

But this was just dinner and helping her plan security for the wedding, not an interrogation.

He took plates down from an upper cabinet and silverware from a drawer. "So I guess you heard that I'm Tristan's best man?"

"Yes, but of course he chose you."

"You make it sound as if he didn't have other options. He could have chosen a friend from his bull-riding days. I'm honored he asked me."

"Rina and I feel the same way about Chloe. Unfortunately her friend that she wished could be there is on location shooting a film in Europe and can't attend the ceremony. She asked Rina to be her maid of honor, and I'm acting as an honorary one, since I have to remain free to coordinate the ceremony."

"How is the planning going?"

"Good." Zurie shook the salad in the colander over the sink, getting rid of the excess water before putting it in the bowl. "Rina is primarily responsible for the cake, but Philippa's going to help with decorating it, I think. And Philippa's also handling the food for the reception. They have a ton of ideas. I understand, it's Chloe and Tristan's day and they're excited for them, but we're going to have to pare things down to the best options. I can help them do that. Chloe and Tristan said they were okay with me choosing the menu, based on the things they said they liked, to save time, but I think we can loop them in with a family get-together at Tristan's or Rina's house. That way we can meet up without it being too suspicious."

The buzzer on the stove went off. He took the chicken out of the oven and set it on one of the unlit burners. "Sounds like a good way to get things done."

"I hope so. The other big thing aside from the ceremony details and security is Chloe's dress. She found this place that operates like one of those on-line personal shopping companies where they send you clothes to try on based on your preferences. But the try-on limit is three dresses. I'm afraid she'll just end up choosing one because she won't have time to send them back and get three more."

"That doesn't sound like a good option. And isn't the dress a big deal? When my sister tried on wedding dresses before she got married, she had my mom, her future mother-in-law and two of her close friends with her. From what I understand, it was a memorable bonding moment."

"That does sound really nice." Zurie mixed the

parmesan cheese and croutons into the lettuce. "But with all the secrecy surrounding Chloe and Tristan's plans, we can't go to a bridal place for her to try on dresses. Unfortunately, it's another thing she'll have to give up, along with not formally announcing the engagement or wearing her ring. I wish it didn't have to be this way for Chloe."

The sincerity in Zurie's face held his attention. She always came across as practical, but she really was disappointed that Chloe couldn't have more when it came to choosing a dress.

"Have you considered sneaking Chloe in under the radar to see Charlotte at Buttons & Lace, like early in the morning or late at night?"

Charlotte Henry and her dress shop, Buttons & Lace, had been a fixture in Bolan for at least a couple of decades.

"We could, but…" She held up the salad dressing packet. "Do you want me to hold off or mix it in?"

"Mixing it in is fine with me if that works for you. You could, but what?"

Zurie opened the packet and poured it in. "We're trying to keep the need-to-know list to a minimum. I'd have to loop Charlotte in on things."

Charlotte didn't socialize with the locals who liked to gossip. She also didn't seem the type to collaborate with the tabloids, but whether or not to trust her wasn't his call.

"What does your gut tell you about trusting her?"

Zurie used the paddles to mix up the salad. "I probably could. I mean, she was a good friend of my mom, and she'd probably love to help. But all it takes is one wrong person to be let in and the plan goes out the window. I need to be sure before recommending that we let anyone else in on what we're doing. What do you think?"

"I'm big on trusting my instincts. When I do, I'm usually right."

"Hmm." The slight curve of her lips came with her contemplative expression. "I'll think about it."

Mace slid carving utensils from the butcher block on the counter. His instincts were definitely telling him something about Zurie. Planning this wedding was important to her, but he couldn't shake the feeling that there was a lot more to it.

Chapter Six

Zurie sat at the table in the dining room adjacent to Mace's kitchen.

While they ate, he went over some basic details about security for the wedding. But her mind kept wandering.

It really should be a crime for him to look that good...

Natural waves traced through his black hair. The shadow of a beard on his cheeks and jawline framed his easy smile, and she couldn't help but stare as it gradually came into his eyes. His shirt and jeans fit as if they were tailor-made for him—snug but not too tight, giving tantalizing hints about the muscle underneath. The total package of Mace was all kinds of distracting.

"So in my opinion, we'll need a security team of at least seven or eight people." Mace picked up the wine bottle and gestured if he should top off her glass. "Most likely, they'll be a mix of the more trustworthy guards from the security company already working at Tillbridge and some acquaintances I know I can count on."

She really should say no to the wine, but it was so good, and she was feeling more relaxed than she had in ages. Zurie nodded yes to the wine. It was so easy to talk to him. The Mace she remembered had always been talkative, but in an immature way, as if he'd been trying to impress her. But the Mace sitting with her now was confident in himself and his words.

When he finished pouring, she took a sip, and the merlot's mellow warmth settled into her. "Isn't that a lot of guards for a small ceremony?"

"Not really. Between securing the perimeter of the property for the outdoor wedding, then monitoring what's going on at the guesthouse during the reception afterward, we'll need them. Tristan's right. Once people start realizing what's going on, they'll get curious. And we'll want to be ready for anything, since Chloe has started getting weird fan mail."

"What? She has a stalker?"

"From what Tristan told me, it's not at that level of concern. Just fans that are really excited for the upcoming movie. It's not unusual, just something that comes with Chloe growing more popular as an actor, along with the loss of her private life."

Zurie paused in lifting her glass. She really hadn't considered just how secretive this ceremony had to be. Or that maybe it might be more of a hardship for Tristan and Chloe to go through with it.

"Uh-oh." Mace interjected into her thoughts. "What's that look about?"

She set her glass down after taking a sip. "I'm starting to wonder if Rina and I made a mistake by pushing the issue of Tristan and Chloe having a ceremony here. I thought they were settling for less, but eloping might be less of a hassle for them."

"No. I agree, they *were* settling. At least, I know Tristan was. When he mentioned eloping to Vegas to me as an option, I could tell it wasn't what he really wanted. When he asked me to be his best man last night, he was really happy about the ceremony, and he said Chloe is, too. You planning this for them is a gift. They wouldn't have said yes if they didn't feel that way.

"I hope so. Otherwise I'm being selfish."

"Selfish? How?"

The story of her doctor's visit with Lily almost slipped out. The wine must have really gotten to her. She'd never considered confiding in Mace in the past. Not that she spent that much time around him. Or made him feel welcome.

Memories flitted in from four years ago, shortly after Tristan had left Tillbridge. Someone had vandalized signs on the back road, and Mace had come by in an official capacity to see if the staff or a guest had noticed anything unusual the night before. As he'd left her office, he'd told her to call him if she needed anything. A part of her couldn't wrap her mind around him no longer being the slightly cocky teen she used to know. And Mace had reminded her of Tristan. She'd made it very clear to Mace that she didn't need his help.

Remorse over the way she'd dismissed him that day stole her appetite, and she nudged her plate away. He'd either forgotten or he'd forgiven her. People forgiving her seemed to be the story of her life lately.

Mace waiting expectantly brought Zurie back to his question. As she searched for answers, one she hadn't thought of until that moment emerged. "I don't know. I guess I wanted to do it because Mom loved celebrating things. Not just national holidays or birthdays or us winning a rodeo event, but things like the last day of school or the first day of summer. And we always celebrated King Day and Juneteenth and, of course, the Tillbridge Spring Fling." Wonderful memories surfacing in her mind made her smile. "And then there were the really obscure holidays like national corn dog or national Popsicle day."

Mace smiled with her. "I remember being at your

house once on national Popsicle day. Your mom made some from fresh peaches."

He remembered that? "Yeah, she used to make all kinds, but the peach ones were her favorite."

"So Chloe and Tristan's wedding is a way of rekindling the way your family used to celebrate things?"

The absence of her mom, along with her father and uncle, hit Zurie, turning her memories bittersweet. "In a way, I guess it is."

Mace laid his hand on hers. The warmth from his touch reminded her of how he'd taken her hand when she'd tried to clean up his shirt at Brewed Haven. Just like then, his firm but gentle grasp felt calming. He let go, and she immediately felt the loss.

Suddenly, needing to do something, she arranged her silverware on her half-empty plate. "If you're going to make me eat cookies, I better start moving around. I'll do the dishes." Zurie stood, and light-headedness assaulted her. As her vision swam, she reached for the edge of the table.

"Whoa, hey, I got you." Mace grabbed hold of her waist and guided her back down to the chair. "Feeling dizzy?"

"Yes."

"Put your head between your knees."

Zurie moved to lean over, but a faint pounding started in her head. "Bad idea." She sat back up, and cold prickles rained over her.

Mace hunkered down in front of her, concern creasing his brow. "I think you should lie down on the couch."

Embarrassment aside, it did feel like she might topple out of the chair. "Okay." Zurie stood. Mace kept an arm around her all the way across the room to the couch.

Once they got there, she sat down, slipped her feet out of her sandals and stretched out. "I just need to lie here a minute."

"Can I get you anything?"

"Water, please." She massaged her temples, which had started to ache. "And some aspirin?"

A moment later he returned with both.

His gaze remained on her as she sat up long enough to pop two pills in her mouth and chase them with water. Then she lay back down on the black-and-white throw pillow.

Mace put the glass she'd handed him on the coffee table along with the bottle of aspirin and sat next to them. "Are you feeling a little better?"

"Yes. I probably just got up too fast."

"Maybe." He studied her. "How much have you eaten today?"

It was confession time. "Probably not enough to compensate for a glass of wine."

"Dizziness and headaches—has it happened before?"

"Dizziness, sometimes. Headaches, yes. More so lately."

"Have you been to the doctor?"

"I have." The genuine concern in his eyes pulled out more. "I saw Lily last week." Everyone knew about Lily and the family practice she'd assumed from her father a few years ago. "She said I'm stressed out. But I've been doing everything she told me to do—getting more rest, trying relaxation techniques, eliminating caffeine."

"Oh, I see." He crossed his arms over his chest. "So when I replaced your caramel mocha yesterday, I was aiding and abetting."

The humor in his tone prompted Zurie to give him a wistful smile. "Yes, you could say that. But I miss coffee so much. I hate giving it up."

"It's hard at first, but it'll get easier. You should give up alcohol, too, until you're past caffeine withdrawal. That's probably why you're having more headaches than usual, and in some people, it can cause dizziness, too."

Caffeine withdrawal? Great. How long would that go on? Defeat and a sudden wave of tiredness hit her at once, and she sank into the couch. "This whole destressing thing is harder than I thought it would be. I'm even failing at meditation, and that's just breathing."

"Does Tristan or Rina know about you needing to reduce your stress?"

"No. And you can't tell them. I don't want to take away from the excitement of the wedding."

"So your version of following your doctor's orders to relieve stress is planning a wedding all by yourself?"

A huffed laugh escaped, and her head protested with a small throb. "I'm on a staycation for the next three weeks. It's the only thing on my calendar. I can handle it."

"Let me help you."

"With what, the wedding? You already are."

"No. I mean not just with the security. Everything. I can even teach you a few relaxation techniques."

"Seriously?" She couldn't keep skepticism out of her tone.

"Is that so hard to believe?"

The Mace she remembered from years ago was a sports junkie and always on the move, never standing still. "I appreciate the offer, but it's not necessary." She went to get up, but he stopped her, placing his hand on her shoulder.

"It's necessary if you don't want me to tell Tristan and Rina that you almost passed out in my dining room. The only way I'm keeping what you told me a secret is if I'm watching out for you. Take it or leave it."

Mace looking after her? The prospect of that didn't sound relaxing at all. But from the look in his eyes, he wouldn't change his mind. Zurie lay back down. "I'll take it."

Mace stuck a detergent pod in the dishwasher and closed it. He'd turn it on later so he wouldn't wake up Zurie.

Earlier, after she'd reluctantly accepted his help and agreed they should postpone talking about the setup plan and security needs for the wedding until tomorrow morning, he'd returned to the kitchen to put away the leftovers and clean up. When he'd gone back to check on her, he'd found Zurie sound asleep.

Maybe he shouldn't have agreed to keep what was going on with her from Tristan. Stress wasn't anything to play with. It was a sign she wasn't taking care of herself. But this wasn't his story to tell. Again. The Tillbridges and their secrets...

A little over four years ago, Tristan had showed up on his doorstep looking as if his world had been ripped apart. And it had. A dumpster fire of lies involving Tristan was threatening to consume Tillbridge. The only way Tristan saw that he could stop that from happening was to leave town for a few years—or possibly decades. And not tell anyone why except Mace. After failing to talk Tristan out of the plan, he'd driven him to the airport in Baltimore the next day to catch a flight out of Maryland.

Tristan had put his family over his own needs. And now Zurie was doing the same.

Mace's phone rang on the counter. He snatched it up and glanced at the caller ID before answering the video call. It was his brother. "Hello."

"Hey." Efraín, a slightly older, leaner version of Mace with light brown hair, frowned at him on the screen. "Why are you whispering?"

"Hold on." Mace left the kitchen and walked down the hall away from the living room and into the first door on the left. "A friend is sleeping on my couch."

"A friend, huh? Is it the one who owns the pet store?"

"She owns a day spa for dogs, and no. It's not her."

Mace shook his head. His personal life always seemed to be up for discussion with his family. As a defense attorney and now head of the family law firm, Efraín was even more relentless than him at finding out answers. But there was nothing to tell. Sure, he'd met a few women for coffee or taken them to dinner, but as far as someone he wanted to spend quality time with—he hadn't found that connection with anyone yet.

But if he mentioned that Zurie Tillbridge was the one on his couch, that would lead to a full-on inquiry and interrogations from Efraín, Andrea and his father— all lawyers.

Their interest wasn't unwarranted. His friendship with Tristan, and Zurie tutoring him years ago, wasn't his family's only tie to The Tillbridges. When his father had practiced corporate law in Bolan, he'd provided legal advice to Mathew and Jacob Till-bridge on more than a few occasions.

Mace quietly shut the door and walked farther into his home office–slash–workout room. "Like I said, she's a friend. You didn't call to find out who I'm dating. What's up? Everything good with you, Gia and the kids?"

"We're all doing great. It's busy now that Gia is back to working full-time at the hospital and the kids are in pre-K. Things are also picking up at the firm."

Mace started filling in the next sentence in his head. The question his family had started asking him ever since he'd completed law school almost a year ago—"When are you taking the bar exam and moving to Nevada?"

The sound of a little girl's voice filtered in through the phone, Efraín glanced down and offscreen. "*Sí, es tú tío.*" Moments later, Efraín's four-year-old daughter, Emilia, sat on his lap staring at Mace from the screen.

A riot of honey-colored curls framed her adorable face. "*Bendición, Tío.*"

Hearing Emilia asking for his blessing of protection, something he, Efraín and Andrea had been taught to do as children to show respect to their elders, made him smile as he sat on the weight bench.

He responded. "*Que Dios te favorezca y te acompañe, princesa. ¿Como estas?*"

"*Bien.* Where are you, *Tío*?"

"I'm in Maryland. Where are you?"

"My house." Efraín whispered in her ear, and she continued, "When are you coming to visit us?"

"I'm not sure. Hopefully soon."

Bored with the conversation, she squirmed on her father's lap.

Efraín smiled down at her and pointed at the screen. "*Dale un beso.*"

Emilia placed her hand over her mouth, and when she took it away, she made a vibrating sound with her lips.

As Mace threw back the kiss, he did the same with his lips and she erupted into giggles. Before he could say, "Bye," she slipped out of her father's arms.

Efraín looked over his shoulder and called out in Spanish for her and her twin brother, Leo, to stop running in the house. He turned his attention back to Mace. "What happened with you coming to visit after you attended that training seminar in Sacramento? Was it canceled?"

Mace pulled up a mental calendar. He still planned to travel to California for the crisis-negotiation seminar. But now that Tristan's wedding was the week after that, and he'd just insisted Zurie let him help with the plans, he'd have to return right after he completed the training to continue assisting her.

But he'd already canceled a prior trip to Reno to see Efraín. Doing it a second time would probably seem like he was stalling on the plan of joining the law firm Efraín and his father had opened when they'd moved to Nevada seven years ago, Calderone and Associates. Especially if he told Efraín he hadn't been studying for the bar exam.

Tension gathering along Mace's shoulders prompted him to shrug it off. It wasn't the end of the world. The deadline to apply to take the bar in Nevada was about two months away. Once he applied and was accepted, he still had six months before taking it. Plenty of time to study and make plans to relocate to Nevada. He just needed to focus on helping Zurie with Tristan and Chloe's wedding first.

"I'm still attending the conference, but something else has come up. I have to return to Bolan earlier than expected."

Efraín's release of breath conveyed a lot. Now that their father had recently retired, Efraín wanted him there to firm up plans to join the firm sooner than later. "So I guess you'll let me know when your schedule frees up again?"

"I will.

Mace switched the conversation to the text they'd received earlier from their mom. Before the call ended, Mace also got a chance to see Leo and say hello to Gia.

Mace checked in on Zurie again. She was knocked out cold.

An hour later, he had showered, shaved, brushed his teeth and dressed in a casual long-sleeve black pullover, jeans and dark Lugz boots. If Zurie wasn't alert enough to drive, he could take her home. After dropping her off, he'd still have time to get to the department and change into his uniform before the start of his shift at nine.

In the living room, Zurie snuggled into the pillow and mumbled in her sleep.

From the smile on her face, she was having a really good dream. Too bad he had to wake her. Crashing on his couch for the night while he was at work was an option, but knowing her, she'd refuse.

Mace leaned down and shook her gently by the shoulder, but she didn't wake up. Not wanting to startle her, he spoke softly. "Hey, Zurie."

Blinking sleepily up at him, she laid her palm to his chest, and her warmth seeped into him. Her full lips parted with a sigh. "Mace..." Zurie raised her head, curved her hand to his nape and kissed him.

Chapter Seven

Zurie let herself fall into the dream. *This is wonderful...*

She held an iced caramel mocha, three times larger than the normal size. Just as she went to take a sip through the gigantic straw, Mace appeared out of nowhere and slipped the drink from her hands. That wasn't very nice of him. She really should be frustrated about that, but his mouth was suddenly more appealing than the iced coffee. In her dream, she gave in to temptation and pressed her lips to his.

As he murmured her name, the deep timbre of his voice spread like melting chocolate on her tongue. Desire stretched and expanded inside her as if it had just awakened after a long nap, refreshed and ready to go. Zurie dived into the kiss, reveling in the decadent warmth of his mouth.

Warmth? She shouldn't feel warmth in a dream.

Wakefulness fell like a line of dominoes, and she opened her eyes. *Oh no...*

As their lips separated, his gaze held questions. But the slight fullness of his lower lip and the faint taste of peppermint on hers answered her own. They'd kissed. Or, based on the bewildered expression on his face, she'd kissed him.

Mortification surged through her, and she sat up, causing him to move back.

"I'm sorry." She snatched up her nearby sandals on the floor and stuck her feet in them. "I'm..." No other words could fully encompass her dismay or embarrassment.

He dropped down next to her on the couch. "It's okay. It's no big deal."

Maybe it wasn't for Mace, but for her this was... She couldn't even look at him. Zurie sprang to her feet, rounded the coffee table and grabbed her purse. "I should go."

"Zurie, wait."

"Thanks for dinner." Her legs couldn't take her out the door fast enough.

Outside behind the steering wheel of her car, she backed out of the driveway. Her tires briefly squealed as she braked, then sped down the street in the middle-class neighborhood with near identical, neatly built houses and manicured lawns. As she reached the main road and navigated through nighttime traffic, she glanced in the rearview mirror. Mace hadn't followed her. A hint of disappointment mingled with relief.

A few stop lights later, she made a left turn and headed to Tillbridge. With miles ahead of her on the less populated, darkened, two-lane road, she set the cruise control and let her mind go back to the kiss.

She couldn't blame what had happened on Lily and the prescription. Yes, Mace checked all the boxes of tall, hot and irresistible, but she'd been the one who'd messed up and kissed him. What was her excuse? Caffeine withdrawal? *Ha!* Yeah, right. The urge to tongue tangle with one of the best-looking guys in town probably wasn't listed as a symptom. And neither was how, during those seconds of losing herself, not one single worry had entered her mind. She'd just wanted to keep kissing him. She hadn't felt that with anyone since…

Nope! Not going there. Dredging up a past relationship wouldn't help. Mace had said that it wasn't a big deal. Why should it be? He had a doggy day spa owner, a personal trainer and a long list of other people he'd dated in town. Kissing her had just been a tiny blip on his radar.

Zurie breathed past the weird disappointment settling in her chest. Once she got home, she'd drown it out along with her embarrassment in a god-awful cup of chamomile tea. And then, after a good night's sleep, she'd figure out what to say to him about it in the morning when he came by to talk about the wedding.

Mace halted his truck at the intersection at the end of the empty tree-lined road. To the left, the sheriff's department was less than fifteen minutes away. To the right, he was even closer to Tillbridge.

Usually he could compartmentalize things and control his thoughts, something he'd learned to do well as a marine. But tonight, not even the string of potholes on the back-road shortcut had shaken the memory of kissing Zurie. Sure, he'd told her the kiss was no big deal. But he'd wanted to kiss her again so badly, he'd had to sit down on the couch afterward and get his head straight.

When he'd first returned to Bolan a few years ago, he'd been interested in getting to know Zurie better. But with all she had going on with her family, and Tristan entrusting him with his secret before leaving town, asking her out hadn't been close to the right thing to do. Zurie shutting him down and refusing his help had made it even easier to let go of the possibility of ever dating her.

But that kiss she'd given him less than an hour ago… Maybe he'd just imagined the desire he'd felt from her. Had she really whispered his name? Or had

Zurie been half-asleep, dreaming of kissing some other guy, like the one in Florida who'd taken her to that restaurant?

Needing answers, Mace turned right.

As he drove down the smooth paved road, the smell of lush green trees and grass filled the cool night breeze coming in through the open driver's side window. The earthy smell of horses reached him just before he spotted the dark railed fence surrounding the acres of land owned by the Tillbridges.

Bypassing the turn that would have taken him along the pasture to the stable, he drove farther down to the twenty-room guesthouse. Since he'd taken the shortcut out of town, he'd probably beaten Zurie home.

He pulled into the full lot and drove past the two-story white building with a pitched roof.

A couple sitting in rocking chairs on the lighted porch in front of windows framed by green shutters looked out over the gently sloping grassy incline that flowed into a fenced-in pasture lit up by moonlight. The horses that grazed there during the day were either gathered in the run-in on the other side of the field or had been taken back to the stable. Night or day, the view was beautiful.

As he approached the far end of the parking lot, his headlights illuminated Zurie's Mercedes in her reserved space. She was just getting out of her car.

Mace backed in beside her, turned off the engine and got out of the truck.

Lights from the porch of the guesthouse helped lessen the shadows.

Surprise and something he couldn't place was on Zurie's face. "Mace, what are you doing here?"

"You forgot something."

"What?"

"An explanation for why you kissed me."

"Isn't it obvious?"

Not in the mood to guess or try to figure her out, he got straight to the point. "No. It isn't. You either liked kissing me or you didn't. Which is it?"

"Does it matter? You said it was no big deal." She gave a shrug of indifference, but the slight hitch in her voice indicated the opposite.

"I know I said that, but I was wrong." Mace stepped closer to Zurie. "You kissing me, it matters."

"That kiss. It can't happen again."

"If that's what you want."

She closed her eyes and shook her head. "Why did you have to follow me?"

Chances. He'd taken more than his share in his life. But answering her question was one of the biggest ones yet. "I liked kissing you. And I wanted you to know that."

Her long lashes raised from her cheeks, and what they revealed took his breath away. Before he could recover, she gripped his arms and sealed her mouth to his. As she parted her lips, he glided in, tasting the desire he'd witnessed a minute ago in her eyes. His heart went haywire.

Mace curved his hands to her waist, bringing her closer, and need hummed through his veins as he explored the curves and hollows of her mouth.

If only he had more time.

He eased back, breathing out at the same time she did as they let go of each other. He cleared his throat. "Glad we got that settled."

"Have we?" The appealing fullness of her lips, and the slightly stunned look on her face, almost pulled him right back in for another kiss.

"Yes. Or at least the important part is settled." The kiss at his house and the one they'd just shared weren't small occurrences they could just ignore. But as far as what to do about them… Mace backed away. "I need to get to work. We'll figure this out in the morning."

Chapter Eight

Zurie walked into her private suite of rooms on the second floor of the guesthouse and shut the door. As she leaned back against it, she touched her mouth, recalling the wonderful feel of Mace's lips on hers.

When he'd pulled up in the parking lot earlier, she'd gone through a mental inventory of her possessions, thinking she'd left something behind. Keys, phone, lip balm. She hadn't accounted for Mace's confession. Or kissing him again. But she'd needed to know if she really had enjoyed it or if she'd just been caught up in her dream. And now she had an answer—and no idea what came next.

Pushing away from the door, Zurie tossed her

purse on the navy couch and went to the adjoining bedroom. A nice long shower and a good night's sleep would help give her some perspective.

Later on, she sat under the crisp white sheets on her bed, leaning back against a pillow on the headboard. She drank a dreaded cup of chamomile tea, waiting for sleep to creep up and knock her out in the tranquil sanctuary she'd carefully cultivated with ash wood furnishings, a large white rug on the light wood floor and warm beige textured walls.

"I liked kissing you. And I wanted you to know that..."

Why hadn't Mace just left the first kiss at "no big deal"? Now that they both knew that they liked kissing each other—and, judging from that second kiss, they liked it a lot—what could they do with that? He said he wanted to talk to her, but it wasn't like they could take things further. No matter how easily those kisses took away her troubles.

But what about how she'd felt around Mace tonight when she hadn't been kissing him? Somewhere between prepping the salad and sitting at the dinner table, her anxiety had naturally lessened. Just like when she'd spilled coffee on him at the café and he held her hand. But it was ridiculous to think that he was some kind of sexy, magic chill pill. And even if he was, the relief would be temporary at best. Look at his dating history. And hers. While he dated around, she didn't go out often. And when she did, it was always when she was out of town. That way she didn't have to answer questions or put up with speculation about her personal life. And if she and Mace were to take things further, it could become a little too personal, since Mace and Tristan were friends.

So that settled it. The answer to getting involved with Mace was no…right?

At six in the morning, Zurie gave up on sleep and sat up in bed. If she tried again, she'd just fall into the same sensual dream of her and Mace that had plagued her whenever she had managed to drift off. But just as bad, the desire she'd felt in the dream still warmed inside her.

Mace would be at her door in a little over two hours. It was going to be impossible to look at him and not see those images. She needed them harnessed and under control before she and Mace talked about last night. Going over the wedding plans first, away from her suite, would give her the mental distance she needed before the "we kissed, now what" conversation.

She picked up her phone from the nightstand. Maybe Tristan would be able to meet her and Mace at the south pasture pavilion later that morning. The pavilion was where Tristan and Chloe wanted to say their vows. After meeting there, the three of them could take a quick drive around the property to discuss the security plan Mace had in mind to keep things in order during the ceremony and the reception at Pasture Lane. Having Tristan at the meeting with Mace would help prevent other distractions.

Zurie fired off a quick text to Tristan asking if he could meet them at eight. Less than a minute later, he responded that he could.

A small rush of relief went through her as she set the phone back down and got out of bed. Maybe her attempt at adding a new normal to her routine—meditating in the morning—would help as well.

After an hour of separating clothes to drop off at the dry cleaner's and completing a few loads of laundry, she was ready to give clearing her mind a chance. Zurie unrolled her blue yoga mat between the flat screen on the wall and the glass coffee table in front of the couch.

She got into position and closed her eyes.

Mace had said they'd talk in the morning. When he arrived in about a half hour, what was he going to say to her? What would she want to say to him? When she saw him, would every ripple of muscle underneath his clothing remind her of what she'd dreamed of last night?

Suddenly, her white tee and blue yoga pants felt warmer than a parka. She dropped her head in her hands. Was she feeling this way because she was in some sort of man drought? Or had those two kisses with Mace really changed how she felt about him?

A knock reverberated through the room.

Her heart bumped against her rib cage as if it were trying to leap out of her chest. Zurie rose to her feet. *You've got this.* She wasn't a teenage girl with a crush. She was a grown woman.

Zurie checked the peephole, then opened the door.

He stood in front of her, even sexier than her dreams.

As Mace stared, as if taking her all in, her expanding heartbeats took up space, not leaving her much room to breathe. "Hi."

"Good morning." He crossed the threshold into her space.

The appealing scents of sandalwood and citrus enveloped her. Every pore of her skin opened, welcoming the heat of his, and her resolve to distance herself from her attraction to him started dissipating into thin air.

A small smile tipped up his mouth, and in her periphery, she spotted the flexing of his bicep. As he started to reach for her, she stepped back, opening the door wider for him to walk in.

She caught the infinitesimal raise of his brow.

Accepting her silent invitation, he came inside. "Did you sleep well?"

As she turned from him to shut the door, denial sat on the tip of her tongue. No, she wasn't a teen with a crush, she was a grown woman who knew how to handle problems. Big ones. And she'd always dealt with them head-on...along with facing the facts.

She'd liked kissing him. What had avoiding her attraction to Mace done for her so far? Nothing but raise her anxiety level and rob her of sleep. Being near him did make her feel more relaxed. Maybe in some odd way, Lily's prescription was right on the nose. And staring right at her now.

Zurie faced him. "No. I didn't sleep well at all."

He frowned. "What kept you up?"

"You." Before she could second-guess herself, she let the whole truth out. "You caused it."

Mace studied Zurie a moment. He walked over to her, and the same inviting warmth she'd felt a minute ago when he'd gotten close moved over her like a slow, gentle caress.

His gaze held hers. "How can I fix it?"

In his face, Zurie saw what she was fighting—desire. But she was losing the battle.

"I'm not sure if that's a good idea." Still, a light-as-air sensation guided her forward onto uncertain ground. A place where there were so many unanswered questions. And possible consequences.

"If you want me to leave, I will."

"No. I don't want that."

His unwavering gaze held hers. "What do you want, Zurie?"

Anticipation and excitement, a long-buried heady mix she used to harness right before a barrel-racing event, surfaced. He curved his hands to her waist, and it rushed in even stronger. Her heart rate ticked up. For nearly seven years, she'd played it safe and not let herself get close to the edge like she had as a competitor—to go fast on her horse with all the trust in the world that she'd be able to control the outcome.

Running Tillbridge required steadfastness and practicality at all times. But right then, she wasn't in charge of running the stable. She didn't have to keep her actions or herself in check. She could do the one thing being the primary keeper of her family's legacy didn't allow her to do—just feel.

Hunger for just that had her lifting up on her toes as Mace leaned in. She met his mouth halfway. Relief and longing brought a moan out of her as she escaped into the drift and glide of an unhurried, deepening kiss. This is what she wanted—real, unadulterated passion and not just memories or a dream. She wanted him.

Mace picked her straight up, and she wrapped her legs around his waist. Having helped Tristan configure the alarm system in her apartment, he knew exactly where to go, but kisses that grew more urgent with need halted the journey every three or four steps.

He picked up the pace, and in a few short steps, they reached her bedroom. As soon as he set her feet on the floor, their clothing became a minor obstacle they raced to take off each other. The final reveal was him sliding down his briefs.

Desire uncoiled inside Zurie.

Mace glided his hands around her bare waist and brought her flush against him. From breast to hip, she melded to his deeply muscled torso. His sweeping, openmouthed kisses down the side of her throat mesmerized her, and the grip of his fingers along her hips made her heart speed up. Mace molded his hands to her butt, pressing his hardness to her lower belly, and her legs became weak.

He backed her up to the bed and followed her down to the mattress. As he explored every inch of her, she eagerly arched up for his kisses and caresses. Her palms traveled over him, meeting rippling muscle under heated skin.

Mace paused to roll on the condom he'd tossed on the bedside table, then guided himself inside her. The outside world faded and narrowed to just that moment. Soon, her shaky breaths became moans as strokes and glides grazed over needy places, awakening more want.

Joined with him, moving with him, she stared into his whiskey-colored eyes, falling deeper into desire.

Pleasure built. Tantalizing her. Teasing her. It drew out cries of *yes* that she couldn't contain and left her hovering on the precipice before she dropped into ecstasy…more wonderful than any stretch of her imagination.

Chapter Nine

Zurie lay in Mace's arms, tucked into his side. Her hand on his chest rose and fell with his slow, even breaths as he slept.

Contentment and the embers of desire ready to spark again—they drifted inside her. Along with something unexpected. Peacefulness. Mace radiated it in his sleep. Usually, she couldn't stand to lie around this late in the day, but right there next to him, she just wanted to stay snuggled to his side.

Her phone buzzed with a text on the bedside table. Careful not to wake Mace, she slipped from his embrace, picked it up and glanced at the screen.

I'm running behind. Can we meet at 8:30 instead?

Crap! She'd forgotten about meeting Tristan.

Mace, still asleep on his back, turned his cheek to the pillow. He needed to rest. And when he woke up, they needed to talk.

Something came up. Can we try again tomorrow?

Dots floated across the screen as Tristan responded.

Even better. Will 8:15 work?

Relief pushed out a breath.

Yes.

Good. Tell Mace I'm sorry. Packed schedule.

Will do.

Tristan gave her reply a thumbs-up emoji.

A small seed of guilt started growing larger as she lay on the bed. What if Tristan had asked her what had come up? Would she have lied to him?

Zurie glanced at Mace. They had to get a handle on things before the situation got too far out of control.

* * *

Mace walked out of the bathroom, fresh from the shower, tightening a blue towel around his waist.

In front of him, the bed was empty.

Where did Zurie go? A small bit of unease pinged in his gut. He snagged his jeans from the side chair, where she'd laid them, and put them on.

He'd awakened at around noon, slightly disoriented and surprised to find Zurie asleep in his arms. Happiness had quickly followed along with the realization he needed to rethink his game plan. He'd left her sleeping and hopped in the shower to get his thoughts in order.

On the drive over to Zurie's place that morning, he'd worked through the various scenarios of what would happen when he arrived. One, she'd immediately want to hit the reset button and forget what happened last night. Two, she'd admit she felt something when they'd kissed, but hesitancy would keep her from wanting to move forward. Three, they'd be on the same page about spending time together.

The curveball she'd thrown him when he'd walked in a few hours ago had been entirely unexpected, but not unwelcome. Zurie wasn't easy to read, but if he guessed, the two of them sleeping together didn't automatically default to option three.

Where was his shirt?

A quick glance around the room didn't reveal its whereabouts.

In his bare feet, he walked out into the living room.

Zurie sat on the couch with her legs curled under her, scrolling through info on her computer tablet, wearing his black pullover shirt. It fit her like a loose dress, draping over her knees. She'd rolled the sleeves up to her wrists.

Her feeling comfortable enough to wear his shirt was a good sign, wasn't it?

She glanced up and then looked back down again. Her dark hair hid her face. "We'll have to postpone going to the pavilion and walking the property until tomorrow."

He went over to the couch, but she still didn't look at him. "Why? What's up?"

She swiped her finger across the screen. "I asked Tristan to join us this morning, but he couldn't make it, and now a rainstorm is coming in."

Mace caught her hand in midswipe. "I'm sure we can find other ways to occupy our time. Like talking about what happened this morning."

As he gently tugged Zurie to her feet, he slipped the computer tablet from her hand and laid it on the glass coffee table. The scent of soap wafted from her. She must have showered in the other bathroom. But afterward, she'd still preferred to put on his shirt. He couldn't stop a pleased smile.

"Mace, I'm…" She lifted her other hand as if to lay it on his chest but stopped short. "I'm not sorry about what just happened between us this morning. But I shouldn't have allowed it to get in the way of what we were supposed to be doing. Tristan and Chloe's wedding should have been the priority."

He caught her hand before she dropped it and brought it to his chest with his. "Yes, Tristan and Chloe's wedding is the priority, but we're still going to get the things we need done. I don't see any reason why we can't balance planning the wedding and being together."

Being together... There, he'd said it. The ball was in her court now.

A long moment passed.

Zurie flattened her hand against him, and the heat of her palm on his skin brought up memories of her soft caresses earlier. His heart rate picked up. "If we were to keep seeing each other, we couldn't tell anyone, not even Tristan, Rina or Chloe. My personal life has never been a factor at Tillbridge, and I wouldn't want it to become one now."

Mace rested both hands on her waist. Not telling Tristan could go either way for him in the consequences department. But Tristan knew the type of person he was and that he'd never hurt Zurie. He'd always treat her with respect. But this wasn't about Tristan. This was about Zurie preferring to keep her personal life private. That was a legitimate ask.

"If you don't want to tell anyone we're seeing each

other, we don't have to. If that changes, it's because we made that decision together."

Zurie's brow furrowed slightly.

Uh-oh. Something else was on her mind. He gave her a slight squeeze. "What's bothering you? Tell me."

"Well—" Zurie sighed. She lifted her other hand to his chest. Her absently stroking over his pecs raised goose bumps. "While I'm off from work for the next three weeks planning Tristan and Chloe's wedding, I can do things out of the norm like sleep until noon or indulge in having fun. But once I'm back to managing the day-to-day here at Tillbridge, that has to be my sole focus."

Was she saying she couldn't manage Tillbridge *and* enjoy life? Mace studied her resolute expression and saw traces of how he'd been years ago.

He'd balanced undergrad studies and the marines, then law school and working as a deputy as his main priorities. He'd been the hamster on the wheel, living off spoonfuls of sleep and massive cups of coffee to survive. When he'd graduated law school and had time to sleep, work out, date, just hang out with friends or do things he liked, he'd realized how much of life he'd missed.

Enjoying the good moments was important to him now. Zurie being stressed out enough for Lily to advise she take time off was a sign she needed to learn to do a lot more of the same. It wasn't about eliminating fun and relaxation but finding a balance between the two. He could help her see how necessary that was while he helped her plan the wedding...and maybe they could continue to see each other afterward. He wasn't heading to Nevada for a few more months.

Mace widened his stance and brought her closer. "Okay. So it sounds like we have a lot to fit in over the next five weeks or so. Plan Tristan and Chloe's wedding. Teach you how to relax. Enjoy spending time together."

She shook her head. "We have three weeks."

"But the wedding is in five." Giving in to curiosity, he leaned in, searching out the scents of lavender and vanilla on the side of her neck.

"Yes, but three is when..." Sighing softly, she tilted her head, giving him better access as he swept kisses near her earlobe. "Mace, you're not listening to me."

"I'm listening, but maybe we should consider an even number, like five weeks. It's easier for me to remember."

Her hands paused in inching up toward his shoulders. "Five isn't an even number."

"Damn. After all these years, I still have problems with math." Mace covered Zurie's mouth with his, kissing away further objections.

Chapter Ten

Zurie drove the golf cart down the narrow paved trail bisecting the north pasture, headed to the stable to meet Tristan. Once she swung by and picked him up, they'd head to the south pasture pavilion to catch up with Mace at eight fifteen.

On one side of her, horses grazed in the pasture. On the other side, vans and trailers belonging to the movie production crew were parked near the indoor horse arena. The large sandstone-colored structure had been built to accommodate the needs of the filming, but the building was also something Tristan had wanted for years.

And he'd been right about the advantages. They

could bring in more income by conducting riding clinics in the indoor arena and offering it as a practice space for local competitors who participated in events like dressage and show jumping or other rodeo events. Or at least they could once the filming stopped.

The golf cart shuddered as it went over a cracked paver. That was the second one she'd encountered so far. She'd better remind Tristan to send the groundskeepers out to make repairs. Eventually, the jagged edges would rise. The last thing they needed was for a guest to trip and fall.

She reached the end of the paved trail that intersected with a wide gravel path. To the right, in the circular, fenced-in outdoor arena, one of the staff was giving riding lessons. The man and woman were riding Tillbridge-owned horses. Most likely they were visitors from the guesthouse.

Out of habit, Zurie took a long pause before she turned left. Satisfied there weren't any oncoming horses being ridden or led down the path, she took her foot off the brake, eased down on the accelerator and headed toward the stable.

As she approached, Tristan and one of the grooms walked out of the open double doors of the sandstone-colored building with a navy roof and trim.

She parked the cart on the side in the narrow graveled space outside the adjoining paddock on the left and waited for Tristan to join her.

But Tristan walked to the driver's side of the cart instead of getting in the passenger seat. Mild irritation was in his eyes.

Zurie picked up her phone from the cup holder between the seat and turned off the reminder alarm for their meeting that had started to chime. "Everything okay?"

"It could be better." He adjusted his navy ball cap with the Tillbridge logo—a white horse and *T* with a lasso. "We ordered pavers to replace the cracked ones on the path leading from the guesthouse to the stable. But the home improvement center delivered the wrong ones. Apparently, our order went someplace else. And they're all out of the ones we need for at least three weeks."

He had noticed the pavers. Good. "Did you try that company we used before in Virginia?"

"You're on a staycation, remember? I got this." Tristan glanced around, making sure they were alone. "Chloe purposely let it slip that you and Mace are helping her plan my early surprise birthday party. And with our meeting today, I told a few key people that Mace and I are reevaluating security protocols on the property because of the movie."

That made sense. A private security company currently monitored the property, including the movie set and base camp—the area where trailers for housing and production were set up for the cast and crew—in the west pasture, but Mace was the unofficial liaison between the security at Tillbridge and the sheriff's department. He was also Tillbridge's go-to consultant on security concerns at the stable.

"You mentioned you and Mace. What's my excuse for being here today?"

A small smile tipped up Tristan's mouth. "I told them that you can't stay away from business, despite being on vacation."

Yes, that *was* probably believable, considering her track record.

He took his phone from his back jeans pocket and checked the screen. "You up for a ride to the pavilion? We've got time. Thunder needs some exercise, and I'm sure Belle wouldn't mind tagging along. We can let them graze in the pasture near the pavilion while we check out the rest of the property. Mace won't mind stowing our saddles in the back of his truck while we ride around."

She quelled the urge to continue the conversation about suppliers for the pavers. "Sure. Let's do it."

A short time later, they were on the trail riding in companionable silence as birds chirped around them. Morning sun beamed through openings in the trees, warming her through her pale blue button-down and jeans.

Belle, a chestnut bay who fit her name, walked regally next to Tristan's ebony-colored horse.

Zurie settled into the Western-style saddle. The gentle ruffling of Belle's dark mane in the breeze, along with the sway of Belle's ears in front of her along with her rhythmic gait, were all like a sooth-ing balm.

It was just as calming as the vibrational healing meditation app Mace had downloaded to her phone yesterday before he'd gone home for a power nap and to change clothes for work.

It was one of the relaxation techniques he used to help him sleep when he got home in the morning after work. He'd been right. The music along with the hypnotic voice guiding her through a relaxing vi-sualization actually *had* helped her drift off to sleep.

Zurie shifted her thoughts from Mace. "Other than the paver issue, is everything else all right?" She caught the pointed but indulgent look Tristan gave her. "I'm not prying, just making general con-versation."

"Yeah, other than the pavers, the only thing giving me a headache is Anna Ashford practically demand-ing that I make time for her to come to the stable so she can interview me. Just because she's got politi-cal connections in Bolan doesn't give her the right to demand anything."

The mayor's sister-in-law, also known as Annoy-ing Anna, was in charge of the town's online news-paper, the *Bolan Town Talk*. The weekly paper was more like a blog filled with gossip and speculation than informative details about current events.

A piece of news that wasn't on her calendar or

the notes she'd passed on to Tristan before her staycation dropped into Zurie's thoughts. "Actually, she does. Remember that side conversation I mentioned having with the mayor at the business mixer about using his influence to change the order of construction for the main and back roads?"

"No." He groaned. "Tell me you didn't make that trade with him?"

"What choice did I have? It was either the interview with Anna or face the consequences of the construction schedule. She just wants the scoop on our future plans for the indoor horse arena once the filming of the movie is over."

"The pothole-infested road would have been easier to deal with. And you've been had. Last I heard, she was still bent out of shape about the mayor visiting the set of *Shadow Valley* without her when the filming started. The mayor made that trade with you because it was the only way he could free himself from her. This interview is a fishing expedition. Anna is either interested in digging up news about me and Chloe and the supposed love triangle with Nash Moreland or what's happening on the movie set."

Zurie huffed a chuckle. "Now who's dealing in gossip? If you're too afraid of her…"

Tristan gave a derisive snort. "I can handle Anna. But once I'm done fielding questions about me and Chloe and why I'm not taking her to the movie set,

I'll probably need a happy hour staycation at the Montecito Steakhouse bar. Let's change the subject. How *are* things going with your staycation? Other than planning the wedding, and not worrying about the stable, what else have you been doing to occupy your time?"

A memory of being with Mace for most of yesterday flashed in, and a mixture of butterflies and heat loosed inside her. "Oh, nothing much."

Were her hands actually getting sweaty? If she couldn't talk about Mace without getting flustered, what would happen when she saw him in less than fifteen minutes?

Sensing Zurie's anxiety, Belle lifted her head and shortened her stride.

As Belle started to lose the easy swing in her gait, Zurie automatically relaxed her shoulders and loosened up her hips, telegraphing to Belle that as her rider, she was still confident and in control.

Tristan glanced at Belle then Zurie. "You okay over there?"

"We're good." Zurie pointed to the gate just up ahead. "Let's go through this one instead of the one farther up. Belle could use a good gallop through the pasture."

"Sounds good to me."

At the gate, they both dismounted.

She managed the horses while he keyed the code into the locking mechanism and opened the gate.

After she led Thunder and Belle into the pasture, he locked the gate and they both got back on their horses.

Mischief filled Tristan's eyes. "Last one to the end of the field buys lunch." Without waiting for a response, he and Thunder started galloping across the pasture.

No, he didn't... Zurie turned Belle. When they were younger, he always used to pull this stunt. She gave Belle her lead, heading after them, and soon Belle's speed merged with the flow of her effortless gallop. As the sky and the empty green field flew past, the same focused rush she used to experience while maneuvering her horse around barrels in the rodeo ring at top speed came over her.

Soon Belle was only half a horse length behind Thunder and gaining fast.

They reached the fence separating the grass in front of the pavilion from the south pasture at the same time. Tristan slowed Thunder down to a trot, and Zurie did the same with Belle.

He grinned at her. "You almost beat me. Not bad for a desk jockey."

"Desk jockey? Look who's talking?" Zurie laughed. "You had an early start, and I still caught up with you."

"Yeah, I guess that is pretty impressive."

They brought their horses to a halt and dismounted. As they secured Belle and Thunder to the hitching post near the covered structure used for parties and special outdoor events, Mace drove his truck through the gate yards away from the opposite end of the pavilion and parked on the grass a distance from the horses and got out.

As he walked toward them, tucking his keys into the front pocket of his jeans, the ends of his casual beige button-down fluttered in the wind.

Zurie shifted her attention to taking her phone from a small holster attached to the saddle. How did she and Mace usually greet each other? A handshake. A nod. Why couldn't she remember?

Mace joined them. He and Tristan shook hands and came in for a brief thump on the back.

Mace gave her a nod and a friendly smile. "Hey, Zurie."

"Hi, Mace."

Now she remembered. Polite hellos were their usual. No friendly pecks on the cheek like he'd exchanged with Rina at the apartment above the café the other morning. If she recalled correctly, even Chloe received a peck on the cheek from him.

Disappointment pushed a quiet exhale out of Zurie. Because that wasn't her usual with Mace, they couldn't start now, especially in front of Tristan. But having a reason to touch him would have been nice. She'd have to wait until they saw each other after touring the grounds with Tristan.

"Does that not work for you?" Tristan stared at her.

Crap. What had she missed? "Why do you ask?"

He chuckled. "You're frowning like you hate Mace's idea."

"No, not at all." Zurie looked from Tristan to Mace. "I'm sorry. I zoned out. Would you mind repeating that last part?" If she'd missed more than that, Mace could fill her in on it later.

"Sure." Mace pointed toward the gate where he'd come in. "We can't let the guests park outside the gate like they usually would when they come here for events."

That left only one alternative. "Then everyone will have to park at the guesthouse and we'll have to transport them here."

"Exactly." Mace nodded. "That way we have total control over who's at the ceremony. Do you know the number of guests yet?"

Zurie flipped to the notes on her phone with the tentative guest list Chloe and Tristan had emailed her. "Twenty to twenty-five for the ceremony and fifty at the reception."

"Have you decided how you want to set things up here?"

"Our best option is a full tent. That's the only way to keep things hidden from view, especially during the setup. A bride's side, groom's side configuration out in the open would just be too much of a tip-off."

"Yeah, probably so." Tristan glanced around with a crestfallen expression. "But one of the reasons Chloe liked the idea of having the ceremony out here was the view. I proposed to her up the hill. She can't see it if we're in a tent."

"There may be a way around that," Mace interjected. "Why not set up the chairs for the guests under a couple of tents, but open the sides during the ceremony? You, Chloe and the minister can stand near the edge of the pavilion to take your vows."

Zurie tried to picture what he said. "But won't the tents still obstruct the view?"

"Depends on how you set them up." Mace gestured for her and Tristan to follow him to the edge of the pavilion.

They all faced forward. Tristan stood on one side of her and Mace on the other.

Mace turned partially toward her as he pointed. "If the tents are positioned on each side at a diagonal, Tristan and Chloe will be able to see the view of the pasture and the hill behind it. And with the front and side of the tents rolled up, the guests can see Chloe walk down the aisle and her and Tristan take their vows."

Zurie clutched her phone in her hand, fighting the urge to lean into where she'd fit so comfortably against his chest yesterday.

She took a step forward, putting space between them. "That could work. The main idea is to not tip anyone off before the wedding. Since the setup plan is supposedly for Tristan's birthday party, we'll label them on the diagram as tents for the buffet tables that we'll never set up. On the day of, it won't take long for us to arrange the chairs instead. So let's talk this through. The guests arrive at the guesthouse, believing Tristan's birthday party is at Pasture Lane, but we'll tell them there's been a change of venue, and we shuttle them out here."

"And then what happens next?" Mace asked.

Images started forming in her mind. "They arrive, someone makes the announcement that it's actually Tristan and Chloe's wedding, and we open the tents. Everyone sits down. Tristan, I think you should already be here with Mace. Chloe should be driven in as soon as everyone's settled. She arrives, walks down the aisle. Wait, back that up. Chloe walks down with her father to Tristan and the minister waiting at the edge of the pavilion." She looked back at Tristan. "You two exchange I dos, and then…"

From the happy look on his face, Tristan could see it, too. He and Chloe finally together as husband and wife. His phone rang, and he checked the screen. "I have to take this. Hold on a sec."

As he stepped away to talk, Mace walked next to Zurie. He leaned in and whispered, "Do you know how hard it is for me not to kiss you right now?"

She kept her eyes straight ahead. So he wasn't

immune. Goose bumps raised on her skin. "I guess you'll have to show me later."

"Yeah, but a lot later than I'd like to. I was tapped to cover an earlier shift. And I'm doing the same tomorrow. When we're done here, I have to head home and get some sleep."

Zurie's happiness deflated. She looked at him. "I understand."

The wind blew hair in her eyes.

Mace raised his hand as if to smooth it back for her, but then lowered it back to his side.

Tristan joined them. "I have to get back to the office. You two are going to have to finish without me. You can catch me up later."

Mace dug his keys from his pocket. "Actually, I was just telling Zurie, I can't go over the security plan today. I've been called in to work early."

Tristan clapped Mace on the back before turning away. "Thanks for coming out."

"No problem." Mace looked to Zurie. The longing she saw in his eyes made her heart swell. "I'll call you."

Chapter Eleven

Late in the afternoon at her place, Zurie sat on the couch checking items from her list on her computer tablet. Order the tents, chairs, portable wood runner—done. Close the guesthouse to reservations the day of the ceremony to just friends of Tristan and Chloe coming to Tristan's fake party—done. Schedule a private party at Pasture Lane for a fake customer to cover for the reception—she could check that off, too. Have fake invitations printed—still narrowing down the best place. Meet with Rina and Philippa to narrow down a menu—on the schedule. Dresses—that had to be taken care of soon.

What Mace had said about trying on dresses

being special had stayed on her mind. Tristan and Chloe's wedding was unconventional in a lot of ways, but finding a way to give Chloe this moment could mean a lot to her—finding the perfect dress, feeling good as she walked down the aisle, no regrets as she looked at her wedding photos years from now because she would see herself in a dress she really wanted. Maybe it was possible.

Zurie mulled over in her mind how her mom had looked forward to those rare free afternoons when she would catch up with Charlotte for lunch. Her mother hadn't been the gossipy type. She'd also valued loyalty and expected the same in return. If Charlotte hadn't shared those qualities, her mom wouldn't have counted her as a trustworthy friend. At least that's what her instincts told her about Charlotte and her mom's relationship. Maybe she should follow her gut instincts like Mace had suggested. Something she tended not to do.

Relaxing mental barriers, she confronted the close to seven-year-old mistake that had been hovering in her mind ever since she'd kissed Mace.

Theo Asher had been part of a group of fund managers from an investment firm in New York visiting Tillbridge. The CEO of the firm had paid Tillbridge a ridiculous amount of money for his people to experience working at the stable for a day.

Her father had given her the task of supervising the group as they mucked stalls, cleaned gear in the tack room, fed the horses, unloaded deliveries and helped with repairs. Some were able to jump right into the work, but Theo had been a disaster at manual labor. The areas he'd been assigned to clean were even messier than when he'd started, and he'd managed to break things no one ever had before. She'd been so frustrated with him, but when a horse had gotten spooked, he'd done the dumbest, bravest thing and jumped in to help. She later found out he'd done it to impress her and hidden that he'd hurt his wrist in the process.

Before Theo had left at the end of the day, he'd asked her out. Instead of basing her answer on reality, she'd acted on impulse and let her inner compass take the reins.

But this situation with Mace wasn't the same. She wasn't diving into a whirlwind romance, naively filled with unrealistic expectations. She wasn't ignoring the most important question—"where is this going?" With her and Mace, there were clearcut boundaries and no expectations. She knew exactly when and how their situation would end in three weeks.

Mace had tried to get her to agree to staying together until Tristan and Chloe's wedding, but what she had with him fit in the same category of her staycation—a diversion that would come to an end as soon as she went back to work. But until then, she'd indulge.

Her phone rang on the coffee table, and she picked it up. *Mace.* Happiness perked up inside her. As she answered, she tucked her feet up under her on the couch. "Hello."

"Hey. How's your day going?"

"Good. I made a dent in the wedding checklist."

"Sorry I couldn't hang around today."

Zurie settled back on the couch and set her tablet aside. "It's not your fault that your schedule changed. Did you get some sleep?"

"Yeah, I got a good six hours."

"Is that enough?" Lily had said she should try to get at least seven to eight hours every night.

"I've survived on less, and I'm powering up with some coffee. Oops. Pretend you didn't hear that."

Zurie's mouth watered. "I'm so jealous."

"I know your pain. I was downing too much caffeine once upon a time, but trust me. And trust Lily. Cutting back will be worth it."

"Seeing you, without the cup of coffee, would help." Oh, that sounded so cheesy. Zurie winced. She was really out of practice with flirting.

He chuckled. "It would, huh? What are you doing this weekend?"

"I'm helping Philippa and Rina pare down food and cake options for Tristan and Chloe to pick from. What about you?"

"I'm off this weekend."

"Well, since you insist on looking after me, I guess you're tagging along for the food tastings."

"Do you want me to tag along?"

What did she want? Answering that question as truthfully as she had yesterday morning—she shouldn't get too used to that indulgence.

"Zurie, it's a simple question. If you don't want me to go with you, just say so. I won't be offended. Looking out for you doesn't include me crowding your space."

"I want you there." As she said it, happiness rippled inside her. But maybe that sounded a little too desperate? "I could use a guy's perspective with the food, and you're perfect since you know Tristan well. Ten thirty at Pasture Lane tomorrow and eleven at Rina's apartment on Sunday. Can you make it?"

"Yes, I can be there for both."

"Good. And tomorrow, after the tasting's over, we could drive around the property and go over the security plan."

"That works for me. And Zurie?"

"Yes?"

"I can't wait to see you, too."

Chapter Twelve

Zurie checked herself out in the tall gold-framed mirror leaning against the wall in her bedroom. The casual, above-the-knee, sleeveless orange-and-white dress was bold and bright. Was it too much?

The dress with the sunflowers she'd worn to Mace's house had also been a departure from the navy, white, black and gray ensembles she usually wore. The simple color palette made it easier for her to mix and match outfits and get ready quickly for work early in the morning. But now she could explore the clothes in the back of her closet that rarely saw the light of day.

Dressing up a bit for dinner with Mace at his

house the other night had seemed appropriate. But today, was she making too much of things? They were just tasting food at Pasture Lane then driving around the property to talk about security. Maybe a casual top and jeans were more suitable.

"I can't wait to see you, too..."

The happiness that had come over her when he'd said it long hours ago made her twice as giddy now. But if that's how he felt about seeing her, shouldn't she wear something that made it worth the wait?

Downstairs, Zurie got off the elevator. The skirt of the orange-and-white dress swished lightly as she walked down a short blue-carpeted hallway.

Ahead of her, in the lobby boasting modern country-living accents, a few guests stood in line at the front desk.

Two smiling young women, crisp and efficient-looking in navy Tillbridge-logoed blouses, staffed the desk.

Zurie turned right and walked past a grouping of side chairs near a wall with gold-framed paintings of horses grazing in lush green fields near mountains.

When she reached the corridor behind the front desk, out of habit, she almost bypassed the glass double-door entry to Pasture Lane, heading for her office. It was so strange not being at her desk every day.

She'd been so tempted to work on the diagrams she'd created for the ceremony at the pavilion on the wide-screen computer in her office, but if she'd done that, she would have also given in to checking her business email. Right now, Kayla was screening her correspondence and only forwarding the ones Tristan couldn't answer to her personal email.

Using her computer or even going inside for something as simple as a paper clip or her favorite pen that was in the drawer of her desk was out of the question. But so far, quitting her office had been much easier than giving up coffee.

Inside the restaurant, she smiled at the young blonde woman in a crisp navy button-down and black slacks standing behind the podium. If Zurie remembered correctly, she'd recently been promoted to working at the host station.

Without glancing at her name tag, Zurie recalled her name. "Hi, Bethany."

Bethany smiled widely. "Good morning, Ms. Tillbridge."

"Am I at my usual table?"

"Yes. It's all set up for you."

Bethany moved to escort Zurie inside, but she politely waved her off. "No. You can stay here. I'm fine. Thank you."

The space with light wood tables and lime-green padded chairs was half-full. Most of the patrons sat next to a wall of glass overlooking the lush scenery that lay beyond a narrow wood deck. At ten thirty, it was the calm before the crowd that would steadily trickle in closer to noon.

Zurie set her phone on the four-top corner table tucked in the back of the dining room and sat down.

Two water glasses and two black coffee mugs were on the table, along with a carafe of coffee and a pitcher of ice water.

She automatically reached for the carafe but steered her hand toward the pitcher of ice water instead and filled up a glass.

Across the restaurant, Philippa, a tall woman in her late twenties, emerged from the kitchen through the faux-wood, double swinging doors. The lime-green bandanna securing her dark locks matched her chef's coat and the Crocs visible under the hem of her green-and-black-patterned pants.

As she drew closer to the table, Philippa smiled. "Good morning, Zurie." A faint southern lilt accented her words.

Zurie smiled back. "Good morning."

As Philippa moved to sit down, she hesitated, glancing at Zurie's empty coffee cup and full water glass. Her smile morphed into a concerned frown. "Is the coffee not brewed right? I'm sorry. The repairman who came into fix the machine this morning must have missed something. It wasn't just the water valve. I'd better go tell the servers to—"

"No, wait, Philippa. If you didn't get any complaints about the coffee at breakfast, I'm sure it's fine. I'm just not drinking coffee."

"You're not?" Philippa sat down and blinked back at her with an expression of disbelief.

Zurie conjured up her best "I'm okay" smile and sipped water. She really was okay. And no, the slight tremor in her hand wasn't because she was fantasizing about grabbing the carafe, ripping off the lid and guzzling down the coffee inside it.

Out of the corner of her eye, she glimpsed Mace walking in. Zurie took another sip of ice water, soothing her suddenly dry throat.

As he got closer to the table, he gave them a slightly lopsided smile. "Sorry I'm late." He sat in the chair to the right of Zurie and set his phone on the table.

"Hi, Mace." Philippa gave Zurie a quizzical look. "You're right on time. I think?"

Oh, that's right. She hadn't told Philippa that Mace was coming. "Mace is here to provide a male viewpoint on the food for…the party."

"Ah, got it, the party." Philippa smiled knowingly and nodded. "I'm serving you myself. That way you can tell me directly which items you want on the menu."

As Philippa walked away to get the food, Zurie turned her attention to Mace. He smelled of all things good. His slightly damp hair brought out its natural waves. A small, thin cut stood out on his angled jawline. Had he cut himself shaving?

He reached for the coffee carafe, nudged it away and poured water instead.

The teasing comment on her lips about his shaving skills stalled as she glimpsed a line of long cuts trailing up his hand from the back of his wrist. "You're hurt."

As he set the pitcher down, he glanced at his hand. "I'm okay." Mace gave her a tight smile, hints of weariness and something else appearing in his eyes.

"What happened?"

Mace's gaze slid over the room in a casual yet deliberate way then came back to her face. He lowered his tone for only her to hear. "There was a bad accident involving two cars on the main road leading to the interstate early this morning. Another deputy and I had to pry open the door to get to the young woman driving the car."

For a fleeting moment, Zurie's mind went to her mom, who'd lost her life in a car crash, and Rina, who'd almost died in one. Those moments were two of the worst days of her life. Her stomach dropped. "Is she okay? What about the other driver?"

"He's okay." Mace sat back in the chair. "But the young woman was airlifted to the hospital."

She couldn't completely understand how he felt about what happened, but it clearly weighed on his mind. "If you don't want to be here now, I understand."

"I could use the distraction. But I also don't want to bring down the mood, either. This menu is for a happy occasion."

"No. You're not bringing down anything." She almost reached over and laid her hand on his arm. "If it helps you to be here, stay. And if you need to talk, I'm here to listen."

"Thanks. I appreciate that, but I'm good." He gave her a small smile then glanced across the room to the kitchen doors. Philippa held a folded tray stand in one hand while expertly balancing a tray with plates on her shoulder. "Looks like the first course is up."

Zurie folded her hands in her lap. He didn't seem to be good. If only she knew what else to say to him. But if not talking about it any more was better for Mace, she'd leave it alone.

Philippa unfolded the stand and set up the tray. "We're starting with the appetizers. Anyone not eat anything or have allergies?"

Mace and Zurie both shook their heads.

"Good." Philippa gave them both small plates and silverware rolled in cloth napkins. "Let's get started."

Bite-size and mini portions of appetizers, based on foods Tristan and Chloe had said they liked, came and went from the table.

A little over a half hour later, Zurie and Mace had made their top choices, and Philippa had left them to finish the even harder task of narrowing them down while she plated up entrée selections.

Mace pointed. "The mini chicken sliders, nacho scoops and vegetable kebabs definitely get my vote."

Zurie dabbed a white napkin to her lips. "They were good. I also liked the gazpacho soup in a shot glass, the shrimp cocktail shooters and the mac and cheese bites. The spinach balls were good, but I wouldn't want to risk people walking around with spinach in their teeth."

"True. What about the mini tacos and the grilled cheese?"

"I'd choose the mac and cheese bites over the grilled cheese. Less crumbs to worry about. The tacos are kind of similar in taste to the nacho scoops."

"And less messy." He pointed between two plates. "Pretzels or loaded waffle fry cones?"

"Not sure. What do you think?"

Mace munched on one of the mini cones. "Definitely these." He chuckled. "They remind me of a particular dart game Chloe and Tristan played."

"A dart game. What does that have to do with waffle fry cones?"

He beckoned her closer. "More than you think…"

Mace whispered to her about a dart game at the Montecito Steakhouse bar between him and Tristan against Chloe and one of the grooms who worked at the stable. A plate of loaded fries had been ordered during the game where things had gotten interesting between Tristan and Chloe.

As he relayed the story of the moment he believed had brought Tristan and Chloe together, he cracked his first genuine smile since he'd walked into Pasture Lane. Soon she was fighting to contain her laughter over what he described.

Philippa came back with a server who cleared away what remained of the appetizers and helped serve small portions of the entrée selections. Philippa sat down and chatted with them as they narrowed things down to apricot chicken, her famed smoked prime rib and spring vegetable pasta—a much easier task than with the appetizers.

"So I think we're good." Philippa tapped notes about all their selections into her phone. "Now we just need to set up a time for the final tasting." The one where Tristan and Chloe would approve the menu for the reception.

Zurie and Mace said their goodbyes to Philippa. Near the entrance, they slipped past the small crowd perusing menus while waiting near the host station to be seated.

They reached the corridor and headed toward the front desk.

He looked over at her. "You up for a short walk before we drive around the property?"

"Definitely. Actually, we could walk to the stable,

grab a golf cart and use it to ride around instead of using one of our cars."

"Sounds good to me."

Outside, a few guests enjoying the view and the mild afternoon mingled on the porch and walked the paved trail where they were headed.

When they were partway down the path dividing the north pasture, Mace's phone rang.

He slipped it from his front pocket. His expression sobered as he glanced at the screen. "I should take this."

"Go ahead." Zurie walked farther down the path, giving him privacy.

Her gaze gravitated toward where she'd noticed one of cracked pavers the other day. She couldn't find it. The delivery issue had been solved and it had already been repaired, thanks to Tristan.

Her gaze strayed back to Mace.

He rubbed the back of his neck as he stared at the ground, listening to whoever was on the line.

Anxiety rose inside her for him. Was it bad news?

Chapter Thirteen

Mace ended the call and caught up with Zurie.

He waited for her questions, but she didn't say a word, just started walking with him.

Mulling over how to break the silence, he tapped his phone to his thigh. "That was the deputy who was with me this morning at the accident. His wife is a nurse at the hospital where the young woman was airlifted. She made it through surgery. It looks like she's in the clear."

Zurie paused. "That's wonderful news." Smiling widely, she laid her hand on his arm.

On a reflex, he put his hand over Zurie's, needing just a few more seconds of contact with her as he allowed himself to fully absorb the good news. The helplessness and frustration that had balled inside his chest long before sunrise that morning began to dissolve.

He did his best not to carry the job home. He couldn't if he wanted to function. But when he'd gotten the car door open and looked into the young woman's scared but trusting eyes, he'd seen a grown-up version of little Emilia.

A breath escaped him along with the rest of the invisible weight he'd been carrying. "It's great news. Peyton's going to be okay."

As people walked around them, he dropped his hand from Zurie's, and she took hers away as they stepped to the side of the trail.

"Peyton? That's her name?" Zurie said. "What happened to her? What caused the accident?"

Realizing he'd said the young woman's name jarred him.

Normally he avoided talking about his job, even with his own family. Some things were hard to explain to anyone who wasn't a first responder. And because of his time in the marines and being a deputy, some people assumed his feelings chip had been removed. Yes, there were deputies who chose to wall off compassion, leading them down the dangerous road of not seeing people as people. But that wasn't him.

Mace looked down at Zurie's upturned face. He'd

opened up this conversation by mentioning Peyton's name, and his mood at Pasture Lane during the tasting probably did warrant more of an explanation.

"Yes, Peyton, that's her name. The other driver had been texting and driving and swerved into the wrong lane."

Zurie shook her head. "I don't understand why people think messing around with their phone while they're driving is a safe thing to do."

"At three in the morning, that road is mostly empty, so he probably thought he could take the risk. Luckily for Peyton, after the accident, he was able to call 911."

Mace recalled the scene when he'd first arrived. The nineteen-year-old-boy, bleeding from a head wound and feeling shaky, had still been in his SUV that was in the right-hand lane but facing the wrong direction. From the tire marks, Peyton's small two-door had spun out before flipping over on the side of the road.

Focusing back on Zurie, Mace continued. "She was conscious when the other deputy and I arrived, but she was wedged in. We couldn't get her out without possibly making her injuries worse. For some reason, she grabbed onto my hand instead of the other deputy's and held on. I stayed with her until fire and rescue arrived and got her out of the car and into the helicopter."

After they had airlifted Peyton out, he'd done his

job at the scene, but for the longest time, it was as if he could still feel her smaller hand in his.

Zurie reached down and clasped the same hand Peyton had held firmly in hers. "You say you don't know why Peyton reached for you instead of the other deputy. I do." As Zurie tightened her grasp, hints of soft emotions filled her eyes. "She knew you wouldn't let go."

Mace locked his truck parked at the curb on Main Street. Tucking his keys in his front jeans pocket and carrying his phone in his hand, he walked down the sidewalk toward Brewed Haven.

A couple of spaces behind him was Zurie's car.

After they'd ridden around the property yesterday, they'd spent time at his place, where he'd let her know how beautiful she looked and how much he'd appreciated her listening to him about the accident. And not saying the two responses he dreaded the most—"I'm sure she'll be okay" or "I'm sure you did the best you could."

When people said things like that, it always led him to change the subject. What could he say? Thank you? But with Zurie, he hadn't experienced that awkwardness, just understanding.

He was trying to give her the same when it came to them seeing each other, but sometimes it was hard. He'd been able to convince her that instead of settling for just a few hours at the stable, they could have more time together at his place. Unlike the neighbor-hoods in Bolan where many of the locals had lived for years, the newer subdivision he lived in consisted of recent transplants—couples by themselves or with younger kids. They were too busy living their own lives to notice or care how long her car was parked in his driveway.

Finally, they'd been able to really relax as they'd discussed wedding plans. Afterward they talked in between her devouring her new binge watch, *Star Trek Discovery*. It had surprised him how she'd be-come mesmerized with the sci-fi series.

He'd almost talked her into spending the night to keep watching it, but around nine, she'd insisted on driving home. She'd claimed that walking through the Tillbridge guesthouse lobby in the wee hours of the morning to get to her suite would have kicked up too much curiosity.

Mace crossed Main Street using the brick path winding through town square.

Days and nights were slipping by without them spending quality time together or having the oppor-tunity to really know each other. Their undercover relationship was starting to play out like a tasting menu, where he could only have small bites, but he wanted the whole dating package with Zurie. He wanted to be able to hold her hand and kiss her when-ever he wanted to in public, to take her on a date somewhere without her worrying if someone would see them. He wanted to see her let loose. Color outside the lines of what she deemed acceptable and live a little. But expectation ruled her choices. Could he ever get her to see past that? Did they have enough time?

Bypassing the entrance to the café, he jogged up the stairs to Rina's apartment and knocked.

The door opened, and Zurie stood in the threshold. A light breeze ruffled the skirt of her casual magenta dress, and her hair hung loosely around her bare shoulders.

"Wow." He gravitated inside, standing in front of her. "You look beautiful."

"Thank you." She looked up at him, and her smile made him want to stay right there, taking it in.

If he was going to get her to color outside the lines, this was as good a time than any.

Mace leaned in, holding her gaze, willing her to stay still and just let it happen.

The clang of what sounded like metal utensils landing on tile made him look down the hallway and caused Zurie to jump back.

So much for saying good morning to each other properly.

"Shoot!" Rina's voice came from the kitchen.

Zurie shut the door. "Rina's a little moody this morning since she was up baking for the half the night. I hope you didn't eat a big breakfast."

A few steps down the hall, as he glanced into

the kitchen on the left, he saw what Zurie meant. More than a half dozen decorated eight-inch round cakes sat on the counter. The way he was eating this weekend, he'd have to put in a workout every day next week.

Rina, dressed for work at the café and wearing a yellow apron, looked up from where she was sweeping coconut flakes from the floor into a dustpan. "Hey there."

"Do you need help?" Zurie stood beside him.

"No, I'm good." Rina dumped the flakes into the trash. "Take a seat in the living room. I'll be ready in a minute."

In the living room, the packed boxes, sofa and coffee table were gone, replaced by a lone six-foot table with a white tablecloth surrounded by four foldable chairs. Several forks, napkins, a stack of small plates and two empty glasses were in the center of the table, along with a small photo album with pictures of cakes.

The sound of utensils rattling in a drawer came through the archway up ahead on the left.

Mace set his phone on the table. As he held out one of the chairs for Zurie, and she sat down, he took his chances and pressed a kiss low on her neck.

Zurie turned her head to look at him and whispered, "What are you doing?"

"Saying good morning. You really do look beautiful."

"Good morning and thank you. Now will you please sit down and behave?" She looked more pleased than exasperated.

He grinned. "No promises, but I'll try."

"I'm ready." Rina carried in a cake from the kitchen, along with a small serrated spatula, and set both on the table. "Let's start with the basics. Vanilla cake with vanilla cream frosting topped with raspberries."

She gave details about the cake's ingredients and pointed out pictures in the album of how it might look as a tiered wedding cake. Then she cut a thin slice, cut it in half, and put the halves on two small plates before giving them to Mace and Zurie.

While Rina went to get water to cleanse their palates between tastings, they sampled the cake.

Sweet vanilla woke up his taste buds. "This is good." He sampled another generous bite.

Zurie sat down her fork. "It's definitely a possibility, but it might be a little too simple."

"What? Too simple?" he teased in a low voice. "I thought you didn't like complicated?"

"It's not that I don't like complicated. I just don't always have time to deal with it. But when I do, complicated is very…tempting. Like now." She glanced over at him.

Was she talking about cakes or something else? He leaned toward her. "Just how tempting *is* complicated right now?"

"Very tempting."

Her lashes dropped and raised as her gaze moved over him. When she looked into his eyes, his heart rate ticked up and almost obliterated his promise to behave.

And from her coy smile, she knew the effect she was having on him.

"Okay." Rina came from the kitchen carrying a pitcher of ice water and another cake. "Next up is red velvet with passion fruit filling and cream cheese icing."

Although she was known for her pies, Rina's cakes were equally delicious. But five cakes later, Mace suffered from a tiny bit of sugar fatigue.

Rina stacked saucers with the remains of cake, then picked up the half-full pitcher of ice water.

"Need a hand?" Zurie asked.

"No, I got it," Rina replied. "You two relax." Carrying plates and the pitcher, she went to the kitchen.

Mace sipped water. "How many more to go after this one?"

"Just two. I think." Zurie sank back in the chair. "Cake tasting is hard work. After this, I don't think I'll want to see another cake for weeks."

Rina came back in carrying the full pitcher and a white frosted cake dusted with coconut and topped with curls of dark chocolate. "This one's a little different. It's…" A ringtone like a doorbell sounded from the phone in the pocket of her apron. "Hold on." She answered the call. "Hey, Darby. Oh?" Her brows raised. "How many are broken? Yeah, that's a problem. Hold on. I'm coming down."

Rina ended the call. "I have to run downstairs for a minute. Zurie, can you take care of cutting this one? I won't be long."

"Sure." As Zurie picked up the cake cutter, Rina hurried out of the apartment. "I hope everything's all right."

"She said she won't be long, so maybe it's not serious."

Zurie hacked at the cake, cutting into it with less finesse than Rina.

He winced. During Tristan and Chloe's reception, she definitely needed to be kept away from helping to serve the wedding cake.

Mace resisted grabbing the spatula from her and motioned with his hands. "You might want to use the serrated side of the spatula, then slide it under to…"

She wiggled the spatula against the side of the slice and dragged it out.

"Or you could do it that way."

The small, mangled slice of the white cake with pale yellow filling barely made it to the plate before toppling over in a heap. "I'll take that one." She licked her thumb.

Her low moan of pleasure raised the hairs on his arms. "It's that good?"

"Oh my gosh, you have to taste this. It's part

cheesecake." Zurie snagged a clean fork, cut a bite from the messy slice and held it out to him.

He ate it, and the rich flavors of sweet coconut, tart lemon and hint of bitterness from the dark chocolate made him a release his own moan of contentment.

Zurie grabbed another fork, and they both gobbled up the slice.

As they licked their forks, their eyes met.

Before he could reach for the spatula, Zurie grabbed it and lopped off a much bigger, messier slice than the first. "Plate."

"Got it." His mouth watered as he caught the slice on a small plate and shoved another one under the second slice she dragged out.

They sorted out the slices and dived in.

"This is beyond good," Zurie said between bites.

He paused long enough to answer. "I don't know what she put in this, but she needs to patent it."

"She should."

A short moment later, Mace cleaned crumbs from his plate with this fork.

Zurie dropped hers on the empty plate and sat back in the chair. "I feel like I just had the most amazing out-of-body experience."

He could relate. Her leading the way to devour almost half a cake was totally unexpected.

Her gaze landed on the decimated dessert. "Rina isn't going to be happy about that. Once we were done with the tasting, I think she planned on selling the cakes downstairs."

"I'm sure she'll forgive us." His gaze was drawn to frosting clinging to the corner of her mouth. "You've got cake on your face."

She turned to him. "I do? Where?"

He picked up a napkin. Hell, she'd already gone way past the boundaries of expectation. Why not see what he could get away with?

Mace tipped up her chin with his finger and kissed the frosting away. "There got it. Wait. No, there's a bit more over here." He pressed his lips to hers. Instead of protests, her mouth grew pliant under his, inviting him in for a longer kiss that served up desire. Cupping her cheek, he went in for more, deepening the kiss.

The apartment door opened, and they broke apart.

Rina breezed into the room. Her gaze landed on the table, and her mouth dropped open. "What happened to my cake?"

Zurie's cute wide-eyed guilty expression made him snicker.

She shot him a look, but her lips twitched, and then Zurie did he last thing he ever expected. She snorted a laugh.

Chapter Fourteen

Zurie strolled out of Buttons & Lace dress shop on Main Street with a smile on her face, carrying a boutique shopping bag. She'd had a productive Tuesday morning meeting with Charlotte about wedding and bridesmaid dresses, and she'd even found a dress even prettier than the blue-and-green paisley one she had on.

She'd talked to Tristan yesterday about letting Charlotte in on the secret wedding and the possibility of doing something special for Chloe to find the right dress. Tristan had agreed, wanting the best and more for Chloe.

As anticipated, Charlotte had been excited to help.

She could even handle altering the suits Tristan had picked out for himself, Mace and Chloe's brother, Thad, who was now an honorary groomsman. But Charlotte also had a few ideas for alternatives that she thought Tristan might want to consider.

After Chloe's father and Thad mentioned going on a fishing trip instead of attending Tristan's "surprise birthday party," Chloe had let her family in on the plans for the ceremony. Aside from Chloe's family and Charlotte, Tristan had also told the stable's office administrator, Gloria. As a longtime employee at Tillbridge, Gloria had also been a trusted confidante and friend of Zurie's parents and Uncle Jacob. She'd volunteered to lend a hand with anything that was needed before or the day of the ceremony.

Blake, one of the trusted trainers at the stable, who, on occasion, filled in as driver for the guest-house van, had been approached to assist with transportation the day of the wedding. He was organized, dependable and like a vault when it came to keeping matters confidential. On the day of the ceremony, with Blake corralling the guests and getting them to the ceremony, she could focus on synchronizing Tristan's and Chloe's separate arrivals at the south pasture.

Zurie neared the wine bar and shop. Contacting the sommelier at the shop to set up a time to sample wine and champagne for the reception dinner and toasts to the bride and groom was on her to-do list.

It was ten thirty. The business opened at eleven. Instead of calling, maybe she should wait around and make an appointment in person. After that, she'd stop by the florist. Then she had to get home and find out why the invitations for Tristan's "surprise birthday party" hadn't come in yet.

She crossed the street to the brick sidewalk surrounding the town square, where a sprinkling of pedestrians strolled through the grassy area with park benches and a fountain in the center of it. Walking to one of the benches nearest the fountain, Zurie took a seat and set her bag and purse beside her.

More cars and a tourist bus that hadn't been there when she'd gone into the dress shop over an hour ago filled parking spaces along the curb.

The casually dressed window shoppers were easily identifiable as tourists, while the locals gravitated like magnets in and out of the establishments lining the street. The rest remained engrossed in phone calls or sending text messages.

While she waited, maybe she could call Mace? He'd just been off that past weekend, so that meant, based on his two-two-three rotation schedule, he'd just come off work that morning and would go in again that night. So he was sleeping.

She missed him. They hadn't seen each other since getting in trouble with Rina over the cake. As Zurie thought about the moment, a smile crept up her mouth. Once they'd stopped laughing long enough to explain how good the cake was, Rina had tasted it herself. It was her first time making the coconut cake–lemon cheesecake combo, and even she had admitted she'd nailed it.

It had also inspired Rina to recall a nice memory. Whenever their mom had made lemon–poppy seed muffins, she'd have to hide them from Tristan and his father, because they shared a love of lemony desserts. But Tristan and Uncle Jacob were the perfect tag team, always managing to follow the clues of the lemon juicer on the drying rack, a bit of lemon rind in the sink or the discovery of lemon glaze tucked in the back of the refrigerator.

Like the loaded waffle fries, Rina's lemon coconut cheesecake creation appeared to be the perfect choice because of a personal connection to Tristan or Chloe.

"Aside from sitting there looking gorgeous, what do you do for a living?"

The familiar deep voice behind her, and what had to be one of the lamest pickup lines she'd ever heard, nurtured a smile. "Please tell me that line hasn't worked for you."

"You didn't like it? I've got a better one."

"I can't wait to hear it."

Mace rounded the bench and dropped down on the other side of her purse and bag. Based on his blue athletic shorts and gray shirt and his phone tucked in the pocket of a band wrapped around his arm, he was ready for a run.

He leaned. "Are you a parking ticket? 'Cause you've got *fine* written all over you."

"What? Seriously? That's the best you got?" She waved him off. But as *fine* as Mace looked in his running gear, that one may have worked for him.

He raised his brow in mock surprise. "Oh, you wanted my *best* line. Are you sure you can handle it? Because it just might make you want to crawl over here and kiss me."

She didn't need a pickup line for that. "I'm sure. Go for it." Zurie schooled her features to neutral.

"Okay. I tried to warn you." He leaned in and looked into her eyes. "Have you been covered in bees recently?"

"Bees? Uh, no, I hope not. Why?"

"Because you look sweeter than honey."

"Sweeter than…" Laughter bubbled out of her. "That one was even worse."

"How about, if you were a phaser on *Star Trek*, you'd be set to stun."

She actually was stunned by how bad that one was. "Stop. You're done. I can't take it."

"Wow. That really hurts."

"I'm just trying to save you from future embarrassment."

He sat back on the bench and grinned.

"Shouldn't you be in bed, resting up for work instead of practicing horrible pickup lines?"

"I should." His smile dimmed a little. "But I couldn't sleep."

"Oh no. Did something else happen at work?"

"No. Nothing like that. I'm good." He gave her a small smile and looked straight ahead for a moment and glanced back at her. "How did things go with Charlotte this morning?"

I'm good. That's what he'd said on Saturday before the tasting, and he'd given her that same small smile, but something had been wrong.

Pushing aside concern, Zurie went with the topic switch. "Really good. She's confident she can find the exact wedding dresses Chloe had planned to try on with the online dress service. And Charlotte is picking out a few other styles for Chloe to try on, just in case."

"You mentioned sneaking Chloe into the shop one night. Is that still the plan?"

"No. This morning Charlotte and I came up with a better one, pretty much guaranteeing Chloe's privacy *and* giving her a chance to have fun while trying on dresses."

"What?" He rested his arm between them on the back of the bench and turned partially toward her.

Zurie angled herself more toward him. "An all-girls' afternoon–slash–dress try-on party this Sunday. I sent Rina a text, and she's agreed to host it at her house. It will just be me, Rina, Philippa and Chloe, and Charlotte will stop by with dresses for us to try on."

"That definitely sounds like a better plan. It's kind of a bachelorette party."

"Maybe, or possibly closer to a bridal shower. What about Tristan? Are you planning something for him?"

"He doesn't want to do anything special. I'm sure if his two bull-riding buddies who are coming to his pseudo–birthday party were in on the wedding, things would be different. I'd like to give him some sort of send-off, though. The day of my brother's wedding, the guys gathered in his dressing room for a toast beforehand." Mace huffed a chuckle. "Efraín was so nervous, he needed that drink to settle down, but we can't do that at the pavilion. Tristan and I will just probably have drinks at the Montecito one night."

"Could you do it afterward? Maybe toward the end of the reception? Before he and Chloe leave for their honeymoon, they're changing clothes. Maybe you could quietly grab his two friends and have a toast in one of the guest rooms upstairs?"

Mace's eyes narrowed as if thinking it through. He nodded. "That could work."

"I'll arrange the room, then." Zurie grabbed her phone from her purse. "It's funny how the list of things to do keeps getting longer rather than shorter."

"I'm sorry. I didn't mean to add to it."

"No. It's not like that." She added reserving the room to her list along with checking in with Rina about how they were organizing the all-girls' afternoon party for Chloe. "What you're doing for Tristan is so important. He needs special moments just like Chloe does. I just…" The teeny voice of anxiety, the one she had to keep tamping down so it wouldn't swirl wedding details around in her mind, crept in. "I worry about dropping the ball on some small detail that will ruin their day. But I try not to think that way, because it just messes up my focus."

"Like now?"

She slipped her phone into her purse and met his gaze. Was he leaning on his general instincts about people or had she become that transparent to him? "A little."

He turned more toward her. "Do me a favor and close your eyes."

"Close my eyes? Why?"

"Just go with the flow a minute."

Was he going to try and sneak in a kiss? No. Mace understood which boundaries not to push against. He wouldn't kiss her in the middle of town square.

She obliged. "Now what?"

"Take a long meditative breath, then tell me three things you hear."

Zurie did as he asked and took a long breath in,

and as she slowly released it, she listened. "Cars, people talking…birds."

"Good. Now take another breath and tell me two things you smell." Hints of his woodsy scent wafted toward her. She'd keep that one to herself. "A bit of car exhaust…" The smell faded but was replaced with something more unpleasant. She murmured, "And someone didn't use the bags in the doggy station."

He chuckled. "You weren't the only one who noticed. It's being taken care of. Now take another breath and tell me one thing you feel."

"You mean like hungry or tired?"

"Not *how* you feel. What you sense that you're touching or is touching you."

"Oh, got it." She breathed. "The breeze on my face."

It blew strands of her hair forward on her bare shoulder. What felt like the barely there graze of Mace's fingertips gently smoothed it back. It was comforting and goose bump–raising all at the same time.

"Now open your eyes," Mace said. "Compared to a minute ago, how do you feel?"

"More relaxed." She looked to him. And even more aware of how badly she wanted to move her things out of the way, slide closer to Mace and have his arm lying on the back of the bench embrace her.

Zurie let her gaze slide away from his face to her

things on the bench. She reached for the boutique bag and her purse. "Thank you, that helped. The wine shop is open. I need to make an appointment with their sommelier to pick out wine." She rose from the bench. "What's the name of the vineyard you said I should check out? Maybe they carry their wine."

"They might. Or you could let me take you there for a long weekend." Mace rose to his feet. "It's not just a vineyard and winery. They have lodging on the property, a tasting room and a great farm-to-table menu. It's three hours away. Not too many people around here know about."

Was he suggesting what she thought he was? "You want us to spend a weekend together?"

"Yes." Mace stood in front of her. "Sitting here on the bench a minute ago, I couldn't hold your hand, and, right now, I can't kiss you goodbye because someone might see us."

Hand-holding and kisses—she wanted those things, too, but going away because of that was too risky. "I understand, but—"

"No, Zurie, I don't think you do understand. I want a chance to find out if you hog the bedsheets or if you wake up grumpy or happy in the morning. What types of songs do you sing in the shower? Do you like crispy bacon and eggs or do you prefer pancakes instead?" A man walked by them, and Mace looked down, releasing an audible breath, as he waited for them to be semialone again. When he looked back up, weariness and hints of frustration were in his eyes. "The two of us together for one long weekend, Zurie. That's all I'm asking."

Mace ran past city hall at a steady pace.

"I need time to think about it..."

That's what Zurie had told him about going away together.

Maybe he'd screwed things up between them by catching her off guard a few minutes ago and asking her that question, but he couldn't let the opportunity pass. When they'd agreed to start seeing each other, he'd tried to talk her into extending their time together until the wedding, but she'd said no. And even if he could have persuaded her to go beyond three weeks, their time would still be limited. Studying for the bar exam, giving his notice to the sheriff's department, packing up and putting his house on the market, plus finding a place in Reno, all in preparation for his big move—like Zurie, he needed to focus on the challenge ahead of him.

Efraín had called that morning to remind him of the deadline to apply to take the Nevada bar. Like he could forget. It stayed on his mind. He'd mentioned to Efraín that he was considering waiting to apply for the next exam date, a little over a year from now, and not moving to Nevada until then. That suggestion had floated as well as a rock on water. Efraín had even questioned his priorities. The bar exam,

Nevada, the family firm—they were still at the top of the list, weren't they?

Frustration fueled Mace as he veered onto the running trail just off the sidewalk shaded by trees, joining the few other joggers who were also getting a jump on the lunchtime exercise crowd.

The natural movement of his body and the breeze wicked sweat from his skin as he ran the winding path. With each stride forward, he let go of everything and cleared his mind. Three miles later the trail intersected with another one that surrounded the soccer field, basketball court and playground nestled in a grassy park. Once he completed running the oval twice, he was done. To cool off, he'd walk the short block home.

Just as he made the first curve and planned to pick up speed on the straightaway, a custom ringtone sounded in his wireless earbuds. His runner's high deflated as he slowed to a stop. It was his sister. Knowing Efraín, he'd called Andrea as soon as he'd hung up with him that morning. The tag-team effort had begun. Mace answered.

"Hey, Andrea, what's up?" Mace walked onto the grass.

"You're awake. I thought I was going to have to leave a message. You sound winded. Where are you?" The quick tapping of what sounded like high heels on tile indicated she was working. Her position as a defense attorney at a large firm in Naples, Florida, kept her busy.

"I'm out for a run. Hey, how's Justin? Did he get that promotion?"

"He's good, and yes, he got it."

"Tell him I said congrats. And Lucas. How old is he now? Seven months?"

"*¿Serio?* Are you honestly trying to distract me right now by asking me questions about your nephew? I'm calling because Efraín says you're having reservations about taking the bar exam."

"He did, huh?"

"What's the problem? Haven't you been studying?"

"No. I've been working."

"And your excuse is? You finished undergrad while you were in the marines. You went to law school part-time while working as a sheriff's deputy. You were able to study then. What's the difference now?"

Her blunt question unearthed an answer, improbable on the surface, but as he took a seat on the grass, it stood out as the truth. The drive that had gotten him through undergrad while serving in the military, and then later working as a deputy and commuting to law school in Baltimore, wasn't in him anymore when it came to becoming a lawyer.

But he couldn't admit that to Andrea. She wouldn't understand. *Driven* was her middle name.

He wiped sweat from his brow. "There isn't. I just want to make sure I'm ready."

"Don't think too long about that or you'll get stuck there. Trust me, I get it. You've had months without the weight of school on your shoulders. Getting back into studying for the bar plus working long hours can seem like climbing a mountain, but you can do it. Take some bar review courses. Get back into the habit of studying again. A couple of associates that just took it here, and passed, used a study program along with review courses to prepare for it. I'll find out which one it was and send you the information."

"Sure. I'll take a look." Whether he said yes or no, she would probably send it to him anyway.

"And remember, Efraín and I are here for whatever you need. And when it feels really difficult, just think of how proud *Mami* and especially *Papi* will be when you pass the exam and join the firm. Power through this. I know you can. I have to go. A client's waiting for me. Love you."

"Love you, too."

The call ended, but his thoughts continued. Mace closed his eyes.

"Think of how proud Mami and especially Papi will be..."

A vision of his parents, both in their early sixties, but with the energy of someone half their age, came to mind. When he'd finished law school, he'd walked across the stage for his diploma strictly for them.

The happiness reflected in their eyes and smiles had made the effort worthwhile. Afterward, he'd spent the weekend with them in DC, as well as with Andrea and her husband, Justin, and Efraín and his wife, Gia, who'd all flown in for the occasion, doing the tourist thing as a family.

He'd loved being with them those few days, but it had been a relief to return to Bolan, where no one outside of Tristan and his direct supervisor at the department knew that he'd officially completed his law school journey.

Taking time off after graduation, before studying for and then taking the bar exam, was only supposed to be a three-month pause. But three months had turned into four, then more months had suddenly slipped by him. The only thing that had kept it on his radar was his family questioning him about his plans...like now.

The reality he'd just unearthed, talking to Andrea, bore down on Mace. He hung his head. The certainty that had allowed him to know and not question if he'd take those final steps to becoming a lawyer and join his family's legacy...it wasn't there anymore. And he wasn't sure how to get it back.

Chapter Fifteen

Rina put a stack of small paper plates imprinted with blue flowers on her new white distressed coffee table in front of the cream couch.

The couch, along with matching side chairs and other furnishings, melded well in the sunlit, modern, farmhouse-themed living room decorated in hues of bright white, earthy green, beige and gray. Artfully placed nooks and corner shelves held green plants, wood-framed photos and candles. A multipatterned rug delineated the seating area on the polished floors.

The cozy space was perfect for the Sunday girls' afternoon surprise for Chloe. Everything looked great, including their coordinated outfits of dark leggings with a side pocket and blue T-shirts printed with "Bride Squad."

Zurie stood beside Rina unwrapping blue napkins. She slipped them into the caddy with the silverware. "Are you sure there's enough space for the food? Maybe we should set everything up on the dining room table."

"Having the food here will make it easier for us to enjoy. It's really not that much." Rina counted the items off on her fingers. "Mini melon and berry mozzarella skewers with yogurt dip, a veggie platter with ranch dressing, tortilla chips with guac, salsa and queso, mini chicken potpie turnovers, chocolate fondue with berries and pound cake, and if we run out of anything, I have chicken wings as a backup."

"I thought the theme was sip and dip? Drinks plus foods that you dip. What are we dipping potpie turnovers into?"

"Gravy."

"It's not gravy," Philippa called out from the adjoining kitchen, separated by a breakfast bar passthrough.

"Right, I forgot." Rina mocked a snooty voice. "It's a velvety chicken velouté, otherwise known as *fancy* gravy."

Philippa paused in stirring the contents of a pan on the stove. She looked back over her shoulder and stared at Rina. "A velouté is one of the five mother sauces in classic cuisine. It is not gravy."

Rina laughed and gave Zurie a conspiratorial wink. "Whatever you say, Chef Hoity-Toity."

Philippa pointed a spoon at Rina. "Where's the queso dip you wanted me to heat up? Did you use the fresh chiles like I told you to?"

A new debate started between the two over the right way to make queso dip.

Zurie internally shook her head as she left Rina and went into the kitchen.

Rina and Philippa had been friends for so long, they bickered like an old married couple. She tuned them out, letting the conversation slide over the surface of her thoughts as she unwrapped heavy plastic tumblers with "Drink Up" printed on the side and stacked them on the beige marble pass-through counter. She had her own pressing problem. What was her answer to Mace about going away for a long weekend?

For the past five days, she'd gone back and forth between yes and no in her mind. And Mace hadn't pressed her for an answer. Being understanding and not pressuring each other to talk about things was just one of the areas where they got along. What if going to the vineyard together actually ruined their chemistry or they just got bored being around each other for three days straight? Why risk ruining what was working for them? No. It was just working for her and not so much for Mace.

The side door of the house opened. Footsteps echoed from a back hall leading from the garage.

Scott walked into the kitchen. The blond stuntman shouldered a bag of ice and carried two small boxes of canned flavored sparkling water under his other arm. A small wet spot spread from the bag down to the front of his short-sleeved tan pullover.

Zurie hurried over to him. "I'll take those." She slipped the boxes from his hands and put them on the kitchen counter.

"Thanks." His hazel-green eyes reflected his easygoing smile. As he passed by Philippa whisking chicken stock into the pan, he peeked at what was inside. "Smells good. What are you putting gravy on?"

Rina cackled from the living room as she plumped the pillows on the couch.

Philippa gave him an indulgent smile. "It's not gravy. And I hope you're not too fond of your girlfriend, because I might have to strangle her before the day's over."

He grinned. "I do like her. So if you could refrain from doing that, I'd appreciate it."

Philippa sighed. "Well, since you asked nicely…"

As he finished tucking the ice in the bottom freezer drawer, Rina strolled in through the archway nearest to him.

He shut the door and looped an arm around Rina's waist. "The other bag of ice is in the garage freezer.

They didn't have any more lime-flavored sparkling water, so I got a grapefruit one instead."

"Perfect." Rina rose to her toes and smacked her lips to his.

They were so cute even Philippa smiled as she glanced over at them.

"Do we have an ETA on Tristan and Chloe?" Zurie asked.

It was Chloe's day off, and Rina had invited them to lunch as a way to get Chloe to the house.

"Tristan called me before they left," Scott replied. "If traffic doesn't hold them up, they should be here in about twenty minutes." He unwound his arm from Rina and dropped a kiss on her nose. "I need to change my shirt. I'm riding with Tristan back to his house." Scott left the kitchen the way Rina had come in and went upstairs.

Zurie worked with Rina and Philippa to finish setting up.

Just as Zurie and Philippa arranged the last of the food on the coffee table around the centerpiece of lavender, white and gold "Bride 2 Be" balloons, the doorbell rang.

Rina set a pitcher of spiked lemonade on the pass-through counter next to the cups and the cans of sparkling water. "Let Scott get the door." She hurried into the living room to join them by the coffee table.

Scott opened the front door that was around the corner from the living room.

Exchanged greetings echoed from the entryway along with Chloe's question. "Where's Rina?"

"She's in the living room," Scott said.

"What are we going to say when she walks in?" Rina whispered.

Philippa feigned a baffled expression. "Maybe something earth-shattering like, gee, I don't know... surprise?"

Rina bumped Philippa's arm. "Why are you my friend again?"

Happiness that their plan for Chloe had come together along with Philippa and Rina's antics pulled a laugh out of Zurie. "Philippa's actually right."

"Hey, what happened to family loyalty?" Rina interjected with a smile.

Moments later, Chloe walked around the corner. "Hey, Ri—"

The three of them shouted, throwing their hands in the air, "Surprise!"

Chapter Sixteen

Chloe's stunned expression quickly morphed into a huge smile. "Oh my gosh! What is this?"

"It's a Chloe celebration," Rina replied as she, Philippa and Zurie swarmed her with hugs.

Chloe glanced at Tristan. Lately, they seemed so much in sync, they even dressed almost alike. Her olive T-shirt and ripped jeans paired well with his khaki button-down and jeans.

"Now it makes sense." She pointed at him. "You didn't forget to bring the salad I made. You left it behind on purpose, didn't you?"

He smiled. "You can apologize for fussing at me about it later." He kissed her cheek then glanced at Scott. "We should head out. Mace is meeting us."

Hearing Mace's name snagged Zurie's attention. *He's working tonight, isn't he?* She pulled up short from calculating how many hours of sleep he may have gotten. Worrying about him. She couldn't get in the habit of doing that.

Tristan and Chloe shared a brief kiss while Scott and Rina shared a double lip smack and *I love you*s.

Scott gave a general wave as he and Tristan filed out of the living room. "Have fun, ladies."

Rina grabbed a blue gift bag with white tissue paper inside it from the couch. She held it out to Chloe. "We got you a little something to put you in the mood."

Chloe laughed. "I'm already there." She set her purse on the side chair and perched on the end of the seat. Digging through the tissue paper, she pulled out a gold "Bride 2 Be" headband and veil, a white T-shirt printed with the same wording, and dark leggings. "How cute. I'll go put them on." She hurried to the bathroom.

Philippa sat in a side chair. "So Scott and Tristan are hanging out with each other now?"

"Occasionally." Rina poured lemonade into cups. "Scott helped Tristan with a plumbing issue at his house, so they got a chance to know each other a little better, and we've had a couple of Friday date nights with them."

Zurie accepted a full cup from Rina. Date nights. If she and Mace were really a couple, they'd be part of the group. She hid disappointment behind a long sip of lemonade.

"I wonder how Tristan getting married will affect his friendship with Mace," Philippa said.

"I don't know." Rina set the pitcher back on the counter. "Maybe he'll start coming on date nights with us and bring whomever he's dating now."

"Now that's a mystery." Philippa chuckled. "Unless you believe the crazy rumor about him and Zurie."

Panic leaped in Zurie, and she coughed down the next sip of her drink. "What rumor?"

Philippa flicked her hand as if waving off an annoying bug. "Just silly gossip someone tried to float around the kitchen." She laughed. "You and Mace. Don't worry, no one believed it."

But why not her and Mace? Was it that far-fetched? The objection hovered on the tip of Zurie's tongue. Why were people so into who was dating who, anyway?

The answer was so obvious, she didn't bother saying it aloud. Bolan was growing as a town, but there were those who still had enough time and boredom on their hands to stick their nose into everyone's business and gossip about it. And that's why she shouldn't go away with Mace for the weekend. If they were both out of town at the same time, people might start putting two and two together and come up with the right answer about her and Mace.

Chloe rejoined them, and the party officially kicked off. She settled back in the middle of the couch with a plate of food and munched a mini pot-pie turnover drizzled with Philippa's sauce. "Wow. This is good. The chicken velouté is just right for these, not too heavy."

"Thank you for noticing." Philippa released an exaggerated breath of relief.

"I have to confess," Chloe added, dusting her fingers over her plate, "the cooking show *Dinner with Dominic* is the only reason I know what a chicken velouté is. Last time I watched his show, he was making mini chicken potpies with this sauce."

Rina leaned over from the end of the couch, grabbed a kebab and spooned yogurt dip on top of it. "Ooh, *Dinner with Dominic*. I love that show. He's delicious, and his recipes aren't bad, either."

Chloe laughed. "If you think he looks good on-screen, you should see him in person. I went to a dinner party last year where he was the chef. If I wasn't a happily engaged woman…"

"I'll have to look up his show." Zurie, sitting on the other side of Chloe, dipped a baby carrot into ranch dressing on her plate. Cooking was something Mace had mentioned might help her relax.

Philippa rose from the chair, scooped up guacamole dip with a chip and dumped it on her plate. "Dominic Crawford is an okay chef who got lucky. And I've tasted his potpie recipe. Mine is better."

Rina studied Philippa. "That's right. You've met him."

"Yes. We've met."

From the look of distaste on Philippa's face, that meeting hadn't been a good one.

Just as Rina looked ready to ask Philippa a question, the doorbell rang. "I'll get it." As she got up, she glanced at Zurie. Excitement was in Rina's eyes.

Zurie felt the same sense of anticipation.

"Is someone else coming?" Philippa asked, playing into the moment.

"Actually, it's more of a special delivery for Chloe."

Chloe paused in the midst of nibbling a kebab. "It is?"

Rina came around the corner with Charlotte.

The older woman with a silvery-blond bob, dressed in skinny jeans and a loose black long-sleeved pullover, had a timeless glow. Smiling, she walked over to Chloe. "Hello. We haven't met. I'm Charlotte Henry."

Chloe shook her hand. "Hello. We haven't met, but your name sounds familiar."

Zurie answered, "She owns Buttons & Lace, the dress shop in Bolan. She's here to help you find the right wedding dress."

Charlotte gently laid her other hand over Chloe's that was still in her hers. "Zurie showed me the dresses you were going to choose online. I found them and others that are similar, plus some other styles I think you might like. You can try them on and decide."

"Really? Like, now?" An expression of glee came over Chloe's face.

Charlotte nodded and smiled. "Right now. They're all in my van outside."

A short time later, Rina's empty downstairs guest room was transformed into a fitting room with floor-length mirrors, a rack of wedding gowns and the necessary accompaniments.

Charlotte kept things in order, using her experience and eye for detail to help quickly eliminate the styles that weren't right for Chloe.

Watching Chloe try on and model the gowns made from satin, chiffon and silk with intricate beading and lace made them all sigh and tear up a time or two.

And of course, Rina indulged her obsession with capturing memories by taking tons of pictures with her phone.

A few dresses in, Chloe tried on one of Charlotte's original creations. Zurie, along with Chloe, Rina, Philippa, was stunned into silence. This was *the* dress.

Charlotte simply nodded with a knowing smile.

Bridesmaid dresses were taken off the rack for Zurie and Rina to try on.

Chloe insisted they choose ones they would wear again.

The style they selected—a chiffon dress, with tied shoulder straps, a high-low hemline and a blue-and-peach floral pattern—was elegant enough to wear to another formal event after the wedding. Or it could be shortened so they could dress it up or dress it down for a more casual occasion in the future.

A little over two hours later, they gathered in the entryway of Rina's home to tell Charlotte goodbye.

Charlotte looked at Chloe, Rina and Zurie. "Everything worked out in our favor today. I don't have to do any major alterations on the dresses. So it's settled. We'll meet again in two weeks at Rina's old apartment for another fitting."

They all nodded. With Rina in the process of moving, it was the easiest place to meet and carry the dresses in boxes or suitcases without bringing too much attention to themselves.

Charlotte continued, "And don't forget to bring your shoes and what you plan to wear underneath the dresses and settle on how you plan to style your hair on the big day."

Zurie made a mental note. Her hair. Another important detail. Going to her usual local stylist was out of the question. The woman asked too many questions. She'd have to figure out what to do with her hair on her own.

Zurie and Rina thanked Charlotte and hugged her goodbye.

Chloe walked out with Charlotte, carting a rolling bag of supplies out to the van. Once the bag was loaded inside, the two women hugged each other like newfound friends and continued talking.

As Rina and Zurie looked on from the doorway, Rina slipped her arm through Zurie's and gave her a nudge. "You've given Chloe some great memories today."

Zurie nudged Rina back. "We've given her some great memories."

"I was just following your lead on a great plan." Rina slipped her hand away, partially closed the front door and headed for the kitchen to help Philippa clean up. "Take the credit. You done good."

Taking credit wasn't important. Chloe having happy, memorable moments leading up to the wedding was. And, honestly, that afternoon, trying on dresses, might not have happened without Mace's input.

Giving in to the sudden urge, Zurie slipped down the hallway to the unfurnished, beige-carpeted guest room. Through the window facing the front yard, she could see Charlotte and Chloe still talking in the driveway.

She slipped her phone from the side pocket of her leggings and called Mace's number.

He picked up on the fourth ring. "Hello. Hold on a minute."

Tristan's voice filtered in from the background.

Shoot. That's right. Mace couldn't just take her call. He had to go someplace private.

Moments later, he came back on the line. "Okay. I can talk now."

What she'd planned to tell him suddenly seemed small compared to the effort he'd just made to take her call. "I just wanted to tell you everything went well here."

"I'm glad to hear it."

"What you said about your sister having a bonding moment trying on dresses, that helped. A lot. Thank you."

"You're welcome. I'm here to help."

He really had helped her a lot with the wedding planning, and, so far, he'd only asked her for one thing.

Zurie tamped down the part of her that caused her to overanalyze things. "I don't sing in the shower. I like my bacon crispy but not burned. I'm not crazy about eggs, but I'll eat them. And I like waffles topped with warm syrup and butter. And as far as the rest of what you wanted to know, you'll have to find out yourself…when we're at the vineyard."

Chapter Seventeen

Zurie slipped a neatly folded pink T-shirt into the blue paisley travel bag sitting on her bed. Now she was ready. Hopefully her long weekend with Mace would pass as slowly as the time had since she'd agreed to go with him. Four days of continued anticipation had almost driven her nuts. But thankfully, her caffeine withdrawal headaches had subsided and she could fully enjoy the wine-tasting experience that weekend.

Her phone rang on the nightstand, and she glanced at the screen. *Mace.* He'd texted her that morning, confirming they were leaving at 10:00 a.m. for the Sommersby Farm Vineyard and Winery. That was in a couple of hours. Why was he calling her now?

She answered, "Hi."

"I'm at the store buying snacks for the road. Do you want anything in particular?"

"It's only a three-hour car ride. I'll be fine."

"Okay. Just don't be offended if I won't share my gummi bears with you."

"Gummi bears, huh?" The thought of him hoarding the bag of candy made her smile. She could probably convince him to give her a few. "Regular or the sour ones?"

"I was thinking of getting one each."

"Get two of the sour ones."

He chuckled. "I knew you'd see things my way about snacks. I think I saw some on the other aisle. There's a place on the way that makes wood-fired pizza. I thought we could stop there for lunch or would you rather bring something?"

"The pizza place sounds good. Can you grab drinks?" She named the brand she wanted.

"On it. And I've got water for us, too. So I think that's it. We're ready."

"Yep." Flutters of excitement loosed inside her.

"See you at the house."

Just as she went to slip the phone into the side pocket of her bag, a call rang in. It was probably Mace again.

She answered without checking the screen. "If you're calling to ask if I'll share my sour gummis, I will if it's an even trade."

"Uh, no, that wasn't why I was calling."

Crap. Not Mace. It was Tristan. A small laugh escaped Zurie. "I thought you were someone else."

"So I guess you're busy?"

The dejected tone in his voice snared her attention. "No. I'm free. What's going on."

"I have a problem." His long exhale filled the silence. "I lost Chloe's engagement ring."

Zurie's heart dropped. "What? When?"

"Sometime yesterday afternoon. Chloe accidentally brought the ring with her to the set, and I picked it up from her. I stuck it in my pocket, went to the office and got busy. I forgot I had it. Chloe got home late last night and didn't ask me about it until this morning on her way out the door. I couldn't tell her I didn't know where her ring was. I'm retracing my steps starting with here at the house."

"Do you want me to come help you look for it?"

"Actually, I was hoping you could take care of something else for me. Anna Ashford is supposed to interview me this morning. She'll be at the office in about twenty minutes, and Gloria's off today."

"Don't worry. I'll handle the interview. Is there anything else I can do? Do I need to check on the staff?"

"The stable is fine. Blake is in charge. Could you look around my desk for the ring? Damn. I can't believe I messed up this bad. If I can't find it, I'll give Chloe two engagement rings if she'll forgive me."

He sounded miserable, and Zurie's heart went out to him. "Don't give up. I'll take care of Anna and look around the office."

"Thanks."

After she hung up, Zurie's gaze landed on her travel bag. If Tristan didn't find the ring, she couldn't just leave town and abandon him. The reason he was so busy was because he was doing her job as well as his own. She had to pitch in and help find the ring.

Zurie grabbed her ID case and keys from her purse, which was inside the travel bag, slipped her feet into the wedge-heeled sandals by the bed and rushed out of the suite. Her jeans and black T-shirt would just have to be good enough for the interview. Hopefully Anna wouldn't take pictures of her.

A short time later, at the entrance to the paved parking lot behind the large horse stable, the guard recognized Zurie and waved her inside.

Having increased security on the property because of the film was still a bit strange.

After parking in a vacant space in the half-empty parking lot, she stuck the ID case in the middle console, grabbed her phone and got out.

A dappled gray horse and two bays were on the closest end of the adjoining paddock on the right of the stable. On the far end, a groom raked and cleaned the area. The pungent smells of horses, hay and grass were in the air.

Anna's blue four-door wasn't in the parking lot yet.

Good. Zurie used the key fob to lock her car and hurried from the parking lot to the paved narrow path leading to the back side door of the stable. She had at least a good five to ten minutes to look around for the ring in the office before the interview.

She unlocked the door and walked into the light-tiled hallway. To the right, up ahead, black- and silver-framed photos hung on the walls. Voices and the brays and whinnies of horses echoed from the interior of the modern stable farther down.

A few of the horses were looking out the top part of the horizontally split navy Dutch-style doors, watching the comings and goings of people and other horses being led up and down the wide rubber-floored aisle.

Trainers were headed for the outdoor exercise ring while locals who boarded their horses at the stable were saddling up for rides.

At this time of the day, Blake would double-check that the stalls were in order along with the tack room. He'd also make sure they were ready to conduct afternoon horse-riding lessons, tours and trail rides for guests staying at the guesthouse.

Zurie unlocked the door in front of her and walked into the beige-tiled white-walled space Tristan shared with Gloria, the stable's office administrator.

Smart windows along the wall on the left had darkened to a smoky blue gray, keeping the office cool and letting in light. Zurie flipped the switch on the wall, fully illuminating the office.

She walked past Gloria's wood-topped metal desk on the right. All of Gloria's papers and files had been stored, and only her wide-screen desktop computer and a caddy with pens and desk supplies sat on top of it.

Tristan's wood desk was the opposite, with several stacks of files, papers, a tube of horse liniment and sample packages of horse treats that a company rep had probably dropped off.

Zurie looked around and underneath the desk first. Nothing but a couple of stray paper clips.

She set her phone near the desktop computer and searched the desk. As she shifted things around, a stack of papers and packages of treats slid to the floor. What looked like a mess to her was Tristan's organized chaos. She didn't want to disturb things too much, or maybe he wouldn't care if she did since finding the ring was a priority. Either way, she was going to have to wait until after the interview to really move things around and look.

Her phone buzzed, and she checked the screen before picking it up. It was Mace.

"Hi." She picked up the fallen papers and bags of treats.

"Hey. I was wondering. I got all my errands done. How do you feel about leaving a little earlier?"

A knock sounded on the open door.

Anna stood in the hallway.

"Hold on," Zurie said to Mace. Smiling politely, she waved the late-thirties blonde inside the office. "Hi, Anna. Come in and have a seat." Zurie gestured to the chairs in front of Tristan's desk.

"Hello." Anna walked in. Her navy blazer with pushed-up sleeves over a T-shirt and cream beige chinos looked casual but screamed expensive. And so were her artfully worn brown ankle boots.

A tinge of admiration for Anna's outfit intertwined with Zurie feeling underdressed in comparison. "We may have to alter our plans. Something has come up."

"Alter as in we can't go?"

Anna took her time, setting her large tan bag in the chair. She tucked a strand of her long hair behind her ear and cocked her head as if listening to the phone conversation.

"Hold on." Zurie held the phone to her chest, muffling her conversation with Anna. She pointed to the beverage station in the corner. "There should be water and juices in the fridge. Feel free to grab something. I'll be done in minute."

"Is Tristan joining us?"

"No, I'm afraid not. Something unexpected that he really had to attend to came up. I'm taking his place for the interview."

"But I was expecting to talk to him. Why didn't

Gloria call me about the change before I drove all the way out here?"

"It's been a little hectic today, and we didn't want to hold you up from publishing your article by re-scheduling. Your questions are about the new indoor arena, right? Or did the mayor misunderstand you?"

Anna didn't even try to disguise her annoyance. "Well, yes."

"Then we're good." Zurie pasted on a slight smile. "Just let me finish up this call, and I can answer all your questions."

She went out of the office, shut the door behind her and went out the side door. "Sorry about that. I'm back."

"I couldn't hear everything, but your tone during that conversation didn't sound vacation friendly. Are you at work? What happened?"

"That was just Anna Ashford." Zurie let go of ir-ritation. "I'm at the stable in Tristan's office, but I'm not working. Just subbing in on an interview she was supposed to do with Tristan. He couldn't do it be-cause he lost Chloe's engagement ring."

She filled him on the details.

"Damn, that's rough," Mace said. "He spent a lot of time searching for the right ring. I know he's probably beating himself up about. Yeah, we can't leave him like this. I'll head out there now and give him a hand."

Gratefulness went through her. Of course Mace

would understand. "Once Anna leaves. I'll take the office apart. If I don't find it, I'll meet you there."

"Hopefully you won't have to. Aside from the office, you may want to retrace his steps from the stable to the parking lot. It's a long shot, but sometimes things turn up in the places you don't expect to find them."

"I will.

"And good luck with Anna. I heard she's persistent. My bosses at the department avoid talking to her."

"I can handle her. And thank you."

"For what, wishing you luck or buying you gummi bears?"

"For being you." She didn't have to see him to imagine his smile.

"You can thank me later. After we find Chloe's ring. 'Bye."

She ended the call. Just as Zurie reached to open the door, she paused, taking Mace's advice to glance around the small concrete landing and the grass immediately surrounding it. Nothing shiny stood out. If only she had time to check the path. And she needed to find out where Tristan had parked his SUV yesterday. But she needed to deal with Anna first.

Zurie walked inside the office and sat behind Tristan's desk.

"Do you mind if I record?" Anna held up her phone. "That way I don't have to write so much."

"Sure. So, let's talk about the new indoor arena."

Anna gave a relaxed smile, crossed her legs and sat back in the chair with a pen and notepad. "Yes, let's talk about that."

Over the next forty minutes, Anna surprisingly asked questions strictly about the stable and the plans for new arena.

Maybe it was better that Tristan hadn't done the interview. Anna was staying on task.

Anna flipped through her notes. "I think that's it except for one more question. The love triangle that Tristan is in the midst of with Chloe Daniels and Nash Moreland—any updates about that?"

So now the fishing expedition. Too bad Anna was about to come up short. "It's a silly rumor that we're not going comment on. If you have more questions about the arena or Tillbridge Horse Stable and Guesthouse, I'm happy to answer them."

The side door opened.

As Tristan and Mace peeked into the office, Tristan's grim expression and Mace's empathetic one told her all she needed to know.

Anna glanced over her shoulder. "Tristan, I'm glad you could make it."

He pointed down the hall. "Actually, something urgent has come up that I need to look into. I'm sure Zurie's filled you in on everything you need to know."

"Oh, not everything." Anna put her pen and notepad into her tote sitting on the chair beside her. She pulled out Chloe's engagement ring and held it up. "I found this under your desk." With a self-satisfied smile, she glanced at Zurie, then Tristan. "Care to comment?"

Chapter Eighteen

Anna had had the ring the entire time of the interview? Zurie sprang from her seat at the same time Tristan and Mace walked into the office.

As she rounded the desk, she caught a glimpse of Tristan's face and his forthcoming confession. It wasn't fair for him and Chloe to have their happiness ruined. She couldn't let him do it.

He went to speak, but Zurie interrupted him. "It's mine."

Anna blinked back at her. "Yours?" She laughed. "We all know that's not true."

The slight slipped through, hitting a place inside Zurie that made her pause in reaching for the ring.

"It is true." Mace came forward, emanating confidence. Anna's laughing smile disappeared as he slipped the ring from her grasp and went to Zurie. "It just happened a few days ago. We're planning to make the announcement after the filming of the movie is over and the stable is back to normal."

As he slid the diamond on Zurie's ring finger, the weight of the ring and a weird excitement hit her at the same time.

Once the diamond was in place, he held Zurie's hand and her gaze. "We need to get this resized, *mi amor*. It keeps slipping off your finger. We're really lucky Anna found it."

Her heart sped up as he kissed the back of her hand. "Yes, we're very lucky. But that's why I brought it with me. I thought we could take it to the jeweler's today."

"Oh, no." Anna shook her head and pointed at Mace. "You were dating two other women up until at least a month ago."

"Circumstances change," Mace said. "If you don't believe me, I'll show you my credit card receipt for the ring—if it'll stop you from selling whatever false story you planned on cooking up about Tristan and Chloe."

Anna's eyes widened slightly before her expression turned smug. "If I were selling a story somewhere, that's not a crime."

The crime was Anna believing it was her job to

turn Tristan and Chloe's personal life into entertainment when that's not what they wanted. Zurie tamped down anger. "No, it's not, but I'm not sure the mayor would be on board with his sister-in-law spreading false stories about a member of his community."

"Yeah, that probably wouldn't go down well," Tristan added, taking a seat behind his desk. "Especially if he's looking to get reelected."

Anna looked from Tristan to Zurie to Mace as if calculating the value of the information she had. And what she didn't.

She rose from the chair. "It's a busy day. I have to get to my next appointment." Her smile didn't veil the condescension in her eyes. "I'll be in touch to see when it's a good time for the photographer to stop by and take pictures of the new arena. I can't wait to share about it." Her gaze landed on Zurie and Mace. "Or your impending nuptials once you decide to make the announcement." She walked toward the door.

"Anna," Tristan called out, and she turned around. "Your phone." He pointed to where it lay on his desk.

"Oh. I completely forgot." Her cheeks grew pink as she went back and snatched it from the desk. Turning up her nose, she stomped out.

The outer door shut, and as Zurie thought about the bullet they'd just dodged, she leaned on Mace.

"Good thing you caught that. Her phone was on record. She probably left it behind on purpose."

"I can't believe her." Tristan lifted his hand and dropped it on his desk. "If I didn't know any better, I'd swear Anna was related to my dad's ex-wife. Do you think she bought it?"

"Doesn't matter if she did or not," Mace replied. "The key is she knows we're on to her."

"Thanks for jumping in like that—both of you." Tristan gave a nod their directions.

"That's what we're here for. Nothing's going to stop your wedding." Zurie released Mace's hand. She went around the desk to Tristan, slipped off the platinum band with the sparkling diamond and handed it to him.

He stared down at the ring. "Maybe we should call the ceremony and reception off. Planning a secret wedding is one thing, but forcing you to keep pretending you're engaged like you did in front of Anna, that's too much to ask."

The sadness on Tristan's face contrasted sharply with her memory of his happiness at the pavilion as he'd envisioned getting married there. And of Chloe's glee at the party, trying on dresses.

Zurie looked to Mace. Staying together longer and pretending to be engaged until the wedding wasn't that much of a hardship…was it?

As if he'd read her mind, Mace nodded.

Zurie walked over to him, and as he held out his

hand, she took it. The firmness of his grasp conveyed what she felt. They were in this together—saving the wedding, making sure Chloe and Tristan had their day…and revealing their own secret.

She faced Tristan. "No, it's not too much to ask."

Tristan opened his mouth as if to object, but he remained speechless as she and Mace intertwined their fingers. His brow raised. "You two are together? Since when?"

Mace answered, "Since we started planning your wedding."

She jumped in, answering the questions reflected in Tristan's face. "No one knows. I've always kept my personal life private, and Mace agreed to honor that. It also didn't make sense to tell anyone because we're only together for a few weeks."

"Okay. I wasn't expecting this." Tristan sat back in the chair. "I guess what matters is that you're both good with what's happening. You know what you're doing." He looked at both of them, but his gaze stayed on Mace a beat longer.

Mace looked back at him. "Everything's under control."

Zurie picked up the subtle undercurrent in the room. This wasn't about her. The two needed to talk as friends.

She spoke to Tristan. "Yes, everything *is* under control. We all just have to maintain what we're doing until the wedding, and that's only three weeks away. Don't worry about us. Just put that ring in a safe place." Zurie looked to Mace. "I'll meet you at the guesthouse?"

"Yes, I'll see you there."

Mace kissed Zurie on the cheek. Before he let go of her, he gave her hand a squeeze to let her know that things were still good.

Zurie gave him a soft smile.

Her moving out of her comfort zone to help Tristan and Chloe wasn't surprising, but after Zurie acted on impulse, she tended to let things get into her head. Luckily, they had whole long weekend to sort through her worries together.

The door clicked shut behind her.

Mace sat in the chair in front of Tristan's desk. "I know you're not worried about how I'll treat Zurie. So what else is on your mind?"

"You're right, I'm not worried, because you know if you did hurt her, I would find you and feed you to the wolves. What I am concerned about is what you and Zurie are doing. It's really easy for feelings to get involved."

Tristan didn't have to finish saying what he was thinking. Mace understood. When feelings got too involved, people got hurt. "If it starts to look like it's becoming a problem for Zurie, I'll make sure we work it out."

"Zurie?" Tristan huffed a chuckle. "I'm not worried about her. I'm worried about you."

"Me? Why?"

"A couple of months ago, when I was twisted up over my relationship with Chloe, you were sitting in that very chair when you told me that if you could be with the woman you wanted to be with, you would."

"And you think I meant Zurie?"

Tristan gave up a shrug. "You tell me."

"I think you're reading way more into what I said. Back then, it was obvious you wanted to be with Chloe, but you were too afraid to admit it at first. I was just trying to wake you up to the fact you didn't want to lose her over some boneheaded decision you made."

"You're right. And I'm glad you were there to help me see it. I'm trying to do the same for you." Tristan leaned forward on the desk. "A short-term thing plus pretending to be engaged—things could get complicated…for all of us." He looked Mace in the eye. "Don't make my wedding present having to choose between family or my best friend."

Mace parked just past the front of the guesthouse. Zurie walked out the front door and down the porch steps, sunglasses on the top of her head, wheeling a paisley-blue travel duffel behind her.

He'd sent her a text before he'd left the stable a few minutes ago, after assuring Tristan his points were noted but not a concern. He wasn't going to put Tristan in the position of having to choose between keeping his friendship with him or loyalty to family.

He got out, and by the time he'd walked to the front passenger side, she'd reached him.

"Everything okay?" she asked. The smile she gave him rated less than passable on the happiness scale.

"Tristan and I are good." Mace slipped the handle of the bag from her hand, collapsed it and put her bag on the back seat with his duffel and the cooler he'd packed with their drinks. "But you're not." He shut the door.

"No, I'm fine."

Mace took her by the waist and gently pulled her into a loose embrace. "You don't have to pretend with me. What's going on in your head right now?"

Bracing for her to pull away because they were in public, she surprised him by laying her hands near his shoulders. The sadness in her eyes caused a strange tug in his chest. "I almost ruined Tristan and Chloe's wedding day. I never should have left Anna alone in Tristan's office."

"No. You don't get to do that. You don't get to take responsibility or assign blame for someone else's screwed-up actions. What Anna did was wrong. What you *do* get to do is remember how you, Tristan and I solved the problem."

"Did we? Or did we just add on another one? We're fake engaged. You know Anna isn't going to keep it a secret. She'll tell everyone out of spite because we embarrassed her. By the time we get back, it will be all over town."

"And I like it, because now we don't have to pretend in public that we don't like each other."

"But—"

Mace captured her mouth, and her lips curved into a smile under his. She leaned away slightly. "You're just going to keep doing that if I keep talking about this, aren't you?"

"Yep. If we have to talk about it, I'd rather do it at the vineyard, drinking wine, eating great food and having a good time watching a movie under the stars."

"They have an outdoor theater?" Her eyes lit up.

"Sort of." He released her and opened the front passenger side door. "But you won't get to find out about that, along with all other great things they have, if we don't leave."

Before she stepped up into the truck, she kissed his cheek.

"What was that for?"

"Just trying out the whole PDA thing."

Glad to see humor in her eyes, he was anxious to get underway. "You'll get lots of practice this weekend."

Chapter Nineteen

A little over three hours after the start of their road trip, Zurie opened the front passenger side window, eager to get a closer look at the view.

Mace looked over at her and smiled. "What do you think?"

"It's beautiful."

Sommersby's simple website hadn't quite captured what unfolded in front of her. Rows of grapevines nestled in a valley of lush green trees under a blue sky with dashes and puffs of soft white clouds.

The breeze drifting over her skin held hints of coolness and warmth. Instead of the earthy smell of horses, it was filled with the scents of rich soil, lush plants, green grass and hints of a sweetness from flowering bushes lining the road.

From what she'd briefly read about the place online, it was a family-owned operation, like Tillbridge, and had been around for generations. It had started out as a farm with livestock, and over the past ten years had transitioned into a vineyard and winery. They also maintained a small orchard and grew a few seasonal vegetables.

They entertained only a few overnight guests at a time in their four-room lodging house, which was open just Friday through Sunday to the general public.

It was the perfect place to unwind and unplug. She and Mace had agreed to go all in on the unplug part of things. Neither one of them had packed a computer tablet or a laptop, and they were taking a break from their phones. They would check for voice mails and texts in the morning. Outside of that, no calls. No social media checks. If there was an emergency back at Tillbridge or something that concerned Mace, Tristan knew where to reach them and so did Kayla.

Mace slowed down as the road curved. Back on the straightaway, they drove past a large red building with white trim designed like a barn with a double-pitched metal roof complete with a weather vane at its peak. A wraparound porch decorated with floral arrangements in metal pitchers on top of wine barrels awaited occupants to sit and take in the view of an open lawn from Adirondack and wood rocking chairs.

"What building is that?" she asked.

"The winery and tasting room."

At the end of the road, a sign pointed right to Summer House Lodge.

He turned left.

She pointed back at the sign. "Lodging is that way."

"I know."

A short distance later, he turned off the road. Farther back in the trees sat a small, modest white house with a red door and trim.

Mace parked in front of it. "This is where we're staying. Come on. Let's check it out. Leave the bags. I'll come back for them."

"Don't we need a key?"

"They use remote check-in." At the door, Mace keyed the code into the pad above the lock.

As soon as the door opened, she was drawn into the white-walled space with dark wood ceiling beams and trim. A king-size bed with built-in wood headboard sat to the right. On the left, a high black marble counter sectioned off the corner kitchen. Next to it was small wood kitchen table with four chairs. On the other end, a brick fireplace with an ottoman and russet side chairs formed a cozy seating area.

He shut the door behind them. "What do you think?"

Pleasant surprise and excitement made her smile. "It's wonderful. I didn't see anything about this on Sommersby's website."

"They don't really advertise it, but they actually have two cottages on the property."

Mace opened the back door, and they walked out onto a wood deck surrounded by a low railing.

Zurie couldn't stop smiling as she took in the vineyard and the green hills beyond.

He pointed. "In front of us is one of the sections where the grapes are grown. To the left, where the rows look similar, that's actually part of the apple orchard. The trees are grown in the espalier method."

"What's that?"

"The trees are trained to grow on a frame instead of freestanding. They also grow olives and make their own olive oil. I don't think we can see that from here. You have to get their *insalata caprese*. The tomatoes, basil and olive oil come from here, and the mozzarella is from a local dairy."

"You really know a lot about this place."

"But not everything. They have all kinds of hidden surprises." Mace embraced her from behind, and she leaned back against him. "I learned about the cottages the last time I stayed here."

The last time... He'd probably been there with someone else. Happiness deflated a little inside her.

Mace kissed her temple. "Instead of guessing, you could just ask me what you want to know."

Wow. She really was that transparent to him. "There's no point in asking. You weren't a monk before we started seeing each other. I know that."

"I've been here three times—on my own. I discovered this place the first time by accident when I had to take a detour on the way back from driving to New York. The second time, I came out here for the day after a rough week at work. The third time was about a month ago. You're tensing up. You don't believe me?"

Note to self: she needed to never play poker with Mace or get much better at hiding her thoughts. "I do believe you. You coming out here by yourself instead of with someone or a group of people is just a little…surprising."

He held her tighter. "Is that a bad thing?"

Like the vineyard revealed surprises to Mace, he revealed them to her about himself. The more she discovered, the more she wanted to be with him.

"No, it isn't." She snuggled back in his arms. "How in the world did you get this cottage on such short notice? Isn't it booked out way in advance?"

"Yes. Usually it is. But they had a last-minute cancellation. When I called this morning to let them know we might arrive later than expected, they offered it to me at a discount." He chuckled. "It wasn't intentional, but it kind of fits in with our fake engagement."

She glanced back at him over her shoulder. "Back

in Tristan's office, when we were getting fake engaged. You said *mi amor*. That means my love, doesn't it?"

"Yes, literally, that's what it means. But it can also mean honey or sweetheart."

"And if I'm remembering my high school Spanish correctly, fiancée is *novia*?"

"No. *Novia* means girlfriend." He pointed to her. "*Tu eres mi prometida.*" He pointed to himself. "*Yo soy tu prometido.*"

She chuckled ruefully. "If we're going to pull off this fake engagement, I guess I better brush up on my Spanish. So, have you ever had a real *prometida*?"

"First, great pronunciation. And no. I've never been engaged. You're my first. What about you?" He gave her a squeeze. "Have you ever been engaged?"

"Let's see…" She silently counted numbers on her fingers.

When she got past three, he spun her around by the waist to face him. "You've been engaged four times?"

"Um." The stunned expression on his face made it impossible to keep in a laugh. "No, I'm kidding, just once."

"So you really were engaged?" He studied her face. "Tristan had never mentioned it. When was this?"

As it did a minute ago, Zurie's silence spoke as loud as words to him. The way she fiddled with the small gold loop in her earlobe and released a heavy exhale now in his arms, those were her major tells.

As he debated between waiting for an answer or suggesting they check out what tours were available that afternoon, she looked up at him. "About seven years ago. His name was Theo. We met when he and his colleagues visited the stable. We connected. Managed to work out the long-distance part of things with him in New York… In time, things got serious." She dropped her gaze.

"He proposed, and I said yes. But a month later, he was offered a better job in Dallas. It was an opportunity he'd really wanted. And to get where he wanted to go in his career, he needed all his attention there. Not on building a relationship. By then, we had started drifting apart. And I had Tillbridge to worry about. No one really knew about him and we hadn't announced our engagement, so were able to end things quietly."

The job opportunity was what Theo had really wanted? Why had the guy bothered to propose to her in the first place if she wasn't a priority to him? Irritation on her behalf wove through Mace. Had her family known about Theo, maybe they would have bounced the guy out before he hurt her. But seven years ago, Tristan had still been in the military. Her father and uncle had been alive, but wasn't that around the time Rina had eloped to Nevada? Knowing Zurie, she'd not only quietly ended her engagement but also quietly endured the pain, prioritizing being there for her family first.

Mace slid his hands from the sides of Zurie's waist to her back, bringing her closer. "I'm sorry that happened to you. From where I stand, if his job was more important than you, it was probably better that he moved on and out of your life."

She laid her left hand on his chest as she looked up at him. "It was. I know that now."

As he looked down at her, the recollection of slipping the ring on Zurie's finger in Tristan's office that morning came into his mind. When Anna had laughed as if were impossible for Zurie to have anyone, it had ticked him off. And from Zurie's expression in that moment, she'd seen Anna's take on her as the truth. Claiming the ring and slipping it on Zurie's finger, he'd done it for Tristan and Chloe, but he'd also wanted to erase the smug look on Anna's face and the stunned hurt on Zurie's. And he'd succeeded at both.

Zurie stared at her hand on his chest. "I really hope Tristan takes a minute to drive home and put Chloe's ring away."

Funny. She'd been thinking of the ring, too. "That's definitely on his agenda. Along with straightening the house. He'd torn through most of the rooms before I got there to help him look. It's messed up that Anna was the one to find the ring, but I'm glad she did. At the house, when Tristan had finally decided to give up and retrace his steps back to Tillbridge to keep looking, he was pretty devastated. I've seen him at low points before in his life, but this was different."

"I know what you mean. He was really disappointed in himself and worried about letting Chloe down. I recently complained about him smiling all the time lately, but I'll gladly take that over seeing him like he was this morning."

"You complained about him smiling?"

"Kind of, but not really." Chuckling, she nudged his arm. "Stop looking at me like that. I know it sounds terrible. It's just weird and wonderful at the same time, seeing him with a goofy I'm-in-love grin on his face. For some reason it reminds of when he was five years old. He used to run around in Superman pj's with a red towel for a cape, excited about the dollar the Tooth Fairy had left him under his pillow."

A laugh escaped Mace.

Zurie playfully wacked him. "Don't you dare tell him I told you about that."

"Why would I?" Mace laughed. Yeah, Tristan wearing Superman pj's was definitely something he'd bring up when Tristan least expected it. But now was the time for them to enjoy themselves.

He glided his hands up and down her back, enjoying the freedom to just hold her without restrictions. "We can still make the afternoon tour of the vineyard and winery if you're interested."

A pleased smile lit up Zurie's face. "Let's do it."

Chapter Twenty

The tour of the vineyard, learning about the careful process of nurturing the grapes currently ripening on the vine. The visit to the winery to learn about the process of producing and aging wine. Time with the vintner experiencing the first pour from a barrel, comparing it to the current vintage and tasting how the wine would evolve. Mace was there for every moment that had happened yesterday, but he barely remembered them.

He'd been captivated by the relaxed softness in Zurie's face, the slight furrow in her brow as she contemplated the differences in the wine they'd sampled and the subtle widening of her eyes when she'd tasted something she really liked. The smile on her face as they'd walked the paths to the vineyards had warmed him more than the sun.

That Saturday morning she'd bitten into a fresh peach in the orchard. A rich, bubbling laugh had erupted from her, and he'd been undone by the beauty of the sound. And the look in her eyes when she'd offered him a bite had caused him to bypass the fruit and go straight to her mouth for a taste of sweetness.

Time was going by too fast. They were headed home tomorrow.

Mace absorbed the reality of that, sitting on a blanket with Zurie on the lawn just past the restaurant in the Summer House Lodge.

Almost every table on the wood patio attached to the simply built, two-story white clapboard structure was full with patrons enjoying food, wine and conversation. The lawn was dotted with couples sitting on blankets enjoying an intimate picnic under the stars.

In less than a half hour, the mystery-comedy movie *Knives Out* would play on the screen yards away from them.

Mace added more *insalata caprese* to his smaller plate from the one sitting in front of them, along with a slice of herbed chickpea bruschetta.

Instead of eating the food on her plate, Zurie glanced around them, absently swirling her glass of rosé. In a simple beige tee and pink shorts, with her hair in a single braid, she looked comfortable and at ease with herself.

Mace took a bite of the *insalata*. The blend of fresh tomatoes, mozzarella and basil with olive oil and a light sprinkling of oregano was as delicious as when they'd had it on Friday.

A server dropping off a basket of warm crostini and crackers for the fig and olive tapenade shifted Zurie's attention back to the food. She slipped her wineglass into the wood holder that also had a carved-out section to hold the bottle of wine. "I could just eat this alone and be satisfied. It's so good."

Mace took a bite of crostini with the tapenade.

"I was starting to wonder if you liked it. You're not really eating, just staring out there. Do you see something or are you looking for something?"

"Maybe a bit of both." Smiling, she brushed crumbs from the bottom of his black T-shirt and then his bare thigh just below the leg of his beige cargo shorts. "With your brother and sister being married, do you ever feel like you're behind in the relationship department?"

It didn't sound like she was questioning him but trying to work out something in her own mind. Was that how she felt with Tristan getting married and Rina being in a serious relationship?

Instead of indulging his curiosity over the source of the question, Mace summed up his dating relationships over the past few years in his mind. "No, I don't feel behind. My circumstances have just been different from theirs. When I was in the military, the first four years, I wasn't interested in getting into anything serious. The last four years, multiple deployments made it hard to maintain a relationship. Afterward, finishing law school took up most of time."

She whipped her head around and looked at him. "Wait. You finished law school? When?"

"Last year. Didn't I mention it?" They'd talked about so many things that weekend, he honestly thought he had.

"No. I would have remembered. How am I just hearing about this now instead of when it happened?"

"We weren't exactly communicating back then."

Something bordering on regret passed over her face.

He hadn't said that to make her feel bad. Mace placed his hand over hers, resting on her thigh. "Outside of my family, Tristan and few people at work, no one else really knew."

"But becoming a lawyer, that's a big deal. Your dad's a lawyer. Your brother's a lawyer."

"My sister is, too."

"See? It's the family business. Are you planning to leave the sheriff's department and work at a law firm?"

"I haven't even applied to take the bar exam yet."

"When are you planning to do it?"

The familiar question pinged around his mind as he scooped up more tapenade with a cracker.

After he'd spoken to Andrea that day in the park, he'd printed out the instructions document for the bar exam in Nevada. The list of things he'd needed to pull together was long—his college transcripts, DMV report, letters of reference and his military discharge papers. And Andrea hadn't just found out the info on the study system, she'd sent it to him. Admittedly, it would be a complement to the review course he'd signed up for online. Everything was in motion. He just needed to get his head back into it.

But he'd figure out how to do that once he got home.

Zurie waited for an answer.

He handed her the cracker. "I'm taking it when the time is right. And right now, we're not supposed to talk about anything work related, remember?"

"Yes, I remember." Her mouth flattened as if she was stopping herself from blurting something out. She nibbled on the cracker with tapenade. When she finished, she looked out at the vineyard and released a barely audible sigh.

Where was on her mind now? They had less than twenty-fours left together. The two of them together, right then, that's where her attention should have been.

Mace leaned over, pressed a kiss near her ear and

whispered, "If you're thinking about Tillbridge, stop. If you're trying to compute the distance to Mars or the formula for gravity boots in your head, double stop. If you're thinking about me becoming a lawyer, stop. Whatever you're thinking about, it can wait until you get back."

"Okay. Fine. I'll stop." She gave him a playful eye roll. "The formula for gravity boots? Please, that's too easy. I could do that one in my sleep."

"Yeah, I bet you could, Miss Smarty-Pants." He poked a sensitive spot on her side.

Laughing, she batted his hand away. "Now you stop. Remember how the last tickle war you started with me ended?"

Yesterday morning, he'd started it as they'd made the bed. Zurie had ended it later during breakfast. She'd caught him off guard while he was drinking orange juice, and he'd snorted some up his nose.

Mace wrapped an arm around her from behind. "For the record, that was an unfair sneak attack."

Smiling, she shrugged. "Oh, well." Her smile faded slightly as she leaned into him. "I wasn't thinking of Tillbridge, not in the way you're thinking. It's just interesting to me—at Tillbridge, the priorities are filling the cottages and rooms at the guesthouse, booking every table at Pasture Lane and every slot possible at the stable. Here, it's different. Their focus is that." She pointed out at the vineyards surrounding them.

"You think it should be different?"

"No. It's just so…fragile. If Mother Nature is in a bad mood and there's too much rain, wind or frost, the vineyard is in danger. In my opinion, that's a frightening position to be in." A slightly puzzled, faraway look came over her face. "The day after Uncle Jacob died, I walked through every pasture. All that was out there was just me and the horses. As I looked around and thought about not losing what he and my parents had built, I realized that the horses and I weren't enough. That's when I decided to build the guesthouse and Pasture Lane Restaurant." She gave a quick smile that fell short of true happiness. "And that's why I'm not in charge of an agricultural enterprise. I'm obviously not cut out for it."

For a brief moment, Mace glimpsed the vulnerability in her that she'd experienced back then. Something she'd probably started masking from the world, the moment she'd lost her mother almost ten years ago and then her father a few years after, and through Rina and Tristan both not being at Tillbridge or able to help her.

Empathy unexpectedly welled inside him. Mace pulled her close, and as he pressed a lingering kiss to her temple, he breathed in her lavender and vanilla scent. She'd carried all that on her young shoulders and succeeded. But what had it cost her?

After the movie, as they walked into the cottage,

Mace couldn't shake what Zurie had told him or what he'd realized about her.

She walked to the kitchen counter and picked up the property brochure. "A stay at the cottage comes with an opportunity to plant something on the farm. I think I read somewhere that at this time of the year, we'd be able to plant something in the garden."

As she continued talking and Mace shut the door, he couldn't stop himself from taking a good look at her. In the past, he'd witnessed Zurie with her walls up, and like many, including her only family, he'd viewed her at times as cold and unfeeling. But to be the person she'd needed to be to keep Tillbridge together all these years, she'd had to shut off her emotions to a certain extent. Because of that, she'd become fiercely independent, driven, and she'd developed some crazy belief that she couldn't have a life of her own and run Tillbridge. Theo leaving the way he had probably reinforced that in her. Without an outlet or someone she could count on to share her burdens with, it made sense she was stressed out.

But she wasn't alone. And she was wrong when she'd said that she wasn't enough for Tillbridge. She was more than enough, and she'd done enough. She just didn't see it. And knowing her, she wouldn't even hear him if he tried to tell her that. What she needed was for someone to show her and remind her on a daily basis that she deserved the same happiness that Tristan had found with Chloe and Rina had with Scott.

But he didn't have time. They had three more weeks together. Less than that when he factored in the days he'd be away in California. And even if he could convince her to agree to keep seeing him beyond the wedding, they'd only have a few more months.

Frustration and a weird sense of helplessness he couldn't define went with Mace as he walked over to Zurie.

She gave him a perplexed smile. "So is that look on your face a yes or a no on planting in the garden tomorrow?"

"If that's what you want." He brushed his lips over hers, planning to end it at that. They were going to have to get up early if they were going to the garden.

But one brief kiss wasn't nearly enough. He gave in to the need to hold her, to pull her against him. To hold her tighter as she wrapped her arms around him. She was more wonderful than any sip of wine he'd ever tasted.

As Mace backed her up toward the bed, brief stops allowed for the removal of shoes and clothing. Urgent kisses made up for the wait, and they intoxicated him. Soon all he could focus on was the softness of her lips and the lush warmth of her mouth. The silkiness of her skin gliding beneath his palms.

He followed her down on the mattress, anxious

to claim her mouth again. Need rose inside him as her passion matched his own. She arched up to meet his touch as he stroked over her breasts, down to her lower curves and between her thighs. He savored her moans and the breathy whisper of his name.

Moments later, sheathed in a condom, he entered her. She fit so perfectly around him, he lost a breath as she wrapped her legs low on his waist and he grasped on to her hips. Moving with her robbed him of thought and threatened to take away his sanity as his mind centered on one thing—pleasing her before he allowed himself to fall with her in that sweet place of release.

"What should we call him?" Zurie, kneeling in the dirt, wearing gardening gloves with yellow suns printed on them, held a foot-high tomato plant just plucked from the pot in her hands.

Midmorning on Sunday, they were the only ones in the greenhouse yards away from Summer House Lodge. The large, clear structure was filled with rows of tomato, pepper and strawberry plants and lettuce, peas and other greens along with flowers in pots on a shelf.

The earthy sweet and green scent of the plants that hung in the air was vented through an opening in the curved roof.

Mace took a knee beside her. The excited gleam

that had been in her eyes since she'd bounded out of bed that morning was still there.

He swiped a streak of dirt from the curve of her cheek with his bare fingers. "I have no idea what to name a plant. You choose."

She studied the plants. "I think he looks like an Ollie."

"Looks like an Ollie? Wouldn't that be a better name for an olive tree?"

"No." She sang out the word with a slightly affronted look. "Naming an olive tree Ollie would so cliché. That's the same as naming a tomato plant Tiberius or Thaxter."

"As opposed to Tom?"

Zurie gave him a hard stare. "You just don't get it." She looked to the plant. "But you do, don't you, Ollie?"

She was talking to a plant? Who was this woman? He liked her a lot. "So, what do we need to do to get Ollie into his new home?"

"First, you have to put on your gloves."

He slipped a match to her gloves, a gift from the farm, from his back pocket and put them on. "Okay, now what?"

Zurie ignored the small slip of instructions on the ground next to her and pointed. "I've already dug the hole."

She'd actually handled the garden tool with finesse when she'd done it. Something that had surprised him, considering how she'd wielded the cake spatula like a weapon at the tasting.

Maneuvering the plant carefully, she gently set it inside the space created for it. "Now I'm going to hold him upright while you fill in the hole."

He scooped up the dirt she'd dug out of the hole, and as he filled in the space around the plant, his shoulder bumped lightly against hers. "Like this?"

"Yes. But don't pack it in. It needs to be loose. The water will mold it to the soil and roots of the plants."

"You sound like you've done this before."

"We had a small garden at the back of the house until I was about, I don't know, ten or eleven, maybe? What about you? Have you ever planted anything?"

He took his hands away, allowing her to better arrange the soil. "My mom would plant flowers every spring. I reseeded my lawn at the house. Does that count?"

Smiling, she poured water on the soil from a watering can. "Your grass isn't dead, so yes." Setting the watering can aside, she gently laid straw underneath the plant then tore up the instructions and mixed the paper into the ground cover.

While Zurie surveyed her work, he surveyed her. She was beautiful like this, all lit up from the inside out.

She sat back on her heels and sighed. "It's up to you now, Ollie. I expect to see you with lots of tomatoes."

How could she see Ollie with lots of tomatoes? Maybe she'd visit on her own like he had, just to get away. Or maybe she'd bring someone else. A vision of her coming back with some faceless guy and enjoying the vineyard with him sprang into his mind.

Zurie nudged him. "Why are you scowling?"

"I'm not." He stripped off the gloves.

Making a conscious effort to relax the muscles in his face, he stood. As he held out his hand, she took it and he pulled her up to her feet and into his arms.

Mace pressed his lips to her forehead, which was warm from the temperature of greenhouse.

The sun was rising higher. Signaling the coming shift from morning to afternoon.

"Breakfast and then we hit the road?" *I wish we didn't have to leave...* That's what he wanted to say, but what was the point? They had to go back to Bolan...and pretend to be engaged.

"Yes. Breakfast first sounds good." From the dimming of the light of happiness in her eyes, Zurie felt the same way he did about their weekend coming to an end.

Chapter Twenty-One

Zurie turned off the 5:00 a.m. alarm on her phone. Responsibility warred with the part of her that wanted to stay in bed until seven or eight. It had been that way since she'd returned to work two days ago.

She sat up and slid her legs from under the sheets, but instead of rushing to stand up, she sat there with her eyes closed, just like the app Mace had downloaded on her phone the first morning and afternoon they'd spent together had taught her. She wasn't going to let those first fifteen minutes slip away from her. That's what she'd vowed two days ago, on Monday, when she'd made a promise to herself to make it habit. Along with the other changes she'd made.

Herbal tea still wasn't her favorite thing, but the rooibos blend that she was drinking as her current substitute for coffee was…tolerable. But the one habit she was still struggling with was not seeing Mace.

Three whole days had passed since they'd left the vineyard, and it felt like weeks since she'd seen him. He'd been working. She'd been catching up at her desk. They'd sent a couple of text messages to each other, but she'd refrained from sending more. She didn't want to appear too needy.

But the problem was that during her staycation, she'd had the freedom to see him whenever he wasn't working. Back then balancing her time and attention hadn't been an issue. Now it was, and in a big way.

The distraction of Mace, that's what she'd hoped to avoid by cutting things off with him when her staycation had ended. She still could, in a way. Couldn't she? Just because they were fake engaged didn't mean that they had to be together every day. And Mace working nights was the perfect explanation for spending so much time apart. They were on different schedules.

On the drive home from Sommersby, they'd also come up with a strategy to handle curiosity and keep hiding the truth. They would neither confirm nor deny that they were engaged. A grin from him, a coy smile from her, and Anna's rumor running amok would take care of it. They wouldn't have to really say or do anything to keep the ruse going.

So, there it was. She could wean herself off seeing him if that's what she wanted. But she didn't. She wanted more trips to the vineyard with him. More movies under the stars. More nights in his arms.

The reality of that sliced through her peacefulness, following her as she got ready for work. Everything suddenly felt off. The navy pantsuit she put on felt restrictive. The sensible black pumps she'd worn so many times in the past seemed too tight. Her schedule too full.

At eight o'clock, sitting at her desk in her office, she scrolled through the calendar on her desktop. A virtual meeting with Kayla at eight thirty. A meeting at nine with a company rep to look over a new point-of-sale system. And she needed to review and give input on the activity schedule and budget Tristan had drawn up for the new arena.

Meetings and tasks lined up one after the other on her schedule day after day all week. Just looking at it made her head spin. But it wasn't a lot. She used to thrive on every hour being filled. Was it just because of Mace? It couldn't be. Post-staycation blues… was that a thing?

Googling it… Not for staycations for definitely for vacations—same difference. Zurie pulled up the article. Reestablish sleep. *Check.* Use memories of your vacation to reduce stress. Ooh, she liked that one. Realize how much you enjoyed being out in the world and...*take a staycation*. Well, that advice wasn't helpful.

Her phone rang on her desk. She glanced at the screen. Hit ignore, that's what she should do. One more habit to build starting today. Don't talk to Mace every day. As if her hand had a mind of its own, she snatched up the phone and tapped the answer icon. "Hello."

"Good morning." Mace's low, laid-back tone signifying he was at the end of his day sent a rush through her more potent then caffeine.

"How did last night go at work?"

"Busier than usual, and not in a good way. But the calls I handled last night weren't the most interesting part of my shift."

"Oh? What was?"

"One of my colleagues pulling me aside to ask about the rumor he'd heard about me being engaged to you."

"And what did you say?"

Mace chucked. "I neither confirmed nor denied, just like we said. What about you? How's your morning going?"

"Good. Strange. Getting back into my schedule still feels...different. It's hard."

"That busy?"

"Yes and no. I miss you." The confession slipped out.

"You do, huh?" He chuckled softly. "In that case, you should probably open your door."

Mace strode down the mostly empty corridor past Pasture Lane, headed for Zurie's office. He'd planned to stick to text messages as their prime way of communicating for a few more days. That's what she seemed to want, and he didn't want to crowd her space.

But just now on the phone, it had sounded like she wanted to see him as much as he wanted to see her.

The door at the end of the hall opened, and Zurie stood in the threshold of her office, too tempting for him take his eyes off her.

He picked up the pace.

Security cameras high above in the corners were clocking his every move. He'd supervised their installation. But right then, he almost didn't care who was watching them on the monitors downstairs in the security room.

When he reached her, somehow, he managed to pull up enough restraint to wait until he was inside, and the door was shut behind him, before he kissed her.

Zurie's lips curled up in a smile against his. She slipped her arms around his neck as he held her by the waist. "You taste a little like coffee. Are you trying to torture me?"

He leaned away a little. "Sorry. No, that wasn't the plan."

"What exactly was the plan?"

"Holding and kissing you like I've been thinking about since I got off work." And like he'd been dreaming of every night since they left the vineyard.

She smiled up at him. "I like your plan."

"Speaking of plans, what's on your agenda for this week?"

"I still have work to catch up on, and Chloe, Rina and I have a dress fitting Thursday night. Why?"

Mace stepped back and reached into his front pocket. He'd never done what he was about to do with anyone before, but with Zurie, it felt right.

He slipped out his spare house key, took her hand and dropped it into her palm.

Her gaze moved from the key to his face. "Why do you want me to have this?"

Mace read wariness in her eyes and suddenly realized the confusion that was probably going through her mind. Giving the person you're seeing a key to your house was considered a big deal. *Damn.* He was doing it all wrong. He should have set it up better, not just put the key in her hand.

Smiling, he took hold of her other hand. "No pressure. I thought you should have it in case you wanted to stop by my place Friday night. I'll be at work, but there might be some wine and other special things in the refrigerator for you then. And if you did decide to drink the wine, you wouldn't be able to drive home afterward, so you'd have to sleep in my bed, which shouldn't be too much of hardship since it's much bigger than yours."

Relief opened up his chest as humor replaced the wariness in her eyes. She closed her hand around the key. "That's quite a plan."

"Oh, but there's more." He tugged her closer. "If you did decide to do all that, we could have breakfast when I got off work in the morning. And afterward, I don't know, all that cooking and eating could make you tired, and you might need a nap."

Zurie laughed as he laid his forehead to hers. "How long did it take for you to come up with this?"

"All of the hours I've been missing you since the vineyard." That admission should have bothered him. He should have been concerned about getting to this place in his head with Zurie so soon.

Maybe his feelings had gotten involved, like Tristan had predicted. But staying away from Zurie right now made less sense to Mace than being with her. He leaned back and looked into her eyes. "Say yes. Please."

Chapter Twenty-Two

Zurie climbed the steps to Rina's apartment carrying a large tote with the shoes and the shapewear she planned to wear with her bridesmaid dress. At nine thirty at night on Thursday, Main Street was mostly deserted. Just a couple of people walking their dogs and workers from the wine bar and shop heading to their cars parked on the opposite end of the street.

No one was paying attention, but as the wedding got closer, a part of her half expected someone to jump out of nowhere with a camera and a mic demanding to know what was going.

But so far, at least tonight was going as planned. Rina had gotten all three dresses upstairs in boxes without hitch, along with Charlotte's sewing machine in a rolling bag. Everything would go back out the same way, but the dresses would go to Rina's house for safekeeping until the day of the wedding.

Zurie knocked on the door.

Moments later, Rina opened it. They'd both had the same idea about clothes—leggings, T-shirts and ballet flats.

"Hey." Zurie paused to give Rina a hug before walking into the entryway.

"Hey, yourself, Miss Engaged Lady." From Rina's mischievous smile, she already knew it was a fake engagement.

"When did you find out about it and who told you?"

"Last Friday night. Darby was the first one to corner me about it. She'd heard it from a customer. I tried to call you, but you didn't answer, so I reached out to Tristan, and he told me everything. Including what happened with Chloe's ring. I can't imagine what those hours were like trying to find it."

"It was really hard on him. Luckily it turned up."

"I don't know if I'd classify Anna as lucky, but you're right. At least the ring was found."

They walked into the living room. The same table and chairs from the day of the tasting sat in the space. The ceiling lights reflected in the large tinted windows.

Just as Zurie was about to ask if Chloe was there,

Chloe's voice along with Charlotte's echoed through the apartment.

Zurie put her tote on the table and sat down.

Rina sat in the chair beside her. "So were you and Mace together before or after you spilled your iced coffee on him?"

That day seemed so far in the past. "After."

"So you spilling coffee on Mace wasn't just an unfortunate accident."

"Oh no." Zurie warned her off. "You are not going down the road of how me spilling coffee on Mace was similar to Scott running into you."

Rina shrugged with a smile. "Whatever you say. Once Chloe and Tristan are settled into their routine, we need to sync our schedules for a triple date night—me and Scott, Tristan and Chloe, and you and Mace."

Zurie hesitated.

"Why the face? Don't tell me you two aren't into date nights. It'll be fun."

"No, that's not it, but…" Saying it out loud felt so wrong but it was the truth. "Mace and I won't be together after the wedding."

"But why not?" Rina's face morphed from confusion to surprised realization. "You two are just hooking up until the wedding?"

Zurie didn't like the sound of that any more than what she'd admitted to Rina, but what Rina said was also the truth. "Yes, but that wasn't the original plan.

We were just supposed to be together over my staycation, but then the fake engagement extended things until the wedding."

Rina grinned and flipped her loose braids over her shoulder. "Look at you making the most of your time off. But why the limitations?"

"Trying to manage Tillbridge and balance a relationship is hard." Giving in to the need to unburden herself, Zurie added, "I can't focus. I'm fighting the distraction of Mace on my mind every day." And it was even worse since he'd given her the key to his place. She hadn't fully committed to spending Friday night at his place, but it was tempting.

"And you think that when you stop seeing him, that will magically disappear." Rina chuckled. "You're fooling yourself. It will probably get worse. The whole absence-makes-the-heart-grow-fonder thing is true. Trust me, I know. Why fight it? Especially since being with him is so good for you."

"Good for me? What do mean?"

"You look fabulous. And you're actually relaxed. You've been here ten whole minutes just talking to me and you haven't reached for your phone once."

Zurie's gaze drifted to her tote. That was true. She hadn't thought about her phone at all until Rina just mentioned it. And she was more relaxed and did have Mace to thank for that, but still… "Things are good between us now, but if we stayed together and things didn't work out, it could get awkward. He and

Tristan have been friends longer than Mace and I have been together. That wouldn't be fair to Tristan."

"I see your point. It could be risky." Rina reached over and squeezed her arm. "But what if it worked out?"

Zurie slipped the key into the lock and opened the door to Mace's house.

The alarm panel beeped, and she keyed in the visitor code that he'd given her to disarm the system.

The floor lamp in the corner of the living room automatically came on, illuminating the simply furnished space with a gray couch, wood coffee table, side tables and a large screen in a built-in cabinet situated between two gray and blue abstracts.

The ceiling light had also come on in the hallway to the left, leading to the main and guest bedrooms.

After closing and locking the door and putting the alarm on stay mode, she walked into the living room and dropped her purse and small blue overnight bag on the couch. She'd been to Mace's house plenty of times, but being there without him in the simply furnished space felt familiar and strange at the same time. Was she imagining it, or could she smell his woodsy cologne hovering in the air?

A text buzzed in on her phone, and she took it from her purse. Mace had mentioned that he would get a message on his phone alerting him that she'd gone inside.

You good?

Yes

Make yourself at home. Don't forget to check out what's in the refrigerator—bottom shelf. See you in the morning.

The morning seemed so far away. But she had work to keep her busy and the surprise Mace had left her in the fridge.

After slipping off her sandals by the couch, she went into the kitchen. She flipped on the wall switch, and light flooded the space. Just like the rest of the house, it was clean and neat with a plate and silverware on the drying rack by the sink.

She opened the refrigerator and peeked inside. An artfully arranged assortment of fresh grapes and dark chocolate–dipped pineapple, apple wedges and strawberries in a domed container sat on the bottom shelf along with a bottle of white wine from the Sommersby vineyard.

Unable to resist, Zurie partially opened the plastic container, slipped out an apple wedge and took a bite. *Delicious.* The man just knew how to make her day.

A short time later, she'd changed into her favorite gray leggings and blue-striped crew-neck shirt with the sleeves pushed up. She settled on the couch with a glass of wine in her hand and some of the fruit on a small plate on the side table next to her.

Zurie took a sip of chardonnay, and contentment settled inside her. After talking to Rina last night during the dress fittings, she'd made up her mind about staying overnight at Mace's house...and broaching the topic of them staying together beyond the wedding.

The weeks they'd spent together had been really good so far. And their weekend at the vineyard had been nothing short of perfect. If anything, why not stay together for more of that?

More time together, that was probably something he'd be interested in, too, wouldn't he? When they'd first gotten together, he had settled for three weeks because that's what she'd insisted upon, not because that's what he wanted. Mace had told her to trust her instincts, and they were telling her that she and Mace were on the same page.

An hour or so later, content and pleasantly drowsy, she washed the plate and glass she'd used and went to the bedroom.

Mace's king-size bed with a tan comforter dominated the room.

After brushing her teeth and doing her facial cleansing routine, she started to crawl into bed. Her phone...she'd left it in the living room, and it needed to be recharged. The battery life was at less than thirty percent when she'd been texting with Mace.

Zurie went to her overnight bag, searching inside it for her charging cord. Wait. No. It was in her car. She was ready for bed and the house was locked up. She wasn't going outside now.

Make yourself at home. That's what he'd said in his text. And she really needed to charge her phone. He had spare cords. She'd used one before. He'd gotten it from his office.

Flipping lights on along the way, Zurie walked down the hall and into the bedroom he'd converted into a home office–slash–workout space. She walked past the weight bench and behind the desk on the far wall.

No cords on top. Shoot. Wait, no, there it was underneath some papers on the right. As Zurie slipped out the phone cord, the heading on a paper caught her eye.

State Bar Exam Nevada

She reached for the paper but then drew back her hand. She wasn't a snoop…but she needed to know. Zurie's stomach dropped as she sat in the desk chair to look through the stack of papers. He was working his way through an instructions list, and most of the items were there…along with one that had dates for the exam. The one that was six months from now was circled.

Mace was moving to Nevada. And it made perfect sense. Most of his family was there. He didn't have anyone in Bolan. At the vineyard, Mace had said he'd take the bar exam when the timing was right. And apparently, that was just a few months from now. When had he made the decision? Before or after their trip?

Zurie sat back in the chair, numbness setting in as she ran the evidence through her mind and faced reality. One, Mace didn't owe her any explanations about what he planned to do now or months from now. What they had was temporary. Two, she'd been through this before. Years ago, she'd known from the start that Theo was ambitious. But she'd foolishly believed that she'd come before his drive for success.

Mace had ambitions, too. He wanted to become a lawyer and practice in Nevada and be with his family. That was his priority. Not her or their relationship. And it was time for her to accept that... starting now.

Chapter Twenty-Three

"Raccoons? That's what all that noise was about? Are you sure?" The woman in her late seventies, standing in the brightly lit foyer of her home, stared skeptically at Mace. "It sounded like someone was breaking into the shed. They made such a ruckus."

"I understand, Mrs. Davies." He slipped his Maglite into the tactical belt around his waist. But I chased the raccoons out and made sure the shed was locked. They shouldn't bother you any more tonight."

"Well, good." Relief flooded her light tan face, framed by soft white curls, as she lifted a hand and clutched the collar of her light pink robe closed over her chest. "Thank you for coming out here. I always feel so much better when it's you."

A noise in the woods past the backyard of her older one-story house. A possible vicious dog on her property, a cat stranded in a tree. That was just the short list of reason why Etta Davies called the sheriff's department at least once every other week. Some of her calls required some sort of minor action. Many did not.

The habit of her calling and reporting suspicious activity around her home at night had started a year ago, after her husband had died. Some considered her a nuisance, but she was just lonely. It was an unspoken understanding that if she called in and Mace was on duty, he'd take care of her.

Mace reached for the doorknob. "Be sure to lock up behind me."

"Wait. I just baked some banana nut muffins. I'll get you some."

Before he could stop her, she'd hurried off.

It was a slow night. He could wait. If he didn't stay for this part of what had become a ritual, her feelings would be hurt.

A moment later, she returned with the muffins wrapped in foil and handed them to him. "Here you go. A half dozen should get you through the night."

"Thank you." He turned to leave.

"You know, years ago, I used to make my Joe a snack to take with him to Tillbridge…"

Mace turned, patiently listening to the account he'd heard more than few times about Mr. Davies, who had been a groundskeeper at Tillbridge.

Long minutes later, she patted his arm. "I'm glad you found Zurie Tillbridge. You're a good man, like my Joe. You deserve someone good to come home to."

Anna's rumor was traveling far and wide. "Thank you."

"When's the wedding going to be?"

Playing the confirm-or-deny game wouldn't work with Mrs. Davies. She'd just keep asking questions. "I don't know. I have to go now. You get some rest."

The end of his shift came later than expected. After finishing paperwork and changing into his street clothes, he skipped the usual catch-up time with the other deputies in the locker room and went straight to his truck and headed home.

At eight thirty on a Saturday morning, traffic was steady.

You deserve someone good to come home to...

When was the last time he had someone actually waiting for him to walk through the door? It had been so long he couldn't remember. Excitement moved through him as he thought of Zurie at his house. He couldn't wait to see her.

Mace pulled into his subdivision. A few turns later, he drove down his street and spotted Zurie's car in his driveway. His heart beat faster as he resisted breaking the speed limit. He parked behind her Mercedes in the driveway, jumped out and strode down the stone path leading to the front of his home.

Unlocking the door was suddenly a tedious task he couldn't get done fast enough. He opened it. Was that bacon he smelled? After shutting and locking the door behind him, he followed the wonderful smell of food to his kitchen and Zurie.

Mace paused, taking in the sight of her checking something in the oven. She'd already gotten dressed in jeans and a loose light purple top with thin shoulder straps. He'd hoped she'd stay awhile. Did she have someplace to go?

As she shut the oven door, she looked over at him. "Hi." Her smile curved up her lips, but it didn't flood her face with the happiness he'd expected to see.

"Good morning." He walked over to her, and as he went to embrace her, she laid her hands on his chest, subtly holding him back as she gave him an all-too-brief kiss, then slipped from his arms.

Prickles subtly danced along his nape. His internal warning system. Or maybe he was just reading her wrong.

"You had frozen waffles, so I made them. They're in the oven." She took plates down from the cabinet.

"Thank you for making breakfast. Was there something wrong with the toaster?" He pointed to the appliance in the corner to the right of the stove.

Zurie stared as if seeing it for the first time. "Oh, I missed it." She reached for the silverware drawer.

Unable to ignore the unease that now radiated into him, he took hold of her hands. "What's going on?"

"Going on? I'm making breakfast." Zurie gave him a smile that was even weaker than the one she'd given him when he'd first walked in.

He pulled her toward him then slid his hands up to gently grasp her arms. "You've used that toaster at least twice. What's wrong? Tell me."

She closed her eyes for a moment. And when she opened them, he saw the Zurie he used to know. The one who put up walls to keep people at a distance.

She released exhale. "I can't do this."

Dread and frustration tightened in his gut. "Do what?"

"This." As Zurie looked around, she lifted her arms slightly from her sides, gesturing to the kitchen and loosening hold. "Us."

She laid her hand lightly over his heart. In a minute, she'd feel it in her hands, because her words were carving it out of his chest.

Zurie looked up at him. "I loved the week we spent together during my staycation. I loved our getaway trip to the vineyard. But trying to be girlfriend and boyfriend for the long term, it's just not me. I love my job. It isn't so much that Tillbridge has to be the priority. I want it to be."

He looked into her eyes, searching for the lie, but all that was there was sincerity. She meant it.

Mace's heart twisted painfully in his chest as he let her go. "I understand. I get it."

Her priorities lay at Tillbridge and his lay in Reno. It was as simple as that.

Chapter Twenty-Four

Four long days. Ninety-six hours, and if she really thought about it, Zurie could break it down to minutes, maybe even seconds since she'd walked out of Mace's house and out of his life. And she'd used the breathing techniques she'd learned over her staycation to keep herself together while each word she'd told him had felt like a tiny paper cut opening in her chest.

Zurie sat back in the chair in her office, still feeling the hurt all the way into her bones. Along with the irony of it. Not lying to him had made it easier, too. It wasn't so much that Tillbridge had to be the priority. She wanted it to be. Loving Tillbridge was safer. It wouldn't break her heart.

A knock sounded at the door.

She clicked the camera icon on her desktop screen. A man she didn't recognize stood outside the office. Her door didn't have a sign on it. Someone must have directed him to where she was.

Zurie got up, smoothing down the front of her dress as she schooled helpful politeness on her face. She opened the door. "Hello, may I…"

No. It couldn't be. It wasn't him. She was conjuring him up in her mind. But it looked like him—right age, too, probably in his late thirties, except this guy had a shaved head instead of short hair. He wasn't clean shaven, but a close-cut beard and mustache shadowed his brown face. And he was wearing a button-down shirt and jeans instead of an impeccable designer suit and silk tie.

"Hello, Zurie."

But the voice was unmistakable.

Theo gave her a tentative smile as if he wasn't sure what to expect from her.

"Hi. This is…unexpected." They hadn't parted acrimoniously when they'd ended their engagement. She didn't hate him. She'd just never anticipated seeing him again.

"I hope you don't mind that I just showed up like this. I tried to call you last week, but your assistant said you were on vacation until this week. I'm passing through. I took a chance on catching you." He pointed back down the corridor. "Any chance you're free for coffee?"

"You came here to ask me out for coffee, right now?" The universe, fate, they were mocking her. That was the only answer for this.

"Yes, I am. This is probably going to sound funny to you." He chuckled as he looked down and scratched the back of his head. "But I'm here to talk to you about buying a horse."

As Zurie sat at her table in Pasture Lane, her mind wandered to Mace sitting in the chair where Theo now was. In weird way, it felt like cheating, but it wasn't. She and Mace weren't together. And Theo—even if she wasn't hurting right now, she'd never consider getting back with him. Hopefully he wouldn't go that route.

As Theo sipped from coffee from a cardboard cup, he glanced at the tea in hers with a slightly puzzled expression. No doubt he was remember how she lived for coffee.

A lot had changed in seven years. She was drinking tea, and he was interested in equines. "So, how's life in the investment world?"

"I wouldn't know. I gave it up about five years ago."

Wow. He must have really hit it big if he'd walked away from that life. "What do you do now?"

"I own a plant nursery in Dallas."

"Plant nursery—you mean like a tree or a flower farm?" Something massive, no doubt, with a good return.

"No. Just a plot of land next to a local flower shop."

"You own a flower shop and a plant nursery. That's...wonderful."

"It is." His serene smile pulled her in to look at him more closely.

When she'd dated him, he'd always been confident with a tiny trace of arrogance. By now he would have bragged a little bit about how big his flower shop was or how much money his plant nursery was making.

Puzzled, she asked. "So why do you want a horse?"

"For my wife as an anniversary present."

Zurie coughed down a sip of rooibos. When they'd broken up, he'd mentioned probably not considering marriage again until he was in his forties.

He clapped her on the back. "You okay?"

"Yes." Curiosity, too many unanswered questions—she had to know. "I'm sorry. What happened? You were on your way to the top of the investment world."

"I was." Theo smiled ruefully. "But then something unexpected happened."

"You met your wife?"

"That happened later. A year or so after I got to

Dallas, I was winning as an investment manager, but then I came down with pneumonia. I didn't know that at first. I was taking meds for the flu and working from home. I got worse. No one noticed or cared that I hadn't been in touch with anyone at the office for almost a week."

"No one noticed?"

"Nope." He sat back in the chair. "Someone from my cleaning service found me. I was lucky."

"That's horrible. Not that the cleaning service found you, but the rest." Surely if she didn't come down from her suite for a few days, Tristan or Rina would come looking for her.

But during end-of-year budget analysis, she was known for barricading herself in her suite for a couple of days with the threat of losing a vital body part for anyone who interrupted her until she was done. Not even Tristan or Rina dared to interrupt her. But Mace probably would. He'd make her open the door. Kiss her senseless. Then feed her and make her take a break. And if the tables were turned, she would do the same for him. Or at least she would have if...

She swiped the thought aside. "So, right after that, you quit your job."

"Pretty much. For a couple of years, I worked independently as a financial adviser. Bought a house. Really got into the landscaping part of things. Something about putting plants in the ground intrigued me more than numbers."

Ollie, thriving in the greenhouse under the sun, flashed into her mind. "Putting down roots, maybe?"

"Yeah, I think that's part of it."

She hadn't meant to say that out loud. As Zurie studied Theo, she let her mind roll back in time, envisioning what might have been if they'd stayed together. Two people driven by their careers, their obligations, trying to make a marriage work. It wasn't pretty.

That day at the vineyard, she'd told Mace that she'd known her and Theo's breakup was for the best. But saying that had always been a knee-jerk reaction to the hurt of coming in second in Theo's life. Yet seeing him now, so happy in his life, she actually believed it. They'd both ended up right where they belonged.

Chapter Twenty-Five

Mace walked outside onto the deck at his brother's house carrying a dish of vegetable kebabs that his sister-in-law Gia had given him.

Late-afternoon sun beamed down, but an awning covering a built-in grilling station, picnic table and deck chairs shadowed the space.

His khaki cargo shorts and a tan shirt would also keep him cool.

Efraín, similarly dressed to beat the heat of the outdoors and the grill, glanced over at Mace as he rearranged pieces of chicken on the rack. "I forgot we were doing those. Go ahead and stick them in the mini fridge."

Mace did as his brother asked, opening the fridge built into the end of the station closest to the beige brick two-story house. He sat down at the picnic table and picked up his bottle of beer. "Thanks for letting me jump on your laptop."

"No problem." Efraín snagged his own bottle from the table. "Were you able to check in for your flight okay?"

"Yep. I'm all set. Gia asked about taking me to the airport, but you don't have to. You already took days off to hang with me. I can take a Lyft to the airport." Mace took a sip of beer.

Coming to Reno after the five-day crisis negotiation seminar in Sacramento hadn't been the plan. But he'd had vacation days he'd needed to use, and it had been the right time to take them. And he'd needed to clear his head before seeing Zurie at Tristan and Chloe's wedding that coming weekend.

Efraín waved him off. "I got you. One of the perks of being your own boss is that you can take off pretty much whenever you want. You'll see."

"Yeah, I guess I will."

And maybe he would sooner rather than later. Moving to Reno in the next couple of months was something he was considering. He could work under Efraín, getting his feet wet with corporate law cases, while he studied to take the bar. The more he thought about it, the more he could see it as the motivation he needed to make those final steps to becoming a lawyer.

Sounds of an argument traveled from the lawn.

Emilia tackled Leo onto the grass, trying to wrestle the ball from him.

"Watch the grill." Efraín shoved the tongs into Mace's hand and hurried to his children. "Emilia… Leo…no. *Ven acá.*"

The four-year-old twins immediately stopped tussling, and the ball rolled away. Following instructions, they got up and went to their father. As Efraín leaned down and spoke quietly to them, the two hung their heads. A moment later, Emilia and Leo hugged each other. Emilia retrieved the ball and handed it to Leo.

A strange sense of awe and pride opened up in Mace. His older brother was a dad. And he was using the same tactics their parents had used to settle arguments between them when they were kids. What had their parents used to say?

You should be taking care of one another, not fighting each other.

Efraín returned to the deck. Shaking his head, he reached for his beer on the picnic table. "Those two."

Chuckling, Mace turned the chicken. "Kind of reminds me of us growing up and you causing trouble."

"Me?" A laugh shot out of Efraín. "You were the one always testing the waters and getting away with it."

"No, that was Andrea."

Efraín opened his mouth as if to object but then changed his mind. "You're right. She was always talking us into things. Why did we go along with it?"

"Because she had us wrapped around her finger."

"She did. Just like Emilia has Leo wrapped around hers." As his brother looked to the lawn at his kids, love filled his expression.

A strange longing opened up in Mace. "You really like being a dad, don't you?"

Efraín grinned. "I do. It's a hard job sometimes, but Gia and I keep each other sane." As he sipped his beer, he studied Mace. "What's that look about? Are you actually considering settling down and going halves on a kid with someone?"

No sat on the tip of Mace's tongue, but the vision of two children around the age of Emilia and Leo, two little replicas, the best of him and Zurie, rose in his mind. Sharing the responsibility of raising kids. He could easily envision them doing that together. But he and Zurie didn't want the same things. She cared about Tillbridge. Not him.

As the image went away, the loss of that possibility hurt like a punch. It pushed out an answer. "I was. Not now, but maybe someday. But I was wrong."

"Seriously?" His brother sat down at the table and turned down the volume of the music on his phone. "This is new. With who?"

Mace held on to the word dying to come out. This

was the type of conversation he would have had with Tristan. But he couldn't. And he needed to talk it out so he could hear himself say it was really over. "Zurie Tillbridge."

"Really?" Surprise came over Efraín's face. "I knew you had a crush on her in high school. So that actually progressed to something when you got back to Bolan?"

"It did. But we're not seeing each other anymore."

"What happened?

Mace turned the chicken. "I wanted more, and she didn't." Okay, there, he'd said it.

"Wait, more as in marriage?"

Gia breezed onto the deck carrying an empty glass dish for the chicken. "Who's getting married?"

"He is." Efraín pointed to Mace as he took the dish from her. "Or at least he was. She said no."

"She who?" Gia asked.

"Zurie Tillbridge," Efraín said. "He had a crush on her when he was in high school."

"A high school sweetheart?" Gia looked to Mace with a puzzled frown. "How come I've never heard of her before?"

"Because we weren't high school sweethearts." As Mace brushed sauce on the chicken, rising smoke amplified the feeling that he was the one being grilled. Good thing he didn't mention the fake engagement. "I only started seeing her a few weeks ago."

Efraín's brows shot up. "You were only dating a

few weeks and you wanted more with her? Possibly even kids?"

"I'm confused," Gia said. "Did you ask her to marry you or didn't you?"

Weariness over the conversation grew inside Mace. "It doesn't matter, because she doesn't want more."

"But—" Efraín interjected. "Did you actually ask her that question?"

Mace halted the conversation with a raised hand. "*Ya. Terminé de hablar de eso.*"

Efraín and Gia exchanged a look.

Mace set the tongs down on the shelf. He wasn't trying to be evasive, but he really was done talking about it. What was the point? He and Zurie weren't getting back together.

Just as he was about to tell them that, the doorbell rang and Efraín and Gia both went inside.

Moments later, two couples and two boys around the twins' age walked out on the deck with Efraín. The kids ran off to play with Emilia and Leo.

Introductions were made, and soon laughter and conversation took over the space. Relieved the focus had shifted, Mace joined in.

One of the women owned a software company. The other worked with Gia at the hospital. The husband of the woman who owned the software company was an attorney like Efraín. The other man,

Jake, was a real estate agent. During dinner, Mace talked to him about houses in the area.

Emilia cut the conversation short when she grabbed Mace's hand and pulled him to the yard to play a game the kids had made up. It combined chase, hide-and-go-seek, and soccer and the rules seemed to change every ten minutes.

Chapter Twenty-Six

Hours later, with covered paper plates laden with leftovers and sleepy kids in tow, the couples left for home.

While Gia gave Emilia and Leo baths and got them ready for bed, Mace helped Efraín clean up the kitchen and the deck.

Once they were done, they both plopped down in the padded deck chairs.

Efraín loosed a jaw-cracking yawn. "Thanks for helping out. It's great to have people over, but it's a lot of work, especially with the kids. Sometimes just watching them run around sucks the energy out of me."

Mace glanced at his brother and smiled. "Or maybe you're just getting old."

"Go ahead and crack jokes." As he looked ahead, Efraín rested his head back on the chair. "Your day will come when you're chasing your own kids 24-7 instead for a few hours. When it does, I'll remind you of this conversation."

"I know you will."

Efraín glanced over at him. "You spent a lot of time talking to Jake about houses."

"Yeah. I figured I should get a jump on things if I'm going to move out here in the next couple of months."

"One minute we can't get you out of Bolan. Now you can't wait to leave."

"And changing my mind is a problem? I thought you were anxious for me to move here."

"Not if it isn't what you really want. What changed your mind? Was it Zurie?"

Mace couldn't lie to his brother or himself. "Yes." He let the need to talk overtake him, explaining everything that happened with him and Zurie from beginning to end to Efraín. "She's got this idea in her head that Tillbridge is all she needs. I did my best to show her. I think what Theo did to her is still driving her thinking. She's afraid to take a risk."

"I see your point, but look at it from her standpoint. The guy left her for his career. She probably needs reassurances before she takes a chance with someone where that same scenario is a possibility. Did you talk about how a long-distance relationship might work between the two of you so she could understand it was less risky?"

"No, because I didn't tell her I was moving here."

"Oh." Efraín remained silent.

"Oh, what?"

Efraín leaned in. "You're either really confused or you are lying to yourself. You went to law school. Line up the facts. You said you wanted more with her. You didn't tell her you were planning to move here, and you've been stalling on taking the bar. The answer is clear as glass. As least it is to me."

Mace considered what Efraín was suggesting and he couldn't lie. "I admit. I wasn't sure if I was ready to take the bar yet. Not from a studying-for-it standpoint. Just life. But I felt that way before I met Zurie. As far as not telling her, I guess I didn't want to put that out there if I didn't have to because she was already putting limitations on our relationship. It was frustrating. There was nothing I could do to change her mind."

"Sometimes it's not about doing something. It's about being."

His brother sounded like a self-help manual. "It's more complicated than that."

"It's complicated because when you're used to making things happen, not doing anything to fix a situation doesn't compute for you. I get it. Do you remember when Gia and I were first trying to get pregnant?"

"Yeah, I remember it being a tough time for the two of you."

"It was. For me, one of the hardest parts of the process was seeing all that Gia had to go through physically and mentally. She's strong and tough, but even the strongest, toughest people in the world need a break, and I couldn't help lighten the load or reduce the expectations that she was putting on herself. Between the hormones and the disappointment month after month, she struggled, and at one point, she felt not being able to have children was a deal breaker for our relationship. Of course it wasn't. Even though I told her that, she started walling herself off from me. I could sense it, and there was nothing I could say or do to stop her."

The memory of Zurie telling him she couldn't continue their relationship came to his mind. In that moment, he'd felt that there was nothing he could say or do to stop Zurie from walking away.

Efraín continued, "One night, Gia and I got into a really bad argument. A lot was said, and I almost left. But before I walked out the door, I glanced back at her face, and I saw this look of acceptance as if she were telling herself, 'See? I was right. I knew he would leave.' And it pissed me off."

"What did you do?"

"I didn't leave. I told her that having children

might have been a question mark in our lives, but me loving her wasn't. No matter how hard she tried to push me away, I was going to be there for the rest of that day, and every day after that, because I loved her, and she needed to deal with it."

"And that solved everything?"

"Well, that, and what happened after I kissed her." Efraín grinned. "Close to eight months later, the twins were born." His smile sobered as he reached over and thumped Mace on the arm. "If Zurie means something to you, don't give up on her so easily."

"You realize if I go that route and try to get her back, I can't do it from here."

"Yeah, I know." Efraín released a slow breath. "Will I be disappointed if you don't move here and help run the firm? Yes. But if you're happy where you have a chance to build a life with someone you care about, I'll get over it. I just want you to be happy."

As Mace's plane lifted off from Reno-Tahoe International Airport, he closed his eyes, exhausted from lack of sleep. Last night, so many things had occupied his mind. They still did. His conversation with Efraín about Zurie. Mrs. Davies's life story with her husband. Zurie's question at the vineyard about if he felt behind in the relationship department.

Maybe he was behind when it came to relationships. He'd never committed to anyone fully. Not even Zurie. His brother was right. He hadn't been straight up with Zurie about Reno or how he felt about her. He'd given her no reassurance about him or their relationship. Instead he'd left room for doubt. And the more he thought about it, he may have instigated it that night she'd stayed alone in his house.

After she'd left that morning, he'd needed to charge his phone, and he'd looked for the cord he'd last used in his office. He'd been so frustrated about not being able to find it and Zurie leaving, he'd batted papers from his desk. He'd later found a charging cord neatly looped in a circle on his nightstand. He hadn't done that. When she'd gotten that cord from his desk, what else had she found? The Nevada bar exam checklist sitting right there on his desk?

Efraín was right—he hadn't been lining up the facts. If he had, he could have fixed it and made better decisions. When he reached his seventies, like Mrs. Davies, he wanted to look back on his life with happiness like her, not regret because he hadn't stopped long enough to share his life with someone. Funny. He'd always thought in terms of connection— that he and the right person would fit together, but maybe that wasn't what it was about at all. During his long weekend with Zurie, he'd shared a part himself with her. He'd also shared what he enjoyed, and she'd enjoyed it with him. And it had felt good to do that with someone. No. Not just someone. Zurie.

Seven hours later, Mace's flight landed in New York. His connecting flight wasn't for hours. Duffel bag on his shoulder, he walked through the terminal, not searching for his gate but for one that had the fewest number of people around.

He found a suitable space, dropped his bag in a chair by the window and took out his phone. He dialed the familiar number. His father picked up.

Mace took a breath and entered into the most difficult conversation of his life.

Chapter Twenty-Seven

Zurie glanced out the living room window.

At seven in the morning, instead of a clear blue early-morning sky, it was still as dark as predawn with various shades of light blue to gray providing a backdrop for the clouds.

A forty percent chance of rain later that morning was the forecast, but it looked more like eighty.

Should the wedding stay at the pavilion or should they move it to Pasture Lane Restaurant? An outdoor wedding with a view of the pasture and the hills was what Chloe and Tristan had wanted. Everything was still in place to make that happen. Switching to Pasture Lane would require changes that would need to start happening in the next hour or so to still pull the wedding ceremony off at one that afternoon. But what if she suggested moving the ceremony to the restaurant, and the weather morphed from rain into the perfect sunny day? She would be responsible for robbing them of the picturesque moment. But if she didn't urge them to make the change and the dark clouds forming in the distance delivered what they promised…

Images flitted through her mind of Chloe in her beautiful wedding dress and Tristan in his tux, huddled under the pavilion, or one of the tents with their guests, trying to escape the rain as puddles of mud rose higher and higher in the grass around them.

Anxiety curled into knots in her stomach. Zurie looked to the rooibos tea in her cup. She just couldn't drink it today. It wasn't satisfying her. She dumped it in the sink, praying that, unlike the tea, the wedding wasn't headed down the drain as well. Of all days, this was not the one for a downpour. Or to not have an objective sounding board. She missed Mace.

A longing for him blanketed her worry in something that made her want to scream. Sadness. She'd never been one to feel sorry for herself. She'd never had time for it in the past, and she didn't have time for it now. She and Mace were over. She'd broken up with him because it was the necessary thing to do.

Tristan and Chloe were taking an important step forward. Being their wedding planner was just like being in charge of Tillbridge—she had to let go of what was unimportant and keep her focus on what mattered. And keep her personal feelings out of it. This wedding had to be a beautiful memory Tristan and Chloe would cherish, rain or shine.

Just as she was about to pick up her phone from the counter, it rang. Tristan's name flashed on the screen. Perfect timing. He'd spent the night in the cottage he still owned on the property instead of his house. Chloe was staying with her family in a two-bedroom suite downstairs.

At the cottage, he actually had a better view of the south pasture than she did. Maybe by some miracle things looked hopeful from his point of view.

Zurie answered her phone. "Good morning."

"Good morning. So I'm sure you've been monitoring the weather. Chloe and I have been texting each other about it all morning. We keep going back and forth on the decision. What do you think we should do? Take a chance on staying in the pasture or go with the indoor plan?"

The window was closing on being able to set up Pasture Lane on time for the wedding.

What's your gut telling you?

The question Mace would have probably asked her hovered. She wanted the best for Tristan and Chloe, and she couldn't guarantee that with the weather working against them. Still, it was a tough call.

Zurie took one last look outside her living room

window, hoping to see a ray of hope, but only larger, darker, more ominous clouds existed. "I don't think we should risk it. Let's move the ceremony to Pasture Lane."

"Okay, then." He blew out an exhale. "Being able to see the hill where I proposed to Chloe while we took our vows, she was looking forward to that. I just hope she's not too disappointed."

It wasn't just Chloe who'd been looking forward to it. Tristan had, too. "She's marrying you. How could she be anything but happy today?"

He chuckled. "Thanks for saying that. I feel the same way about her, too."

"This is only one little hiccup. We'll get through it."

"Actually, there's two. Mace isn't back in Maryland yet. He called me last night. The same thunderstorm that's coming our way hit New York yesterday. His connecting flight from there to Baltimore was delayed, then canceled."

Mace had called Tristan instead of her. That made sense. They hadn't spoken to each other since she'd broken things off with him at his house. And burned the waffles. Smoke rising from the oven had capped off one of the worst moments in her life. He hadn't wanted her help in cleaning up the mess, so she'd left. And cried all the way home.

Stop. *Focus on what's important.* Remember? "Is

there a chance he'll be able to fly out this morning? It's a short flight."

"That was the plan, but his early-morning flight had a mechanical issue. He's having problems getting rebooked again. And they're still dealing with storms. He's going to try and rent a car."

But road conditions probably weren't that great, either. He'd be driving into the storm. Concern for Mace's safety started to well inside her, and she tamped it down. As a sheriff's deputy, he knew the risks of driving in inclement weather. If it wasn't safe, he'd stay off the road.

But there was still one more issue with Mace and the wedding that had to be addressed. "Did he say anything about security for the ceremony?"

"He did. It's taken care of. His friend Dean is in charge. And as far as best man, Thad will take his place."

Crappy weather was one thing. Not having his best friend at his side as his best man because of it—that wasn't fair. "I'm sorry."

"It's not your fault. The weather is to blame."

But maybe Mace not being there *was* her fault. Guilt pinged. His original plans hadn't involved him being gone this long. "Is there anything I can do?"

"Check on Chloe for me?"

"I will. Once I get everything arranged in Pasture Lane. I'll text you what time to be downstairs. You remember the contingency plan entrance, right?"

"The loading dock. Tell me the time and I'll be there."

Zurie said goodbye to Tristan. As she slipped on her tennis shoes at the door, she went through a revised mental checklist for the day. *Yikes.* The minister. She'd almost forgot about calling him. And then she needed to text Rina about the change. And get in touch with Blake to make sure the tents were taken down at the pavilion before the rain.

Downstairs, after making those two important calls, she met up with Philippa in the dining room.

It had already been set up for the reception with the DJ in the far corner along with a portable dance floor.

Floral centerpieces with candles were already on the white linen–covered tables. Fanned beige napkins plus silverware were also set up. And now everything had to be shifted around.

Zurie gave Philippa an empathetic glance. "Everything looks beautiful. You and the staff did a wonderful job setting this up. I'm sorry we have to move everything around."

"Thank you." Philippa shrugged. "The tables will get a little messed up moving them back and forth. We'll just have to herd everyone out into the corridor immediately after the ceremony so we can put everything back in place. What about the kitchen and dining staff? Are we keeping them in the dark still about this being Tristan and Chloe's wedding ceremony until the last minute?"

"Once they see the tables lined up along the sides and chairs lined up forming a center aisle, they'll probably guess it's a wedding. But they still won't know who. Maybe hold off until a half hour before the ceremony? Don't forget to give them the cell phone talk."

"Oh, I definitely won't forget that."

No pictures of the wedding and no posting of info about the wedding on social media until after the reception was over was the courtesy they were asking from everyone, including the guests in attendance.

With the help of a few of the service staff, they rearranged the tables and chairs. Two tall ferns in brass pots were spaced out up front in the center of the room. Tristan, Chloe and the minister would stand between them.

All that was left was rolling out the white runner down the middle. But that wouldn't happen until the start of the ceremony. That way it wouldn't get dirty before Chloe walked on it.

Last stop was the suite where Chloe and her family were staying.

Zurie knocked on the door.

A more mature version of Chloe answered the door. The sleeves of Patrice Daniels's peach dressing gown billowed as she welcomed Zurie inside the suite and gave her a hug. "How's everything downstairs?"

"We're ready," Zurie replied. "How's everything here?" She allowed herself a moment to soak in the embrace.

Patrice gave the best hugs. Long and comforting with a nice tight squeeze before she let go. "We just finished a light breakfast. Have you eaten today, or have you been too busy running around?"

Zurie's stomach answered for her with a low growl.

Patrice, a dietitian, gave her an admonishing maternal look. "You'll have a muffin and some fruit before you leave. We can't have you passing out in the middle of the ceremony."

"Yes, ma'am." Feeling properly scolded, in a good way, Zurie followed her into blue-carpeted living area.

Chloe's father, Dr. John Daniels, a balding medium brown-skinned man with glasses, sat on the tan couch drinking coffee and talking on his phone. The cardiologist was already dressed for the wedding in dark slacks, a crisp white shirt and a blue tie.

He mouthed "good morning" to Zurie as she followed Patrice into small kitchen alcove adjoining the living room, where a catered continental breakfast of muffins, fruit, coffee, juice, water and packages of oatmeal were laid out on a wood table along with small plates, paper napkins, glasses and flatware.

Patrice picked up a small plate, put a banana muffin and grapes on it, and handed it to Zurie. "Start with that." She gestured for Zurie to have a seat at the table.

Zurie complied and munched a grape. "Thank you. Where's Chloe?"

"In the bedroom, getting ready and texting Tristan." Patrice chuckled and shook her head. "You'd think they hadn't communicated with each other in months. Once they're married, they'll have their whole lives to talk to each other. Even when they don't want to."

Patrice's dignified eye roll made Zurie laugh as she broke apart the muffin and ate a small piece. "I'm not surprised they're texting each other. They've been like twins, joined at the hip for months now. They even almost dress alike."

"I thought it was just me noticing that."

"Noticing what?" Chloe breezed in wearing a white robe. She kissed Zurie on the cheek then poured a glass of water from the pitcher on the table. Even with makeup, her complexion was dewy with a natural glow. Her curly hair was pinned into an updo.

"Nothing important." Patrice eyed Chloe's glass of water. "Make sure you ease up on the fluids before the ceremony. Nerves have a way of sneaking up on you once you're zipped into a gown. The last thing you want is to have to visit the ladies' room in your wedding dress, or worse…"

"Yes, Mom." As Chloe slipped into a chair at the table, a slight dimple appeared in her cheek with her small smile. "I will avoid having to make a pit stop right before the ceremony at all costs."

Zurie absorbed positive mother-daughter banter and loving energy swirling around her. Her mom would have gotten along with Patrice and adored Chloe. And Uncle Jacob would have spoiled Chloe. A pang of bittersweetness hit. The way Tristan looked after Chloe with such care and love, she saw glimpses of Jacob in him.

After dutifully finishing every bite of food on her plate under Patrice's watchful eye, Zurie rose from the chair. "I need to check on a few things before I head upstairs. Call if you need anything."

"Oh." Chloe laid her hand on Zurie's arm. "Two things you should know. Anna Ashford, the town journalist, cornered me yesterday, wondering if her invite to Tristan's party was lost in the mail."

"*Journalist* is a loose term when it comes to Anna. I definitely didn't send her an invite."

"Well…" Chloe gave a slightly sheepish look. "I added her to the guest list. I know she's a pain, but from my experience, it's better to win someone like her over with a bit of honey than waste time and money trying to get rid of them with repellant."

Chloe could have a point. "If you're comfortable having her here, then I am, too. What's the other thing?"

"My agent and publicist insisted on hiring a photographer. It's sort of a wedding gift–slash–make-
sure-we-get-the-right-photos-for-publicity thing.
Tristan already gave his name to security. Any word
on Mace?"

"No. I haven't heard anything." Zurie tossed her
paper napkin in the trash and put her plate in the
sink with the rest of the dirty dishes. She'd have to
get used to the "where's Mace" question, since many
people thought they were engaged.

Chloe stood. "I hope he makes it."

Zurie did, too…for Tristan's sake, of course, not hers.

Chapter Twenty-Eight

Zurie faced the twenty-five guests standing in the seating area where the host podium was located, separated by a wall from the dining room of Pasture Lane Restaurant. Friends of Tristan and Chloe were attired in afternoon cocktail to dressy casual clothing.

She took a breath, trying to calm the butterflies in her stomach. Once she'd slipped on the chiffon dress with the high-low hemline and a blue-and-peach floral pattern, the feeling had erupted. This was it. In less than twenty minutes, the ceremony would start.

Flagging everyone's attention, she raised her voice over the crowd's conversations. "Hello, everyone.

Thank you for being here today for Tristan's surprise early birthday party."

Cora, a thin, birdlike older woman, waved her hand. "The invitation mentioned Chloe Daniels. Is she here?"

Cora's husband, Wes, a thin older man with a smooth bald head and a deep brown face, who was also the stable's farrier, gave her nudge trying to shush her.

"Good question." Anna Ashford joined in. "I believe I'm supposed to have an exclusive interview with her today."

Zurie had to stifle a derisive snort. Honey versus bug repellant. That's what Chloe had said, so she had to stick to the script. "There are actually a few surprises happening today. But I'm afraid that you're going to be the ones surprised…in a wonderful way."

Varying levels of confusion, doubt and wonder crossed the guests' faces. Anna and Cora leaned in with most eager expressions of all.

"Instead of celebrating Tristan's birthday…you're here because Tristan and Chloe wanted you to witness their vows and celebrate their union. Welcome to Tristan and Chloe's wedding ceremony."

Exclamations of surprise rose from the guests along with applause.

Zurie smiled along with them. "I know. Isn't it wonderful? And to keep it that way, we need to ask a huge favor." She have Anna a direct look. "Please don't text anyone that you're here right now or take photos or post about this affair on social media. Allow Tristan and Chloe a chance to have their day. There'll be plenty of time to share the good news tomorrow."

Many of the guests nodded in agreement. Anna dropped her phone back in her purse.

"In the dining room, we've lined up chairs along the aisle. Please sit there instead of at the tables. All right, then. Follow me."

Inside the dining room, the floral centerpieces with candles were lit. Combined with the natural light coming through the windows and the view of the gray-blue sky and intermittent rays of light peeping through the clouds, the space had an ethereal glow.

Slow love ballads, played by the DJ in the far corner, came through the speakers situated near the small dance floor.

Once the guests were seated, Zurie nodded to Philippa, who peeked into the kitchen.

A moment later the minister came out through the swinging door in a dark suit.

Tristan walked behind him.

Charlotte's instincts about the style of suit had been right. He looked beyond handsome in an impeccably tailored cream-colored tux paired with a white shirt and navy satin vest, tie and pocket square.

Instead of Thad… Mace walked out behind him.

Zurie's legs grew weak. *He made it.* Tristan must be so relieved.

GQ-worthy from head to toe in a navy suit with a white shirt, cream vest and tie, he stood near the ferns with Tristan and the minister.

Tristan looked solemn and a bit nervous as he adjusted the cuff links in his sleeves.

Mace clapped Tristan lightly on the back as if to let Tristan know he was there for him.

Tristan smiled and nodded.

Zurie tore her gaze away from Mace and sent a text to Rina that it was time for Chloe to arrive. Instead of coming through the lobby, Rina, Chloe and her parents were coming the back way to the corridor.

As she hurried out of the restaurant, she gave Blake a nod.

The trainer, who looked like a slightly older Bradley Cooper, had worn a dark suit for the occasion. With Scott's help, he would roll the white runners down the center aisle.

In the corridor, buffet tables had been set up on the right for the heavy hors d'oeuvres Philippa would serve after the ceremony. On the left, farther down, were two portable bars.

Two of the security detail Mace had organized stood on each end of the hall in dark suits. According to the plan Mace had sent her before they'd broken up, more security guarded the front door and were patrolling the grounds.

Coming from the direction of her office, Zurie spotted Chloe with a cream cape covering her dress and wearing a delicate floral tiara. Charlotte, in a tangerine dress, walked beside her.

John, now fully dressed in his dark suit, walked with Patrice, who'd put on a sky-blue dress and had styled her hair in messy bun that complemented her delicate features. Thad, a taller, leaner version of his father, with short, neatly clipped hair, walked with them. He wore the same suit ensemble as Mace.

Rina also walked with them, carrying the calla lily bouquets.

As they got closer. Chloe gave Zurie a huge, tremulous smile as she smoothed a tendril of hair from her cheek.

Charlotte untied the cape and slipped it from Chloe's shoulders. Chloe looked even more stunning then she had that day at Rina's house when she'd tried on the strapless mermaid-style dress with appliqués, beads, lace and a chapel-length train.

Zurie squeezed Chloe's hand. "You look beautiful. Are you ready?"

"Yes." Chloe squeezed back before accepting a pink calla lily bouquet from Rina.

Rina held out one of the two single white calla lilies in her hand to Zurie.

"Why are you giving this to me?" Zurie asked.

"You're walking down the aisle as a bridesmaid, too, since you don't have to run around anymore. Thad's standing up front with Mace and Tristan."

"I'll hold on to this for you. And don't worry, I'll take care of Chloe." Charlotte slipped the phone from Zurie's hand.

There was no time to argue.

Like clockwork, as Zurie had planned, Thad escorted his mom down the aisle to her seat.

Rina walked down next, and then it was Zurie's turn.

As she walked down the aisle, a million details swarmed in her mind. *I shouldn't be doing this. I need to make sure everything is ready for the reception.* Halfway down she met Mace's gaze, and every thought dissipated. Her heart swelled with happiness in seeing him there and hurt for the loss of him in her life at the same time.

Before she took her place, she looked to Tristan. Flooded with genuine happiness, she smiled at him and he smiled back.

The DJ cued up a classical string quartet version of the bridal chorus.

Head high and smiling, Chloe walked regally down the aisle on her father's arm.

Zurie caught a glimpse of Tristan. Stunned, captivated, happy—seeing his face as Chloe walked toward him brought tears to Zurie's eyes, and she blinked them back.

Chloe's and Tristan's gazes remained locked on each other, breaking away only when Chloe's father hugged her and then Tristan.

Chloe gave Zurie her bouquet, then turned back to Tristan.

Clearly in love with each other, Tristan and Chloe faced the minister.

...to have and to hold from this day forward, for better, for worse, for richer, for poorer, in sickness and in health, to love and to cherish, till death do us part...

The solemn, reverent words seem to hover in the air like a blessing.

Rings were exchanged, and a short time later, Zurie handed Chloe her flowers.

Now husband and wife, Chloe and Tristan walked back down the aisle.

And then it was Zurie's turn to walk with Mace. She looked into his eyes, and suddenly it felt as if her high heels were bolted to the floor.

Rina's subtle elbow nudge propelled Zurie to take one step and then another until she reached him.

She looped her hand through the crook of his arm. His strength, the weight of his hand resting lightly on hers, the cologne wafting from him. They all hit her at once. It was like being caught in a sudden downpour without a raincoat or an umbrella. She looked straight ahead, training her eyes on the end of the runner. That's when she could let go. What if she couldn't? What if she kept holding on to him like a part of her so desperately wanted to do?

A few steps before she should have, Zurie slipped her hand from his arm.

She joined Tristan and Chloe in the corridor. The two emanated pure joy as she hugged them both. "Congratulations."

"You did it!" Rina came over and gave the couple hugs and kisses.

"This way, please." A thin, silver-haired man with a camera waved them down the hall.

Chloe picked up the skirt of her dress. "We should go now before the guests start coming out, otherwise we won't be able to break away."

"Go on." Zurie nudged them forward. "I'll wrangle the guests and catch up with you in a minute."

"Security has it handled." Mace walked over to her. "They'll keep the guests in the corridor while we take pictures."

"Oh. All right." He stared down at her, and, once again, she suddenly found it hard to move. His scent—a mix of cologne and how it warmed on his skin—made her heady.

Guests filed out of the Pasture Lane, and as promised a blond member of the security team directed people toward bars and buffets with appetizers.

"We should catch up with everyone." Mace laid his hand on her back to guide her.

A spark of attraction and familiarity struck, but

icy reality replaced it, prompting her to walk faster and get away from his touch. They weren't together anymore. She had pull herself together. She couldn't fall apart or turn into a puddle every time he looked at her.

The photographer took candid and posed photos of Chloe and Tristan and the entire bridal party in the lobby and on the porch.

Staff members who'd just found out about what happened came to the lobby to see what was going on and to congratulate the couple.

Tristan and Chloe relaxed the no-photo rule to take a few pictures with the staff.

He called out, "Hey, guys, do us a favor and don't text or post them until we're gone, okay?"

Before Zurie's eyes, Tristan slipped into the role of celebrity husband, giving Chloe space to interact with her admirers, not taking offense when they didn't want him in a photo.

The hired photographer wrapped up taking photos of them.

Using the excuse of holding Chloe's train, Zurie avoided being near Mace and lessening the pull of proximity.

It was going to be a long afternoon.

Chapter Twenty-Nine

Food, dancing, conversation, laughter—it all flowed freely at the reception, along with the wine.

At the table during dinner, Zurie sat next to Chloe's father. He took a sip of the full-bodied red wine and nodded approvingly. "This is from a local vineyard?"

"Yes, it's just three hours away." As Zurie shared details about Sommersby, she relived a few of the moments from her trip there with Mace.

John staring at her alerted Zurie to the fact that she'd been talking nonstop.

She reached for her phone. "I have the info. I can airdrop it to you if you're interested."

"Please." He took his phone from his inside jacket pocket, and she sent him the info.

"Thank you." He slipped his phone back into his jacket. "What you described sounds like a great day trip to take before we leave. Next time we're in the area, we'll have to plan an overnight stay there. No offense to Tillbridge."

"None taken. It's a wonderful place. If you stay in the cottage, before you leave, you can plant something on the property and…" *Stop talking. You're boring the poor man.* Zurie shook her head. "I'm sorry. I'm rambling." She laughed. "Maybe it's because of the wine."

John gave her an indulgent smile. "Or you just enjoyed a memorable trip there with someone you care about. I understand. Patrice and I have experienced some great trips together. Special places, like the vineyard you mentioned, are our most unforgettable getaways. If you want my advice—keep doing them together. That's what's kept us together for thirty-five years."

Zurie pulled up a smile and nodded. Mace walking out the restaurant with Tristan caught her eye. There wouldn't be any more vineyard trips for them. Only memories carefully stored like a precious vintage in her mind.

At the bar in the corridor, Mace, Tristan, Thad and Luke, one of Tristan's bull-riding friends, raised shots of whiskey in a toast.

"Here's to Tristan," Luke said. As the dark-haired man, who looked more like a surfer than a bull rider, raised his glass a bit higher, he flashed a grin. "May his marriage to Chloe be a lot more successful than his bull rides."

Tristan laughed. "Okay. Don't make me go on YouTube and pull up some footage on you."

"Seriously, though." Luke's expression sobered. "I'm happy to see you this happy. And I wish you all the best in the years to come. To Tristan and Chloe."

Mace and Thad echoed the toast, and all four of them clinked their glasses before drinking the shot.

More toasts were made to Tristan before Thad and Luke returned to the dining room, leaving Mace and Tristan behind.

Tristan glanced over at Mace. "I know the drive wasn't easy in the storm. Thanks for making it today."

"Couldn't miss it."

Tristan stared down at the platinum wedding band on his hand. He shook his head. "On some level, this feels unreal. She married me."

Tristan's love-struck grin pulled a chuckle out of Mace. "If it helps, I can't believe she married you, either. If you want to keep her, my advice to you is burn all the photos of you as a kid wearing Superman pj's and a red towel as a cape. All that bull-rider street cred you have, gone. Don't do it."

"Oh, man. Who showed you those? Rina?"

"No. Actually, I haven't seen them. Zurie happened to mention it. She told me not to tell you I knew, but..." Mace shrugged. "Hey, I just couldn't let it pass."

Tristan chuckled. "Of course you couldn't." He studied Mace. "You and Zurie have been avoiding each other all afternoon. Is everything good between you two?"

Mace signaled to the bartender for two more shots. As far as avoiding, he wasn't. That was all Zurie. "Not as good as I'd like it to be. Remember when I told you that if I had a chance to spend time with the woman I want, I would, and then I told you it wasn't Zurie?"

"Yeah, I do." Tristan propped his elbow on the bar. "But let me guess, now she is."

"Right."

Tristan gave him an empathetic look. "Anything I can do? Do you want me to talk to her?"

"No." Mace took a drink from his glass. "This is something Zurie and I have to settle on our own."

Bubbles floated into the sunny sky along with the well-wishes and cheers as Tristan and Chloe hurried to the waiting black limo. As it pulled away from the curb and out of the parking lot, they waved goodbye and Chloe blew kisses out of the open window.

The crowd dispersed. Some went to their cars in the parking lot, while others went back inside the guesthouse. Standing off to the side of the entrance on the porch, Zurie gave in to fatigue and leaned her shoulder on Rina's, who stood beside her, still radiating energy.

Rina, scrolling through photos on her phone, released a happy sigh. "Oh, look at them. They look so wonderful." She held up her phone so Zurie could see the montage.

Somehow, Rina had managed to be everywhere at once, capturing candid, lovely, cute and humorous photos of Tristan and Chloe during the reception.

Rina paused on a photo of the two of them with Chloe in the suite after she'd changed into the cute pale blue midthigh dress she'd worn for travel to her and Tristan's mystery honeymoon destination. Chloe had given Zurie and Rina pale gray Stetsons with a personalized leather hat band with their name. Tristan had given the same with a different design to Mace and Thad, and she had pictures of that moment, too. They all looked good, but Mace held her attention.

Rina kept scrolling and slowed on photos of Mace and Zurie when Tristan had humorously shared that Zurie and Mace weren't really engaged.

The picture of Anna's sour-looking expression was priceless.

But one photo, of Zurie and Mace, pricked Zurie's heart. She and Mace were both faking a laugh in the photo. Pretending everything was okay. Could it get any worse? Actually, it could. They had pretended to be engaged, and now she had to pretend that everything was okay when she was around him…until he left in a few months. It hurt too much to think about it.

Zurie looked away from the picture. "I'm going upstairs to change. I'll be back down to help Philippa with cleanup." She turned to go through the door and smacked into a human wall.

As she faltered, Mace lightly grasped her arm. "Careful."

Zurie stared up at him. Seconds passed before she realized her hand rested on his chest. "Sorry." She went to move away.

He held on to her with one hand. The hat Tristan had given him was in the other. "Do you have a minute?"

"I should really go ch—"

"Sure, she does," Rina interjected, looking pointedly at Zurie as she walked inside. "I'll help Philippa."

If only Rina knew her matchmaking was in vain. Zurie pulled up a smile. "Well, I guess I do have a minute."

People scooted past them.

Mace let her go. "Can we go somewhere private? Like your office?"

"Sure." Zurie led the way inside the guesthouse.

As they walked side by side down the corridor, staff members folded up the buffet tables.

Once inside her office, Zurie shut the door behind her and Mace.

She tried to muster up indifference but couldn't. Especially as the walls of her office seem to shrink, making the space smaller.

Zurie broke the silence. "I heard you had a hard time getting out of New York. What time did you finally get here?"

"I couldn't get a flight out in time. I had to drive."

That explained the shadows under his eyes. Wait. Had he moved closer or had she? "How was the training in California?"

"Good." Mace definitely stepped closer.

"Thanks for assigning Dean to help out. I really appreciate that." She needed to stop babbling.

"I'm sorry I wasn't here." He dropped his hat onto one of the padded chairs in front of her desk.

"You were busy. You have a lot to do now that you're moving to Reno."

Mace's brow raised a fraction.

Oh... She hadn't meant to say that. Now she'd have to explain how she knew. But she hadn't been snooping around his desk that day. Zurie started to explain.

"I'm not moving to Reno."

"You're not? Why?"

"You know why." Mace walked into her personal

space. "Because of you." He took her hand, wreaking havoc on her concentration.

"You can't."

"Oh, yes, I can."

"No, you are supposed to be a lawyer in Nevada with your family practice, Calderone and Associates. They're expecting you." She could see the question in his eyes about how she knew the name of the practice. She'd looked it up.

"They *were* expecting me, but now they know the practice will have to go on without me. Bolan is where I live. My job as a deputy is here. My home is here. My life is here. And I want you to be a part of it."

For how long? He'd worked hard to get that law degree. Someday he could change his mind and want what his family law firm could offer him.

Zurie shook her head, saying no to him and herself. "My father put Tillbridge in my hands. Not Rina's. Not Tristan's, mine."

"That's a weak argument. You say you can't because of Tillbridge, but I think some of the people in that room, the ones that work for you, your family, would tell you that you don't have to sacrifice yourself for them. And honestly, when your father put this place in your hands, I don't think that's what he intended, either. Tillbridge didn't thrive because of one person. It's here because of family."

Mace cupped her face in his hands. "I want us to

be family. Seeing your face is how I want to start my day, and you're the one I want to come home to at night. I want to visit vineyards with you, watch movies under the stars with you. I want to watch you stick tomato plants or whatever else into the ground, and I want to hear all the names you pick out for them."

As hard as Zurie tried not to imagine it, she couldn't stop herself. What she saw in her mind looked oh so wonderful. Too wonderful to reach for.

Mace glided his thumb across her cheeks, swiping away tears she hadn't realized leaked from her eyes. "And when the time is right, I want us to have kids and choose names for them together. I want to be there when you bring the best of both of us into the world. I want to be by your side, sleep deprived and happy and in awe of what we made together. And that's just the beginning of what can be a wonderful life for us. But you have to want it just as much as I do. I love you, Zurie. But we can't have all that if you won't trust me. If you won't trust yourself enough to love me back, and I won't take halfway. If you want to be with me, it's all in, just like I'm all in for you."

Mace sealed his lips to Zurie's. As a sob fueled by hope and uncertainty escaped from her, he deepened the kiss, chasing her doubts, fighting her fears, stirring up passion.

He wrapped his arms around her, and little by little, the wall she'd built around what she'd given up on most of her life started to crumble. Happiness. It expanded inside her, searching out the place where it belonged. Her heart. But did she even know how to be happy?

The kiss ended too soon. As Mace laid his forehead to hers, the cadence of her unsteady breaths joined his.

He loosened his embrace, and the soft kiss he brushed near her temple made her close her eyes, trying to stop the flow of tears.

Mace gently squeezed her waist. "When you're ready, you know where to find me."

He let go, and by the time she found the courage to open her eyes, Mace was gone.

Chapter Thirty

Mace strode out the front of the guesthouse, fighting the urge to go back for Zurie. But if he did, what would he do? Throw her over his shoulder and carry her away, caveman style? No, he'd said his piece. And he'd done what he'd needed to for Chloe and Tristan's wedding. It was time for him to go home.

He took his phone from the inside pocket of his suit jacket and called Dean. "We're done here. Everyone can head out. And thanks. Drinks are on me at the Montecito next Friday."

"No problem," Dean said. "I'll spread the word about next Friday."

As Mace ended the call, Rina walked out the door of the guesthouse.

"Hey." Rina nudged his arm. "Can you believe it? We pulled it off. Chloe and Tristan's day went perfectly."

Ignoring the viselike feeling around his heart, Mace summoned a smile. "Yep. Just like we planned."

She looked to Scott, walking toward them from the parking lot. "He delivered plates of food to your security guys."

"Thanks for doing that."

"We all really appreciate them being here. Did you grab some food to take home?"

"No, I missed out."

She laughed. "I can definitely rectify that. Most of the leftovers are in my car."

As Scott came closer, Rina headed toward the steps. "A few people are coming by my house tonight to help finish them off. You have to stop by. Can you tell Zurie, too? I lost track of her."

"I don't know where she is."

Scott had reached the bottom of the steps. As Rina walked down them, she paused in taking his out-stretched hand. "She's not with you?"

The constraint around Mace's heart grew tighter. "No. Zurie's not with me."

Varying levels of confusion and realization dawned on her face. "Oh… I thought…" Her mouth remained open as if she wasn't sure what to say.

Scott took hold of Rina's hand and gently tugged.

"We should get home so we can put the food in the refrigerator." He gave Mace a bro nod of solidarity. He understood Mace's pain.

Rina slipped her hand from Scott's, walked to Mace and gave him a kiss on the cheek. "If you don't make it by, I'll save you a plate. You can pick it up later."

"Thanks."

As Rina and Scott walked to the car with their arms wrapped around each other's backs, Scott kissed her temple.

The memory of his last kiss with Zurie earlier flitted through his mind. The loss of her followed him as he trekked to the far side of the parking lot. At the truck, he tossed his jacket into the back seat and his tie on top of it.

He glanced toward the guesthouse.

The door opened, and a couple walked out.

Disappointment sat heavy inside him. Yeah, dinner at Rina's house definitely wasn't happening. He was still planning to live his life the best way he could without Zurie, but he needed a minute before he got started on that.

Mace got into the driver's seat and turned the key in the ignition. Before putting the truck in Reverse, he opened the window, needing some fresh air. Glancing behind him as well as in the rearview mirror, he started backing out.

He heard Zurie's voice calling his name. But he

refused to look. *Damn.* He missed her so much, he was hearing her voice.

"Mace!"

Zurie's voice reached him loud and clear through his open window, and he turned, looking for her.

"Mace, wait!" She waved at him from the top of steps. As she hurried down them, she paused to slip off her sandals and flung them aside.

Equal parts of shock and memorization held him in place as she ran toward him down the sidewalk, gray Stetson in hand, her hair streaming behind her, dress clinging to her curves.

He shut off the engine, got out and walked around to the front of the truck.

Zurie slowed to a walk, and he met her halfway.

She was slightly out of breath.

As the wind blew one of her curls over her forehead, he balled his hand in a fist, resisting the urge to smooth it back.

Zurie brushed the strand from her eyes and looked up at him. "You forgot something."

Of course, she was bringing him the hat.

"Thanks." He reached for it.

Zurie held it behind her back and shook her head. "No. You forgot something else."

Before he could ask what, she curved her hand to his nape, urging him to lean in as she lifted on her toes and sealed her mouth to his.

Unable to resist holding her, Mace grasped her by the waist.

When Zurie finally came up for air, his heart was pounding hard and he felt a little light-headed. But that didn't stop him from chasing her mouth for a longer kiss.

Whoops from across the parking lot caught both their attention.

Rina happy danced next to Scott. As she threw her hands in the air in victory, her shouts of *yes* traveled on the breeze.

Zurie's laugh vibrated into Mace.

She'd come to him, but he needed to hear her say why. Mace gave her waist a light squeeze. "What did I forget?"

"Me." She cupped his cheek. "I love you, too. I have to be honest, I'm a little scared. I'm so used to being on my own and handling things myself, but what you promised me in my office a minute ago, I want that with you. If you can be patient with me, I'm ready to go all in."

The trust and love in her eyes made happiness well inside him. Mace bent down, swept up her legs and picked her up his arms. "What took you so long?"

Zurie put the Stetson on her head, freeing up her hands to loop around his neck. "Sorry for being a little late."

"I forgive you, *mi vida*." Mace kissed her, capturing her smile as his own. Zurie was his life…his heart…his love.

* * * * *

MILLS & BOON

Coming next month

MATCHMAKER AND THE
MANHATTAN MILLIONAIRE
Cara Colter

"I don't need a refund. I need to be engaged!"

"That's ridiculous. And impossible."

"She hasn't done it, has she? She hasn't made me a match."

"No, I don't believe she has. I can't –

Jonas regarded her stormily for a long enough that it felt as if she was going to stop breathing.

"What about you?"

"Excuse me?"

He stepped toward her. He didn't reach out and he didn't touch her, and yet Krissy felt as if he had taken her glasses off and was planning on running his hands through her hair.

"Yes, you'll do," he decided, a touch too clinically. "There's a little of that librarian look to you. Wholesome. The girl next door. Yes, you'll do."

Krissy's heart was beating madly, as if he had removed her glasses.

"I am not going to be your temporary toy!" she said. She wanted to sound firm, but her voice had an unfortunate squeak to it. *Librarian, indeed.*

He cocked his head charmingly at her, as if he was not being completely ludicrous.

"Toy," he said, his tone mulling. "No, no I don't think so."

Why on earth would she feel vaguely insulted by his dismissal?

"That could lead to complications," he explained gravely, "That's, in part, why I turned to your aunt. No complications.

Still, we would need to get to know each other first, before we made it official. It's important to know each other."

"You think?" she asked. He seemed to miss her sarcasm.

"It's for a family reunion in the Catskills, the long weekend in July. My sister would know, instantly, if you didn't know what my favourite colour was. Restaurant. Movie. That kind of thing."

What kind of weakness was it that Krissy suddenly wanted to know what his favourite colour was? Restaurant? Movie? Plus, the long weekend in July. She had always spent it with Aunt Jane, who knew, as her own parents had not, that occasions – birthdays, Christmas, Easter, the Fourth of July – were important to families.

His invitation felt like a reprieve from the looming weekend alone, but more, it felt as if she was being invited to step into the pages of a story, a very interesting story with all kinds of twists and turns and characters she knew nothing about.

Krissy did not like temptations. She did not appreciate her sudden awareness that the nice, safe, predictable life she had so carefully constructed for herself might be slightly, well, boring.

That was her aunt's word, after Krissy had brushed off her enthusiasm about having found the perfect man for her.

You're too young to be so set in your ways, so allergic to adventure. Life is not meant to be such a bore, my dear.

"Come on," he said persuasively. "It will be fun."

Fun. So no matter what he said, there was an element of her being his toy in there. Temporarily.

What do you do for fun?

Continue reading
**MATCHMAKER AND THE
MANHATTAN MILLIONAIRE**
Cara Colter

Available next month
www.millsandboon.co.uk

Copyright © 2021 Cara Colter

COMING SOON!

We really hope you enjoyed reading this book.
If you're looking for more romance, be sure to
head to the shops when new books are
available on

Thursday 18th February

To see which titles are coming soon, please visit

millsandboon.co.uk/nextmonth

MILLS & BOON

LET'S TALK
Romance

For exclusive extracts, competitions
and special offers, find us online:

 facebook.com/millsandboon

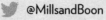 @MillsandBoon

@MillsandBoonUK

Get in touch on 01413 063232

For all the latest titles coming soon, visit
millsandboon.co.uk/nextmonth

WANT EVEN MORE

ROMANCE?

SUBSCRIBE AND SAVE TODAY!

'Mills & Boon books, the perfect way to escape for an hour or so.'

MISS W. DYER

'Excellent service, promptly delivered and very good subscription choices.'

MISS A. PEARSON

'You get fantastic special offers and the chance to get books before they hit the shops.'

MRS V. HALL

Visit millsandboon.co.uk/Subscribe
and save on brand new books.

MILLS & BOON
A ROMANCE FOR EVERY READER

- **FREE** delivery direct to your door

- **EXCLUSIVE** offers every month

- **SAVE** up to 25% on pre-paid subscriptions

SUBSCRIBE AND SAVE

millsandboon.co.uk/Subscribe

MILLS & BOON

THE HEART OF ROMANCE

A ROMANCE FOR EVERY KIND OF READER

ODERN

Prepare to be swept off your feet by sophisticated, sexy and seductive heroes, in some of the world's most glamourous and romantic locations, where power and passion collide.
8 stories per month.

STORICAL

Escape with historical heroes from time gone by. Whether your passion is for wicked Regency Rakes, muscled Vikings or rugged Highlanders, awaken the romance of the past.
6 stories per month.

EDICAL

Set your pulse racing with dedicated, delectable doctors in the high-pressure world of medicine, where emotions run high and passion, comfort and love are the best medicine.
6 stories per month.

ue Love

Celebrate true love with tender stories of heartfelt romance, from the rush of falling in love to the joy a new baby can bring, and a focus on the emotional heart of a relationship.
8 stories per month.

Desire

Indulge in secrets and scandal, intense drama and plenty of sizzling hot action with powerful and passionate heroes who have it all: wealth, status, good looks…everything but the right woman.
6 stories per month.

EROES

Experience all the excitement of a gripping thriller, with an intense romance at its heart. Resourceful, true-to-life women and strong, fearless men face danger and desire - a killer combination!
8 stories per month.

ARE

Sensual love stories featuring smart, sassy heroines you'd want as a best friend, and compelling intense heroes who are worthy of them.
4 stories per month.

To see which titles are coming soon, please visit

millsandboon.co.uk/nextmonth

JOIN US ON SOCIAL MEDIA!

Stay up to date with our latest releases, author news and gossip, special offers and discounts, and all the behind-the-scenes action from Mills & Boon...

 millsandboon

 millsandboonuk

 millsandboon

It might just be true love...

GET YOUR ROMANCE FIX!

MILLS & BOON
— blog —

Get the latest romance news, exclusive author interviews, story extracts and much more!

blog.millsandboon.co.uk

MILLS & BOON

HISTORICAL

Awaken the romance of the past

Escape with historical heroes from time gone by. Whether your passion is for wicked Regency Rakes, muscled Viking warriors or rugged Highlanders, indulge your fantasies and awaken the romance of the past.

Six Historical stories published every month, find them at

millsandboon.co.uk/ Historical

MILLS & BOON

HEROES

At Your Service

Experience all the excitement of a gripping thriller, with an intense romance at its heart. Resourceful, true-to-life women and strong, fearless men face danger and desire - a killer combination!

Heroes stories published every month, find them all at:

millsandboon.co.uk/Heroes

MILLS & BOON
MEDICAL
Pulse-Racing Passion

Set your pulse racing with dedicated, delectable doctors in the high-pressure world of medicine, where emotions run high and passion, comfort and love are the best medicine.

Eight Medical stories published every month, find them a

millsandboon.co.uk